VAMPIRE

IMPALER

The Immortal Knight Chronicles
Book 6

Richard of Ashbury
and Vlad Dracula
1444 - 1476

DAN DAVIS

Vampire Impaler

For information contact :
dandaviswrites@outlook.com

ISBN: 9781092863018
First Edition: April 2019

1

The Battle of Varna

1 4 4 4

A HUNDRED THOUSAND TURKS faced us across the plain. Banners snapped in the wind coming down from the hills and from the Black Sea close behind us.

It was to be the last battle of the last true crusade. The last time the kingdoms of Europe united to wage holy war on the enemies of Christ in a great battle.

"What do you reckon, Richard?" Walt asked me. "Biggest army you ever seen?"

We sat in the saddle in our armour, with the mercenary company I led around us. A hundred good fighting men, well equipped in steel and riding warhorses, plus their attendant squires, pages, grooms, and other servants which made me a minor though welcome addition to the crusade.

I looked out at the swarming mass of enemy horses and men filling the land from hills to hills and beyond, shining in their riot of armours and colours and raising noise enough to startle Heaven.

Across the plain in front of us, the *azab* infantry were robed and armed with spears. They were in effect a peasant militia, unmarried men who fought because they had no choice but were no less dangerous for all that. They might have been armed with just bows and spears, but there were many thousands of them that would have to be overcome.

It was not only low-quality men who were arrayed against us on foot, for the Anatolian infantry behind them wore mail with small plates, armed with spears and shields.

Beyond those infantry, in the centre of the entire army, thousands of elite Janissaries massed behind palisades, in their white or yellow robes, holding powerful recurved bows or the new hand-guns, and long, wicked polearms with spear heads, axe blades and hooks all on the same weapon. They also fought on foot but they were the most well-trained, well-equipped forces that the Sultan could deploy. At their sides were slung long, thin, curving swords that could split a man's flesh to the bone in a single, swift cut. Beneath their robes, they were protected by a light coat of mail, some bore bronze shields with shining bosses and on their heads they all wore tall, white felt hats that made them impossible to miss even from across the battlefield.

The sipahi horsemen from Anatolia and from Rumelia – that is the Turkish-held lands of Europe such as Bulgaria - were heavily armoured, wearing steel turbans on their heads that had mail hanging down to protect their necks and long white feathers trailing from the top. Some wore mail shirts, others wore lamellar armour of hundreds of small steel plates sewn together. Their horses were likewise well armoured in strong, light steel. Their steel shone in the dim light as the masses of cavalry rode this way and that on the two wings of a front two miles wide.

Our great army of Hungarians, a few Serbs, and German and French knights, was far smaller. Vlad II Dracul of Wallachia sent a force of seven thousand men, though he would not join us for the whole campaign and had left us in anger before the battle.

We were led by King Vladislaus of Hungary but the true commander was a knight and great lord named Janos Hunyadi. His countless military successes against the Turks in the Balkans over many years had so invigorated Christendom that the Pope had called the crusade and so it was Hunyadi, as the best soldier in Christendom, who chose our strategy and our tactics.

"Can we win?" Walt asked.

The eyes of my closest companions, Eva, Rob, and Stephen, also turned to me.

I said nothing.

"One Christian is worth a dozen Turks," Rob said, raising his voice. Some of the men of my company overheard and called out in affirmation.

"If we cannot win," Stephen asked, speaking softly as he sidled his horse closer me, "would it not be reasonable to withdraw? Our company, I mean. Richard?"

"I took the cross," I said. "I am sworn to fight. And so my men, who are sworn to me, are sworn to fight this battle also." I looked at him. "You included, Stephen."

"So, then, we fight," Stephen said, scowling. "Even if our deaths are almost certain?"

"Yes," I said.

"Nothing is certain," Eva said, almost speaking over me. "Even our reasons for being here."

I ignored her barbed comment. We were there because William was there, fighting for the Sultan. It was Eva and Stephen's agents who had discovered him but she was right that it was not certain. Even so, I felt it in my bones that he was across the field that day. Hidden from my view by the blur of distance and the swirling of the ranks of men and horse, perhaps, yet there all the same.

And the odds were against us in the battle but we had not meant for it to be so.

Hunyadi's plan for the crusade had been straightforward enough, in concept. We had followed the line of the Danube before crossing it in September 1444 and then westward into Bulgarian lands up to the Black Sea to the town of Varna. Instead of slowing our advance to take numerous, small enemy fortresses we had ignored them.

We knew of a great Turkish army coming to do battle with us but they refused to engage and so our advance to Varna was rapid.

From there, so we planned, we would push south into Turkish Rumelia and throw our enemy from Thrace and Bulgaria. The Turk had been in possession of those European lands for far too long already. And then we would go on, chasing them back across the Bosporus and back into Anatolia.

4

In all this we would be supported by fleets of Burgundian, Venetian, and Genoese ships who would close the Dardanelles and the Bosporus, denying the enemy the chance for reinforcements. Once we had the Turk on the run, we could pursue all the way to Jerusalem and win back the Holy City once and for all.

That was the plan.

But first, we had to defeat the great army of the Turks, led in person by Sultan Murad II.

We had reached Varna on a bitter day at the start of November and were shocked to discover the entire Turkish army camped just two miles away to the west beyond the hills. It was a failure on the part of our scouts and our leadership but once it was done, it could not be easily undone. Our army found itself trapped with the Black Sea to the east and the thickly forested hills in the north from where we had come. Between the northern hills on our right flank and the sea close behind us was an extensive marshland that meant we could not slip away quickly without being surrounded and destroyed.

"It is victory or destruction," I said, raising my hand to point at the Turkish centre. "Besides, William is there."

My companions looked at me once more.

"You do not know that," Eva said.

"I know it."

"You wish it," Eva said. "Because your desire for revenge is so strong that it has overcome your reason. You do not know."

"Your own agents have said he sits at the Sultan's ear, whispering that Christendom must be destroyed. And the Sultan is here, and so William is here." I looked at the vast host. "He would not be elsewhere."

"We are not certain that the man calling himself Zaganos Pasha is truly William," Stephen pointed out. "None of us have seen him with our own eyes."

"They say he is a tall and dark-haired Christian and none knows from where he has come. Some say he is Serbian, others Greek, and others that he is a Frank. It is typical of William to cause such confusion, sewing a dozen stories so that the truth is lost amongst the lies. This Zaganos Pasha has come from nowhere, at no time, and others whisper that he has always been there. He is feared and respected even by his enemies and the other pashas and viziers at the Sultan's court. Who else could Zaganos Pasha be but William?"

"Even so," Stephen began, "we are throwing our lot in with this doomed army without certain proof that—"

"You and Eva will retire to the *wagonberg*," I said to him.

Stephen broke off and turned to look to our rear. Behind us, the centre of our position was a vast ring of a hundred fortified war wagons, emplaced on a section of higher ground.

"I would rather fight at your side," Eva said.

"And I would rather that the work of the Order of the White Dagger continue," I replied. "Should I fall today."

She wished to argue but for the sake of appearances before my men, she simply nodded and pulled back to the *wagonberg*. Those one hundred war wagons were defended by hundreds of expert hand-gunners from Bohemia. The combination of war wagons and firearms were a remarkable military innovation by the

Hussites that had been proven effective in their repeated victories against the great kingdoms of Christendom in the decade or two prior. An innovation embraced enthusiastically by our Transylvanian-born Hungarian leader Janos Hunyadi.

The wagons had high, solid walls on all sides from which the hand-gunners and crossbowmen shot at the enemy, along with men armed with polearms to protect their fellows should enemy cavalry ever reach the wooden walls of the wagon fortress. The solid wood sides dropped down to protect the wheels and the wagons were joined together by strong chains. I had seen wagons pulled into defensive formation before, indeed the Tartars had been well-known for the tactic, but first the Hussites and now the Hungarians had developed the concept into a sophisticated weapon of war that had proved all-but unassailable in previous battles in central and eastern Europe.

Indeed, the day before, when we had discovered the enemy horde were so close, a council of war was called. By that day at Varna, I had fought with Hunyadi for over a year and ever since I had impressed him in my first battle at his side he had invited me to join him at such councils.

It was the king's tent, and King Vladislaus sat in a large chair at the high end of it, but it was Hunyadi who commanded proceedings from where he stood, to the side and two paces in front of the King.

Hunyadi was about forty years old at Varna, in the prime of his life, and he had been a soldier for all of that life already. He was no more than middling height, was rather dark, and he had a heavy brow and a magnificently large nose, but he was not unattractively featured for all that. His eyes were shrewd, pits, twinkling with the intelligence of the man behind them.

In his youth, Hunyadi had served as page for a famous Florentine knight, then as a squire for a great Hungarian lord who loved battle, before serving the Despot of Serbia. Because of his brilliance even as a young man, he had been brought into the retinue of Sigismund, the old King of Hungary, who ordered Hunyadi to join the army of the Duke of Milan so that he might learn the modern ways of battle in Italy. Later, Sigismund brought Hunyadi into Bohemia where the young knight had learned to admire the tactics and technology of the Hussites that he would later replicate.

I had arrived in Hungary, still assembling my own mercenary company, just in time to join Hunyadi in his campaign against the Turks. We fought the Turks in a dozen battles and won almost all of them, though we had ultimately failed to break through the Turkish strongpoints in our efforts to invest the Turkish capital of Edirne, which had once been called Adrianople by the Eastern Romans. Still, we had thrashed the Turks three ways from Sunday and I had been mightily impressed by Hunyadi's tactics and his ability to lead men.

Still, many of his betters were jealous of his rise above them and they doubted his abilities to lead a crusade, even if it was in the name of King Vladislaus of Hungary.

"We are outnumbered and trapped," Cardinal Cesarini had said, his eyes wild. He was a tall man, as finely armoured as a prince, and in the prime of his life. "It is not possible that we should win. All we can do is fortify ourselves within a *wagonberg* and wait for our great fleet to arrive, which surely they must at any moment."

He was not just a representative of the Church of Rome but was a great lord in his own right, as were the other bishops and Church lords who had come as leaders. Each led their own contingents of powerful knights and other men-at-arms, meaning their words at a war council carried weight.

Many of the nobles in the tent called out their agreement.

Janos Hunyadi looked at each man who spoke and seemed to be fixing each of them in his mind as he did so. One by one, they fell silent. Some hung their heads, as if they were chastised boys.

"But even if it did arrive here, would the fleet be large enough to take all of our men from the coast?" Hunyadi asked. The lords spoke in French, occasionally in Latin, and sometimes in Hungarian. My Hungarian was improving every day but thankfully French was spoken by all lords, even those from the mountains of Thrace.

"God willing," Cardinal Cesarini said, to general muttering. "Surely, my lords, with the fleets of the Burgundians, the Venetians, and the Genoese, we shall be saved from this disaster."

"Indeed," a young princeling said, raising his voice. "Indeed, my lords, we must not engage with the enemy. I will not lead my men into a fight they will not survive. We must withdraw tonight under cover of darkness. By morning we could be away toward the Danube."

Voices were raised in agreement and many a man nodded to himself and to his neighbour.

Hunyadi caught my eye and nodded once to me.

I peered over the heads of the men in the command tent and looked down at the princeling that spoke to the great lords of Christendom with such surety. He was a stocky lad with a fluffy beard and moustache beneath a long, sharp nose.

"I beg your pardon but how old are you, little lord?" I called out. A round of stifled laughter flowed through the tent. Even Hunyadi's mouth twitched and he covered it by scratching his cheek.

"Who said that?" the young prince snapped, turning around from the lords at the front. "Some coward who speaks from behind the safety of—"

He stopped as I pushed forward through the men and looked down at him. "I meant no offence, my lord. Your suggestion is not such a bad one. I simply wondered how much experience you have in warfare."

The swarthy young fellow drew himself up as tall as he could and lifted his long nose. "I am Mircea of Wallachia, eldest son and heir of Vlad Dracul, Voivode of Wallachia. I bring seven thousand horsemen and am one of the leaders of this army. Who are you, you great Frankish oaf, to even address me?"

I smiled widely and bowed low. "Of course, now I recognise you. I met your father a few months ago, when he returned to his homeland. I believe your revered father said at that time that we had no chance of victory, did he not? In fact, I recall his very words. The Sultan's hunting party is larger than your entire army, Hunyadi." A few men behind me snorted and young Mircea of Wallachia's dark face darkened further and I quickly raised my voice. "And he was right."

The tent fell silent.

Mircea nodded and spoke warily. "So, you agree with me, sir? We must withdraw tonight, is that not so?"

I lifted my head and pursed my lips, tempted to ask whether he still demanded my name now that he thought I agreed with him but there was no purpose to humiliating the fellow further, especially when he wielded such power. "A withdrawal through the hills at night is possible," I said and turned to address all those present. "For some of us, perhaps. A thousand men might make it out, escaping detection. Two thousand, perhaps." I turned back to Mircea. "Seven thousand, even." His eyes widened. "But any man that attempts to leave this place shall be breaking his oath. What is more, he will be committing a great sin. The greatest sin, perhaps. Yes, any man who attempts to take his men away from the battlefield will not only be abandoning the King of Hungary and his fellow Christians, he shall be abandoning Christ."

Mircea of Wallachia stiffened. "What are you suggesting, sir?"

"Yes," Janos Hunyadi said. "Make your point, sir. There is much to discuss. Surely, you do not suggest dividing our army?"

"My lord," I said and bowed, then I paused while every man looked at me, including the King of Hungary from his throne. "I suggest that tomorrow, we attack the Turk and drive him from Bulgaria forever!" Men cried out and began arguing with me and then with each other. Many seemed to agree with me, especially the French and German lords. But others disagreed, calling into question my sanity and my ability so that I raised my voice above them so I would be heard.

"We do not have the numbers!" the Bishop of Talotis cried.

"Even with God on our side, we cannot defeat so many."

"Do not let your eyes fool you, my lords," I said. "Their numbers are swelled by the many thousands of *azabs* they will throw at us. These men are peasants, with no armour and almost no will to fight. We shall run them down without slowing our horses."

"It is not the peasants but the *sipahis* that concern us," said a young Hungarian nobleman named Stephen Bathory who was the Palatine of Hungary, which I understood to be as high a rank as a man could achieve in that kingdom and he was well-favoured by his king. "The *sipahis* are equal to our mounted men and they have two or three times our number. They are our only concern."

"They are not our equal!" Michael Szilágyi said. He was another Hungarian noble and Hunyadi's brother-in-law. I liked him, although he did not feel the same about me and mistrusted outsiders. Which is right and proper, of course, and I did not hold it against him. "Our armour is stronger and our horses far larger."

"Precisely," said Bishop Dominek of Varadin. "Our beasts shall tire while theirs remain fleet and strong throughout the day."

Hunyadi, watching and listening, glanced at me.

I raised my voice over theirs and silenced them with sheer volume and the refusal to cease speaking. "What else can we do, my lords, but attack them and destroy them? If we take shelter inside the wooden walls of a *wagonberg*, with no army in the field, the cannons of the Turks will blast down our walls and destroy us. Our only way out is over the corpses of the Turks."

Cardinal Cesarini raised his hand and cried out. "We also have cannons, sir, thanks to God. And so with our cannons we shall destroy the Turks first, from a position of safety. Until the fleet arrives."

"There will be no fleet!" Bathory shouted. "If they were coming, they would be here by now, would they not?"

The discussion continued and Hunyadi nodded his thanks, so I stepped back into the crowd and held my tongue until they had talked themselves into action.

There really was no other choice but to attack and Hunyadi won them over with his plans. The king gave all appearances of backing Hunyadi's plan of action and once Vladislaus stated that we would indeed attack tomorrow, the others fell in line or fell silent.

It had always been the case that no matter what anyone said, or hoped, there was no way out but forward, through the Turks.

It was to be a battle.

"He may be just sixteen years old," Hunyadi said, nodding at the back of Mircea of Wallachia as the lords filed out. "But he is not a fool. He has the cunning of his father. And, like his father, he will continue to play both sides in this crusade. He will pay tribute to the Turks with one hand and offer the other to Hungary."

I sighed. "He is a devious little shit if ever I met one. But one can hardly fault a lord for protecting his vassals."

Hunyadi scoffed. "His vassals? Vlad Dracul and his son care only for themselves." He sighed. "But I must give him some credit. The Turks hold his other two sons as hostages and he certainly risks their lives by sending his men to join us. So, Richard, no matter how we dislike them, we must try to not judge him or his father too harshly."

"And we need them."

"I wish it was not so but yes, we need them."

"His men must be guarded in case Mircea attempts to withdraw his men in the night," I said. "It is clear that he believes we cannot win the battle and so he will flee. He does not seem to be a man overly concerned with honour."

Hunyadi sighed again, rubbing his eyes. "Unfortunately, you are right. Yes, they shall be watched. The Wallachians are always watched. But if he takes his seven thousand horsemen away from me, what can I do? Send ten thousand to stop him? Begin the battle by fighting amongst ourselves? If he decides to abandon us, all I can do is let him go."

"We cannot afford to lose seven thousand."

"No."

"Whether or not we win this battle," I said, "we must not allow any Christian land to fall to the enemy, by force of arms or diplomacy. The Wallachians have the most defensible land in the region and they must be brought to heel."

He nodded. "It is easy for you, an outsider, to say such things. You are more right than you know but it is not so easy to do. We shall deal with such matters later. Tonight, we must prepare. Tomorrow, we must fight. God wills it."

"He does, my lord, He does." And so do the Turks, I thought. "With your permission, I will see to my men."

After an uncomfortable night camped on the plain, exposed to the wind off the sea behind us, we rose in the morning and were arrayed in a crescent, with Lake Varna on our left flank and the hills rising to our right. Our forces were spread across a mile or two. My place in the centre was not far from Hunyadi and his enormous bodyguard of superbly equipped men-at-arms.

The thousands of mounted Wallachians were behind us and were under orders to act as a mobile reserve to counter any breaks in the line or any flanking attack that came around by the lakeshore or from the hills. I prayed that young Mircea would do his job well, for if the swarms of *sipahis* could get in amongst us and behind us, we would be finished.

Behind the Wallachians was the *wagonberg*, our wooden fortress protected by the Bohemian mercenaries with their hand-guns and great polearms. If it came to it, we could fall back and rally at the *wagonberg* under cover of the guns. That was where I had sent Stephen and Eva, along with those of our servants who would be of no help in the fighting, and the youngest of the pages and grooms.

"Turks in the hills, now," Walt said, nodding that way. "See the little bastards glinting in the woods on the ridge there?"

I could see little enough in the trees. Walt had good eyes and a good nose for danger, so I believed him.

The Sultan's empire was divided in two by the waters of the Sea of Marmara and the straits of the Bosporus and Dardanelles. With Anatolia on one side and Rumelia on the other, the lands of Europe that had once been ruled by Constantinople or Bulgaria or other Balkan kingdoms. And the Sultan had deployed his army in the same way, with the lords and soldiers of Anatolia on his left flank and those of Rumelia on his right.

"Their Anatolian cavalry will engage our right," I said, "and their infantry will push through the woods, beyond our flank, and get behind them. They will have bows with which to shoot our men and they will have spears to ward them off."

"What can we do about that?" Rob said, frowning as he squinted up at the hills.

"Nothing."

"God damn them," Rob said, turning to spit.

"It is a rather standard ploy, is it not?" I asked. "When one has the numbers on their enemy."

"I do not damn the Turks but our own lords," Rob replied. "Why in the name of God do we have almost no infantry? We need men on foot. Spearmen, peasant levies, even townsmen would do. Have they lost their wits?"

"They believe that infantry would slow them down too much," I said. "Others say they cannot afford to pay for the upkeep of such low-quality men when we already have so many veteran mercenaries, and that the supplies required to feed them would be more than could be procured. Others I have heard state simply that they have no need for such useless oafs blundering about against our Turkish foes, being that our enemy are mostly horsemen themselves."

"Madness," Rob said. "Peasant spearmen could cover the woods up there. They could screen our mounted men here at the front. They could fill gaps in our lines, hold positions out on the field for us to make charges from. Anyone would think our great lords have never been to war before."

"They haven't," Walt said.

I shrugged. "Some of them know. Others know that nothing

can resist a heavy horse charge. Not all the Turks on earth. And they are trusting to that."

"Can't they bloody see how many spearmen the Turks have?" Walt said. "How many, do you reckon?"

Sighing, I pointed out vast formations all across their lines and made an estimate. "Twenty thousand? Thirty? Difficult to see through all the horsemen galloping here and there."

"They have more in infantry than our entire army, Richard," Rob said. "You are certain we must fight this battle?"

We have no choice, I wanted to say. But that is not what my men needed to hear.

"What happens if we do not smash them here? They may push on to the Danube and then along it all the way to Belgrade, and from there to Buda, then to Vienna. Where to then? Prague? Nuremberg? And then into France?"

Walt laughed, shaking his head. "You exaggerate, Richard. A dozen kingdoms would rout the Turk well before then."

"How many men can France put into the field, would you say? Twenty thousand?" I pointed at the Turks. "There stands a hundred thousand veterans, armoured in plate and mail, with more and better guns than us." I jerked my thumb over my shoulder. "How many more men could they bring up from Anatolia, if they needed to? As many as this again? Four times this many?" I pointed at the centre of the Turkish army again. "And William may be there, at the heart of them. Driving them on. It is our duty to be here. It is our duty to defeat the enemy. And so that is what we shall do."

A few men around me cheered but their apprehension was

apparent.

We had around three thousand men in the centre, mainly King Vladislaus' Polish and Hungarian bodyguards, the Hungarian mounted mercenaries, and the Hungarian nobles and their men. The mercenaries were commanded by Stephen Bathory.

Our left flank was commanded by the very capable lord Michael Szilágyi. He had around five thousand Transylvanians and German mercenaries and a few Hungarian lords who were sworn to him. They were enormously outnumbered on that flank by twenty thousand sipahi cavalry, each man with mail or lamellar armour and quality helms, with long lances and shields for the charge. Their horses were fast and could run all day, if handled well.

Still, I hoped that Szilágyi could hold them.

It was clear from the deployment of Turkish light infantry moving through the forested hills that they would attempt to turn or crush our flank there. And it was clear that Hunyadi had seen the danger, as he weighted our strength most heavily on our right. Bishop Dominek of Varadin had six thousand men alone. Cardinal Cesarini commanded thousands of well-equipped German crusaders, and the Bishops of Erleau and Talotsi, the governor of Slavonia, commanded their own contingents.

I prayed it would be enough.

In the centre, the Sultan stood behind ten thousand Janissaries.

These were his best men. They were also men who should have been ours. They were ours by blood and by birth but they had been stolen. Taken, by the Turk's *devshirme*, the Blood Tax, imposed by the Turks on all Christians who they had subjugated. Every year, the Sultan's agents, often Janissaries themselves, would collect Christian boys from the Balkans and make them his personal slaves. These boys would be aged eight or ten or even older boys close to becoming men. When they were taken, these poor innocents were indoctrinated into believing the alien religion of Mohammedanism. They were trained in military pursuits and administration until the age of around twenty and then placed into the Sultan's personal army or the civil service. And they were utterly loyal to the Sultan, and he used the existence of these elite troops to keep his great lords under control.

It was only the Christians under the Turks who were subject to the *devshirme*. Not the Jews, nor the wild Turkmen tribes in the east, or the Mongols of the Golden Horde. Only Christians— whether Anatolians whose ancestors were Romans and Greeks, or Bulgarians from Rumelia—a people strong in body, quick in wits, and loyal to a fault, were desired for the Blood Tax. Some of the highest ability might one day, after a life of service, become landowners and a very small handful might one day become governors or viziers. But no matter how high they rose, they would never be granted complete freedom.

And the Janissaries alone, the most highly trained soldiers in the world, numbered ten thousand. Not only did they hold the centre, on a small hill, they were well dug in behind barricades and were supported by an incredible number of levy troops.

And we would have to somehow overcome them all to achieve

victory.

A sudden wind whipped up from the Black Sea behind us, wailing and powerful enough to stagger us and frighten the horses. Hundreds of banners were blown down and standard bearers pulled off their feet. Only that of King Vladislaus III stayed upright. It seemed to be a sign from God but what meaning the sign had, no one could agree.

"Here they come," Walt said, pointing to our right flank.

Up along the row of hills, thousands of Turkish horsemen advanced in a staggered series of lines.

"By God," Rob said, crossing himself. "They are so many."

"Our men are stronger," I said, sitting as high as I could and peering through the upright lances and banners between me and the right flank that curved forward. "All we need to do is keep our heads."

Even as I spoke, though, thousands of our horsemen on that flank advanced away from our lines to meet the massive Turkish attack.

"What are they doing?" Walt cried. "Why advance now? They must wait."

"They must," I agreed. "Yet they do not."

We watched in horror as the horsemen under the bishops of Erlau and Varadin plunged headlong into the massive Turkish advance. Rather than leave the others to their fate, the two thousand men under the Bishop of Talotsi, also advanced into the enormous melee. All together, our men were outnumbered three or four to one and soon there was little chance for them to withdraw, no matter how frantically Hunyadi's men signalled that they should do so.

With the right flank advancing so far forward, there was now a huge gap between them and our men in the centre.

"Richard?" Rob said. "Perhaps you might ride across to Hunyadi and suggest he close the gap?"

"Hunyadi knows his business," I said. "But tell our men to prepare themselves. We shall see action soon."

It was then that the Turks sent their other wing forward against our left, by the lake. Michael Szilágyi was a capable man and the Hungarians were disciplined enough to meet it in good order. The clash was incredible, with dozens of companies charging and wheeling repeatedly with neither side gaining any immediate advantage.

"There are gaps between us and both flanks," Rob said.

"And if the enemy push between one of them?" I said.

"I suppose we in the centre would counter and crush them from both sides," Rob admitted. "But the Sultan has enough men to attack both gaps and get around our flank on the right."

"He is holding, for now," I said, watching the Turkish centre. The tens of thousands of infantry and horse there were still dug in behind their barricades and in their trenches. "He fears Hunyadi's ability."

"You think the Sultan afraid?" Walt asked.

"He respects Hunyadi's ability," I said. "And so he should. Here is a signal, men."

Trumpets sounded and flags were waved from the centre where Hunyadi and his bodyguard advanced. I ordered my men forward and we moved away from King Vladislaus and his loyal troops who stayed back. I turned my horse to review the state of my men and noted behind them that the Wallachians were advancing to take the position that we were leaving. They would plug the gap and they would help to defend the King. Hunyadi really did know his business.

"Where is he leading us?" Walt called out over the wind and the growing din of battle. "Left, right, or centre?"

"We shall see," I said. The noise of the clashes on the flanks was like a distant sea, rising and falling but relentless and growing louder as more and more men were drawn in.

"Care to wager on it?" Walt asked, grinning.

"Do not be crass," I said as the men-at-arms of my company rode past us. "Thousands of men are about to die."

"Ten ecus says that we attack the left flank."

"You do not have ten ecus," I said, nodding and holding up my hand to this or that man of mine as he advanced.

Walt patted his breastplate. "Got more than that right here, Richard."

"Very well. Hunyadi must seek to save our right before it collapses," I said, confidently. "And that is where we will go."

"Richard wagers we go into the hills, very well, and I say it shall be the left." Walt grinned. "Rob?"

"I do not have ten ecus," he said. "But surely we will attack the centre?"

"Only a madman would assault ten thousand hand-gunners, Rob," I said. "Protected by ten thousand spearmen."

He scratched his nose. "I'll not wager what I do not have."

"Our lads look keen enough," Walt said as the last of our men-at-arms advanced past us, raising their hands or their lances in salute to me as they went. "Hard-hearted bastards, ain't they?"

We had French, Burgundians, Britons, English, Irish, Scots, Welsh, all desperate men seeking fortune and glory. But I had personally tested each one before allowing them to join my company and Rob and Walt kept a close eye on them. Since leaving England, we had recruited those we needed as we crossed Europe and we had expelled those who were found wanting, either in ability or in moral character. Some were brutal men, killers with little education and even less fear, but I would not allow disobedience or men not in possession of self-control. They were a good company and I was pleased with them.

"Will we get close to the Sultan?" Rob asked. "You believe William to be there, at his side. But if the centre is unassailable..."

"The more that I think on it, I believe if we drive off the flanks, we will have a stalemate. We cannot assail their central position and I doubt they will attempt our *wagonberg*. If his *sipahis* are crushed, the Sultan will likely withdraw. William will have to wait for another day."

"If he's even there at all," Walt said.

"The time for discussion is over," I snapped. "Come, let us catch Hunyadi and his men and do our duty."

With a final glance back at the great banner and bodyguard of King Vladislaus and the vast *wagonberg* behind him, I closed the visor on my helm. I could see ahead through the slits and down at my body through the breathing holes but due to the solid armour covering my neck, I had to turn my shoulders along with my head in order to see to either side. My nose was filled at once

23

with the sourness of my breath.

We galloped forward and with surprise I saw Hunyadi's banner continuing straight toward the centre of the enemy. We were yet far enough away that their Janissaries' handheld firearms would not reach us but still I thought I had overestimated Janos Hunyadi. He was going to charge straight into a hail of deadly lead balls and the battle would be lost. All would be lost.

But I should have had faith for, with a waving of signal flags and blaring of trumpets, he finally ordered us to attack the enemy flank.

Not toward the hills where our right was crumbling, as I had wagered ten gold pieces in expectation of, but instead to our left, where Szilágyi's Hungarians were holding.

We had advanced so far that we crashed into their flank and slipped behind them, attacking the rear.

"Keep the men together!" I ordered. "Stay together!"

My company formed up together on either side of me and we charged into the *sipahis*. I thrust my lance into a Turk and shoved him out of his saddle before pushing on into the man behind him. The press of men was enormous and the sea of horses swelled and crashed under the weight of our charge. My men knew not to advance too far, too quickly, and we helped each other to disengage and pull back. Once we and our horses had paused for breath, we dressed our line and advanced again into a charge at their crumbling flank.

As their centre pulled back to meet our charges, Szilágyi pushed them further with his own men. Hundreds died in the charges and hundreds more in the press of the fighting but they were unnerved due to being surrounded and their will crumbled until the *sipahis* fighting us fled in something close to panic.

"Stay here!" I ordered, and Walt and Rob and my other key men ensured my company stayed together. There was little better in life than pursuing a fleeing enemy and many a soldier let it go to his head, whooping and cheering as he chased the *sipahis*. But the day was far from over and we would need every man on the field and so my company reined in and came back to the centre with me.

Other captains and lords were not so fortunate in their soldiers as was I. For the Turks fled so far that the chasing Hungarians disappeared along the lakeshore. Later I would hear that they in fact got fully behind the Turkish lines and began looting enemy camps that they found there. The damned fools filled their purses with loot and sport as they ran through panicking camp followers and servants while the rest of us fought on.

As Hunyadi attempted to rally us back to him in the centre, Walt rode up, shouting and pointing his bloody mace behind me.

Opening my visor, I turned to look up at the hills.

Our right flank was destroyed.

The men there were outnumbered in horse but they had also been surrounded by Turkish archers in the woods, shooting down at our knights as they fled the field. Some of the Germans were pulling back to the *wagonberg*, still in good order with banners raised, but the flank was still open.

"Are we finished?" Rob called. "Should we return for Eva?"

"The Wallachians must hold the line in front of the wagons,"

I cried. "The battle is yet in the balance, men. We have won a flank apiece but both centres hold. All is well. We shall yet win the day."

But I had underestimated Mircea, son of Vlad Dracul, and his Wallachian horsemen, for they did not hold, nor did they engage the enemy. Even as the rest of the Christians watched, they galloped their seven thousand men, perhaps a fifth of our army, along the banks of the lake through the gap the Hungarians had opened up by crushing that flank. Later, I would discover that young Mircea stopped only to join in the looting of the Turkish camp before continuing on all the way back to Wallachia.

"Those duplicitous bastards," I shouted as they cantered by in their thousands. "Treacherous little shit. I swear by Christ I shall have his head."

"Is that it?" Walt asked. "We can't win, now, can we?"

"No," Rob said. "Only a matter of time before some other lords decide to follow the Wallachians."

"We are not lost! But we must assault the horsemen on our right," I shouted to my men, pointing up at the hills. "The only enemy cavalry on the field is there, do you see? We can still kill them all. Do you hear me? We will kill the enemy cavalry and then the day is not lost." When wearing a helm, it was difficult to hear a lord's voice especially with the wind and the roar of battle, and so I shouted something clearer my men would understand. "We will kill them!"

Hunyadi and his Hungarians were forming up to do just that and I led my men forward with them. We rode slowly across the field and squires and pages handed out water and wine and some men stuffed bread or slices of sausage into their mouths. Exhausted horses were exchanged, and damaged weapons replaced. It appeared that some of the Hungarian nobles who had remained in the centre with the king were moving rightward to join us in the rising ground. I wondered whether the Turks would chance an assault against the King, but we were now between him and most of the enemy's remaining horse so it seemed likely he would be safe where he was.

The Turks were superb horsemen. Their horses were well-bred and trained for war, just as the men riding them were. Big fellows with bow legs and broad chests, just like the Mongols and other Tartars from whom they were descended. Hundreds of years of success on the battlefields of the steppe, and the hills of Anatolia, and the plains of Thrace and Bulgaria, had made them experts at war and had provided them with enormous riches plundered from the collapsing Roman Empire of the east.

Even so, there was nothing in all the world that could stand up to a charge by the knights of Europe. We were superb horsemen, too, raised in the saddle, practised in the proper use of the lance from boyhood. Our steel armour was the finest the world had ever seen, whether Italian or German made, and as long as we were led by a lord who knew the limitations of the charge, there was no hope for an enemy that attempted to resist it.

Hunyadi ensured that each of his companies were formed up before he ordered the attack on the Turks. His bodyguard were the centre, and Hungarian lords surrounded him. Near to the centre, Walt and Rob harangued my company into a line with voices louder than thunder. Contingents from Germany formed their own lines above us to the right. The Bishop of Talotis, God love him, somehow brought his defeated men back to join us in a renewed assault.

The order was sounded to advance and six or seven thousand of us moved toward the Turkish *sipahis*. They were busy chasing down the poor remnants of the right flank, desperately defending themselves from the wheeling Turks. When they saw us coming, the enemy galloped in all directions, attempting to form up against us. I thought that they would certainly do it but as we got closer and slowly increased our pace, they were still attempting to regain their order and were yet in several great, confused masses rather than ordered formations. At the last moment, our scores of companies charged in a staggered, broken line that must have been a mile wide.

I saw little of it, as I lowered my lance and raked my spurs against my horse, trusting that my men would be beside me. I thrust my lance into a Turk's helm with such force that he was certainly destroyed immediately. On, I charged, and my lance took the next man low on his flank as he turned to flee and his horse fell along with him. My lance broken, I used an axe to break through the Turks I came to. Beside me, my men attacked and we pushed on into the darkness of battle, with the cacophony of war filling my head so that all I could hear was a roar and the laboured breathing from my own lungs as I drove deeper into the enemy.

All of a sudden, there was daylight and sky, and no more enemies to kill.

They had broken and fled. Bodies lay everywhere underfoot

and horses with no riders galloped in confusion this way and that.

Our men were celebrating our victory. We had killed the Beylerbey of Anatolia along with thousands of horsemen, and now the crusaders were the only horsemen left on the field.

"Now what?" Walt called, after we collected our surviving men and took stock of the damage done. Only six of my men had been killed. We were bruised and battered, some men nursing bad wounds, but my company had tasted a victory and only wanted more.

"No man loots the bodies," I shouted. "Unless it is to replace a weapon he has lost. We must reform on Hunyadi and either attack that damned fortress of a Turkish centre or withdraw."

"Richard?" Rob said, looking down the hill to our centre. "In the name of God, Richard, what is he doing?"

By *he*, Rob meant King Vladislaus III, who was riding at the heart of his enormous bodyguard. Thousands of heavily armoured horses and knights advanced along the flat of the plain straight at the Turkish centre.

"By God," I cried. "He means to attack himself."

"Stupid bastard," Walt said, pausing to spit a mouthful of blood to one side. "He wants some of the glory for himself, does he not?"

"He must be blind," Rob said. "Or mad."

"Glory," I said. "He seeks glory."

Walt scoffed. "He'll find a spear shoved up his arse instead, the silly bastard."

"Long has he been in Hunyadi's shadow. A lord should not be outshone by his vassal. And Vladislaus is a king."

"So he means to steal Hunyadi's victory and claim it for his own," Rob said, nodding.

"He's a fool," Walt said.

"What do we do?" Rob asked.

I looked for Hunyadi's banner. He was forming up his men but we were so much further away and the King, astonishingly, did not appear to be waiting for us. The trumpets sounded and we made our way across the slant of the hill toward the massive Turkish centre. By that point, we had been fighting for hours and our men and horses were exhausted. If we rushed toward the enemy, we would be on our knees by the time we reached them and so we were able to watch as the flower of Hungarian nobility charged the Turkish centre. It was the king's finest men against the Sultan's ranks of infantry, thousands of them, in prepared defensive position.

In front of the ranks of waiting Janissaries were lines of *azabs*, the peasant spearmen. These were swiftly overcome by the power of the Hungarian charge and the spearmen fell or were scattered as the nobles and their men rode them down and continued on, barely slowing or needing to reform. It was a magnificent display of bright colours and shining steel.

Behind were ranks of armoured infantry, armed with spears and axes, and wearing metal helms. But these men fled as the Hungarians rode down the thousands of peasant levies in front of them.

That left only the Janissaries between the King of Hungary and the Sultan of the Turks.

"He's going to do it!" Walt shouted. "Bloody hell, Richard,

the king is going to kill the Sultan after all."

Many of my men and the others around us believed the same, for they raised their weapons and cheered, urging their king on. There were ten thousand Janissaries but their lines looked rather thin compared to that of the peasants the king had just run down. The Janissaries were barely armoured.

My heart fluttered at the thought that we might just do it after all. *If the Turks break, we shall have to pursue William through Bulgaria*, I thought.

As the king and his men approached the hill upon which the ten thousand Janissaries formed, the foremost ranks of the elite Turkish soldiers raised their long weapons to their chests, pointed them, and almost as one fired their hand-guns.

I had seen small hand-held cannons here and there for years. In Milan, decades earlier, I had watched a company of mercenaries displaying one such weapon which they propped up at the front with a long, forked stick and a man held at the rear with the pole attached to the iron barrel. When another of the fellows held a burning rope to the touch hole, the small cannon belched out a great stinking cloud of smoke with a sound so loud it caused my ears to ring for a day. The poor fool not only missed the target but fell over backwards after the shot, no doubt more from fear of mishap than from the force. How we laughed.

"Absurd of them to suggest such a device could replace a crossbow," I said to Walt, both of us grinning at the notion.

Fifty years later and we yet used crossbows but often they were used beside hand-gunners, whose firearms had developed into reliable weapons fired by couching the thing in one's arm at chest height while touching the firing pan with a lit rope. The Bohemians used them to great effectiveness from the safety of their wagons, as did the Hungarians who had taken up their arms and methods.

But the Janissaries had them also and trained to use them in the field and had done so with great success against Turkmen tribes in the east and against the poor people of the Balkans and so were well practised in technique and application. Far more than I had realised until that moment.

Thousands of Janissaries fired their guns in a great billowing of smoke that belched from their lines.

Moments later, the massive sound of it reached us and boomed and rolled from the hills.

Down on the plain, the royal and noble riders and horses fell in their scores but still they came on, their horses drumming their hooves on the earth. Before they reached the Janissaries, another volley of smoke and noise crashed and more knights fell tumbling back or rolling beneath their horses.

It was a slaughter. It reminded me of English archers shooting their longbows into French knights so many decades before. But instead of joy, I now felt horror.

Even though so many fell, the mad charge of the Hungarian nobles reached the Janissaries lines. We still rode closer and as we descended, it became more difficult to see but their charge crashed into the Janissaries at many places. They rode down the enemy palisades and then broke through the Janissaries' lines. Once through the first ranks of hand-gunners, they pushed deeper in.

I still had hope.

The king's banner wavered and slowed but it, and the king beneath it, pushed deeper into the Turk's camp to within a stone's throw of the Sultan's great tents.

But the enemy numbers were too many.

By the time we came down the hills and reached the flanks of the enemy lines, there was little we could do to reach the King, deep in the centre. We killed thousands of spearmen on our approach, we bowled over the armoured Anatolian infantry who had fled the king's charge, and we rode down Janissaries and cut at them. And yet they did not break. Far from it, in fact, and when they recovered from the shock enough to begin firing their hand-guns at us, we were forced back in our thousands and we retreated out of range for another charge.

"Come on!" I shouted. "We must break them. We will break them!"

No one wanted to charge against such an implacable enemy but I rode up and down the front rank of my company.

"We must not, Richard," Rob said. "It is madness."

"William is there," I roared. "He will be there, by the Sultan. This is our duty."

"Very well," Rob said, exchanging a look with Walter. They closed their visors and waved my men into line.

I led them forward and our charge was mighty indeed. We ran down the foremost ranks of the Janissaries and got in amongst those behind, cutting down scores of them.

"We are surrounded!" Walt shouted. "We must break free or be lost."

"Damn you, man," I swore. But he was not wrong and I ordered us to retreat once more.

It was a bloody and desperate battle. Even then, after so many of us had been lost, we might have won the day. Might have reached the Sultan and ended him and his son before all the devastation that they and their descendants would wreak upon Christendom.

But King Vladislaus III of Hungary was killed.

The cry went up along the line that the king had fallen and all remaining fight went out of the crusaders.

It was over. We knew we could not rally after such a loss.

I joined Hunyadi and we attempted to rescue the king or recover his body, at least, but scores of men fell all around us and it quickly became clear that we could do no more without bringing the remaining army to disaster. The Janissaries advanced on us and we had to retreat.

Our forces did not collapse and we disengaged carefully, though arrows fell and their hand-guns fired, we pulled away out of range. They were reeling from our assaults and their infantry could never have pursued our cavalry anyway.

We retired to the *wagonberg*, and together fled the field in some semblance of good order. The surviving Turkish cavalry limped after us but they never attempted a proper assault. In our various national groups, we formed up and fled beyond the Turks, either along the lakeshore or through the hills or marshes and we all attempted to get as far away as fast as possible. Indeed, we rode through a portion of the night before stopping to rest and tend our wounds.

I had just over fifty men left in my company and those that lived were battered and tired. Our remounts were needed but even those were exhausted and many of my servants rode two to a horse. We had left the company's wagons and much of our supplies back at the camp but there was nothing to be done about that. Eva was angry at the decisions that had been made but I think mostly she was annoyed that she had missed out on the fighting. Stephen fretted about what it all might mean for Christendom, muttering of dark things, but Walt told him to hold his damned tongue. We had no time to indulge in anything but flight.

The enemy did not have enough cavalry left to defeat our fleeing forces, for at least six thousand of our soldiers had survived. But we left ten thousand or so dead on the field and the Turks pursued us for days and weeks, as we rode back toward Hungary in a fog of defeat.

It was a hard ride. We could not stop for long without falling behind and those that fell behind were in danger of falling to the Turks chasing us.

But stop we did and word spread amongst us about what had happened at the end of the battle and I sought out witnesses.

Later, during the journey, I found a Polish knight who had survived the charge alongside the King. The knight was recovering from multiple wounds, and the ones on his head seemed at first to have robbed him of his wits. Or, perhaps it was the horror of the battle that had done so. We crouched, shivering, over a tiny campfire, and I urged him to speak of it.

"Did he reach the Sultan?"

The knight's eyes filled with orange tears that reflected the light of the fire. "Alas, no. It was not in some glorious combat with the Sultan or his son. First, he was shot by a slave armed with a cowardly, satanic weapon at a distance but that did not stop him. His horse was shot also, many times, but it did not slow. He charged on ahead of me, shouting for the Sultan to fight him. The king was almost at his tent when a man stepped forward with a long spear and thrust it up into him." The Polish knight stopped speaking and stared through the fire.

"A man?" I asked. "A Janissary?"

The Pole shook his head slowly. "He was bareheaded and unarmoured, in fine clothes. Not a Turk. He had the look of a Frank. Or an Englishman." He lifted his eyes to mine. "Like you."

A chill that was not from the night air ran through me. "His name is William. I believe they call him Zaganos Pasha, now."

"He was taken in the Blood Tax?" the knight asked.

I shook my head. "What happened after he was speared? You saw him die? Or was he merely wounded?"

The knight looked away again. "Your man, Zaganos Pasha, he pulled the king down from his horse as if he was no more than a child. Lifted him, in all his armour, and ripped off his helm with one hand and then he... he defiled him."

"Did he... forgive me, sir, did he *bite* the King?"

The man's eyes glowed. "Bite? He tore his face off with his teeth while the king screamed for God. And then with a long knife he cut his head from his body. The Janissaries cheered this."

"I am glad you survived to tell me what happened," I said.

He snapped his head up and glared at me. "I did all I could!

My men pulled me away, forced me away, against my will, I would have died to defend him, would have died to defend his corpse from defilement."

I held up my frozen hands. "I meant no offence, sir, and apologise for having caused it. Others have told me of your bravery on the field and there is no man alive who doubts it, least of all me. Is there anything I can do for you?"

"Just leave me be," he said.

The Polish knight died of his wounds two days later. Like many men in that desperate retreat, he was swiftly buried in whatever suitable site could be found before the pursuing Turks caught up. We left a trail of crusader bodies many weeks long as we followed the course of the Danube, seeking support from the local people of Bulgaria and then Wallachia.

With the survivors of my company, I rode with Hunyadi's dwindling group of loyal men. Companies broke off at various points so that each group could slip through a number of valleys and passes on our journey back to Transylvania and Hungary without running into enemy forces.

Perhaps I should have abandoned Hunyadi but I wanted to help to defend him until he reached safety.

One morning we were surrounded at both ends of a steep vale by hundreds of Wallachian horsemen. Some of them I am sure were those who had treacherously abandoned us at Varna.

"We are here to escort you to my lord Vlad Dracul, the Voivode of Wallachia," said the fat nobleman leading them, addressing Hunyadi directly.

Hunyadi was furious but he controlled himself. "My thanks,

sir, but we have no wish to do so. We are returning to Transylvania directly without your escort."

The Wallachian lord smiled through his beard, showing a mouthful of yellow teeth. "Forgive my unpractised Hungarian, my lord, but what I mean to say is that you are my prisoner. And soon you will be the prisoner of the Voivode of Wallachia, Vlad Dracul. Come with me now or we shall kill you here. Is that clear, my lord?"

Hunyadi's men stirred, some drawing their swords. I walked my own horse slowly forward closer to Hunyadi's. We were outnumbered three to one and we were exhausted. But I thought we could break through if we fought together and meant to say so.

Instead, Hunyadi gave himself, and all of us, up as prisoners.

"Damned bastard," Walt cursed him as we were escorted into Wallachia. "Bastard coward. We could have killed these useless dogs and been free."

"He is mortal," I said. "And mortals must preserve their lives where we would risk them. We cannot fault him for this."

Walt was incensed. "You seen this Vlad Dracul with your own eyes. You met his son. Insulted him, to his face. These treacherous Wallachians will cross us and give us up to their friends the Turks, mark my words, Richard. Mark my words."

Looking up at the forested hills of Wallachia, I thought that Black Walter might just be right.

2

Târgoviște

1444 - 1447

WE WERE ESCORTED NORTHWARD through the Wallachian plains to the capital of Târgoviște. At the end of a long valley and at the foot of the hills that rose in the north to become a vast chain of mountains, the town had an attractive river running beside it that came tumbling and twisting down into a meandering course that irrigated the fields, then bare and cold. It would be a place I came to know and host to scenes that would haunt my nightmares for centuries, but the first time I laid eyes on it, it seemed a sturdy and well-appointed city in the German style.

Certainly, the defences of Târgoviște had been attended to, for it was protected by a high and thick stone wall with sturdy towers at intervals around the perimeter and over every gate.

Inside, the buildings were well made and of a good size, if far plainer when compared to the grand and intricate stonework of Buda or the ornate richness of Vienna. It had first been built by Saxon colonists and still retained that German character and, indeed, a large Saxon population who were responsible for most of the trade that went on in the city. But it was far more civilised than I had expected and as I entered through the gates I hoped that our captors would likewise prove to be more courteous than I had imagined.

"Vlad Dracul is in residence," Stephen mumbled, nudging me with his elbow and indicating a great dragon banner hung on the walls of the castle.

"Thought he was supposed to be off waging war on the Turk?" Walt said.

"So were we," Rob replied.

The ordinary soldiers, including my surviving men, were herded into tents in a huge field outside the walls and they would be damned uncomfortable but I reminded them to thank the Christ that the Wallachians had been so generous. They grumbled but they were hard fellows to a man, squires and servants included, and so they took to their quarters with stoicism.

"Do not attempt to run," I warned them before I went into the city. "We will play our parts and all will be well."

"Reckon they'll have work for us, sir?"

"We shall see."

As a leading mercenary captain and knight, I was allotted

quarters for myself and my servants, those being Eva, Stephen, Walter and Rob and a handful of true servants. We were crammed into two dark rooms inside the castle within the city but it was warm and dry.

"This is the finest prison I have ever been in," I quipped as the door was slammed shut. "How lucky for us that warlords like Vlad Dracul rely on the services of mercenaries."

"We need blood," Eva said, her face ashen and eyes dark. "I will bleed the servants. You must free us from this place."

"Certainly, my dear."

I spoke to placate her, because she was suffering from the blood sickness. But I knew it would not be so simple to extricate ourselves. The Wallachians were a people that seemed filled with violence, many appeared to feel vitriolic hatred for the Hungarians and for the people of any other nation who followed the Pope of Rome rather than their own Orthodox Church. We had been captured with Hunyadi and that might have meant we were destined to share whatever fate he would suffer. On the other hand, they had treated us well by providing pleasant quarters.

We bled our servants and my immortals drank, sighing and calming themselves as the blood sickness symptoms retreated. Later, our captors brought bread, cheese, and cured pork, which we devoured, and even jugs of wine. Eva and I shared the main bed, Walt claimed one trundle bed and Stephen did the other. Our servants curled up where they could, and we passed the night in more warmth and comfort than we had experienced for many months. Still, Rob took the first watch and swapped with Walt, who swapped with Stephen. None came to harm us in the darkness. We may have been treated well but that did not mean I trusted our captors.

The next day, I was taken to the great hall where Vlad Dracul sat on his throne with his eldest son, Mircea, beside him on a throne of his own. Light from windows high above the thrones illuminated them, while the rest of the room was lit only with lamps around the walls. A hot fire burned in the huge fireplace behind the throne but it was still cold in the hall.

Vlad II Dracul was about fifty years old and he looked older but he was yet broad in the shoulder and straight backed. His face was fixed into a scowl, just as it had been when I had last seen him across a hall months before. I suspected from the depth of the lines on his face that the scowl was a permanent feature of it and had been s0 for decades. His dark eyes were narrowed beneath a low brow and his blade of a nose jutted from between them. His black moustache was as wide as his face and the oiled ends were curled up like two iron hooks.

Before the prince and his son, on one side of the hall, stood the *boyars*, the great lords of Wallachia. In Wallachia, the commoners were made up from the masses of free peasantry and then there were the lords, who were called *boyars*, above them and then there was the *voivode*, which was a title meaning the Prince of Wallachia. I did not yet understand just how much power those *boyars* wielded in Wallachian society, but I was about to.

On the other side of the hall stood the Hungarian and allied knights and nobles that had been captured along with Hunyadi, although Hunyadi himself was not present. There was an empty gulf between the two groups who stood glaring at each other and muttering amongst themselves. I slipped almost unnoticed into the rear of the hall and nodded to a couple of other knights who saw me. The *boyars* and Vlad Dracul's personal guards were armed and the Hungarians and other survivors looked about them, wondering what was about to occur.

It certainly seemed to me as though we were to be put on trial.

I did not fancy being subjected to judgements that Vlad II Dracul would make.

Almost as soon as I took my place, Janos Hunyadi was escorted into the great hall and every man turned to watch as he walked the length of the room. His servants were held back, and Hunyadi marched with his head held high to the base of the dais.

He and Vlad stared at each other in silence for a moment that stretched and stretched. Young Mircea glared at Hunyadi with a smirk but the mighty Hungarian warlord had eyes only for Vlad. The *boyars* began to shift and glance sidelong at each other.

"Janos Hunyadi, the White Knight of Transylvania," Vlad Dracul said at last, speaking Hungarian, "through your actions, you have brought the great crusade into ruin. And even now, when you have personally caused the death of ten thousand Christian men, and so ruined the crusade to throw the Turk back into the wilderness where he belongs, you stand before me filled with arrogance. I see it upon your features. You dare to cast your eyes at me and be filled with pride, in spite of your utter failure. What will happen now, Hunyadi?"

On the floor before the *voivode*, Hunyadi made to speak but Vlad spoke over him.

"I tell you what will happen! The Turk shall take his revenge. That old goat-fucker Murad will come to my land. He will cross the Danube and burn and destroy all of Wallachia before crossing into Transylvania and he will do the same there. Your own lands shall burn. After Transylvania, Hungary will fall to the endless hordes of the Turk and his demons. And it was you who did this." Vlad tore his mad eyes from Hunyadi and looked to his *boyars*. "I warned Hunyadi of what would happen. Did I not? Some men in this hall heard my words. You do not have enough men to face the Turk in open battle, I said. Your crusader army is smaller even than the Sultan's hunting party that he takes into the plains from Edirne. Take his fortresses, I said. Take his ports and his castles, one by one, and avoid a battle that you are incapable of winning." Vlad Dracul whipped his dark eyes back to Hunyadi and a mirthless grin stretched across his face. "Your arrogance is the cause of all this death. You believed in your own prowess more than you heed the advice of other, better men. You thought yourselves above all others and see where your hubris has brought us. Has brought all Christendom. You thought of yourself as greater than your king and now your king is dead, his body ripped apart and unburied. One wonders if this was perhaps not your intention all along? Will you make yourself king, Hunyadi? Is that what you have wrought with your convenient defeat?"

The *boyars* and watching Hungarians had been mumbling throughout the *voivode's* verbal assault, and increasingly so, but this final accusation brought a chorus of angry cries and outraged denials. The Wallachians shouted down the Hungarians and Poles, who roared their protestations in defiance of the threats

44

against them. They loved and admired Hunyadi, who had led them to a hundred unlikely victories in the mountains of Transylvania and elsewhere over decades.

As subtly as I could, I sidled further away from the *boyars* and placed my hand near the handle of my knife.

Mircea, the son of Vlad Dracul, sat still smirking at the riotous lords. Once I reached the side of the hall, I stayed as still and quiet as I could, feeling utterly adrift in the turbulence of Balkan politics. Also, I could understand only one out of every ten shouted words that filled the hall to the rafters.

"Silence!" Roared Vlad Dracul, slamming his hands on the arms of his throne and standing. He was not a tall man, but he was broad and powerful, with a barrel chest and a herald's piercing voice. Gradually, the lords calmed themselves and Vlad pointed at Hunyadi before sitting down. "You will now speak, Hunyadi. What do you have to say for yourself?"

Hunyadi waited until silence had settled once more and when he spoke it was with his customary clear and strong voice. "All men here know what happened. All men know who stood on the field and fought with honour and for Christ." His head turned toward young Mircea, who blanched and glanced at his father. "And all men here know who did not."

The hall erupted once more, with the *boyars* on one side of the hall pushing and shoving the Hungarians and Poles and other crusaders on the other. Vlad's personal guards pulled lords apart from one another and it took even longer for the noise to settle while Vlad stood with his hands raised.

"For your crimes against Christ, the Church, and the King of

Hungarians," Vlad said. "I sentence you to be executed."

Guards stepped up, ready to stop any violence, as the crusaders raged in shock and dismay at the sentence. I assumed the Wallachian *boyars* would come to blows with the outraged crusaders. And yet, to my great surprise, the *boyars* did not argue with the Hungarians. Instead, the *boyars* sided with them against Vlad and they protested the sentence with almost as much vigour as did Hunyadi's allies. It seemed the *boyars* did not wish to anger the entire Kingdom of Hungary over such an extreme act.

I could not quite follow what was said but it was clear that Vlad Dracul and his son Mircea were also shocked by the resistance to the *voivode*'s order.

And no matter how he raged and threatened, the *boyars* stood as one and defied their prince. Their stance could not be overcome and so, infuriated, Vlad cursed them and strode from the hall with his son on his heels.

The *boyars* muttered to each other when he had gone, not at all pleased by their victory. Instead, they seemed disturbed by the implications. And when Hunyadi and his men sought to thank them, the *boyars* were grim in their acceptance of that thanks. Hunyadi was cautioned to remember what the *boyars* had done for him and then we were ordered to be removed from the hall.

When I was escorted back to my quarters, my men stood and waited, pained looks on their faces as they tried to read my expression.

"What is it?" Rob asked.

"Are we to be put to death?" Stephen asked, aghast. "We are sentenced to death, aren't we. I knew it. What are we to do,

Richard?"

"Had to happen sooner or later," Walt said, with a shrug. "Would have been nice to see old England one last time."

"Be silent," Eva snapped at them. "Speak, Richard."

"We are to be freed and sent on to Hungary," I said. "Along with Hunyadi and all his men."

∞

A week later, we were sent from Târgoviște along with a large escort of *boyars* and their loyal men, heading north into the mountains of Transylvania. The passes were clear of snow but the mountains were heavy with it and the thick forest was dense with shadow.

"I do not understand how they could defy their lord," I said to Stephen as we trekked through a vale with jagged rocks jutting up into mountains on either side. "Why is the prince so weak in his own kingdom?"

"It is a mountain land and they are a mountain people," Stephen said, wiping his nose and looking miserable. "Precisely the same as mountain folk everywhere. Every valley has its lord and every lord is king of his valley. A hundred valleys, a hundred tribes and a hundred petty kings. Their feuds go back who knows how long and are so complicated that no outsider can ever hope to understand."

"Same as the Welsh," Walt observed.

"You would know," Rob said, quickly, a grin on his stubbly face.

Eva rolled her eyes and kept her own counsel.

The cold was astonishing and for the most part we kept to ourselves until we descended on the Transylvanian side of the mountains. Here, Hunyadi visibly relaxed and our Wallachian escort left us, to head back once they had rested and recuperated. For us, the journey continued, and I found myself invited to dine with Hunyadi in a large and fine town named Brasov at the foot of the hills.

"What will you do now?" Hunyadi asked me, once the wine was flowing. His look was at once penetrating and easy to return. There was no doubt he was a remarkably intelligent man and he had turned all his wits to mastering the art of war. But he had suffered a great defeat on the field and for some men who experience such a thing it defeats their spirit. Whether Hunyadi had been broken by it, I could not yet tell.

"I came here to wage a crusade against the Turk," I said. "I shall continue to do so."

His face did not change and yet I could tell that my answer pleased him.

"What of your men?"

"Most shall follow me for a while yet, as long as we have a master willing to pay for our services. Even then, there are some who I suspect would rather wage war elsewhere. Italy is far more civilised, as far as these things go."

He nodded. "And if I do continue to pay for your services, how will you wage this war, Richard, with such a reduced company?"

I drank the wine. It was rather good, if sweet for my taste. "That depends on what happens now, my lord. You were in command of the crusade. That has ended in practice but to my mind, you are the moral leader of the crusade still. If this crusade is considered to be ended, perhaps the Pope might consider calling another?"

Hunyadi took a deep breath and let it out slowly. "The king is dead. His own vanity cost him his life, and cost the crusade victory in the field, but he must be properly mourned. More to the point, however, is that Hungary needs a new king."

I watched him closely, for the men often muttered that Hunyadi should be made king, despite his relatively low birth into the knightly class rather than the upper nobility. It would certainly be unprecedented but they could not find a more able king to lead them in war, of that I was certain. He did have healthy sons, but the crown was not a hereditary one. Surely, if the lords had any sense they would see he would be the strong arm that Hungary needed if it was to resist the Turkish menace. For all his bluster, Vlad Dracul had been right enough about the danger.

"And who will be that king?" I asked.

He smiled. "Not I, if that is your meaning." He waved away my half-hearted protests. "I have the hearts of the minor nobles of Hungary but the truly powerful there shall never vote for me to be made king. No, they will make another wear the crown but it is my wish and my expectation that we shall continue the war. It is my wish also that another crusade be called, for this very year, if there is the will for it. But Hungary comes first. A king must be crowned and soon and then the war may continue."

"A sensible order of business, my lord. But what do you mean to do with Vlad Dracul?"

He raised an eyebrow. "Do? Whatever do you mean, sir?"

I glanced around and lowered my voice. "Surely, my lord, you have a great enemy in this man. His desire to have you executed will now have only grown and should he come into possession of your person once again, he will not hesitate to act, this time without consulting the lords who defied him." I shook my head to myself.

Hunyadi seemed to find this amusing. "The *boyars* revolt against the *voivode* disturbs you?"

"Surprises me, somewhat. That they have such authority against their own prince."

"You would have me believe that the King of England acts as a tyrant?" He smiled. "That he may go against the will of his lords without consequence?"

The thought of the useless, witless fool who was King Henry VI acting as a tyrant brought a smile from me, also. "Nevertheless, Dracul and his son have proved not only duplicitous but treacherous. How long before Vlad resumes his subjugation before the Turk? It is a vast land, the border of Christendom. We cannot afford to lose Wallachia."

"It pleases me to hear you say *we*. But if you had the power to act, what would you do?"

"Whatever has to be done."

"You would murder a prince?" he asked, his voice low and steady.

"What is one life compared to the lives of all of our people?"

"I wonder if I could ever truly trust a man who is so quick to jump to murder," he said, as if speaking to himself. "Do you know why Vlad is called Dracul?"

Of course I do, I almost said but stopped myself. "He is a member of the Order of the Dragon. It is a chivalric order, established by Sigismund, King of Hungary, in order to fight against the Turk. He was another great man who led a crusade against the Turk that ended in defeat, at Nicopolis."

"You were educated regarding it?" he asked.

I remember it, I wanted to say, *and heard from those who were there how victory was snatched away by arrogant knights charging before they should have.* Instead I merely nodded.

"I was raised and trained by men who survived it," he said. "A defeat that hung heavy over them, and so over me, all my life. I wonder if my defeat will echo through our sons." He shook himself from his melancholy. "And yes, my lord Sigismund founded it. The Brotherhood of the Dragon, or the Order of the Dragon, or any one of a number of other names. It is a society with no official name, you see, and yet the members must each bear the symbol of the society on his person at all times. This sign or effigy is in the form of the dragon curved into a circle, its tail winding around its neck. The dragon sign also includes a red cross, in the same way that those who fight under the banner of the glorious martyr St George are accustomed to bear a red cross on a white field."

"I have seen the emblem. And Vlad Dracul not only wears this sign on his person in the form of an amulet but he has made it his personal coat of arms. By doing so, he proclaims to the world his closeness to the Order and to the King of Hungary, whoever that shall be."

Hunyadi smiled. "Precisely. His membership of the Order is no small thing. He cannot simply be murdered."

"I never said he should be, merely that there should be no limits on actions that ultimately defend Christendom. But I suspect that he cannot be brought to heel. Not a man such as he. Can he be deposed? Would the *boyars* allow such a thing?"

"The position of Voivode of Wallachia has never been a stable one." He inclined his head. "If there was a suitable candidate, ready to step in, once the current *voivode* is removed, certainly he could be replaced. There are a couple of leading families that tradition would allow, especially those of the Danesti, who are the great enemies of the Draculesti."

"I assume you have a specific candidate in mind. How would you remove Vlad?"

"How would you?"

"I am a simple man. I would march an army to his gates and demand his surrender."

"If I were to do so, would you and your men join me?"

I hesitated. It was dangerous for a mercenary such as I was to tie himself too closely to one lord over others and some of my men had joined specifically to wage war on the infidel, not other Christians, even Eastern ones. Despite all that, I did not hesitate for long. "He and his son have proved themselves to be treacherous. They cost us the battle and so the crusade. I would see them removed."

"It will have to happen, in time." Hunyadi nodded slowly to himself. "But first, Hungary."   .

Our business concluded, I made to leave but Hunyadi leaned forward and placed a hand on my arm. "Richard. What is your interest in Zaganos Pasha?"

Slowly, I eased myself back into my seat. I considered denying it but it was obvious that men had told him of my enquiries. "I believe he was born a Christian but now he is a man who must be killed."

"Why?" he fired the question at me.

"He means for all Christendom to be destroyed."

"More than other Turks?"

"Yes."

"How do you know this?"

"I know."

"You know the man personally? How so?"

"He is an old enemy of mine."

Hunyadi smiled to himself, no doubt amused by my apparent youth. "He has wronged you personally?"

I had an urge to explain everything to Hunyadi but there was a good chance he would believe me to be a madman. "He has, my lord."

"At Varna, you took your men into an attack on the Sultan's position. It was foolhardy and you lost many of your men and you suffered extensive wounds. After hearing of your interest in this man, it seems to me that you were not attempting to slay the Sultan but this Zaganos Pasha." When I said nothing, he nodded once and continued. "I wonder if, should we come to battle with them again, you could be trusted to obey orders. Your passions may overcome you once more."

"My passions did not overcome me. I am not some fragile king who cannot let better men win glory. I know how to read a battlefield. My charge into the Sultan's position was only possible because Ladislaus acted like a mad fool. He threw away his life and that of his men but it almost worked, did it not? If only we had the Wallachians with us. Seven thousand horsemen would have overrun even the Janissaries and the Sultan and his son would be dead. And so would Zaganos Pasha."

Hunyadi kept very still. He was not distracted by my clumsy attempt to change his focus back to the Wallachians. "Men say that you bleed your servants every day. Why do you do this?"

I shrugged, attempting nonchalance. "All men should be bled every few days, especially servants. It keeps them servile."

"They say," Hunyadi muttered, "that Zaganos Pasha has a taste for human blood. Have you heard this rumour?"

I smiled. "I could very well believe it."

"There are tales in Transylvania, my homeland, of creatures who live by ingesting blood. Creatures who look like men. Who once were men but were turned into monsters by another. Have you heard of such tales, I wonder?"

Holding myself still, I attempted a smile. "There are many tales of monsters and the like amongst peasants. Even in England. There, they are called revenants."

"We have many names also. In Serbia, I heard these monsters called *vampir*. Here in Transylvania, they are called *strigoi*. It is not only peasants who believe they walk amongst us but lords and priests and learned men also."

"And you believe that I am a demon because I have my servants bled each week? Truly, my lord?"

Hunyadi said nothing but sipped from his wine. "My friends tell me that I should no longer associate with you. They tell me that you are unnatural. That many of your men are unnatural. One of your men is even a woman and yet she has the strength of ten knights."

"How absurd."

"But you do have a woman for a squire, Richard, do not deny that to my face when I have seen her with my own eyes. Who is she? Your wife? Your sister? Your whore?"

I flinched at the last word and fought down an urge to strike him. He was attempting to provoke me and knocking his teeth out would be satisfying for only a moment before his men attacked me. But what could I say about Eva? That I had known her for two hundred years? The truth was that we had been man and wife for decades while also fighting our way around Christendom and the East, as mercenaries and as crusaders and for our own purposes. Our love for each other had become friendship and our ardour had turned to tedium. After a mortal lifetime of companionship, she had needed to be apart from me and that was how we had lived for decades more. Many times since, we had found ourselves in each other's arms and beds. It was inevitable. And ever since leaving England for Hungary, three years before, we had slipped once more into comfortable companionship, sharing our bed when one was available and lying curled together under the stars or in a tent when one was not.

How could I explain to Hunyadi that there was no word for the nature of my relationship with Eva? She was not my wife, not really. She was my squire, she fought by my side and saved my life more often than I saved hers. More than anyone else, she understood my stomach, my heart, and my wits, and offered better advice than I could find anywhere in the world. Simply, I suppose, she was my friend but at the same time Eva was such a part of me that I could not imagine life without her in it.

"She is no one," I said.

Hunyadi sighed, exasperated. "I must say that I feel inclined to agree with my friends about your nature. We have seen you and your men training. Seen how you fight in battle. I have seen you move as swiftly as an arrow and I have seen you throw a man, in full armour, clear over a horse. There is something utterly unnatural about you, Richard, and I do not like it."

I nodded to myself, trying to understand what it was he wanted. Reassurance that he was wrong? Or confirmation that he was right. I tried for a middle path. "And yet in spite of my unnaturalness you wish to use me and my men to help you achieve freedom from the Turk?" I said.

He tilted his head. "You do not deny it?"

"Deny what? That I am stronger and faster than any living man? That I have turned the tide of battle more times than I can count? Janos, you have been content to let me fight for you all this time, what has changed?"

"We return to Buda and the court there is far more dangerous, for both of us, than the Sultan and his Turks. I must be above reproach and while you are an asset on the battlefield, you are a liability at court."

I almost laughed, for I had heard that very thing many times before.

"You and I have the same enemy, my lord. Whatever else I may be, I seek to always be a good Christian and a good knight. Mistrust me if you will, I quite understand. I will find another way to defeat the Turks."

He almost smiled again. "All of them?"

"If they stand between me and my enemy."

His smile dropped and for the first time, he seemed uncertain. "I can protect you from rumours at court but you must keep yourself and your men on a tight leash."

"I understand."

"And so you will you restrain yourself until I am ready to act?"

If he thought I was a *vampir* or a *strigoi*, then perhaps he was asking me to stop drinking blood. Or he may have been merely warning a foreign mercenary captain to know his place.

"My lord," I said, "I am a courteous man, in full control of myself and my actions. If it does not take too long, I shall wait like a peaceful Christian for you to once more aim your lance at the Turk."

"Oh, I shall take aim, sir." Hunyadi pointed a finger at me. "And you shall be the point of the spear."

A new king was raised to the throne of Hungary. A young boy of five years, named Ladislaus V, and Janos Hunyadi was named as the Regent. This young fellow was in the physical possession of the Habsburgs in the Holy Roman Empire and they would not let him return to Hungary, so while Hunyadi ruled the boy king remained in the care of his guardian, the Holy Roman Emperor Frederick III.

The politics of the crowns of Europe were complicated beyond my clear understanding, no matter how much Stephen and Eva explained the web of alliances and debts and feuds between hundreds of major and minor noble houses. All I knew was that Hunyadi had been made king in all but name and I chafed to be freed from the luxuries of Buda into the wilds of the southeast once more. The Turks were rampaging through Serbia and it seemed to me that we did almost nothing about it.

I kept my men sharp by leading them into Serbia multiple times each season, where we raided and harassed Turkish soldiers. I pushed my men hard and they won themselves enough wealth from fallen enemies that they were reasonably happy. Two years of such warfare was enough for some and they returned home. Others wanted more. More wealth and more glory.

Hunyadi did not go to war but, as Regent of the enormous Kingdom of Hungary, he was never still. He spoke often of the traitorous Vlad II Dracul who had betrayed the crusade and so had turned against Christendom and God Himself.

And the *voivode* of Wallachia turned once more to the Turks and negotiated the subjugation of his people in return for not being destroyed.

To give the man his due, the Turks held his two youngest sons as hostages, and no doubt that played some part in it. Those two sons were named Vlad and Radu and they had been hostages for many years. The boys were being raised as future Princes of Wallachia, who would be friendly to the Turks when it came time for them to be placed on the throne. The Turks were cunning and forward thinking, in ways that we simply were not. I do not doubt for a moment that my brother was responsible for imparting this deviousness into the barbarous mind of the Sultans.

Whatever the circumstances, Vlad II Dracul once more agreed terms with the Turks in 1447, agreeing to pay the usual enormous tribute in silver as well as the *devshirme*, the Blood Tax that would take the best sons of Wallachia and turn them into the Janissaries who would overrun their brothers and then all Christendom. Vlad Dracul also agreed to give up the fortress of Giurgiu, on the Wallachian side of the Danube, and a key to unlocking the destruction of the country.

"Enough is enough, my lord," I said, when I had finally been granted an audience with Hunyadi. "Vlad is bargaining away Wallachia. The Turks will have free reign to push right up to Transylvania once more. Christendom's border is now a hundred miles closer to Hungary."

Hunyadi seemed to have aged a decade in the two years since he had assumed the regency. Soldiering will keep a man young and vigorous but politics will take his soul.

"Ah, another man who likes to explain to me what I already know. And what would you have me do?"

"What you said you would do. You must act."

"And I shall. And you and your men shall come with me."

Taking a small but powerful force, we travelled to Transylvania and met with a young boyar lord named Vladislaus, who Hunyadi favoured for replacing Vlad Dracul. The fellow certainly seemed agreeable enough, and no doubt for he was being offered a princely crown, but I wondered if he would be strong enough to resist the power of the *boyars*.

We crossed the mountains between the two kingdoms at the end of the year, just before the snows filled the passes, and we descended into the valley like a horde of barbarians and there invested Târgoviște. We had a handful of cannons and these were wrestled into place while soldiers dug trenches and threw up palisades around our camp.

Word was sent demanding that Vlad surrender, though we knew he would not give up his throne without a fight. The city was a strong one and it seemed that we would need to reduce a section of the curtain wall to rubble before we could assault it. Our army was not huge but Hunyadi believed it would be enough to take the walls, if it came to that. There were not enough men to seal the city entirely but it was reckoned we could stop supplies from getting in.

"Why could he not have done this in summer?" Stephen asked, looking up at the snow drifting down on our camp. "It will be Christmas soon."

"Hunyadi has a vast kingdom to rule and a dozen allies who might become enemies. He could not have come in summer."

"The bastards in the city will be warm and dry and we will freeze."

"And come spring, they will have eaten themselves into starvation and they will be ready to talk."

"War is a miserable and tedious pursuit," Stephen grumbled.

"You could have stayed in Buda," I pointed out. "Warm and cosy in bed beside that fat Polish girl."

"Do not remind me," he said, miserably.

And yet we did not have to settle in for a winter siege. Only three days after our arrival, before our trenches and camps were even half established, a great cacophony came from within the walls.

Hurriedly, we assembled in whatever armour we could quickly don, ready to fight off a sally that was surely coming.

When the gates were thrown open, instead of the *voivode* and his knights charging at our camp, it was unarmoured citizens who emerged bearing a flag of truce on a tall pole.

"What is it that they are saying?" I asked Eva, suspiciously, taking off my helm.

"They say they have overthrown Vlad Dracul," she replied. "And they welcome Hunyadi as their overlord."

"Is it a trick?" Rob asked.

Walt scoffed. "Course it bloody is."

Just then, Hunyadi sent for me and I rode up to him. "Richard, would you be so kind as to enter the city and see if what these men claim is true?"

I laughed aloud, drawing sharp looks from his lords and bodyguards. "You want me to risk my life and the lives of my men because you suspect this to be a ploy by the treacherous Vlad?" He turned to look at me for the first time and I laughed again. "Better a mercenary than your friends, My Lord Regent, I quite agree. And of course I shall go, happily, and if it is a trap, I shall slaughter every man in the city."

Some of his men crossed themselves and I brought my men forward to the gates where the *boyars* bowed and urged us to come within.

"You cannot mean to take us in there," Stephen said, his face white.

"He ain't wrong, Richard," Walter said. "Can't be nought but a trap."

"Walt, you will take twenty men and hold the gate while the rest of us go within. If they attack, we shall keep moving and we shall fight our way out."

"God save us," Stephen muttered, crossing himself.

"Grow a spine, man," Eva said. "And ready your sword."

Passing into the shadow of the gatehouse, I saw scores of grim-faced men in the streets beyond. Many were brandishing drawn weapons, and some of the blades and clubs they bore were bloodied. Those men watched us as we rode slowly through the streets, deeper into the city, our horses' hooves clacking on the stones in the frozen road surface.

"Here, my lord, here, you shall see, here he is," one of the men leading us said as we came into the market square. He was dressed in his finery and his hat had an enormous feather in it that bounced and fluttered each time he bowed and backed up, further and further. He was fair haired and I took him for a Saxon. Trailing him came a group of other men, almost all of them were old and fat. Rich townsfolk and merchants, nervous and yet proud.

"What has happened?" I asked them, not bothering to hide my contempt and distrust as I looked down at their worried faces.

"Come, come," they said, beckoning me on.

A large, silent crowd stood at the edges of the square and they turned to face us as we drew to a stop at the corner.

In the centre was a single post, prepared with faggots of wood. A stocky young man was tied to it, his bloody and bruised face a mask of anguish.

"It is Mircea, son of Vlad Dracul," the Saxon man leading me said, nodding and seeking acknowledgement. "Do you see, my lord?"

"By God, it is him," I said. "What is wrong with his eyes?"

"Ah, they were burned out, my lord."

"Merciful Christ," I said. "You burned out his eyes?

"Burned out, as punishment for his crimes."

"What bloody crimes?"

The Saxon townsman blanched and turned to the *boyars*. "Why, his misrule, my lord. His misrule and that of his father. We... we thought you would be pleased."

"He is a treacherous little shit but his blood is royal."

"No longer, for his father has been deposed. And so he will now receive his final punishment."

The lord grinned, raised a hand and called out. A group of men rushed forward and ignited the pyre beneath young Mircea, who screamed and wailed as the fire took him. The crowd stood in grim silence, watching their young prince until his desperate prayers became screams that faded into silence. Soon, the smell of cooking flesh filled the square.

"What of the *voivode*?" I asked. "What did you do to Vlad Dracul?"

The Saxons, merchants and *boyars*' faces dropped. "We did everything in our power, my lord, but he is a very great knight and his men were too powerful. Even with the help of the Saxons, we are simple townsfolk, and—"

"Where is he?" I shouted.

A boyar raised a hand and pointed to the eastern side of the city. "He fled, my lord. But he cannot have gone far. It is a mere half a day since he—"

I turned to Stephen. "Ride to Hunyadi and tell him Vlad has escaped. Send Walt and the rest of the men to me, now." Stephen nodded and his horse clattered through the streets. "Leave anything heavy with your squires and pages, take only food and water. We ride hard and fast." My men prepared themselves. "You will provide me with guides, on good horses. Men who know the country and who can ride like a centaur. Hunters, soldiers, anyone dependable, strong, you understand?"

The *boyars* shakily agreed and began shouting orders. Almost at once, an old man in rough country clothes came forward.

"This man is a hunter and a fine rider," a lord said, presenting him. "He says he will lead you."

"You can find Vlad Dracul?" I asked him.

He looked me in the eyes and nodded once.

"Give him a bloody horse, someone," I said to my men.

"The company is ready," Rob said as we rode through the city to the south gate. "But why don't we let the prince go free? Seems to me we're well shot of the bastard."

Eva answered him. "Because he will raise an army and fight to regain his throne, weakening Wallachia and only making Turkish conquest all the more likely."

"Right," Rob replied, nodding to himself.

"And because he is a treacherous dog who would sell his soul to the Turk if we but let him," I said. "Come on, you men," I shouted as we came out of the city. "Who wants to kill a king?"

My men roared their approval, despite Vlad Dracul not technically being a king at all, and we rode south in pursuit.

He had half a day on us and he knew the country better than anyone. But it seemed clear that he was making for the fastest, straightest route possible toward the Danube, straight down the valley toward the plain and the great river beyond. Whether he was aiming for one of his many fortresses on the river or was contemplating riding beyond into Bulgaria and into the hands of the Turks, I did not know. But clearly, we had to catch him before he reached safety and so I pushed my men hard.

Our horses suffered from the ride and from the intense cold and we were forced to leave more and more men behind every time we paused for rest. The guides provided to us failed in their strength or their will and on the first night one young lad curled up weeping and so we told him to return to Târgoviște at first light. Another man feigned an injury and could not be persuaded to continue, even when Walt lifted him from his feet and spat insults into his face.

Soon, only the grizzled old peasant who had volunteered in the city remained. He rode hard before us, his weathered face set into a wrinkled frown and his narrow eyes pointing ahead.

"Reckon he's got a score to settle," Walt said while we watered our horses halfway through the second day.

"What gives you that idea?"

Walt laughed. "Tough little fellow, ain't he. How old do you think he is? A hundred and one?"

"Younger than you, whatever he is."

He turned from his crouched position and looked at us. "My name is Serban," he said, in French.

Walt and I exchanged a glance. We had been speaking English but he had detected that we were talking about him. I switched to French to ask him a question. "Few men here speak French, especially commoners. How did you come to learn it?"

"In my youth, I travel. I fight. I return to my land. But I remember."

"You were a mercenary?"

He raised his chin. "A soldier."

"You own land?" I asked.

His face darkened. "Once. My family land is lost to me, now." He pulled his horse toward the stream and let it drink just a little before he mounted and rode south again, hooves flinging back sods of frozen soil.

"Best get after him," Walt said, "or he'll kill the lot of them before we catch up."

The winter day was short but we found Vlad as darkness was falling. He had attempted to hide his men in a wooded marsh, on the flat plains by a meandering river, but Serban had found his tracks and he knew where the prince was hiding.

"There is a small place there," Serban said, speaking softly. His voice was like a growl. "Through the trees, high and dry land. Some people live there."

"A village?"

He shrugged. "Some houses. It is called Bucureşti's place. Wet earth beyond, very soft, all the way to the river."

I turned to my men. "Sounds like the prince and his men are camped on something like an island of dry land, protected by that beech wood, there."

Rob scratched his stump. "Easily defended. Especially in the dark."

"We should wait until morning," Eva said. "Hunyadi's men will have caught up with us, then. We can surround the wood, and the marsh, and either he gives up without a fight or he does not. Either way, we have him."

Serban's head snapped around at the mention of Hunyadi's name. "Not wait for Hunyadi. Vlad Dracul is there, now. We go. We kill him."

"I am inclined to agree with you, Serban," I said.

"Hunyadi wishes to use him to keep the new prince in line," Eva said. "He will be grateful if we provide him this prisoner."

"And yet it will not be us who provides him, if the entire bloody army comes down here in the morning to roust him out,"

I said. "Hunyadi will take Vlad prisoner, lock him in Buda and use him in his political games. These people are too keen by far on their politics. Vlad is better off dead. And it is better by far if I am the man to do it. Our influence at court wanes every day. This act shall purchase for us some influence. We go in, now. Tell the men. We take no prisoners."

Eva grabbed my arm and pulled me to the side. Lowering her voice, she leaned in. "How do we know to trust this Serban? He volunteered to help you rather quickly, did he not? Perhaps the prince left him behind in order to lead you into a trap. Vlad may be there, waiting for you. Or he may be miles away in another direction."

Straightening, I turned and raised my voice. "Serban, are you leading me into a trap?"

"No, lord."

"If you are, then you shall be the first one I kill."

"Yes, lord."

"There you are," I said to Eva, who pinched her nose and said nothing.

We followed Serban through the darkness beneath the trees. Admittedly, it was not as eerie a place as the dark green woods of the mountains in the north and beech forests were as familiar to me as the back of my hand. Even so, there was a wildness to Wallachia, even on the lowland plains. Much of it was unpopulated and untamed, and deer and wolves roamed the woods and I half expected us to scare up a boar big enough to disembowel my horse. My men were disciplined and there was not a word spoken as we advanced but still the noise we made crashing through the brittle undergrowth was loud enough to wake the dead, let alone alert Vlad's sentries.

"Faster," I said to Serban just ahead of me. "Faster, man." I turned to Rob beside me. "We shall rush them."

A noise clacked in the trees ahead and a bolt whipped unseen through the darkness.

Rob drew his mace and spurred his horse forward. "Sir Richard!" he cried, not as a warning but as a war cry. "Sir Richard!"

I raced after him and my men came behind, all them taking up the cry.

"Sir Richard!"

The enemy were ready for us, dismounted with their spears in hand, the blades flashing in the twilight, their roars of defiance filling the darkness. "Dracul! Dracul! Wallachia!"

My men dismounted and rushed in close, overwhelming the defenders with our numbers and our ferocity. Crossbowmen on the flanks shot at us and horses in the rear of the enemy position drummed their hooves as their riders galloped away from us.

"Vlad flees," I shouted to Walt, before forcing my horse around the remaining men. Something banged against my helm, a bolt or a spearhead, but then I was through and chasing the fleeing riders through the trees. They thinned and the ground grew soft and my horse began lifting his hooves high and tossing his head. Ruthlessly, I raked my spurs and forced his head up. "On, you bastard, on!"

I was chasing three riders through the dwindling light. The moon, low over the horizon ahead, shone through wisps of cloud even as the last of the day's light faded behind me. My horse splashed through shallow water and then onto dry ground again before running into wet ground once more, softer and slower. Ahead, my quarry had also slowed, though they struggled on toward the silver glint of the river in the distance.

Opening my visor, I raised my voice. "Coward!"

They ran on for a few more strides but their horses slowed and turned. Almost as one, the three of them slid from their horses and came back toward me, standing three abreast with their weapons drawn.

The man in the centre was broad and short.

"Vlad!" I shouted. "There is nowhere to run, now."

I slid from my horse and strode forward through the freezing water, which was almost up to my knees, and the ground beneath sucked at my feet. The three of them had stopped on the edge of a dry patch of land and so they were above me as I came forward, right at them, lifting my feet high as I advanced.

At the last moment, I rushed to the right, spraying icy water everywhere and stabbed up into the groin of the man there, sliding my sword point deep into his thigh as he swung his axe at my head. I continued on, caught his hand and took the haft of his weapon as I slid my blade out.

Vlad Dracul roared like a bull and thrust his sword at my neck. I batted it aside and pushed him as hard as I could, throwing him away from me. The last man caught me on the shoulder with his mace but I swatted him down and finished him on the ground.

The *voivode* got to his knees and launched himself at me, attempting to grapple and pull me down. I swung the axe at his arm, crushing the bone and half-severing his right hand. He cursed me and drew a dagger with his left, still trying to kill me.

I twisted it from his grasp and held him on his knees before me, pulling his helm from his head to ensure I had the right man.

"You," he snarled, speaking French. "Hunyadi's English dog."

"My Lord Prince. You fought with spirit. I will tell Christendom that you died well."

"Ah," he said, suddenly, looking up at the sky. There were tears in his eyes. "My sons. Forgive me."

"You should know that the men of Târgoviște burned Mircea alive after you abandoned him."

He snarled and tried to stand but I held him. "All I have done, I did for my sons. That monster has them, my youngest two. Vlad and Radu. He has corrupted them, by now, I fear but I had to try."

I paused. "What monster? Murad?"

Vlad scoffed, looking at the emerging stars once more.

"You mean Zaganos Pasha?"

He snapped his eyes back to mine. "You know of this monster." It was not a question.

"I shall kill him," I said. "Know that, as you die, the man who has your sons will one day die by my hand."

"But then we share an enemy," Vlad said, quickly. "I did as I was bid by the Turk in order to save my sons. Free my sons and I shall be free to fight the Turk once more."

"You have been a slave to the Turks too often to ever be trusted," I said, shaking my head. "You will not live."

His face clouded again. "Then protect my sons from the

monster, sir. With my last breath, I ask it humbly, from one Christian to another." I hesitated and he continued. "With my death, Murad will seek to place Vlad on my throne. Or Radu, if Vlad is too obstinate. Help them to fight the Turks."

"If the Turks free them, they will be Turkish slaves already in their hearts and they will die, also."

Vlad smiled. "Not my sons. Not the sons of Dracul."

"Any man who fights the Turks will be my ally. That is all I promise."

"Grant me a single favour, then, from one knight to another. Give my sword to my son. My oldest living son, Vlad. And this." Reaching up to his neck with his one remaining hand, he pulled up a circular metal insignia on a thin silver chain. He held it out to me. "My sword and this. Vlad is to wear it always."

"If I can," I said, taking it from him.

He sighed. "God strike you down if you break your word. I am ready. Make the blow clean."

"You are strong, my lord, and you have killed many men in war. Your blood is strong and I shall take your strength into myself. Know, as you die, that I shall use your strength to kill the Turks and drive them from your lands."

He frowned in confusion as I lifted him up, slit his throat and drank the hot blood gushing from his neck. He fought me, with all the will left in him, but his will soon leeched from his body and I drank until my belly was full and his heart slowed into nothing. I dropped him at my feet.

Filled with the power of his blood, I arched my back and let out a roar at the moon.

I turned to find the old Wallachian named Serban a few paces behind me, shaking in what I took to be shock, fear or simple awe. I thought I was going to have to chase him down and kill him before he spoke to his fellows about what he had seen.

Instead, he dropped to his knees in the freezing water. The moon shone down on his wrinkled face.

"My lord, I see that you are *vampir*," he said, shaking. "I would serve you."

I walked forward, filled with a blood rage, and considered taking him also. But I had had my fill.

"You may serve me. Your first act will be to remove the head of Vlad Dracul. I shall bring it to Janos Hunyadi. And then we shall go to war."

3

The Battle of Kosovo

1448

HUNYADI WAS SO FLUSHED WITH the quick success against Vlad Dracul, that he let it go to his head, somewhat. He announced that he was now the ruler of Wallachia.

It did not go down well with the Wallachian *boyars* who had risen up to depose one lord only to find a far more powerful one was now above them. And Hunyadi's own lords and friends urged him to reconsider, on account of him having more than enough to occupy his attention as Regent of Hungary.

"Can't help it, can they," Walt observed one night in Târgoviște, when the arguments were still raging. "Never enough for these great lords. Give them a regency and they want a crown. Give them a kingdom and they want another, and then one more."

"Perhaps he should take them all," Stephen said. "Is that not what our great problem is, sirs?" We looked at him, waiting for him to go on. He always did. "The Sultans, for a hundred years, have sought only conquest. They take us, piece by piece, year after year. No matter if they lose a battle, they keep coming. The sons and grandsons of Turks who were thrown back now live on those lands."

"Does he think he's telling us what we do not know?" Walt asked Rob in a stage-whisper.

"But why?" Stephen said, turning on Walt and Rob. "Why do they come on and on while we fight amongst ourselves?"

"William is there, whispering in their ears," I said. "He was probably there beside the first Mehmed, and perhaps even with Beyazid or earlier, with the first Murad. Seventy or eighty years, perhaps."

"You do not know that," Eva said.

Stephen replied. "But it makes sense, does it not? All that time, they have been pushing into Christendom, taking over or else forcing the Wallachians and Serbians and Moldavians into vassalage. Consistency, across generations."

Eva pursed her lips. "Yes, perhaps. What is your point?"

"It was only possible with a strong leader, who could dictate policy at will. Or close to it. The Sultans have accumulated personal power through all that time until Murad and his son Mehmed can expect to rule almost as tyrants. How can our scattered Christian kingdoms possibly stand in opposition to that?"

76

I nodded slowly. "So, you would have Hunyadi seek to hold the crown of Wallachia."

Stephen crossed his arms. "And Hungary, and Transylvania."

"And then Serbia," Eva said. "And Moldavia."

"You are in this together, I see."

"We are of one mind about this, yes," Eva said, holding up her hand with her fingers spread, before closing her hand tightly. "Only a strong king can hope to unite these kingdoms into one fist." She punched her other hand.

"And who better than Hunyadi?" Stephen said. "He has healthy sons who could rule after him."

"And when better than now?" Eva asked.

I snorted. "Have you two prepared your words before time?"

"Are we wrong?" Eva asked.

"Of course not. But what can we do about it?"

"He trusts you," Stephen said. "You gave him Vlad Dracul's head."

I scoffed. "He does not trust me, Stephen, I assure you."

Eva leaned forward. "He *likes* you, Richard. That is plain."

"He respects what I can do on the battlefield but he fears me. He knows we are different. And his men absolutely do not like me, nor do they trust me. Vlad Dracul's head or not. Whatever position I take, if I take one, they will argue against it purely for that reason." They sighed and I continued. "Listen, both of you. You have bent your attention to the southeast for so long that you have forgotten what lies north and west. The kingdoms of Poland, the Holy Roman Emperor, the bloody Pope, and who knows who else. If Hunyadi attempts to make himself king of so many kingdoms, he will have war on Hungary's northern border as the Habsburgs and all the rest strive to bring him down. And how will that help us resist the Turk?"

Walt snorted. "Without Hungary, all is lost. And that's the truth, no mistake."

Stephen wheeled away and kicked a bedpost. "Why are our people so bloody-minded? Why can no lord follow another?"

Rob answered. "Every free Christian man is the king of his own household, Stephen. Every wife is a queen and their children are princes and princesses." He shrugged. "From Scotland to Italy, and Castile to bloody Wallachia, it's the nature of our people. It just is. I ain't learned much in all my years but I learned that. We do not good slaves make."

"He's right," Walt said, his arms crossed and nodding decisively. "It makes us strong."

Stephen pinched his nose. "No, it makes us divided. And divided, we are weak."

"Our greatest strength and our greatest weakness, then," Eva said. "Be that as it may, Richard, I would have us be *patient*. Clearly, William has laid his plans for decades, perhaps a century or more. These mountains are not easily conquered, nor are these mountain kingdoms easily overthrown, especially by armies of horsemen. You must be patient. If not Hunyadi, then perhaps someone else. Perhaps his son, or the son of another. Or a man not yet born. But we have time."

"You speak as though I am one to rush in without thinking the matter over." After I spoke, Walt burst out laughing and Rob covered his mouth and turned away. "What amuses you, men?" I said, which only caused them to laugh harder. "I shall be patient," I said, "if you damned fools cease your bloody mirth-making."

"We must discuss also the new man you have taken into your service," Eva said.

"What is there to discuss?"

"He saw you drinking blood. And then offered himself to you."

"Yes."

"Does that not disturb you?"

I looked around at each of them. "Should it?"

Walt shrugged. "The old boy must have been shitting himself. He thought he would be next. And he swore to save his own life."

"So what if he did?" I asked.

"If he swore only in the moment to save his neck," Rob said, "then how can he be trusted to hold his tongue about what he saw?"

"He knew what I was. He called me *vampir*. It was a word that Hunyadi used before to describe stories of blood drinking demons. It is a Serbian word. In his own country, the word is *strigoi*. And now this man Serban saw me and calls me *vampir*. Am I wrong in thinking William has his own immortals in these lands?"

"It seems likely," Stephen said. "And if they are here, then we must be careful. We must watch our backs. Any of Hunyadi's men could be one of William's."

"Or Hunyadi himself," Walt said.

"Do not be absurd," I said.

"Right, yeah," Walt said, covering his eyes with a hand.

"Probably not."

"We must watch for enemies in our midst," I said. "But why wait for them? We must seek them out and destroy them first, if we can."

"How do we do that?" Rob asked.

"I will speak to Serban and find out what he knows. He has rooms in the city, I believe."

"Why not summon him here?" Stephen said. "It will be safer."

"He's above that tavern off the square," Walt said. "The one with the good German beer."

"We will go to him," I said. "I will take only Walt, so that we do not overwhelm him."

Walt rubbed his hands together and grinned. "Lovely. I'm right parched, I am."

Serban came down from his quarters above the tavern's ale room and the innkeeper directed us to a table and bench in a quiet alcove, bringing beer, wine, bread, cheese, herb sausages, and pork in jelly.

"I would have come to you, my lord," Serban said as he sat opposite us, staring at the food.

"Eat, please. You must eat and drink. We cannot finish all of this by ourselves." Walt glared at me but I ignored him as Serban grabbed a piece of bread. I poured him a mug of beer and handed it over before doing the same for myself. "Serban, you swore to be my man."

"I did," he said, not meeting my eye.

"Tell me about yourself."

He looked up. "My lord?"

"You were a soldier in your youth. You said you once had land but no longer. I like to know all of my men and I would have you tell me about the things you have done so that I will know how to best use you."

Serban bobbed his head slowly. "Yes, my lord. I was born in the west, near to the Iron Gates."

"The great gorge that the Danube flows through," I explained to Walt. "Near Serbia."

"That is just so," Serban said. "My father had good land. We grew almonds and figs. But there was not enough land for me. I was the youngest. So I go and fight."

"Where did you campaign?"

"Many, many lands. Bulgaria, Albania. And across the sea to Italy."

"Is that so? We fought there, also. On occasion. Where did you fight?"

"Oh, for this lord against that. A duke against another duke. Milan against Venice. Venice against Genoa. When I return home, a new lord ruled over my father's land and had given my family land to another. My parents had died. My brothers and sisters fled, or died. I was lost. But there is always work in Wallachia for a man who fights. I come here. That is all."

Walt and I exchanged a look and Walt shrugged.

"When you offered me your service," I said, lowering my voice. "You called me something. You knew what I was."

Serban held my gaze. "Yes."

"How did you know?"

He stuffed a large slice of sausage into his mouth and took his time chewing it, looking around the room, in every corner, rather than look directly at us. Walt's eyes twinkled with amusement but I was impatient.

"You have heard tales of these things?" I prompted.

Slowly, he nodded, pointing to his ear. "I hear things."

"Have you ever met one before?"

He scratched at the stubble on his chin before answering. "All people know these stories."

"All people of Wallachia?"

"And other places. These hills have long hosted *vampir* and *strigoi*."

"So they are two different things?"

He shrugged, as if he did not care to answer. The man seemed nervous but was trying not to show it. "Different, yes. One is more powerful. The *vampir*. But both..." he lowered his voice. "Drink the blood of man."

"Tell me more."

"More?"

"Where are they found? Where do they live, Serban?"

"Why do you want me to speak of such things?" he said. "Do you not know these things yourself? You are one of them. You must know. No?"

"Humour me," I said.

He frowned.

Walt cuffed his lips and spoke with his mouth full. "He means tell him what you know anyway."

Serban nodded. "I know very little. Stories all mothers tell their sons and daughters. Do not go out at night, or the *strigoi* will catch you. They will drink your blood. If you are lucky."

"What if you are unlucky?" Walt asked.

With a small smile on his lips, Serban continued. "The *strigoi* take the little children back to their master, the *vampir*. And there you will be eaten. Or some other evil thing. It was not clear."

"So it is just tales to frighten children?" I said. "What do you know of real men who are *strigoi*?"

"Forgive me, my lord, but are you afraid of them?"

"Of course not," I said. "I simply wish to make their acquaintance. Perhaps we might become friends."

"I do not know of any," he said. "But there are old folk in the villages. They may know more."

"Older than you?" Walt said, grinning.

Serban stared back. "Perhaps I can find one who knows more. They would need paying."

I nodded to Walt who stared at me for a moment in contempt at my gullibility but he pulled a few silver coins from his purse and, scowling, pushed them across the table to Serban.

"And not a word of this to anyone," I said before he took them. "One word from you to another lord and I will cut off your head and drink you myself, do you understand?"

"Yes, lord."

∞

He may not have been able to make himself into an emperor, even if he wished to do so, but Hunyadi's dominance of the political and martial landscape was far from finished.

After pushing for support from the Pope, he organised a new crusade to be launched against the Turks, this time to save Serbia.

Serbia had capitulated to the Turks just a few years earlier, under their leader George Branković. The Turks had occupied his lands and, caught between two great powers, ultimately, Branković had simply been more afraid of the barbarous Turks than the Hungarians and so he had promised the usual great sums and the *devshirme*, the Blood Tax. What is more, Branković held a number of territories within the borders of southern Hungary and these he passed over to Sultan Murad II as part of his capitulation. Of course, this was never completed in practice, because physical possession is a fact that legal documents cannot themselves overcome and so Hunyadi had simply seized these lands for Hungary, considering them forfeited by the Serbian capitulation.

And Branković had even refused passage of the crusader armies through Serbia before the battle at Varna. Now, in 1448, Hunyadi demanded that Serbia join the new crusade. Not only did Branković refuse but he denied passage of the Hungarian army through Serbia.

Hunyadi swore that once he defeated the Turks, his very next act would be to destroy Branković and place a worthy prince on the Serbian throne.

"Branković is finished," Stephen declared, as we rode south with the new crusader army. "He cannot be allowed to defy us like this. Hunyadi will set all Serbia aflame for this continued

84

defiance."

"One task at a time, Stephen," I said, looking ahead at the thousands of men spread out over the march south.

"It is worse than defiance," Eva said, turning in her saddle to speak to Stephan. "After refusing to join us, refusing passage, what do you think Branković did? There is no doubt he sent word to his master, Murad II, and so there is no doubt that the Turk will be fully prepared to meet us. There is no doubt, also, that Serbians are watching our advance and taking stock of our composition and dispositions. The enemy will be able to intercept us at will and offer battle."

"You do not seem confident in our grand crusade," I said. "What would you suggest we do?"

She was silent for a time before she replied, looking out at the hills in the distance. "Hunyadi seeks to retake Southern Serbia and Macedonia, to drive on to the coast and so split Turkish Rumelia into two parts, with Bulgaria on one side and Greece on the other."

"A fine plan, is it not?"

Eva turned to me. "If it works, certainly it is. If it fails, then all is lost."

Stephen laughed. "One can say the same with all plans!"

"What I mean, Stephen," she said, glaring at him, "is that it is both unspecific and dangerous."

"Describe to us a better plan," Stephen said, "If you would be so kind to impart your wisdom."

She ignored his goading and spoke to me. "If the Serbians had joined us, it would be different. But not only has Branković refused to take up the crusade, he is opposing us. He sends word of our movements to Edirne, or to the Sultan's army, if it is already in the field. Worse still, Branković has forbidden the lords of Serbia to join us. This means our army is smaller than planned for and we have fewer men who well know these lands."

"Some Serbians have joined us," Stephen pointed out.

"A fraction of what we expected. What we need. And how does Hunyadi react? We are pillaging and burning through Serbia, treating it as an enemy land but without conquering it."

"What would you have him do?" Stephen asked. "We have been defied."

"Either make the Serbians our allies, or destroy them in battle, and make them a vassal." Eva glared at me. "Hunyadi instead takes a middle path so that we march through and leave an enemy behind us."

Rob came cantering back along the line to where we rode and fell in beside us, his squire and servants trailing behind. He was sweating, though the air was cold.

"Thank Christ you have returned," I said. "It has been days. What news?"

Before he even opened his mouth, I knew it was not good.

"Skanderbeg and his Albanians cannot reach us," Rob said, wiping his dry lips and calling for water. "The damned Serbians under Branković himself are blocking the passes and fords between Albania and Southern Serbia."

"God damn that man," I said. "Still, surely there is time. Perhaps we can meet further south, in Macedonia. No?"

He cleared his throat, took a long drink of water and frowned at the sky. "There is a hope that we can meet Skanderbeg's forces on the plain of Kosovo, yes. And that is where we are now headed."

"And the Sultan has not returned?"

"Hunyadi's agents say again that the Sultan is campaigning in Anatolia," Rob said. "I asked about local forces but every one of the bastards told me either to not concern myself with such matters or to flat out mind my own business. And then I was asked to return to my master."

"What did you do?" I asked.

"Nothing," Rob said. "Nothing at all. I simply seized the man who had told me to mind my own business and I pushed my bare stump into his face and explained to him that killing was my business. Other than that, I was entirely courteous."

"To the Kosovo plain, then," I said. "Is there anything we can do to speed Skanderbeg along his way?"

"No," Eva replied, before Rob could reply. "Skanderbeg may be the most competent commander for a thousand miles." She looked at me. "Present company included. He does not need our help. If there is a way to get to us, he will find it."

"I think our Eva is enamoured with the new ruler of Albania, Richard," Stephen quipped.

I ignored him. "What makes you so confident in him?"

"Look at what he has achieved already. He was raised by the Turks, trained by them. He will certainly have come across William in that time. We must speak with him. If Hunyadi falls, Skanderbeg is one who may be able to take up the mantle, who may be able to lead all these kingdoms to victory together."

"He has won a few skirmishes," Stephen argued. "No more. Perhaps he has potential but let us see it in the coming crusade before jumping to conclusions."

I agreed. "That seems like a good notion."

Walt scoffed. "No one from a civilised kingdom is going to follow an Albanian, Eva."

"Let me tell you about Skanderbeg," Eva said to me. The wind whipped at a strand of hair streaming from beneath her cap. She tucked it back inside. "His name is George Kastrioti, and according to all reports, he served the Ottomans loyally until he deserted them at Nis, the year before Varna. The Turks called him Iskander Bey, and so we called him Skanderbeg even now, though he has since proved himself to be a loyal son of Albania and a good Christian. Which is remarkable in itself, as Albania, do not forget, was long a vassal of the Turks. He was sent to Edirne as a noble hostage, and it was the Turks who trained him in battle. He even became a Mohammedan, completely embracing the religion of the infidels. Or seeming to, at least. He was rewarded with a timar, near to the territories ruled by his father. His loyalty to the Turks was tested, time and again, and always he proved himself to them. There was a rebellion in his homeland and his relatives invited him to join them but he resisted and the Turks rewarded him with further advancements. They made him a cavalry commander, a sipahi, and after the revolt was put down the Turks installed him as a governor, for a time. But he was better suited to war and they gave him a cavalry unit of five thousand men."

I whistled. "He cannot have been deceiving them, surely he was a committed Mohammedan and loyal to Murad."

"Perhaps. Who can know what is in a man's mind? But he was rewarded again and made Sancakbey of Dibra. It was now that he must have been in contact with the people of his homeland. Had he already decided, long ago, to rebel against the Turks? Or did someone change his mind?"

"Seeing his homeland," Walt said, suddenly. I had not known he was still paying attention. "A man is tied to his homeland, to his ancestors, by the blood of his people and the soil of his homeland, is he not? Bloody foolish of the Turks to send him home and expect him to resist what cannot be resisted. It's inevitable."

"But a man who has turned against his own people, then turned against his masters," I said, "can he be trusted not to turn once more?"

"He can never go back," Eva replied. "It was a year before Varna, at the Battle of Nis, when he was fighting for the Turks, that he took himself and three hundred Albanians from the Turkish ranks and fled the field. From there, he went to Kruje, in the heart of Albania." Eva smiled. "He handed the governor a forged letter, supposedly from Sultan Murad, and gained control of the city. He overthrew those loyal to the Turks and proclaimed himself lord of the city. Then he conquered a dozen fortresses in the area and raised his battle standard, which is a double-headed black eagle on a red field and proclaimed himself a Christian. What is more, any Mohammedans in his lands, by birth or by conversion, he commanded to embrace Christ or face death. Somehow, he united the disparate Albanian princes under his leadership."

"I remember when the Sultan sent armies to stop him," I said. "But he defeated them."

"I heard it from a Serbian mercenary who was there. Ali Pasha had thirty thousand men and Skanderbeg just half as many. Skanderbeg, knowing how Turkish armies fight and deploy, pulled the enemy into battle at a place of his choosing. Prior to the arrival of the Turks, however, he had already placed three thousand of his strongest cavalry unseen in a forest to the Turkish rear. The Turks were surrounded and crushed. The Albanians killed ten thousand Turks that day. He smashed two more armies. At Otonete, he surprised them in their camps and slaughtered at least five thousand, taking only three hundred prisoners. Then it was just this summer when he beat Mustafa Pasha in the field at Diber."

"He has had a good run," I said, "no one would deny that. But is he a Hunyadi in waiting? We shall see in the coming battles what this Skanderbeg can do. And yes, I shall request an audience with him and ask him about William. Let us all pray that he can throw off the Serbians and join us at Kosovo."

We advanced southward where we were met, finally, by the Wallachians under their new *voivode*, Vladislaus II, who was loyal to Hunyadi. A handful of Skanderbeg's men made it to us but they only confirmed what we dreaded; that the main army was caught up manoeuvring against the damned Serbians. At a vast plain named Kosovo Polje, our army rested and waited for our allies to arrive before we continued on to begin assaulting Turkish-held cities in the south.

On the morning of 17th October 1448, an uproar spread

through the camp until it reached us.

"What is it?" I cried, throwing back the flaps of my tent.

Walt approached, his face grim. "It's the Turks, Richard. Sultan Murad is not campaigning in Anatolia after all. He is here."

∞

"My lords, we have two choices," Hunyadi said to the assembled leaders of his army within the vast command tent. "The Turks have got behind us to the north, cutting off any chance of direct retreat back toward Hungary, and so if we are to retreat, it must be southward, towards Macedonia."

The men were grim and quiet but they grumbled their dislike of this proposal.

"That would be madness," one of Hunyadi's companions said. "We would move closer to their routes of supply and reinforcement and further from ours. Manoeuvring will be possible but only for a time and we will be dependent on what can be foraged or taken by force as we move deeper into winter."

"We must cross the mountains into Albania and join with Skanderbeg," another lord said.

Hunyadi sighed. "Using those passes, with an army of this size, makes it likely we are drawn into skirmishes and perhaps a battle with our backs to the mountains. And that says nothing about the Serbian army of Branković out there. If we attempt Albania, we will be trapped between Branković and Murad. What is more, much of Albania remains Turkish. We cannot go that way."

"So, my lord," I said, in my rough Hungarian, "our choices are between retreating south or something else? Perhaps you would provide us with the alternative."

A few of the greater lords scowled at my speaking out of turn, which I had a reputation for, but other men smiled because every one of us knew what the alternative was.

Hunyadi lifted his head. "We may retreat. Or we may fight."

The lords wanted to fight but they were rightly cautious. Once more, we found ourselves outnumbered. Perhaps more important was that we were not prepared in our minds for a great battle.

"How might it be done?"

"We have three thousand German hand-gunners, war wagons, and scores of artillery pieces," Hunyadi said. "The Turk cannot assail our position and overcome us."

"Then why would he attack at all?" I said. "They have only to prevent us returning to Hungary or trail us into Macedonia and need not risk an assault against our wooden walls." Some lords shouted me down and told me to mind my tone. I ignored them and looked only to Hunyadi. "And if we wait, the Turks can bring reinforcements from a number of directions."

"No," Hunyadi said. "Their most likely reinforcements will come from the passes to Albania." He turned to one of his men. "Alex, take a thousand of the Transylvanian light cavalry and take the passes. They must take them and hold them. We cannot be surprised at our rear or all is lost."

"How might we assail their position?" A German mercenary

leader asked. "They are yet taking their places on the field but it seems the Sultan is deploying with the River Lab at his rear, so we cannot get behind him easily. There are hills on his left flank, and the River Sitnica will no doubt guard his right. He has nested himself in tight."

"Do we know how many they are?" I ask. "Their true numbers, I mean, not panicked guesses."

"It appears they are sixty thousand," Hunyadi said, to nods from his men. "*Sipahis* from Rumelia and Anatolia both and of course his Janissaries are in the centre protecting his camp. We shall see what their final dispositions are but it seems the Anatolian peasant levies are being sent out to his right which we assume means the Rumelians will be put on the left, out by the hills."

"No cavalry at all in the centre," a Polish knight said. "My men confirmed it. Just lines of infantry, mostly *azab* levies with spears. And then artillery and behind are the Janissaries. A tough centre to break with cavalry but it can be done. A massed charge of heavy horse to overwhelm them and send them flying into their own guns and on to the Janissaries. We almost broke through at Varna, we can do it properly here."

"Begging your pardon, my lord," I said. "My own men have ridden so close to the enemy today that some were wounded by hand-gunners. They report that between the front line of *azab* levies and the Turkish guns, the enemy are digging deep and wide lines of trenches. We cannot ride over with ease."

They grumbled and some doubted me enough to send their own men forward to see for themselves. But Hunyadi did not question my assertion.

"We form the *wagonberg* on the hill here," he said. "The German and Bohemian hand-gunners will man the war wagons. The artillery will position between the wagons and from there fire across the field into the Turks. Within the *wagonberg* we will have the crossbowmen and the archers. We shall keep a unit of Wallachian horsemen safe within, also, who will follow up when the Turks break under our fire and shot. All our cavalry will be on the wings. The Albanians and Wallachians, the horse archers, and the men-at-arms also. Before the *wagonberg* in the centre, we shall have light horse in the first line and heavy horse in the second. I shall command the second line in the centre, with the royal troops, my mercenaries and the Transylvanians. I want the Wallachian lords under their own banners with me." He then pointed out which great Hungarian lords he wanted on which wing and what they were to do and we were dismissed.

"Sir Richard," Hunyadi called and I crossed to him. "You will be with me and I would have you and your men kept out of the fighting for as long as possible, until the time comes. It may not come until late. Do you think your men can restrain themselves?"

"They can. Each knows if we slay the Sultan then he will be famed and showered with wealth."

He grasped my arm. "When you strike at his heart, it must be with everything. Those damned Janissaries will be hard to break."

"I shall not need them to break if I kill them all instead."

He shook his head at my arrogance and said I could go.

"How's the boss?" Walt asked as I joined him outside.

"Worried."

"Ain't we all."

It was a tense night on watch, half expecting a horde of Turks to come screaming out of the night. I went from man to man in my company and explained that we would need to avoid fighting until late in the battle, even if it started before dawn. But the sun rose in the morning and we assembled in our thousands and stood watching each other across the plain.

"The Turk ain't ever going to attack," Rob said. "Why do we not push forward?"

"Hunyadi knows his business," I said.

"God save us," said Stephen, crossing himself. "This shall be another Varna."

"Look out there, Stephen," I said, pointing. "Do you see those massing lines of levies? Behind them, the field guns? Behind them the Janissaries, beneath the Sultan's banners? There stands William de Ferrers. Our enemy. We have a chance to end it once more, today. You should be filled with joy."

Stephen nodded. "You are no doubt correct, yet I am filled with the sense that our illustrious leader is going to repeat the mistakes he made at Varna and so I am retiring once more to the *wagonberg*. Eva, are you coming?"

She stared across the field. "I am not."

"Very well, I wish you well and look forward to joining you for the victory feast."

"Bloody coward," Walt muttered. "Always slipping away, ain't he. Back there, sipping on wine while we do the work."

"We all have our strengths and weaknesses, Walter," I said. "You would best him in feats of arms and yet in a battle of wits, you would be defeated even by a drunken Stephen."

Rob snorted. "Walt would be defeated in a battle of wits by a drunken chicken."

"Our men are wheeling ever closer on the right," Eva said. "They are goading the enemy."

"That'll do it," Walt said. "The Turk can't control himself."

We watched as best we could. Our light horse advanced, shooting arrows into the Rumelians. When they countered, our heavy horse came up to fend them off while the horse archers retreated behind them. It was a highly effective manoeuvre and the Turks were growing frustrated, pulling ever more forces into attempts at counter attack. So much so that our flank was reinforced also.

"This is it," I said. "It cannot be resisted now."

Sure enough, Hunyadi was forced to send knights and light cavalry from his centre lines onto the right. It was then that Murad ordered his Anatolians against our left, where the light Wallachians met the enemy advance.

It was difficult to make out what was happening but suddenly the Wallachians, essentially our entire front line on the left, suddenly broke and fled straight back away from the Turks.

"Damn them," I said, with a sinking feeling in my guts. "The Wallachians are the most useless bloody men in Christendom!"

Hunyadi led us out from the centre, two thousand heavy horse, to stem the collapse of the left. I kept my men back from the press of the fighting, as ordered, though it galled me to do so.

Now that we had weakened our centre, Murad sent forward masses of the *azab* infantry to attack us there. I watched from the flank with my fresh and unused company as thousands of Turkish infantry marched right behind us and straight toward the *wagonberg*. Our last line of heavy cavalry in the centre charged the *azabs* and I was certain they would run down the weak, useless levy infantry. Instead, it was our heavy horse that broke and fled to the flanks.

"Good God Almighty," Rob said. "What is happening here? God is against us."

Walt sneered at the cavalry fleeing from the peasants. "Useless bastards."

"All is well," I said. "They shall not break the *wagonberg*."

The German mercenaries inside unleashed the power of their hand-guns and blasted away the *azabs* in a hail of shot and smoke. Our cannons fired into the masses of Turkish levies and drove them back. Hundreds were killed, and then thousands, and they edged back from the storm of fire and massed together like frightened sheep. Finally, our damned cavalry returned and charged into the panicked *azabs*, cutting them down gleefully as the Turks fled back to their own lines and the safety of their cannons.

It was growing late and we had stopped the Turks on both flanks and in the centre. With the spare men in the centre, Hunyadi reinforced the right further and broke that flank, sending the Rumelian cavalry fleeing into the dark hills or back to the Turkish camp.

Darkness fell and we drew back into our camp.

∞

Our cannons continued their firing as night fell, and the Turks did the same. I had never seen such a thing before, the flashing of the cannons in the darkness and the endless repetitive crashing of the guns. It unnerved everyone, the horses especially, but Hunyadi insisted that they continue.

"We must force them from the field," he said in his tent. We all ate and drank standing up in our armour, even those lords who had taken light wounds.

"Perhaps an attack in the night, my lord," a Hungarian noble suggested.

Many scoffed. "Such a thing would be chaos. No man could see what he was aiming for."

I cleared my throat. "What if a small company was to make an assault on the enemy guns, my lord? They are flashing and banging for all to see. We could come at them from the flanks and so avoid their danger. Kill the crews manning each cannon. That would give us a fine advantage tomorrow, would it not?"

For once, no one shouted me down. They were tired, having fought a battle and were dreading fighting another the next day. Anything that might make their task easier was worth considering.

"Who would lead this attack?" Hunyadi asked all those present. The lords suddenly found the contents of their cups incredibly interesting. It was not that they were cowards, far from it. It was simply that only a madman would take his men in a night attack.

"I will do it, gladly, my lord," I said. "It is just that I have a mere fifty men to lead. Even with the advantage of surprise and the confusion of the enemy, we could only do so much with so few men."

"I want your men fresh, Richard," Hunyadi said.

"Then I will leave my men in their tents and lead others. If any are willing."

Hunyadi looked around the scores of lords crammed beneath the canvas walls. "Who here will place his men under Sir Richard's command for this attack?"

Again, men shuffled their feet and cleared their throats but said nothing.

"I would happily lend some of my men," a lord said. "Alas, they cannot see in the dark."

Others murmured their assent.

"This discussion is all for nought," another Hungarian snapped. "Who here has ever heard of a Turkish army staying on the field for more than a single day?" There was muttered agreement. "Even now, their army will be retreating behind the guns and in the morning we shall find that they have withdrawn, only to offer battle elsewhere on another day. Or perhaps to move on altogether. We certainly hammered them today. Hammered them hard, my lords, did we not?"

There was much agreement to this and my suggestion for a night attack was dismissed as unnecessary. Certainly, these men, their fathers and grandfathers had been fighting the Turks for decades and I was willing to believe their expertise.

Despite the endless cannon fire, I lay down in my tent and slept for what seemed like a few moments before Eva shook me awake and bade me come outside.

The sun was lightening the sky in the east and already we could see the glints of metal and fluttering colours of the banners in the blackness across the field.

"They did not move," I said, shaking my head. "Damn them."

"What are they playing at?" Walt said. "Who wants to bet they come straight at us today? Stephen, how much gold do you have?"

"If we had some prisoners," Eva said, "we would not have to bet." I turned to look at her and saw that old glint in her eye. "We would know."

"Rouse the men," I said to Rob. "Prepare the horses. We are going to snatch up some Turkish sentries before the sun rises."

At the command tent, as a haggard-looking Hunyadi made his finishing remarks, I strode in, covered in dust and sweat, breathing hard. They turned to look at me, scowling.

"By God, you did not make a night attack alone after all, did you man?" some knight quipped.

"My lord," I said, "just before dawn, I took a small company out to the left flank and we brought back five sentries to the camp where we questioned them, separately. Two were Greeks. Well, Thessalians. They said almost the entire Thessalian cavalry was sent far around our left flank in the night. A small number of them were left with banners, so that we would not notice they had left the field. They will attack our left flank from the rear once battle is joined."

Everyone began speaking at once until Hunyadi's men

100

shouted them down and commanded silence. Eyes fell on Hunyadi.

"Where are these men?"

"Outside. I brought them, in case you wished to question them yourself."

Hunyadi nodded to one of his men who ducked outside the tent to do just that. "If what you say is true, Richard, then we must strengthen the left at all costs. The only way to do that is to take men from the centre. And also from the reserve. And so that is what we shall do." He turned to the German mercenary lords. "And also ensure your hand-gunners are ready for a cavalry assault on the *wagonberg* from the rear. If there is nothing else? Then, God be with us all."

Hunyadi crossed the tent as they went back to their units and he grasped my arm in two of his in a powerful grip, nodding. His eyes were watery from exhaustion and the lines of his face were deeper than ever.

"They will come at us hard, today," he said, letting me go. "Harder than yesterday."

"You still want my company to assault the Sultan, my lord?"

"You still wish to do so?"

"More than anything."

"And if it is a choice between your enemy, Zaganos Pasha, and the Sultan?" He peered at me. "What will you do?"

"I would slay the Sultan, of course," I said, which was a lie.

"Then God be with you," Hunyadi said.

Stephen elected to join us on the field, clad in the most expensive Italian armour that could be bought, though he was careful to ensure he hid its brilliance behind poorly-applied paint and unremarkable cloth. He had no desire to be mistaken for somebody of importance.

"The Germans seem to think they will be attacking today," he said to me. "And I do not relish being guarded by the camp followers and the wounded."

I slapped him hard on the back. "That's the spirit, Stephen. And remember, if a cannon shoots in your direction, ensure that you duck."

"Very amusing," he said, closing his visor.

The battle began much as it had before but both armies were full of tired men and perhaps it was my imagination but everyone was tense and fearful. The entire plain was soon filled with the drumming rumble of thousands of horses and the blaring of trumpets and banging of drums.

The Anatolians came hard against our left but we had so many men there now that it held. On the other side of the plain, the Rumelian light horse almost turned our flank but the reserve drove them off.

With our flanks holding, Hunyadi committed his entire centre and all our infantry into an attack on the Turkish centre. The *azab* infantry were pushed back by our hand-gunners who advanced and fired, advanced and fired. Our cannons were pulled forward and deployed again behind our advance.

When we came into range of the Janissaries, our hand-gunners and the Sultan's elite soldiers stood in ranks and shot into each other. The Janissaries had the advantage of their prepared positions, their trenches and palisades, which protected them from our infantry's fire. Even when our cannons opened up on them, blasting holes in sections of their palisades, it made little difference. Battalions of infantry in lines, shooting their firearms into each other would in coming centuries become a familiar sight for me. But at the time, it was truly astonishing. Billowing clouds of smoke and the endless crash of the guns filled the air while we watched from a distance.

Our Germans began edging back from the withering fire of the Janissaries.

"Prepare to attack!" the cry went up and down our line and the men-at-arms in their armour prepared to charge the Janissaries lines.

"Lances!" I cried and my men called for the same from their squires. "Lances!"

"By God, no," Stephen said. "It shall be Varna all over again, Richard. You must stop them."

"No man can stop this now, Stephen. The battle has become a beast with its own mind. All we can do is ride it and try to hold on. Come, we shall join the charge."

We were many thousands of heavy cavalry and our front must have been half a mile wide. Ahead of my company, I watched the steel clad men and horses weaving through the trenches on their way to the Janissaries and I led my own men through safe routes.

The Janissary line broke against our charge, fleeing in sections until the entire line turned and fled. Our cries of victory went up all along the line of our attack and we pushed deeper in toward their camp, cutting down fleeing Janissaries left and right. Our horses were tired and the men's arms grew heavy but the elation that we had won gave strength to us all.

Ahead, the flags atop the Sultan's great tents fluttered in the breeze.

"Pull the company together!" I roared at Walt and Rob. "We make a final charge there, do you see?"

Eva threw her horse against mine and nudged me with her bloody mace. "What is that? Richard? What is that, there? There!"

I followed her pointing and saw the advance of a reserve unit of Janissaries coming forward in good order, shoulder to shoulder, about five hundred of them. The front ranks with their guns levelled and pointed. They were equipped as Janissaries, with the long robes and headdress, with polearms, hand-guns, bows, and side swords at their waists.

But their robes and long felt hats were dyed a vivid, blood-red.

"There!" Eva cried, jabbing her mace.

I tore my eyes to their right flank, on the far side of the formation from me.

William.

Riding an enormous iron-clad warhorse, he wore heavy mail, and had a Turkish helm on his head, with his face exposed. I would know it anywhere, as I knew his bearing and manner. A chill shot through me.

William's unit of blood-red Janissaries stopped as one and couched their gunpowder weapons.

"Halt! Pull back!" I ordered and led my men away from the front of the firing line. Just in time, as the Janissaries fired and scores of Hungarians fell to the volley.

I expected more gunners to step forward and take another

shot but instead, the Janissaries dropped their guns and advanced quickly, drawing their wicked swords. Others in rear ranks raised their polearms, long spears with axe blades on one side.

Another order was called and they broke into a run, advancing like lightning on the Hungarian horsemen.

"Good God," I muttered.

They moved with unnatural speed.

Inhuman speed.

In moments, they crashed against the advancing men-at-arms and killed them. Their spears flashed and their swords whirled into men and horses. The red-robed Janissaries swarmed up onto mounted knights in the saddle and killed the riders. They grasped horses with their hands and dragged them to the ground, crushing the men's helms with maces or cutting off their heads with their swords.

"William!" I roared.

Eva had hold of my horse's bridle and would not let go. She commanded Walt and Rob to hold me back.

"He has five hundred immortal soldiers, Richard!" Eva shouted. "We cannot defeat them. Richard, we cannot! We must live so that we may kill him."

I allowed them to pull me away and I ordered my men to retreat away from the advancing immortal Janissaries. The red-robed monsters cut a swathe into the rest of our army before the retreat was sounded and we fell back, riding across the plain all the way to our reserves before the *wagonberg*.

Instead of pursuing us, William held his Janissaries back and the mortal Turks came forward to occupy their positions amongst the trenches and surviving defensive works. Our men were shocked and confused by the sudden reversal in the battle but they saw we were safe for now and they trusted Hunyadi to see them through and order was restored.

"What now?" Stephen asked, flipping open his visor. "Can even our entire army defeat so many immortals?"

"God damn his soul," I said. "God damn that bastard."

"Can we get around to his rear?" Walt suggested, gesturing with his weapon. "Slip through between their flank and centre, and circle in to the Sultan's camp and close on William's position?"

"He's right," Rob said. "We go around those red-robed bastards and avoid them altogether."

"We shall do it," I said. "Ready the men."

"Richard," Eva said, her tone level, pointing at our centre, where the surviving knights were preparing for another mass charge at the Sultan. "Hunyadi must be warned not to attack again."

It would undoubtedly be suicidal to assault hundreds of immortal soldiers, that was true, but there was a problem. "What can I say to him? What reason can I give that he would believe or even understand?"

None of them had an answer.

It was at that moment that the Turk's Thessalian cavalry finally arrived on our left flank in their thousands and assaulted the rear of the men still engaged there. We watched from our position in the centre near to the rear as our men were surrounded by the flanking manoeuvre.

"All is well," I said to my concerned men. "Hunyadi heeded our warnings and placed the Wallachian reserves there, you see? They are advancing and the Thessalians will themselves be pinned by the Wallachians. The flank will be ours again and their horsemen will be destroyed."

But it dawned on me that something was very wrong.

The Wallachians were not fighting.

"By God, those treacherous dogs are at it again!" Walt cried. "Do you see? Do you see it?"

"What is it?" Stephen asked us, turning from me to Walt, to Rob. "What is happening?"

"The Wallachians," I said, knowing then that the battle was lost. "The Wallachians, thousands of fresh horsemen, our reserve. They are surrendering to the Thessalians without offering battle."

"What?"

"We are betrayed. The Wallachians are surrendering! The battle is lost."

4

Dracula

1448 - 1452

HUNYADI MIGHT HAVE BEEN DEFEATED but he and his Hungarians again showed their ability and experience during the retreat, saving much of the remaining army.

The Wallachian's treacherous surrender allowed the Anatolian *sipahis* to overwhelm our left flank and so Hunyadi ordered the retreat. Their professionalism allowed the left and centre to disengage, with units taking turns to hold the Turks at bay while we did so.

However, the entire right wing was isolated and destroyed. We were still pulling back into the dark of the night. He left behind a screen of infantry to man the camp and sent cavalry to feint attacks while the majority of us slipped away. It must have taken the Turks all the next day to overwhelm the *wagonberg*, even poorly defended as it was, because they did not pursue our army. The men we left behind were slaughtered, of course. God bless their souls.

And despite the sudden change in the course of the battle, we still lost only about six thousand men while the Turks certainly lost forty thousand.

Their enormous losses were the main reason we were not pursued far and we broke into smaller groups to travel back to Hungary, for we would have to skirt far around the Turks on our way back north.

"It is like Varna," Stephen said during our flight. "Like Varna all over again."

"Yes, yes, you were right, Stephen," I said. "Be quiet."

Throughout the journey, riding hard through cold passes and sleeping on thin, hard, freezing soil, I could think only of William and his red-robed immortal army. In the hills many nights later, we crowded into the shelter of a roofless hovel and outbuildings but I was too angry to rest easy.

"If not for William and his immortal Janissaries, we would have killed the Sultan," I said, leaning against the ruined wall and watching the growing fire my men had lit in the centre of the room. "And his son. We would be throwing the Turks out of Europe. If not for William. How could he do such a thing? How could he make so many? How does he find enough blood for them?"

"The Turks have learned to be efficient," Eva said, looking up through the ruined beams at the clear sky above.

"How can we hope to defeat so many?" I asked. "We five against five hundred."

"There is always a way to achieve a goal," Eva said. "Now, sleep. Have patience. Trust that we will yet cut off his head and burn his foul body into ashes. Dream well."

Disaster followed disaster, however, and when we reached Hungary, we discovered that Hunyadi had once again been caught in his defeat by an enemy. George Branković, the ruler of Serbia, had chased down and captured Hunyadi as he and his men cut across his territory, threatening to hand him over to his Turkish masters.

Hunyadi immediately promised a vast ransom if he could be released, to which Branković agreed. The Serbian despot was like a whipped Turkish dog but he saw gold showering down from a desperate Hungary and so he let Hunyadi go. Still, the delay in returning, and doing so in such an ignominious fashion, took more of Hunyadi's remaining lustre and Christians began to wonder if the great Janos Hunyadi could be so great after all, if he only ever lost the battles that truly mattered.

In his defence, it was undeniable that on the field he had done everything correctly, even brilliantly, and yet still he had lost. It was not his fault that he faced an immortal regiment of Janissaries. Even then, he might have saved his army if not for the betrayal of the perfidious Wallachians.

The Turks were on the rise again and Hunyadi had been brought low in the minds of many. The Turks focused now on taking Albania and they invaded in 1449, and in 1450. Each time, the brilliant Skanderbeg threw them back. It seemed for a time that he might truly be the brilliant leader who could unite eastern Christendom, but then he promised peace and entered into negotiations, promising to pay six thousand ducats and swore he would accept Turkish suzerainty. I was saddened by the news but it was all just another clever ploy on his part as he never paid the promised sum and then renounced his subjugation when it came time to pay. Immediately, he began raiding Turkish forts and the invading army, he attacked supply caravans and carried off enormous quantities of booty, eventually forcing the Turks from the field without ever fighting a grand battle.

"Perhaps that is the way to do it," I said, on reading the reports and after listening to men who had been there or claimed to have been. "Force them to withdraw."

"That'll work for mountain lands," Walt pointed out. "What you going to do on the plains, when they can see you coming and chase you down when you flee?"

We were comfortable once more in our house in the city of Buda but it seemed so far from the action.

"Is it time to travel to Albania?" I asked Eva and Stephen, seeking their advice.

"How many men can they put in the field?" Eva asked. "Ten thousand? Lightly armed, at that. Enough to protect their hills and valleys but would Hungarians follow an Albanian, no matter how successful he is in raids and small battles?"

"Damn these people, all of them. The Wallachians most of all."

"Patience, Richard. We have time. Years, decades. We know where William is, now. He has shown inhuman patience and so must we."

"You need not repeat yourself," I said.

"I think I do. You wish to fight. Always. I know. But to defeat William you must first defeat that need to always fight and kill."

"I know, I say. I know, woman, now leave me in peace."

The Turks assaulted the city of Kruje, led in person by the Sultan, but the garrison defeated every attack. The Turks attempted to cut the water supply, and undermine the walls, and they offered vast bribes, literal fortunes to any man who would open the gates. Every attempt failed and Skanderbeg's brave Albanians resisted. The Turkish siege was struck by camp sickness and eventually the Turks, clutching their painful, watery bellies, limped back to Edirne in defeat.

And there, in early 1451, Sultan Murad II died.

He had ruled the Turks for thirty years and had been fighting and winning for most of that time. Christendom rejoiced at his passing and there was a sense that things may just improve, now. The Sultan's son came to the throne as Sultan Mehmed II. He was very young and already in his life he had been the Sultan, when Murad had attempted to retire in his old age and hand the reins of power to his very young son. But the boy Mehmed was not capable of ruling a vast empire, nor could he lead vast armies. Indeed, the young Mehmed had supposedly been Sultan when the crusade of Varna had been launched.

We had heard that young Mehmed II asked his father to reclaim the throne but Murad II refused. Our agents had reported that Mehmed wrote to his father thusly. "If you are the Sultan, come and lead your armies. If I am the Sultan I hereby order you to come and lead my armies."

It sounded to me like the sort of thing William would say but whatever the cause of it, Murad had returned for Varna and for every battle since.

"We shall pray that the boy Sultan remains incompetent," Stephen said.

"Was it incompetent to command his father to return?" Eva said. "Or was it in fact the only thing that saved their damned empire from destruction?"

"It was William," I said, "Whispering in the boy's ear. I have no doubts. But the old man is dead and now we have this young fellow. What is he now, nineteen years old? In command of a vast empire. No, William will have this lad wrapped around his finger, mark my words. We may wish for incompetence but we must plan for further conquest."

"Have you thought any more about making us our own immortal army, Richard?" Rob asked. "To counter the Janissaries in red?"

"I think of little else," I said. "But the questions remain, Rob. Who can we trust enough? Can I make a hundred Hungarian immortals and trust them to keep the secret? If I make a hundred, let alone five hundred, how will we find blood enough for them? Already, there are endless rumours about us here and the drinking of blood. William had Murad to shelter him and now he has Mehmed. Who do we have? You think Hunyadi would comprehend it? He is already walking a knife edge and if we brought him into it, his lords would overthrow him and then we would have chaos. And if there is chaos, William will walk right up to the gates of Buda."

A knock at our door proved to be one of Hunyadi's messengers. "My lord wishes to speak with you, sir. At your earliest convenience."

That meant immediately. My servants prepared my finest clothes and I made my way through the city to the royal palace, whereupon I was brought at once into Hunyadi's private audience chamber.

"Vladislaus II has not proved himself to be the ruler that I hoped he would be," Hunyadi said, inviting me to sit with him by a window overlooking the Danube below.

"You mean he is not obeying your commands," I said. "And you were the one who placed him on the throne of Wallachia."

"I do not issue him commands," he snapped. "But I have just had word that Vladislaus has sent a delegation of *boyars* to congratulate the new Sultan."

I shrugged. "Wallachians are duplicitous. None can be trusted."

Hunyadi eyed me, weighing up his next words. "And yet some can be trusted more than others. And it seems that Vladislaus can be trusted to throw in with the Turks, just as Vlad Dracul had done. We need a loyal man on the throne, or at least one who hates the Turks more than he fears them."

"You need a man who hates the Turks more than he does Hungary," I said, which did not please the Regent. "Are there any such men in Wallachia?"

"Perhaps there are not," he admitted. "Not amongst the *boyars* in Wallachia at this moment. But perhaps there is one who feels this way who is not in Wallachia?"

"Very well," I said. "Who is this man?"

Hunyadi looked out of the window before speaking. "We have had word that the Turks recently released a Wallachian who was their hostage for many years. He is the eldest of the two surviving sons of the former *voivode*, Vlad Dracul. The son's name is also Vlad. He is coming here."

I nodded. "The son of the man I killed is coming to Buda?" As I spoke, Hunyadi smiled. "And you wish me gone before he comes, is that it?"

"It would not be for long. You see, I have a task for you. We must begin to move against Vladislaus by taking at least two of the fortresses on the border of Transylvania and Wallachia so that we control the passes and not him. And while you are away, taking possession of these places for Hungary, I will speak to this young Vlad and I will see how he feels about things. And, yes, it might be best if the man who cut off his father's head was not present when he arrives. It may have an undesired effect on the young fellow."

"I am pleased to hear that he is coming," I said. "When I do meet him, I will be able to fulfil a duty that I swore to uphold."

"A duty? Swore to whom?"

"Before he died, Vlad Dracul asked that I look after his sons. He gave his sword, and a dragon amulet, into my care, and requested that I pass them to his eldest, this Vlad. I wondered if I would ever get the opportunity."

"Truly? Well, that is well. Perhaps the bridges can be mended, in time. Nevertheless, the Transylvanian fortresses must still be taken. There will be no fighting, but the garrisons must be replaced, you see."

∞

The fortresses in the duchies of Fogaras and Amlas were willing to give up without a fight but honour demanded they go through the motions of demanding the legal proofs and the commanders stated they had to receive confirmation from the lords before vacating the defences.

Although I took my company and four hundred other mercenaries in Hunyadi's pay and Hungarian soldiers, there was a lot of talking and even more waiting. I did my best to be courteous to all and remembered that it was supposed to take a long time. I was supposed to be keeping out of the way while Vlad, son of Vlad, made himself at home in Buda.

"Perhaps we can raid into Wallachia a little," I suggested to Eva. "Keep the men busy."

"Because you are bored," she replied.

"It would make Vladislaus look weak," I said. "And his people would demand his removal. Which is what Hunyadi wants."

"He does not want lawlessness on his borders, and he does not want the Wallachians subject to raids by Hungarian soldiers. Or soldiers loyal to Hungary."

"We would disguise ourselves," I said, warming to the idea. "Perhaps we could find some Turkish armour?"

"You should train against Walt and Rob. Take out some of your excessive vigour."

I scoffed. "They are no challenge. They have only three hands between them."

"We will not raid Wallachia, Richard. You would not be so rash. Once, perhaps, but not now."

"Have I changed so much?"

She smiled. "There will be war enough even for you, soon. Have patience."

After a few weeks on the Transylvania-Wallachia border, my business was concluded. The towns and fortresses had written letters to the *voivode*, begging for forgiveness for accepting the protection of the Hungarian crown. My Hungarian soldiers and most of the mercenaries I left as garrisons in the towns. They would not be enough to resist the Wallachians should the *voivode* decide to take them back by force and instead the garrison soldiers were there to keep an eye on the towns. And no one believed Voivode Vladislaus would go so far as taking the towns back by force.

When I returned to Buda, the young Vlad had been welcomed into Hunyadi's service and had sworn allegiance to Ladislaus V, the King of Hungary. Even so, I felt it best to keep my distance, literally. Until I was once again summoned by Hunyadi to the palace.

I knew what to expect. At least, I thought I did.

The summons was to his private quarters and I expected that the conversation would again be a quiet one with just him and his chamberlain and other servants.

Instead, when I was escorted in, there were dozens of men and lords present, surrounding Hunyadi. He was somewhat hidden behind those lords, engaged in serious conversation while wine was served and men drank in small groups, and I waited until his business was completed.

Some men nodded in greeting but I was not well liked by most lords, great and small, and most ignored me. I was an outsider and also I made no effort to play the game of politics by building friendships and alliances, which was unusual and so made the men who would be my peers mistrust me even more. Some looked down on me as a mere mercenary knight and others wondered if I had some secret motivation to have remained at the Hungarian court for so long.

Of course, they were right to be suspicious. I was indeed there for secret, ulterior motives, and I did not care what they thought of me. I was not a part of their society, or any society, existing outside of it. And Eva said I had a stillness that disturbed people, and I moved with a fluidity reminiscent of a wolf. Some lords were so powerful that no lesser man, even an unnatural one, was a threat to their position and so I was welcomed by kings and princes.

It was fine by me. Their opinions on warfare were idiotic, and I often listened to impassioned arguments for one tactic over another where both men were woefully wrong. Even those infuriating discussions were preferable to the fools discussing the minutiae of this piece of armour over that, or a new weapon they had obtained. Worse still was the ravings over items of clothing that they were having made, or even the absurd shoes they were wearing. Other than that, it was complaints about their sons, fathers, wives, daughters, their servants, or their vassals. It was incredibly tiresome.

"Who is that man there?" an outraged voice cried out in Hungarian.

The room fell silent and I looked up. Across the chamber, Hunyadi was on his feet and beside him a short, young lord stood glaring at me with his hand outstretched and his finger pointing at me.

Nobles on either side of me cleared their throats and stepped backwards, creating a space around me.

Hunyadi looked anxious but restrained, watching me carefully.

The top of the young man's head came up to Hunyadi's nose but he was otherwise powerfully built and had a strong face, with a long, sharp nose and the beginnings of a fine moustache beneath it. His clothes were of rich cloth, in red, with sable edges.

"I am the mercenary captain known as Richard of England," I said and bowed. "And who are you, my lord?"

I knew who he was.

"I am Vlad Dracula, son of Vlad Dracul, the former Voivode of Wallachia." He stalked forward, approaching slowly with a face fixed in an unreadable expression. "I have heard of you," he said, his voice deep and steady. "You are the man who did slay my father in the marshes."

Lords and knights shuffled further away from me.

"I am," I said, looking him in the eye. "And I did."

He stopped just an arm's span from me, looking up through

heavily lidded eyes and thick black eyebrows. "In that case," he said, speaking slowly. "I must thank you, sir. My beloved father was for too long a friend to the Turk. And so it is right and proper that he was removed from power and a loyal Christian put in his place."

Around me, I heard many a breath being released.

Still, it seemed rather convenient to be swiftly and publicly forgiven.

I bowed my head a little. "I am glad you feel that way, my lord."

"However, Sir Richard the mercenary captain, we do have a problem, do we not?"

"We do, my lord?"

"Why yes. Certainly, we do. For there is now one on the throne of Wallachia who has also forgotten his duty to God. He also must be replaced by a man who knows where his true loyalties lie."

I glanced at Hunyadi, who stood motionless across the room. He met my eye but I could not read his expression. "I hope that such a replacement of the Voivode of Wallachia can be swiftly brought about, my lord."

"Will you help me?" Vlad asked, suddenly. He cleared his throat and spoke more slowly. "That is, if you would agree, I would much value your assistance in claiming the throne that is mine by right."

Over his shoulder, Hunyadi made the smallest nod of his head. "My only desire is to kill Turks," I said, watching closely for his reaction. "My only goal is to drive them from Europe, once and for all."

"Your *only* desire?" Vlad raised his eyebrows and smirked. "Truly?"

In fact, my only desire is to kill William and the Turks are in my way, I thought.

"Yes, my lord," I said.

He smiled beneath his moustache. "I am pleased to hear it. And since that is my only desire, also, then you should help me."

"I should?" I said.

The young Vlad frowned, his eyebrows lancing down over his dark eyes. "You would be paid, of course. You and your men. You are a mercenary company after all, are you not? And you are currently unemployed."

"It seems to me, my lord, that you have much work to do before you begin slaughtering Turks. Not least of which is taking the throne that you say is yours by right. When you have armies to throw against our enemies, I will gladly fight beside you. Assuming, of course, that my lord Janos Hunyadi, who currently pays to retain my company for his service, grants us leave to take up employment by the new *voivode*."

Vlad scowled and turned to look at Hunyadi, who appeared annoyed.

"The Turks have a new Sultan, Richard," Hunyadi snapped. "And they will be on the march once more. Our new ally, Vlad Dracula, has accepted responsibility for guarding the Transylvanian border against Turkish incursion. If Vladislaus has indeed thrown his lot in with the Turks, they will march straight through the Wallachian plains and seek to cross the passes. Vlad

Dracula, therefore, shall indeed soon be engaged in your favourite pastime. And because, as you say, I pay you well in order to retain your service, I will ask that you join him in his new responsibility."

Vlad Dracula turned back to me, his dark eyes full of expectation.

It seemed quite possible that he intended to get me alone, away from the court, and out in the wilds so that he could take revenge for his father's murder. There was no chance at all that he meant what he said about being glad I had killed the older Vlad. No matter how one feels about one's father, no man alive could break bread with his killer, much less serve beside him in battle.

On the other hand, he seemed willing to throw himself into the fight. Perhaps his long years amongst the Turks had created in him a desire to destroy them, or at least resist them, as it had done for Skanderbeg in Albania.

There was still a good chance that the young man was in fact a Turkish agent, biding his time until he betrayed Christendom and opened the gates to the swarming hordes beyond. He would not be the first Christian hostage to convert to his captors' religion and throw his lot in with them. If that was his plan, to kill me, and to betray his Christian brothers, then the best place to stop him would be at his side.

No doubt Hunyadi was playing his own games. Indeed, although he paid to retain my service, I was not sworn to him and could refuse a task. Breaking our contract would not go down well with my men, who would feel their reputation was at risk of being tainted and who always made more money on campaign than sitting idly.

By arranging for me to be confronted by Vlad publicly, Hunyadi was hoping to pressure me into accepting the task, even if I had doubts about my safety and the young lord's chances of success.

But I thought I could protect myself against an inexperienced young knight. And if he failed, then I would not have lost much. More important was keeping Hunyadi on my side.

I bowed. "I will guard the border with you, my lord."

And I will guard my back from you, I thought.

"Do you consider yourself an equal to me?" Vlad asked, watching me like a hawk.

Just in time, I stopped myself from bursting out into laughter.

Instead, I bowed. "You are a great lord, who will one day soon be Prince of Wallachia. I am a mere knight, albeit one of great renown and personal ability, with a small but loyal company of veteran soldiers."

A Hungarian lord growled from across the room. "He is a mercenary dog who will do as he is commanded, if the whip hand is firm enough."

I smiled. "And you are a fat old man who cannot hold his wine. Would you care to do combat with me, fat old man? You may choose the weapons, as I am your superior in them all."

His face turned purple and he threw his goblet down with a crash upon the floor. "How dare you! I demand an apology!"

"You may try to take it, if you dare," I said, holding out my hands.

"Enough!" Hunyadi roared. "Radol, I forbid you to fight my

mercenary."

"Listen to your lord, Radol," I said. "Or you won't live to regret it."

Hunyadi turned on me. "Richard, you will go with Vlad Dracula or you will leave Hungary forever!"

Sighing, I imagined Eva mocking my inability to hold my temper.

I bowed to him and then to Vlad. "To Transylvania it is, then."

Vlad Dracula watched me with a strange look in his eye. I could not be certain but it seemed as though it was a look of delight.

∞

On the journey to the mountainous southern border of Transylvania, I was sure to keep myself and my company far from Dracula's. His new personal forces, some gifted by Hunyadi, others by loyal Wallachian *boyars*, and a number of Moldavians, outnumbered mine many times over.

Before we left Buda, I had explained to the men of my company that we were heading into danger and that the threat might come from our host, Vlad Dracula.

"But the main threat is to you," a grizzled Frenchman named Claudin said. The leading men in my company had assembled in my tent and it was crowded and unpleasant inside and I wished for it to be done as swiftly as possible.

"Well, thank you for your concern, Claudin," I said. "My heart is touched by your compassion."

Some of the men laughed but he continued. "Without you, my lord, we would have a company no more. But I merely ask whether Vlad Dracula means to kill you and you alone."

"I do not know if he means me harm at all, Claudin, but it is a distinct possibility, would you not say?"

He shrugged and pursed his lips, for he was both deficient in wit and a Frenchman.

"Might he not kill us all?" Garcia asked. He was a young man, forced to leave his homeland in his extreme youth due to some indiscretion or other, but he was a sharp one. "If Vlad Dracula, son of Vlad Dracul, wishes you dead and kills you, might he not wish for there to be no witnesses to his crime? After all, Hunyadi would not wish to see you murdered. It would be a crime to blacken his name. Cause him trouble, no? But if the entire Company of Saint George is killed to a man, he might well swear that it was the Turks that did the deed."

The men muttered and looked around at each other in the tent.

"Indeed, Garcia," I said, "that is the case. So you must each of you be on your guard at all times. We shall ride and camp as if we are in enemy territory. Any Wallachian or Transylvanian that comes near us, day or night, must be stopped and questioned and if he is on proper business then he must be watched and well guarded in every moment."

"What about Serban?" someone called and others chuckled.

"All Wallachians other than Serban," I said. "He is sworn to me. None of you will treat him as the enemy. Do you all understand what we are riding into? And do you all agree to follow me in such circumstances?"

Thanks to God, and the men's love of money, they all came with me into Transylvania.

We rode away from our supposed allies in the day and camped with an established perimeter that we closely guarded. Each night, my close companions and I took turns to sleep, lest Vlad Dracula or his men attempted an outright attack or an assassination.

And each night passed without incident.

"Biding his time," Walt said confidently one morning, after we had been in Transylvania for two weeks.

Rob agreed, as his squire strapped his vambrace on his handless arm. "Luring you in by being patient and waiting until you let your guard down."

"Ah, well," I said, tapping my nose. "Little does he know that I never let my guard down."

Eva scoffed. "Every night, the whole of Transylvania can hear you snoring."

My companions found this highly amusing. "I snore so that you, my friends, will each be wide awake enough to guard me in my slumber."

One by one, Vlad Dracula toured the fortresses of the border that fell under his command, and each commander swore loyalty and agreed plans of action should the Turks attack. A few men he removed and replaced but the tour was largely without incident. Eventually, we took quarters outside a fortress in the east called

Crăciune.

I had kept my distance from Vlad for weeks and what had started out as sensible precaution had begun to look like rudeness and, ultimately, outright fear. I did not like to skulk about and to always be where our leader was not. It made me appear unimportant and disinterested, as well as fearful.

"Perhaps I should join our young commander in the fortress," I said to Eva, who lay beside me in our low, narrow bed inside my tent. "He seems committed to taking his throne and waging war against the Turks after all. If that is true then it is likely he would be a friend to me."

"That would be taking an unnecessary risk."

"If he was going to do us harm, he would have done it already. It stands to reason."

"A man may use reason to convince himself of anything," she said. "Many pathways of reason appear sound all the way to the conclusion and then men choose the one they like the best."

"I am not prone to such failures in reasoning," I said.

"All men do this," she said. "And all women, too. You cannot out-think a problem to a certain conclusion. It is not possible."

"But one may weigh up decisions. Come to a reasoned decision based on this outcome or that having more or less likelihood of success."

"Precisely. For instance, you cannot reason whether Vlad Dracula will be a friend or an enemy to the Turks. Or to you. Perhaps he will be an enemy to the Turks and an enemy to you also. What you wish to be true is that he seeks to destroy his former captives with every ounce of will he possess, and so you look for reasons that this is true. You speak to me of the hatred that must have grown in his heart at being held prisoner by hostile and strange people. And you look for evidence of this in his actions since being freed, or in the words he uses, or the tone he takes, or expression his moustache makes when he speaks of the Turk. But it is all wasted effort, do you not see? Either of your suppositions could be true, or neither."

"Out of all of the women I have ever known, you have the most elaborate way of telling me to shut up and go to sleep."

She tutted. "I am telling you to be patient. Be prepared for any eventuality. Even better, be prepared for every eventuality and you can never be surprised."

I pinched her suddenly on the flank and pushed her gently onto her back, shifting myself over her. "You did not expect that, did you?"

She rolled her eyes and smiled. "With you, Richard, I never expect anything else."

"You expect me to always take your advice," I said.

"Because it is always good advice," she said.

"Perhaps. But how would I ever know if I did not on occasion disregard it?"

She frowned as I slid off of her and climbed from my bed, calling for my valet.

"What are you doing?" she asked, sitting up.

"I will not live like a whipped dog, cringing at the sound of his master's boots. I am going to speak to Vlad."

"At this hour? He will be abed."

"Or drunk."

"Aye, or drunk, which would be far worse."

I grinned at her as my valet entered and pretended not to be staring at Eva's breasts.

"I am going to call on the future Prince of Wallachia so prepare my fine clothes," I commanded and he bowed and crossed the tent to do just that.

"Richard," Eva said, climbing from the bed. "Why would he grant you an audience at this time of night? Why not wait until morning?"

"I have something in my possession that he will want," I said. "He will see me."

Eva scowled and snapped at my valet. "Leave the clothes be, I will see to them. Go and rouse Sir Robert and Black Walter. They are to attend Sir Richard at once. Go, now."

"Thank you, Eva," I said.

"Wear the green jacket with the loose sleeves so you may hide a blade inside each arm," she said, crouching naked by my clothes chest and searching through it.

I bowed. "Whatever you say, my dear."

We crossed the field into the fortress by the light of lamps alone. The sky was low and rain threatened, with a cold wind bringing damp air down from the east.

"You sure about this, Richard?" Walt asked, scratching his chin.

"It does seem contrary to your previous advice," Rob said, carrying the long wooden case that I had entrusted to him.

"All will be well," I said. "Just, for God's sake, be on your guard."

It was a small fortress and the hall was likewise diminutive. When I was escorted in and instructed to wait, the remains of the meal eaten earlier were being cleared away and the trestle tables taken apart. We stood in front of the high end of the hall where the permanent chairs of the lord sat empty. A couple of soldiers sat slumped in the corners, heads lolling onto their chests.

Behind me, Walt scoffed. "Wallachia's finest sons, there."

"Useless bastards," Rob said, before yawning. "Though I wish I was in a drunken stupor."

Walt snorted. "Remember that time in Prague when that little Bavarian lad challenged you to—"

"Will you two old maids cease your prattling?" I snapped. "Someone comes."

Footsteps approached from the rooms beyond the hall and Vlad Dracula entered, followed by a dozen of his companions. All were armed.

He did not acknowledge me until he had taken his seat in the largest chair upon the dais. It was not raised high but still it was a demonstration that we were not equals. Far from it.

"Sir Richard," Vlad said. "What is the danger?"

"My lord?"

"I asked you what is the danger, sir." He gestured with his palm up. "I assume there is some danger imminent and that is why you had to see me immediately. I was just about to get into bed, such as it is."

"There is no danger, my lord."

"Oh? Then what is the meaning of this urgency? After all, you have kept yourself and your company so far from me and from any service that I had concluded that you were workshy. It seems that your reputation as a fierce soldier was no more than lies. You have taken your pay and done nothing of note other than to camp in this field or that with your men. What has changed, sir, that you felt so compelled to insist I see you in this very moment?"

"We are a fighting company, my lord, that much is true. Thanks to Christ, though, that there has been no fighting these past weeks, for us or for you. Clearly, your powers of diplomacy are significant and worthy of praise and you have done so much to secure the lands of Christendom against the Turk. Indeed, I was so impressed by your ability to secure the length of the borderland that I suddenly recalled a duty I swore to perform. This duty is why I have come to you."

I left it there so that he would be forced to ask.

"A duty?" Vlad said. "What duty must you perform tonight?"

"I swore that I would support you, as long as you were an enemy of the Turk."

Vlad sighed, gesturing at me to hurry up. "Yes, yes, you swore to Hunyadi, I was there."

"I stated my terms in Buda and Hunyadi agreed. I swore nothing to him that is not in my contract."

He was confused and growing frustrated. "Well, who did you swear this oath to?"

"To your father."

He and his men bristled and I noted a few hands drifting toward their swords. Most would have spent the last hours of the day drinking wine and would be quick to anger and slow to see subtleties.

"You swore to my father to support me," Vlad said, "before you killed him?"

"I pursued him and his men into the marshes. We fought and he was injured in the arm and neck. Before he died, he asked that I help his sons, Vlad and Radu, to fight the Turks."

Vlad was very still, though I thought I saw him flinch at the name of his brother. "My father would not have said that."

"I beg your pardon for disagreeing, my lord, but he did. He begged me to deliver these to you and to urge you to remember your duty, just as he had failed in his."

I turned to Rob who handed over the long wooden case that he had carried for me from my tent, and I held it out to Vlad.

The case was covered in intricate patterns of moulded boiled leather in a deep red, with gold leaf in recesses throughout. The corners were protected by polished brass. The pattern on the top of the case in the centre was that of a dragon with its tail in its mouth and a cross on its back.

One of his men took it from me, his eyes widening as he saw the beauty of the designs and brought it reverently to his lord.

"My father gave you this?" Vlad asked, rightly suspicious.

"The case I had made in Buda," I replied. "Though it was a Wallachian who did the work. He claimed to have trained in Florence and I did not believe him until I saw his work. It is the contents of the case that were given to me by your father that I might give them in turn to you."

Vlad did not take his eyes from the case as he undid the clasps and opened it. His men clustered close about him and peered over his shoulders.

The interior of the case was moulded to the shape of its contents and covered in red silk.

Vlad reached in and lifted out the sword, staring at it with such fervour that I feared his eyes would pop from his head. With his other hand, he took the dragon amulet on its chain and looked from one to the other as his men took the case away.

Finally, Vlad lifted his eyes to me and I saw that they were damp with threatened tears.

"Did he say anything else?"

"He asked that I protect you."

"Protect me?" Vlad repeated, bewildered. "And you agreed?"

"I said that any man who was an enemy to the Turk would be a friend as far as I was concerned."

Vlad thought for a moment and stood, stepped down from the dais as he approached, still with the sword in one hand and the dragon amulet in the other, its silver chain dangling down.

Walt and Rob slid forward but I waved them back.

"Thank you, Sir Richard," Vlad said, standing before me and looking up. "You have done your duty in this matter. And you have done it well."

"It pleases me to hear it, my lord. As I said to your father. I am here to fight the Turks. The Sultan and his closest men in particular."

Vlad glanced up at me. "I hate the Turk more than any man alive. Once I have my kingdom secured, I shall do everything in my power to destroy them. Every one. The Sultan and his closest men in particular."

For a moment, I thought he was about to embrace me but

instead he dismissed me. As I left the hall, I saw him showing off his father's sword to his companions.

"How did it go?" Eva asked.

"I think perhaps we should throw in our lot with this Vlad Dracula. We might help him to win the throne and if we do, he may well become a great ally. Or even more."

Alas, it was not to be. The Turks were not sitting still and allowing us to make our plans and live our lives. They were bent on conquest.

In the morning, a frantic messenger came from Hungary, with letters for Vlad Dracula but others for Stephen from his agents in Buda.

"What is it?" I asked Stephen when his face turned grey. He continued reading. "Stephen!"

He dragged his eyes from the words. "The new Sultan, Mehmed, is not coming for Transylvania after all."

"Damn," I said. "Where is he headed? Albania? Not Moldavia, surely, they are nothing."

Stephen swallowed. "There is no doubt that he has chosen to concentrate the efforts of his entire empire on the final reduction of Constantinople."

"Constantinople?" Serban said, crossing himself.

"Bastards," Walt said.

"Can it be true?" I asked Eva.

Stephen answered, flicking the letter in his hands. "It is Constantinople herself that calls for aid. Letters have been sent to every Christian kingdom, begging for help before the Turks arrive."

"Then that is what we shall do," I said. "Prepare the men. We leave for Constantinople."

5

Constantinople

1453

THE TURKS HAD LONG SOUGHT CONSTANTINOPLE and yet it was impossible to not see William's hand in this new assault. It was the sort of grandiose monstrosity that he brought forth into the world. Yet it was certainly in the interests of the new young Sultan, for if he achieved his aim it would secure his position within his empire, as well as make him famous everywhere in Dar al-Islam, even in Arabia and Egypt where they looked down on the Turks as barbarian upstarts. Indeed, such fame would help to secure his empire's porous eastern borders, for who would dare attack the man who had destroyed the great Constantinople?

The Byzantines had long been forced into vassalage under the

Turks. Under the terms of their vassalage they had not even been permitted to strengthen the great walls of their city and had been sending troops to fight for the Turks for decades already. Even sixty years earlier, the subjugated Byzantines had sent troops to help destroy the city of Philadelphia, the last Byzantine possession in Anatolia. All that was left of the once great and vast Roman Empire of the East was the city of Constantinople and a handful of outlying ports, fortresses and villages. Such a disgrace and humiliation to suffer and yet the city itself, with its vast walls, had resisted every previous attempt at taking it.

There remained many elements in the city's favour. Provided that Venice and Genoa and other fleets came to Constantinople's aid, the Turks would have enormous trouble crossing the Bosporus without coming to disaster. The Turks were good soldiers but their fleets had always been weak compared to Christian navies. And if they attacked the great chain gate that protected the Golden Gate harbour, they would be risking a counter assault by the Christian ships safe in the Golden Horn.

"Do not think the Turk is unaware of this," the Byzantine officer said as he escorted us along the top of the inner wall of the city's main defensive fortification. The officer's name was Michael and he was a grim fellow though he had welcomed me and my company with open arms when we arrived. "One of the first acts that alerted us to the Turk's intentions was his construction of the fortress six miles north of here, on the European side of the straits. It is at the narrowest point of the Bosporus, do you see? It was when the towers of the fortress grew as tall as our own walls that Emperor Constantine sent his letters requesting aid. That fortress is armed with vast cannons, powerful enough to threaten any ship passing through."

Michael came to a stop beside a tower at the northern end of the inner wall and we looked out through one of the enormous crenels to the empty land beyond. The fields were untended and there were hardly any people on the roads, all the way to the horizon. On our right was the inner portion of the Golden Horn, the protected harbour so precious to the city. Within the harbour, hundreds of ships, large and small, bobbed on the blue waters.

On the other side of the harbour mouth was the walled town of Galata, which was largely populated and controlled by Genoese colonists. Unseen beyond Galata, further along the strait, was the new fortress that Michael had spoken of. It was technically, legally, on Byzantine land but the Turks had not cared about that. They meant to take everything for themselves anyway, so why quibble over such things? The local peasants had protested but there was nothing they could do.

"So they now control the northern half of the straits, at the least," I said. "But still, the Turk cannot truly sail."

Michael scoffed. "No, he takes to the water like a stone," he said and spat. "And may they all drown like rocks, also. But no, they have been building ships everywhere in Anatolia. And they have promised fortunes for Christian crews and captains for a thousand miles and they have answered, the treacherous, mercenary, bastards. With hundreds of new ships and Christian crews, the Turk may be a challenge for the Venetians and Genoese."

"Surely not, sir," I said, thinking him far too fearful.

Eva and Stephen exchanged a look and Stephen began scratching down notes. Walt leaned on the merlon and looked out at the landscape beyond, pointing down at the lower, outer walls and muttering something to Rob and Serban.

"Four hundred Turkish ships in the straits, so they are saying. Eighteen great warships, another twenty galleons and a score or more built only for transporting horses across the straits. They have made a fleet and made it for the sole purpose of contesting the Bosporus and for moving an army across the waters."

Stephen stopped writing for a moment to stare, Serban crossed himself and Rob muttered a short prayer or an oath.

"Even so," Stephen said, "the Venetians alone could defeat the Turks, could they not?"

"That is assuming more Venetians come than have already," Michael said. "They are not a people to be trusted, as I am sure you know. They care only for gold, for making wealth. They are a people without honour."

"They are Christians, sir," I said. "They will come. All of Christendom will come."

He scoffed openly. "An easy thing to say. Yet, where are they?"

Stephen answered. "Constantine has promised to heal the schism between the Roman and the Orthodox Church, has it not? And the agreement allows the Pope in Rome to be the lord of all Christians in the East."

The soldier sucked air in through pursed lips. "Old Constantine has promised it, yes, and the leaders of the Church have agreed. But ordinary people will not have it. Mark me, sir, the people will not be subject to Rome."

"They would rather be destroyed by the Mohammedans?" I said, irritated by his obstinacy, and that of his people.

"They would rather be free to worship as they believe in their hearts."

"But if it is a choice of surviving or being destroyed, surely they can see they would be better off changing the form of their worship somewhat rather than seeing their sons murdered and their wives and daughters raped and sold into slavery."

He shrugged. "They see it as subjugation also. But they believe the walls will save us. And God will save us. This is God's city. He will not let it fall."

I shook my head in disbelief, and Eva placed a hand on my arm.

"Who has come so far, sir?" Eva asked him, smiling pleasantly. "We have seen Venetian ships in the harbour and men of many nations in the city."

His face flushed as he answered, annoyed at being addressed by a woman. Normally, she held her tongue amongst strangers but we were not in normal times. "Catalan mercenaries have been hired but silver was stripped from the churches to pay for them and the people are not happy. Not happy at all, madam. Some of the silver went on repairing the walls, at least, and few men complain about that. The Venetians, though, already lost ships to the great guns of the Rumelia Hisar fortress and so they are keeping clear of it until the battle is won. To that end they have sent us the ships you see, along with two transport ships now departed which was filled with Venetian soldiers."

"So they have come," I said. "In numbers."

"A few hundred soldiers, perhaps. But will they stand or will they set sail when battle is joined?"

I had no answer for him. "Who else has come?"

"Cardinal Isidore arrived yesterday and his men are now disembarking. I believe he has brought hand-gunners and archers but a mere two hundred soldiers. In the streets, the people are rejoicing and saying that this is the vanguard of a vast army which comes even now to save us. After all, why not think this? The Pope could send tens of thousands but he demands Constantine publicly heal the schism first. Outrageous. I tell them that the Pope's army is not coming but few have listened. Even my own family tell me to have faith. Ha!" He turned and spat over the wall, the wind catching it and sending it flying away horizontally. I guessed he had spent a lot of time up on that wall.

"And what of the Genoese? Is there word?"

"They say that they will come. But will they? They are almost as bad as the Venetians and perhaps they are even worse, for they occupy the Galata quarter, across from the Golden Horn, and many are saying that they must remain neutral if there is a battle. Neutral! Can you imagine it? Almost as bad as the Hungarians." He eyed me, watching my reaction, for he knew that we had come from that very place and that my company had been in their employ.

I spoke lightly. "You have reason to hold the Hungarians in contempt, sir?"

He lifted his chin. "I do. We have had word back from this jumped up poor knight made Regent of Hungary, named Hunyadi. He lost the battle at Varna, the bloody fool. And now he sends word in reply to a request for aid from the Basileus himself. Do you know what he says to my lord?"

"I was the one who bore the letter," I said.

Michael scowled. "So, you know. You know that your master Hunyadi says that he will only send soldiers here if we promise him land in Greece in return. Land that is not even in our possession now that the Turk has taken it! It is as if he has intended an insult. Is that what he intended, an insult to the Emperor?"

"I do not know."

After leaving Vlad Dracula in the province of Transylvania, I had returned to Buda and asked Hunyadi how many men he was sending to protect Constantinople. He told me it had yet to be decided and that I was to wait. It soon became clear that the Hungarians were interested only in making the most of it as an opportunity to extract concessions from the Emperor. In truth, there was little he could give, for he had no territory, no men, and no money. He did have historical claims to certain territories and other rights and these were what Hunyadi asked for.

"So, you will not go?" I had asked Hunyadi. "Truly?"

"We may go, by land or by sea, but there must be the will of the council and the lords see Constantinople as a lost cause. We may bring them around yet, Richard. Have patience, sir."

But I did not have patience and could not sit around waiting while the last bastion of Christianity in the East was at risk. And so I had begged that he allow my company to go, at least. When Hunyadi agreed, I had the distinct feeling that he did not expect to see me ever again. At least he had paid me and my men and

143

had helped arrange our ship from Venice.

On the high, inner wall, I turned and looked in toward the city. Below me, protected by the ancient wall, was a huge plain dotted with fields and houses. In the distance, where the peninsular narrowed, I saw the massive dome of the Sancta Sophia and the other grand buildings with the sea around on all three sides. I had been there before, many times, and each time the venerable city had declined. It had become a collection of small villages, communes, dotted about, with the densest areas along the northern and southern walls and in the heart of the old city where the government administrators and merchants lived.

"What will Emperor Constantine do?" Stephen asked Michael.

"He has promised Hunyadi the land in Greece he has asked for. What else can he do? He has embraced humility and is willing to give all in order to save what is left. But these Christian kings think only of themselves. Do you know that Alfonso of Naples demands the island of Lemnos in return for sending his ships? As if it is not his *duty* to do so all the same."

"I agree, it is madness," I said. "But more men will come. I am sure of it. But how many men do you have in total?"

His face coloured and he looked out at the waters. "So far? Not eight thousand proper soldiers. More will come, yes. Yes. They have to."

We exchanged looks. Eight thousand men to defend the greatest city in the world? It was ludicrous. It could not be done.

"What of the militia?"

He nodded. "Yes, we have thirty-five thousand militia under

arms inside the walls. And they have been trained. But they are not soldiers, they are men with weapons."

"Men defending their homes," I pointed out. "Their families."

"Yes," he said, looking wistful.

"You have family still here?"

"Of course," he said, looking both offended and confused.

I thought it best to change the subject. "What of the walls? You are repairing and rebuilding certain sections, I see?"

The walls of the city were famous throughout the world. For a thousand years, they had helped keep the city safe. But they were old. Built for a time that was long gone.

Extending across the peninsula from the Sea of Marmara in the south to the Golden Horn in the north, they were four miles long and dotted with almost one hundred towers. The main, inner wall was forty feet high and the smaller outer one beyond it was thirty feet. Beyond that was an enormous moat sixty-five feet wide and thirty feet deep.

Where they reached the water in the north and south, the walls turned sharply and ran all the way around the peninsula so that the city was entirely encased in stone and brick, with battlements on top.

Repairs and additions had been made over the centuries, of course but there were few emplacements for cannon or firearms. Michael and his men escorted us along the top of the inner wall and showed us the sections they had repaired and other terraces where they had installed small cannons.

"What do you think?" I asked my men.

They were silent, looking in various directions.

"I think it is still a wonder of the world," Stephen said. "Even after so many years of degeneration."

"There are no defences like this anywhere else on earth," Rob said. "The scale is... inhuman."

"I think we were fools to come," Walt said. "This place is doomed."

"There is hope yet," Rob said. "Think of the floating chain, with the massive buoys. It yet closes the Golden Horn, from the Acropolis Point to the sea wall of Galata. It is in place. It is functional. No assault can be made there.

"Stephen?" I prompted. "You saw it two hundred years ago, just as I did. It is much changed, is it not? The walls are still here, yes, but the people are so few. It is like the countryside in here, not a city."

"And yet we must remember that this city has been besieged so many times, Richard, and almost always it has resisted. Look here, behind the walls. Yes, the people are fewer than they were. But we see vast fields under cultivation. Orchards. Livestock of all kinds being reared, sheep, pigs, even cows. Pasture for horses. They bring in great baskets onto the docks every morning, filled to bursting with fish caught just off the many harbours. There are cisterns all over the city storing more water than can be used. No siege can starve us out, that much is certain."

Walt held his hand over his eyes. "But they ain't going to settle in, are they, Stephen? You heard how many men the Turks are planning to bring here? That are already gathering beyond all four horizons." He slapped a hand on the towering merlon beside him. "They mean to break *through*. Perhaps not these walls, perhaps instead by the sea ones there or there. But they mean to break us open. We should not have come here. Eight thousand proper soldiers, Richard. Look at this wall. Look beyond it. Imagine the plain filled to the horizon. How many will William and his pet Sultan bring here? A hundred thousand? Surely, knowing what we know, we must leave while we still can."

I sighed and leaned on the top of the crenel, trying to imagine the army that Walt described.

"These walls have stood every assault," I said. "Well, other than the madness of the crusade in my youth when the Christians of the West took the place by the power of deceit and confusion. But look how high they are. How broad. Of the hundred thousand they might bring, how many will be horsemen? What will horses do against this mighty fortress?"

For fortress it was, more than a mere wall. With its multiple layers, stairs, gates, tunnels, and towers, the word wall did not do it justice. It was a fortress complex, only one that was stretched across four miles.

"All they need do," Walt said. "Is fill the moat with the bodies of their horses and climb over the walls. A hundred thousand against eight thousand? You ain't thinking straight, Richard."

"With the walls under our feet, we will even the odds."

Eva sighed. "There is word that the Hungarian cannon maker named Urban has been casting guns for the Turks for months. Probably years."

"Why is the bastard not making cannons for Hungary?" I asked, irritated.

"He was, and then he came here to do so. But the Emperor

would not pay for the great cannons he wished to build, and they could not procure the metals and would not provide him men with the expertise. And somehow the Turks persuaded him to go to them."

"So because of the weakness of our leaders, the enemy shall have the cannons that we should have," I shook my head. "But surely there is not a cannon that has been made that could bring down these mighty walls."

"Perhaps it has not been built yet," Eva said. "But perhaps it shall be."

I sighed. "William is bringing his Sultan here to destroy this city. It is our duty to stop him. We must stay. But our mortal company are not duty bound to do the same. I will speak to them and give them the opportunity to leave before it is too late."

∞

In December 1452, Constantine XI accepted that the only way he was going to get more men from Christendom was to go through with his promised union of the churches. And so a service was dedicated to the official union in the Santa Sophia, with all the heads of the Orthodox Church agreeing to end the schism with Rome.

The old soldier, Michael, had been right about the mood of the people, however, and that of the lower clergy. Immediately following the service of union, the city erupted into rioting as the furious people felt betrayed.

We stayed well out of it, of course, but it did not bode well. Instead of preparing for the fight of their lives, they were fighting each other. It was madness. It was as though they could not see what was coming.

Or perhaps they could.

Unseen beyond the walls, the Turks were busy. They reinforced Byzantine bridges and cut down Byzantine forests for timber.

All the men in my company had stayed with me and had not deserted. I called a meeting in order to give them a chance to leave with their honour intact and I did not lie to them about our chances.

"It does not look hopeful," I said, looking over the sea of their faces.

We were crammed into the main chamber of a tavern near our quarters and every man had a cup of wine in his hand.

"What do you mean, my lord?" Claudin called out. "We not getting paid?"

I rubbed my eyes and sighed. "We will not get paid, Claudin, because we will all be dead." That jolted them and they muttered unhappily.

"Is it truly so bad?" Jan the Czech asked. "There is no hope?"

The muttering died down as they waited for my answer.

"We are certain to be vastly outnumbered. The Turks are crossing the straits and massing to the west. We were expecting more soldiers to come. Many more."

"Perhaps they will yet come here," Garcia said. "Perhaps there are tens of thousands of soldiers on their way in this moment."

"It may be so. Yet, it seems unlikely they will be here before the Turks close the trap."

"So there is hope?" Claudin said, gesturing so vigorously with his cup of wine that he splashed it on himself. "Hope that help may come?"

"I am giving you all a chance to leave," I said. "The Emperor has forbidden it but I have spoken to a merchant captain who is willing to take any and all of us in his ships, for a price I have agreed per head."

They fell silent.

"What will you do, my lord?" Jan asked.

"I am staying. Black Walter, Robert, Stephen, and Eva are all staying, as are our servants. But I will not hold you to your contracts. You came here to save this city in the name of God, not to die here in a battle we could never win. I will pay each of you your due before you depart."

Again, they fell silent. Some looked at each other, while others looked at the floor or the ceiling above. Outside, a seabird screeched overhead.

"God knows, I do not favour their Church," Jan said. "But I came here to fight for Christ against the heathens. If I run now, I could not be at peace with myself for the rest of my days."

Heads around the room nodded.

"I had a feeling I would die here," Garcia said. "So be it."

Claudin raised a hand. "Could we get our coin paid out now anyway, Richard? If I am to die, I think I will spend my last days drunk as a lord in the brothel house by the Gate of the Neorion."

Not one of them chose to leave. I was touched beyond words but also filled with sadness. It seemed likely they would all die.

Soon after, the first Turkish troops arrived on the horizon and began clearing trees, bushes, and vineyards so that their cannons would have a clear shot at the walls, and so that their horsemen could roam quickly across the peninsula.

Turks set up camps and began digging trenches, banks, and other groundworks. It was early spring 1453 when they brought their massive guns up and systematically took the last remaining fortresses outside the walls.

At the start of April, the great chain was drawn across the Golden Horn, closing it off to ships.

Before the chain was drawn, however, a Genoese captain named Giovanni Giustiniani Longo sailed into the Golden Horn with two enormous war galleys and seven hundred excellent troops. The soldiers were young and enthusiastic and it raised the spirits of all inside the walls to see them. I half hoped that it presaged a sudden deluge of Christian soldiers but in fact, Longo and his men were the last to arrive.

Longo was well known as an expert in siege warfare and his fame was such that he was swiftly given the rank of *protostrator*, made overall commander of all forces in Constantinople, and gifted the island of Lemnos for payment. It was a token, of course, for he would have to save the city in order to take possession of it and perhaps it spoke of Emperor Constantine's desperation more than anything. But Longo seemed a sharp and capable man who knew his business. He treated me with respect and gratitude and gave me clear instructions about what he expected from my company. I liked him.

I do not know when or where it started but there soon spread an excited report that Hunyadi had personally led a great seaborne campaign to outflank the Turks. It soon turned out to be no more than a rumour. I was bitterly disappointed in Hunyadi and irritated at the hope I had felt when I believed it to be true.

Gradually, it dawned on each and every one of us that Christendom was not coming. The mighty kingdoms of Europe, from the Atlantic coast, to Spain and Italy, to the Holy Roman Emperor, Poland, and to the Balkan kingdoms who were already engaged in a war of destruction against the Turks, decided for their own reasons, to abandon Constantinople to her fate. Perhaps some believed that she would not fall, that her walls would prove too strong. Others no doubt expected that the rest of Christendom would act and so they would not need to. Others, I am certain, felt that the city was a lost cause. All were, of course, engaged in their own local struggles against some other kingdom or against over-mighty lords or other rebellions within their own lands. But whatever their reasons, by their actions, a withered, shadow form of Constantinople would stand alone against the mightiest empire in the world.

Turkish troops filled the peninsula beyond the walls day after day until they covered the plain from the waters of the Golden Horn in the north, to the coast of the Sea of Marmara in the south, all the way to the horizon.

Their ships surrounded the city in their hundreds while those allied to us were safe within the Golden Horn. While thousands of us watched from the walls, the Turkish fleet attacked the great chain but they failed to make headway against our superior ships. They tried again three days later but were also thrown back. We rejoiced but we did not yet appreciate their cunning, nor their determination, or the resources that they could bring to bear. For they were building a wooden slipway behind the Genoese town of Galata that nestled in the promontory, unseen behind the hills. This would create an overland link between the waters of the Bosporus to the waters of the Golden Horn at a point behind the great chain, bypassing it entirely.

We did not know but we would discover it soon enough.

A few days after their attack on the chain, they made a sudden night attack on the walls.

We had expected their great guns to spend weeks or even months reducing the walls before they attempted an assault and so we were almost caught off-guard.

Almost.

Our Genoese *protostrator* Giovanni Giustiniani Longo was no fool. He had ensured the walls were manned at all hours and when the Turks attacked, signals were lit and trumpets blared. Walter shook me awake and I sat up to see Eva in her undershirt clambering up the ladder to the roof over our house.

"Assemble the men," I ordered Walt.

He nodded, grim faced. "Rob's already at it."

I climbed the ladder and joined Eva on the roof. She was looking west to the Great Wall, where signal fires were flaring. "False alarm, perhaps?" I said to her. "The militia are a jumpy lot."

"Their families are here," she said, not looking at me. The moonlight softened her features and I watched her face rather than the distant walls. "It is no wonder they are fearful."

"By the time we get there, order will have been restored and we will return to our bed. Perhaps we will have an hour or two of night which we may spend together."

She looked at me and rolled her eyes. "If it is a real attack, it may work."

I scoffed, placing a hand on her shoulder. "The moat alone would stop them. Then the walls. They have no hope."

She shrugged my hand from her. "Imagine fifty thousand soldiers advancing on the walls. How might it be done?" she said to herself. "Five thousand in ten divisions, each assaulting a different section. Might they not bring up boats, or rafts, with which to cross the moat? Ladders to scale the first wall and the second? If they are unopposed, might it not be done in half a night?"

"God damn them."

"Such a combination of daring and disregard for the lives of his men would be reminiscent of someone we know, would it not?"

I looked out at the distant wall and listened to the shouts and footsteps of the men running through the streets toward it. "The Catalans are quartered just behind the wall. They will hold them."

"Come on," Eva said, returning to the hatch. "We must hurry."

It was more than a mile from our quarters on the northern side of the city to the closest point of the Great Wall and once I was in my armour and had gathered my men, most of the fighting was over. When we reached the walls along with thousands of other soldiers, we found the Turks fleeing in the night.

It had not been a massed attack in force, as Eva had feared, but a probing attack intended to take us by surprise and perhaps take a gate and hold it open for others to come through. But our soldiers manning the walls had moved into action, both the city's professional soldiers and the militia, as well as the Catalans who had snapped into action rapidly. The arrows, gunfire and cannons had been enough to send the Turks fleeing without much of a fight.

"Your tactic would probably have been successful," I said to Eva on the wall as the sun rose behind us.

"What tactic?" Stephen asked, his helm tucked under his arm.

"Never mind," I said. "We should find quarters closer to the wall. Can you see to it? And we must find more horses."

Stephen shook his head. "New quarters are not a problem. But each horse in the city is worth a fortune."

"Then we must pay it."

He lowered his voice. "I would rather us retain enough gold and silver to pay our way out of here, should things turn bad."

I sighed. "Damn you, Stephen, but you are right enough about that. Well, do what you can. Even a donkey or two would help."

It was that very morning when their mangonels began their work on the walls. Later in the day, the first Turkish cannon fired. It was a sound we all had dreaded hearing and there it was, splitting the air with its blast. Soon it was joined by a dozen and then scores of others. Before long, the cannonballs were making their mark, blasting holes in the outer surfaces of the walls and towers and working their way inward.

Out of the dozens of guns, a handful were enormous. But there was one beast mightier than them all. The work of that traitorous gunsmith Urban, it was truly enormous. We knew from prisoners taken that it was called *Basilisk* and the Sultan and Zaganos Pasha were very proud of it. Every time it fired, the very air shook, the walls cracked, and the people grew more afraid.

It was less than a week after the night assault on the walls that the Turkish ships suddenly appeared within the Golden Horn, brought there by the slipway. People were confused for hours and then, when they understood that their indestructible chain had simply been bypassed, they grew to wailing and despair. It was almost as if they could not comprehend it. The commanders at least worked quickly to transfer soldiers from the walls and other places to defend the sea wall facing Galata.

But we were surrounded now on all sides.

Because so many Turkish ships had been taken from the Bosporus, it meant there were fewer guarding the actual straits themselves. It was an opportunity to strike back at the Turks and so one night at the end of April, fire ships were deployed. Two big transports were packed with cotton and wool and oil and were sent with the tide and the wind toward the Turkish fleet at anchor out in the straits.

Although the Turkish fleet scattered in terror, our fire ships were sunk before they could inflict any damage. Still, it had been a good idea and one I made sure to remember for the future.

The first breach of the walls was made at the gate of Saint Romanus on 30th April. The militia repaired the breach as well as they could with stones and timber prepared for such an eventuality.

Another new type of gun was brought up. This invention was a long-range mortar that fired up and over the walls, to fall within the city, wreaking great destruction. The first to fall prey to this monster was a Genoese merchant ship which sank like a stone in the harbour.

"Our lads are getting nervous," Rob said as we watched the fires burning.

I smiled. "I'm getting bloody nervous."

Rob laughed. "Couple of them came to me yesterday."

"Oh?"

Rob scratched his stump. "They said they know what we are."

"They what?"

He sighed. "They know we take strength from the blood of our servants. Everyone in the company knows."

"Do they, by God? For how long?"

Rob shrugged. "You know what rumours are like."

"What did you say?"

"I said I didn't know what they were on about."

"What did they want?"

"They wanted to become like us. Wanted our strength."

"Who was it?"

"I promised not to say."

I looked at him. "Rob."

"It was Claudin, Garcia, and Jan."

"Truly? Those three are friends?"

Rob pursed his lips. "I reckon they came representing their friends. Jan spoke for the Czechs and Germans, Garcia the

Castilians and that lot, Claudin for the French and for the idiots."

I sighed. "What do you think?"

"I think we need all the help we can get," he said. "And if they decided to betray our trust, they would not be able to flee from us. And I think that most of them will die anyway. So why not gain a few immortals? What if it is enough to swing the balance in our favour?"

"It will take more than a few immortal soldiers to save this God-forsaken place. But let us discuss it with the others."

"We must do it," Stephen said at once. We had assembled in my new bedchamber which was close enough to the walls to hear the booming of the cannonballs striking them all day long. I considered moving away again lest a giant cannonball fall through my ceiling at night but sometimes one must simply live with danger. And besides, it was a remarkable old building, with many chambers on two storeys above and a long hall below where we could all assemble to eat as a company. "With an entire company of immortals, we stand a better chance of surviving whatever comes."

"Eva?"

"They would have to take our oath and join the Order. They will have to understand it would be a lifetime commitment to serve you and that if they survive this place, they will have to follow you for centuries. What if they then decline? We will have dozens of mortals aware of our existence and our purpose. It could be a greater danger than leaving them as they are."

"That is true. I do not know that I trust all of these men. Where is their loyalty? They are from a dozen or more kingdoms.

Some have already betrayed pervious masters. One or two are certainly criminals."

Walt, leaning by the window, turned and straightened up. "Ain't they already proved themselves loyal, Richard? Some of these lads have been with us for almost ten years, now. You forget how long that is for a mortal. We've seen some of these fellows join us as little more than boys and grow into men under our command. Whatever some of them once may have been, they see themselves as serving you. They're proud of it, have you not noticed? You gave them a chance to flee before coming here and the ones that didn't fancy it, they left. Then you gave these lads the truth about our chances and offered to pay for their passage and send them off with their purses full. They stayed. Every bloody one of the stupid bastards. I reckon they've proved themselves loyal, don't you?"

Eva pursed her lips and shrugged. Rob nodded to himself.

"I had not seen it that way," I admitted. "It is as you say. Ten years passes almost without me noticing sometimes and I often cannot easily recall how this year or that has been spent."

"They'll be giving up their chance to be fathers," Rob said. "Though some of them have bastards, none have proper wives. They need to understand that, at least."

"And some may well die if your blood does not take," Eva pointed out.

"We'll have to bleed more of the servants, and all," Walt said. "Soon as our lads are made immortal, we'll be committed to feeding them regular."

"We will assemble the men only," I said. "No squires or

servants. And we will lay everything out as clearly as we can."

"And those that decline?" Eva asked. "Perhaps we should wait before taking action."

"Perhaps."

"We are out of time!" Stephen said, advancing on me. "We need them. Have you forgotten William's army of red-robed immortals? They are out there, right now. And they will be coming here. How can we hope to stop them if not with an army of our own? If we had any sense we would use your blood to turn the entire garrison. Imagine if we had five thousand immortals, Richard, we could stream out and defeat the Turks in a single blow. We could take their entire empire!"

I stared at him. We all did.

"Would I get a say in this grand plan of yours, Stephen?" I asked.

He sighed and sank down to sit on the top of a closed chest. "Turn our company, at least. What Walt says is true. They are loyal to you now. They will be loyal in this."

"Assemble the men," I said to Rob.

After they filed out, Eva came to me and took my hands in hers. "I know that you do not wish to do this. It is not too late to change your mind. Who knows how they might turn on us or who they might tell? But Stephen is right that we need to consider William's army."

I leaned down to rest my forehead on hers. "If they betray me, I may have to kill them."

"You will have to," she said, softly.

I straightened up. "Do you think it was Stephen who started

the rumours amongst the men? Suggested they come to Rob?"

"It is his nature to do these things."

"Damn him."

"It may be what saves us. It may be what helps you to fulfil your oath."

"Do not defend him," I said.

"He serves you faithfully. In his own way."

"I suppose so," I admitted. "Come. If we are going to do this, we must get started. I can only bleed enough to change so many every night."

When the men were in the hall below, I came down and stood before them, with Walt and Rob at my side and Eva and Stephen behind us. I noted that Serban stood at the side of the hall, watching me closely, his eyes questioning. My men fell silent and stared at me, full of apprehension. I was full of worry myself but I forced it down and drove on regardless.

"The rumours are true. I am not like other men. Nor, indeed, are your captains." I watched them closely as I spoke, watching for signs of fear or revulsion. "We have lived longer than the span of mortal men and are gifted with strength and speed beyond any man here or on any battlefield in the world. Wounds that would kill any of you in hours or days will be healed on our bodies. But these gifts do not come without a price."

"You must drink blood," Garcia said. "We know."

"Oh?" I said. "You know, do you?"

He was wary but he nodded, as did a few others. "We have seen you. Now and then. You bleed your servants, you drink their blood. I saw you after that battle in the woods, with Hunyadi, when that Serb cut your face. Before Varna. I saw you, though you did not see me, and I saw you drink from his throat and the cut across your face turned to nothing."

"By God," I said. "You have known all this time?"

He and others nodded.

"Why did you not say?" I asked.

He shrugged and Jan answered for him. "We were afraid. Some men left, giving false reasons out of fear. Some of them call it the work of Satan. Only one who has a pact with the Devil could have such power. It is witchcraft, so they said. And they left."

"And yet all of you stayed," I replied. "Why?"

"We are not all so ignorant," Garcia said. "You acted always with honour. You treated your men well. We were content to follow one with such power."

"And you always paid up," Claudin said. "Always was fair."

I glanced at Serban and wondered if he had been whispering to the others about us. He stared back, his face rigid.

"Sir Walter was seen," Jan said. "And Sir Robert. We knew it was blood magic. Some of us have long hoped to have this power for ourselves."

"And we saw the Janissaries in red at Kosovo," Garcia said. "They moved like you do. They moved like you, Richard, and Walter and Robert, and Stephen and the Lady Eva. We saw them."

Many of my men nodded their heads, their eyes staring through the floor into the memory of those red devils tearing our army apart.

"And we knew it was the same magic," Jan said. "Somehow."

"We tried drinking the servants' blood ourselves," Claudin said. "Couple of us did, anyway. Didn't work."

"It was hoped you would reveal to us your secrets," Garcia said. "But you did not. And so we did speak to Sir Robert."

"We have seen your power in battle," Jan said. "We want it, also, my lord."

"And you have not aged a day," Claudin said. "Don't think we haven't noticed. None of you. Not one day has marked your flesh. Not one line more, nor one scar. I was as young as you when I joined the Company of Saint George and now look at me. It's the blood what does it. And we want it, and the magic that goes with it, my lord."

"You think that the price for this power is that you must drink blood?" I said. "That is not much of a price. No wonder you are willing to pay it. Slurping up some warm blood fresh from a fellow's arm. It is nothing at all." They regarded me silently, suddenly more tense than before. "But that is not the cause of the power, as you discovered. If you have this power, you will drink blood to increase your strength and heal you, yes. But you must drink every day or two. If you go three days without drinking, you will begin to feel sick. Your stomach will turn in knots and your mind will ache. Go without for longer and your skin will turn grey and then green. Your flesh will blister and your hair will fall out, your eyes will become red and you will begin to lose your mind. You will think of nothing else but drinking the blood of a man or a woman and nothing will stop you from getting it. Is that a price you are willing to pay?"

They stared but some already nodded in agreement.

"There is more," I said, holding up a finger. "Once you are granted this power, there is no going back. You will never be a mortal man again. You will be as ageless as we five before you." Many grinned at that, glancing at each other. "And you will never father a child." Their smiles fell from their face. "You may try for all you are worth but no matter how many women you lay with, no matter how often you do so, your seed will never grow."

They were rightly appalled and I gave them time to consider it.

"It is a steep price," Garcia said. "I had hoped to return home one day."

"And you may do so," I replied. "If you decline what I offer. And if you survive the assault on this city."

"Is there more?" Jan asked.

I nodded. "You will never again feel the warmth of the sun on your skin without it burning you. Wherever sunlight falls on your flesh, it will swiftly redden, and blister, and then burn. You must cover your skin and always cover your head."

"And pray for clouds?" Claudin quipped.

"Even overcast days will burn you, I am afraid. But night will be your friend. You will be able to see into the dark better than any mortal."

"But I have seen you," Jan said, frowning. "I have seen you many times with the sun on your face, Richard. You take pleasure in it, just as any man does."

"Ah," I said. "But you see, Jan, I am different. I am not as you will be. I can make immortals but you cannot."

I did not admit that my immortals could use the same process to make mad, savage revenants. I would hide such knowledge for all I was worth.

"So, where did you get your power?" Garcia asked.

"Let me tell you a story," I said, "about a man named William de Ferrers and the Order of the White Dagger."

After speaking for so long that my throat grew hoarse, I answered their many questions until they fell silent. Serban stared at me in surprise and wonder and I nodded to him before turning back to my men.

"Each of you must decide for himself whether to join the Order. I will welcome you all but you must know that some of you will not survive being turned. I do not know why but some men cannot take it. It is not strength, nor age, nor any other common factor as far as I can see but it is unavoidable for some. With that in mind, I ask that you make your decisions. Certainly, you have been thinking on it for some time."

"I will do it," Claudin said, getting to his feet.

"As will I," Jan said. "I will risk death and pay the price for the power it will give.

Others agreed, one by one, until only Garcia and Serban had yet to speak.

"Serban?" I asked. "You have not been with us for as long as the others but you have been welcomed by all. You knew what I was within days of meeting me, having witnessed me drinking the blood of a fallen enemy. And you have heard stories about people like us in your homeland. What do you say? Will you become one of us?"

He stood upright, looking me in the face, and crossed himself.

Then he fell to one knee and bowed his head. "Please forgive me, my lord, but I cannot. I do not think you evil, nor have I ever divulged your secrets, but I cannot do it."

I shrugged. "Very well. You will continue to serve me faithfully as a mortal."

Serban looked up, relief on his old face. "I will, my lord."

"Garcia?" I said. "You have spoken of your desire to return home and make a family. It is a good wish. You do not need to give it up."

"No, sir," he replied, standing. "I will join you, gladly. It is a worthy cause for a knight. To fight evil. I see now why you named our company after Saint George. I believed that the saint was a warrior of Christ and the serpent was the Turks. But now I see that the saint is us and the serpent is evil. It is your brother William."

"Very well," I said. "You will all take the oath. And I will make you into immortal men."

∞

Before I was halfway through turning the men of my company, the Turks attacked again in the night.

They came in force against many parts of the wall, attacking the partial breaches and crumbling towers. Where the walls were damaged, the rubble fell down and out to fill the gap between the two walls and to partially fill the moats. The piles of rubble created unstable slopes for the attackers to climb up to the top of the breaches and down the other side or up onto the wall walks either side of the breach.

But the militia worked tirelessly every day and through many a night to repair the breaches, to clear the rubble, and to throw up new walls and barricades of timber. These repairs would be blown to pieces by the cannons and the garrison would repair them. Every day and every night, the pattern repeated but the Turks and their cannons were irresistible. We could not repair and rebuild as swiftly as they could destroy.

And so they came in the darkness on the 7th May, crossing the moats on rafts and throwing in vast quantities of earth and rock to create causeways. All the while our men shot arrows, fired cannon and guns at them, killing hundreds. Still, they crossed the moat in many sections and climbed onto the lower, outer walls through the breaches.

I held my men back. I would not lead them down into that hell amongst the fires and the cannonballs unless there was no hope.

And the militia and the proper soldiers of the city did well. The Catalan mercenaries also threw themselves into the thick of the fighting and the Turks were turned back from the outer walls.

We cheered as hard as anyone when the sun rose that day but we knew it had merely been the start. Repairs continued and the cannons fired, bringing down the battlements on four towers in just one day.

As quickly as I could, I turned the rest of the men in my company, each and every one of them, apart from Serban, who still declined. I lost five good men in the process. They were drained of their blood and they drank mine but they did not wake up. We buried them and I felt enormous guilt for their deaths, even though they had accepted the risk. And though I lost five, I gained thirty-nine immortal soldiers who swore to follow me until the end of their days in my pursuit of William and his monsters. Eva said it was a good trade.

"If we meet the immortal Janissaries in battle," I said, "they will still be outnumbered ten to one."

"Far better odds than we had last week," Eva said. It was hard to argue.

It was five days later when another attack came, again at night.

The Turks focused their forces on the north-western section of the walls by the Golden Horn in the Blachernae district. In their attacks there they were supported by their fleet in the Golden Horn and it seemed for a while that they would break through. By the time my company arrived, the fighting on the walls was confused and it was hard to know where best to place my men. I held them back in reserve, ready to counter any breach into the city that occurred.

At sunrise, fighting slowed as the Turks stopped receiving reinforcements and it became clear they would not get through. Still, it had been a close run thing and, no doubt because of their success that night, the Turks concentrated their efforts on that district even more.

Serbian miners had been sent to Mehmed by the Despot of Serbia George Branković, along with two thousand Serbian cavalry. It was the miners, working tirelessly to undermine and breach the walls, that became the greatest danger and many of the tunnels were aimed at the Blachernae district. Our militia dug their own tunnels to counter those of the Serbs before they could undermine the walls or even come up inside the city.

Some of the Serbian tunnels were flooded and others were set on fire and the miners smoked out.

For others, though, where there was danger of them breaking into the city, we had to get down there and kill them.

"It is good work for us," I said to my company. "We can clear out the enemies in the tunnels with our strength."

My men were unconvinced that it was a task for knights and mercenaries.

"Any wounds we receive we can heal by drinking the blood of our enemies and we can do so without being seen by our allies," I said, which they were intrigued by. "Besides, I have already volunteered our services to Longo."

It was horrible fighting. As bad as war can get, and that is saying something. Dark, sometimes black, smoky, often cold but sometimes roasting hot. No room to flee because of the men behind you. It was dirty, awful work and two of my men were killed before I could get blood into them and another was crushed when a tunnel collapsed. But because of my company, we defeated all of the Serb's best efforts.

Our successes in the tunnels and the militia's tireless work in sealing breaches meant that the Turks would only find success through storming the walls. Incredibly, in just a few days, the Turks constructed a bridge across the Golden Horn, allowing them to bring up their troops much faster. Sorties were carried out in an attempt to burn the bridge but it remained intact.

On 24th May we stood on the walls and silently watched a lunar eclipse.

What it meant, whether it was a good omen or bad, none could agree.

Word spread that a vast crusader army was approaching to relieve the city. Many rejoiced at the news but others were cautious. Previous rumours of the sort had proved false and we had received no official word of such a thing and so cooler heads questioned where the rumour had started. For many, this in itself was somehow proof of the army's existence, reasoning that the crusaders would not have sent word that could have fallen into Turkish hands.

During the night of the 27th May, fires appeared all over the Turkish camp. There was further rejoicing, for it was concluded that the Turks had seen the approaching crusaders and were burning their supplies before their flight back to Anatolia. Indeed, many a Greek began drinking to their victory and drank themselves into unconsciousness.

"Sieges can drive people mad," I said to my company. "The fear causes them to lose their wits."

"What if it's true?" Claudin said, grinning. "See the fires burning out there. They must be burning their supplies, what else could it be?"

But in the morning, the enemy was still there. In fact, there seemed to be more than ever before, and the enemy soldiers began coming forward to fill the foremost defensive ditches closest to the walls.

"It was a feast," Stephen said, looking out at the distant scenes. "A celebration of some sort."

"What was?" I asked.

"The fires. The great fires in the night was not them leaving, it was a celebration of the victory to come. A great feast where they ate until they were bursting and they burned their fuel, as they will not be needing it when they take the city."

"By God," I said. "You think that is it?"

He pursed his lips. "Perhaps the Sultan had his supplies burned so that his men would have to achieve victory or starve?"

I sighed. "So you do not, in fact, know anything at all."

"Looks like rain," he replied. "I know that much."

Stephen was not wrong. A great rainstorm started and did not end, drenching everything. The gunners stayed within the towers and fought to keep their gunpowder dry and the fields turned to mud. On the walls, I met the commander of the Catalans, Pere Julia, who cursed the rain and the Turks with equal vigour.

"They will come soon," he said. "Mark my words, Richard, they will come. Look at them, the dogs. You see the stacks of ladders there? They do not care that we can see. They want us to see. They want to break our hearts."

"How are your men?"

"My men are angry. They want the Turks to come. They want to kill them."

"I am happy to hear it," I said.

"Oh, you think mercenaries do not have passion, sir? Is that how it is in England?"

"I am a mercenary, sir," I replied. "And I want to kill them, also."

He nodded, barely placated. "My men love God, Richard. Above all, they love God. They will do their duty for God, mark my words."

"I believe it," I said.

"Look at the dogs," he muttered. "I hope they drown."

The rain continued to fall.

Just a couple of hours before dawn on the 29th May, the Turkish cannons sounded. All of them fired at once and then over and over again, as quickly as each one would allow. As the dawn lightened the sky behind us, thousands of *azab* infantry emerged from the darkness. They were massed at the gate of Saint Romanus where the great cannon, the Basilisk, had created a wide breach in the outer and inner walls.

We brought up three thousand soldiers from the reserve behind the line and filled the walls either side of the gate. Longo himself came, as did Emperor Constantine, though he kept well back.

The *azabs* advanced through the rain in their thousands toward the breach and our cannons fired, blasting them apart. Our gunners fired from the crumbling towers and from the battlements of the inner wall. Crossbowmen shot down at the advancing battalions, killing and wounding hundreds. Before they even crossed the moat, the *azabs* suffered massive casualties.

Along the sea wall in the north, Turkish ships came swarming through the Golden Horn to the base of the walls and threw up ladders for the troops in the ships to scale so that they might breach them and get into the Blanchernae district. Reports came through to Longo that the fighting there was terrible and he sent a few of his reserve forces to the north to ensure that the assault by the river was thrown back.

In front of us, the *azab* assault ground to a halt under our terrific fire. The sound of the guns was endless and trumpets blared and banners hung limp in the relentless rain. I made my way to Longo's position so that I might through him gauge what was happening throughout the battlefield. He sat upon his fine horse with a confident expression on his face, receiving messages and sending riders in all directions. In the distance, the Emperor's guard held position.

"What do we do now?" Stephen asked behind me.

"We wait."

The great guns sounded again, in another timed and almighty barrage that shook the walls over miles at once. As the echoes died away, thousands of Anatolian soldiers came charging out of the rain, attacking the breaches by our position at the Saint Romanus Gate.

All the breaches made by their guns were too high and too narrow for them to walk through but still they tried. The Anatolians were armoured in mail and lamellar and good, steel helms. They crossed the moat and attacked the lower, outer wall and attacked our soldiers there. Longo ordered militia units forward to reinforce those positions.

"Should we help?" Rob asked.

"We keep our men back for as long as possible," I said, and pointed at the breach in the inner wall and the fan-shaped hill of rubble that lead up to the broken top of the breach. "When the

Turks come charging down that slope, we will stop them. Not before. Tell the men."

When the Anatolians retreated, our men cheered for a long time but there was sense of dread settling on the defenders. We were already exhausted by the struggle and yet the Turks had used only a fraction of their strength. Still, we had killed thousands of them and lost few ourselves.

After the Anatolians retreated, we received yet another bombardment and a hit by the Basilisk brought down a massive section of wall at the breach, throwing up an enormous cloud of white dust and sending chunks of masonry and brick flying in all directions. When the dust settled, we realised that the walls were now beginning to crumble with almost every shot and I am sure the dread spread further.

Beyond the walls, the enemy's war drums started again and their horns sounded.

"Here they come again," Walt said, before raising his voice and turning to my company. "Here they come again. Prepare yourselves."

The Anatolians came back to assault the breaches in their thousands, swarming the outer walls. Our gunners shot down from the inner walls above us and the elite crossbow units shot and reloaded and shot again, with incredible speed. In every moment, I expected to see the helms of the enemy appearing at the top of the breach.

And yet we threw them back again. Banners were waved and the men cheered their victory. The wounded and the dead were carried back from the walls and filed past us, heading east toward the rear.

"Jesus Christ, there's a lot of them," Walt muttered, crossing himself.

Riders came galloping in from the north, drenched and covered in mud kicked up by their horses, calling for Longo and other commanders.

I caught Pere Julia, the commander of the Catalans, and asked him what the panic was.

"They assault the Blanchernae Walls also, in force, and threaten to break through. Just Minotto and the Venetians there to stop them."

"Is that where your men are going?" I asked him.

"No," Pere Julia said. "I am ordered to defend the imperial family and the great and the good in the southeast."

"You what?" I said. "Why?"

"The Turks are making an attack also on the Contoscalion Harbour. If they break through the walls there, we must stop them."

"Then God be with you. All of you."

"And with you," he said. I watched him ride away with his men following through the rain. It was a long way and when they got there, they would be on their own and at the opposite side of the city from the ships that might take survivors away.

"Shall I take some of our men north to the Blanchernae, Richard?" Rob asked. "Sounds like it's in danger."

"Everywhere is in danger. And we must stay together. It is for others to guard that way. All we can do is protect this breach. This is where the hammer blows are falling. Here is where the Basilisk has done its work. The Sultan's flag is flying behind it. Here is where we must be."

Later, we had word that the assault in the north was thrown back by the Venetians. Indeed, it had been a long day but we could sense it coming to an end. And we were still standing. There was fight left in the men, whether militia or professional soldiers, and despite the breaches, we had slaughtered thousands of the enemies who had attacked us. We had a sense now that it could be done after all. The Turks had thrown their worst at us and we had done what was necessary, and more. I saw Longo congratulating his men and drinking wine with them.

But the Sultan had not thrown everything he had at us. There was one part of his army that had yet to engage.

"Janissaries!" came the cry from atop the wall. Trumpets sounded and men jumped to their positions, racing back up to the tops of the walls. Our cannons fired again and again.

"Wait here," I said to my men and went forward toward the wall, pushing my way through the crowds. I was one of the few men dressed entirely in plate armour so they tended to let me through and so I stood at the top, looking out through the crenellations at the scene beyond.

Thousands of Janissaries advanced from their defensive ditches. They came marching in tighter formations than I had seen from any infantry in my life until that point. Our hand-gunners fired from the walls and brought down the advancing Janissaries in their dozens but sill they came on without hesitation and without breaking formation. Arrows rained down on them, killing more and their lines became wavered. Still, they reached the filled in sections of moat and the half-burned pontoons and rafts and crossed without hesitation to the lower outer wall, where they threw up ladders.

Our soldiers on the wall below stood ready to meet them either side of the great breach that led through the outer wall to the inner one.

"Those bastards," Walt said.

"I told you to wait below," I said, turning to see not only Walt but Rob and Eva, also. "All of you."

The Janissaries reached the breach, as we had known they would, and cut into the militia, spreading out even as they were shot and killed by the men in the towers and on the inner wall. On they came, relentlessly, as if they cared nothing for their own lives.

"Our lads are getting nervous," Walt said, nodding to the Greeks along the wall. I saw at once how right Walt was. The men were inching back, afraid of the assault. In no time, they would find false reasons to escape from the wall in ones and twos and then they would be in full flight.

"We will hold them," I shouted. "They are no better than us. They are weaker than us. We have the walls!" I turned to my men. "Take up the cry, lads. Spread the word." I raised my voice again and called in Greek as loudly as I could. "We have God on our side. We have the walls. We have Constantinople! Constantine! Constantine! For the Emperor!"

They took up the cry in time, and it spread along the wall until they were cheering themselves. The crossbowmen were a steady lot who took immense pride in their skill and they worked tirelessly. The soldiers with their halberds came forward and climbed down in their hundreds and fought the Janissaries hand to hand in the breach. Bodies tumbled down into the gulf between the walls. The white mounds of rubble turned pink with blood even with the rain turning it to rivers and washing it down. It was brutal, bloody work. Bodies piled up. Guns were fired from both sides and the air stank of filthy smoke and blood and entrails.

We threw them back. The Janissaries cowered below the outer wall, afraid of attempting the breach again and they began falling back in pairs and then in dozens, trudging back toward their trenches beyond the moat.

The day was almost over and the enemy were in retreat. Some of the men indulged once more in congratulatory cheering.

"They did it," Walt said, chuckling. "God love them, the mad bastards, they did it."

"They will have to do it all over in a few days," I said. "And again a few days after that. Assuming the Turks did not break through today along the Marmara wall in the south."

Walt laughed and slapped me on the shoulder, splashing droplets of rain. "You know your problem, Richard, is you're never—"

"Wait," Rob said, grasping Walt with one hand and jabbing his stump out at the field, "there!"

From the smoke and the rain advanced a new formation of Janissaries.

These were clothed in red.

"William's immortals," I said.

"By God," Eva said. "How can we stop them?"

I cried for all guns to be turned on the advancing Janissaries, and all cannons too. Bring back the crossbowmen, I shouted. Return to the walls.

But this next wave of attackers had caught us by surprise. Only two cannons fired, and one missed. The other ball cut a small swathe through the corner of the formation, felling no more than half a dozen, and the rest missed not a step. Crossbowman shot their bolts but they were running low and replacements had not reached us. A few hand-gunners fired but again their ammunition or gunpowder was wet or had been expended and more was not yet in place.

"They are coming on fast," Rob said and he was right. William's red Janissaries crossed the moat and swarmed up the outer wall and spread out along it like a drop of blood falling into a bowl of water.

"We will have to hold them at the inner breach," I said to my men. "We cannot let them inside. You know who they are and what they can do. We cannot let them inside. Come, back to the company. Come, now."

Before I followed my men down the stairs, I turned for one last look at the immortal Janissaries. They breached the outer barricades and rushed forward in a surge, swarming up and over them. Our soldiers came on to meet them and raised their spears and swords and axes but were cut down in moments by the Janissaries' inhuman speed and strength. Our defenders were exhausted and their enemies were faster than they could imagine and they stood no hope.

Even so, they did not break. They knew that if the enemy broke into the city, all was lost. And so they stayed and they died in their hundreds.

"Richard!" Rob shouted from below. "Come on!"

"What is this?" a captain on the wall shouted to his men. "What are they?"

"Whatever they are," I said, "they will not break. Will not flee. They must be killed."

"How?"

"One by one," I said. "A score of ours for one of theirs. It is the only way." I rushed down the steps as quickly as I could and ran across the open space by the breach. I saw Longo approaching the wall with his men around him and hoped that they would stand and fight with us. "This is it, men! Now, we do our duty. For Constantine! For the city! For Christ! Deus vult!"

My men lifted their weapons and roared in response.

"Deus vult!"

The red robed immortals appeared at the top of the breach and began to descend the rubble pile into the city. Above on the wall, the Greeks shot down into the advancing men, no doubt stunned by the speed of this new enemy, and their resistance to arrow and lead. I led my company forward up the loose rubble to meet the enemy, pushing through the ranks of Greek soldiers who held back, no doubt in shock at the ferocity of the approaching red tide.

Suddenly, they were there. With their long red, felt hats and red robes, they were big and powerful men with polearms and swords whipping up and down and thrusting forward. I caught the first one unawares as he descended, spearing my sword point into his face. Still, he fought even as he died and the axe blade of his polearm banged against my breastplate. More came behind him, cutting down the mortal Greeks with ease and stepping forward.

But my men had arrived and spread out along the rubble to stem the rising tide. A part of me wondered if they were surprised to find enemies who fought as well as they did. Better, in fact, for my closest companions had fought more than a hundred battles and lived more than a hundred years and our armour was the best that could be bought and the Janissaries' weapons glanced off when they struck. The rest of my company were as good as could be found anywhere, with decades of experience between them and now they fought with the strength and speed of immortals.

In mere moments, a dozen immortal Janissaries soon lay dead before us, and then a score more. My company cut into them like a scythe, cutting down a field of red wheat.

But we were outnumbered ten to one and my company was swarmed on all sides. They got around our flank and there was nothing we could do to stop them.

"Stay together!" I shouted and cut down the Janissaries in front of me. "Stay together!"

Suddenly, the immortal Janissaries simply pulled back from us. They retreated and avoided our position, like water moving around a rock in a stream, and they pressed on around us into the city.

"With me!" I shouted, and pushed on up the rubble slope to where more came up over the top of the breach. If we could stem the gap, we could cut them off and stop any more mortal Turks from coming in behind them. As I pushed deeper into their ranks they could not so easily get away from me and I cut down all those who stood before me, slicing through their necks and chopping through their faces.

Walt grabbed my shoulder, leaned in and banged his helm against mine and held it there while he shouted. "They have gained the wall!"

I followed the line of his axe and saw dozens of red Janissaries swarming up the breach to the shattered tops of the wall on either side of it where they cut down the men at the top.

"We must throw them down," I shouted.

But now we were close to the top of the breach, we were surrounded by immortals trying to kill us and for a time all I could do was defend from the men all around. Men in my company fell, overwhelmed by the numbers. Still, we held them close to the top until the pressure was relieved. Once again, the Janissaries pulled back and left us alone, refusing to engage with us.

"William must have taught them this," I said, cursing his cunning. "We make for the wall!" I called to my men, turning to see who was still alive.

With shock, I saw that most of my company were gone. Many had been cut down behind me and lay dead on the rubble and others had been carried off down to the base of the rubble hill by the waves of immortals pushing forward. The ones who yet lived, half my company, perhaps, fought the enemy on both sides and behind us. I swore and cursed but nothing could be done. If the Janissaries took the wall then they would take the gate and if they opened it and held it, then all the Turks in Europe would pour through and end the city forever.

"On!" I shouted to my remaining men. "On, on! To the walls!"

I pressed through into the immortals that still came on, cutting down one man and then another. Hands grasped me and I cut off a hand and then sliced through a throat, spilling hot blood. I longed to drink mortal blood, longed for the strength it would bring. We slowed, as the press of men grew dense at the breach itself. Mortal Janissaries had joined the fray and they poured over the breach in their hundreds, mingling with their red brothers who yet fought. The mighty wall was right above me. How I would climb it with so many enemies around, I had no idea. I knew only that it must be done.

A great cry went up and I glanced up, seeing through my helm a quick glance in the smoky, wet gloom. It was Longo's personal banner, up on the top of the wall above the gate, advancing toward the Janissaries there.

Praise God, I thought. *Well done, Longo.*

He had seen the danger and thrown himself into it, to inspire his men by his personal leadership.

It was a view gone in a moment, as the enemy crashed into me again with such force that I was lifted from my feet and thrown down onto my back, tumbling down the pile of masonry. Blades whipped down even as I fell, seeking to end me. I slashed at them and rolled to get up, grabbing at a Janissary and pulling him down. Together we slipped in the loose, wet scree. My sword was pulled from my grasp and I raised my armoured arms over my head as I got to one knee, feeling my armour bend and break from the blows that crashed down on me. Standing, I grabbed a spear and ripped it from my attacker's hands and used it to fend them off, whirling it around until I broke the shaft across a Janissary's face.

There was a great commotion all around but I did not know what was causing it, whether it was to do with me and my men or with the battle elsewhere.

And then suddenly the enemies rushed beyond me. I saw that I was close to the ground once more, having fallen down forty feet of the slope. My men rushed toward me, sliding and falling down.

I wheeled about, peering through the dented eye slits of my skewed helm to see what was happening.

A mighty hand clapped me on the back, in a familiar way, and then Walt was before me, his helm gone and blood streaming down both sides of his head. Eva, Stephen, and Rob were there also and a mere dozen of my company. All around us were bodies, Greek soldiers and Janissaries in red and in white, many writhing and crying out.

Beyond them, our army fled from the wall.

Thousands of soldiers and militia walked or ran or rode away from the wall toward the distant city.

"What in the name of God has happened?" I shouted.

Walt spat a mouthful of blood before he answered. "Longo fell. His damned fool men lowered his banner and carried him off."

I looked at the wall and the Turk's banners were held aloft by Janissaries atop the gate towers. The enormous gates themselves were being prised open.

"Pull back to the city?" Rob said. "Fight them in the streets?"

"We must flee from here!" Eva shouted at me. "Now!"

Beyond the breach and through the rain and by the last of the daylight, I saw thousands of infantry and horsemen approaching.

"The city is lost," I said, turning to the survivors of my company. "We must escape."

6

E s c a p e

1 4 5 3

THE PROTOSTRATOR GIOVANNI GIUSTINIANI LONGO
had not been killed outright, merely wounded by a gunner's shot.
If his men had only withdrawn him a little way and held the line,
perhaps we would have thrown them back. Perhaps we would
have held the wall, and so held the gate, and so held the city.
Perhaps Constantinople would be Byzantine to this day, if only
the handful of men around him had chosen differently. If only
they had loved their captain a little less.

Such is the way of battle and of the world. The smallest
decisions can have enormous and irreversible consequences.

In the chaos of the break through, Emperor Constantine
disappeared also and every man, woman, and child in the city

knew by the spreading panic that it was lost. Darkness enveloped the city, illuminated by distant fires and flashes of cannons and guns, and lamps and torches held aloft by soldiers and citizens fleeing one way or another.

We made for the ships yet moored in the Golden Horn, knowing that even if it was unlikely to be successful, it was our only chance of escape.

And so did thousands of others.

We walked and ran in turn toward the docks, many of our company limping and breathing heavily. Some of my men removed and dropped dented pieces of their armour. Others begged a servant for a cup of blood

"The servants slow us down," Stephen said. "Perhaps we might consider going on ahead and meeting them at the dock?"

"You mean abandon them?" I said.

"No, no," he said. "We shall hold a boat for them."

He knew that in such chaos, once separated, we would never meet up again.

"At least have the courage to make your true argument," I said.

He sighed and shook his head. "Do I really have to make it? If we move at their pace, all of us may be killed. What of the Order, then? What of William?"

I grabbed his shoulder, stopping him. "It is their duty to follow their masters and it is ours to not abandon them. And what will you and the others do for blood if we leave them?"

"There are always mortals around," he muttered but would not meet my eye.

I shoved him so that he would continue on. I went back to

help and to hurry them on. Despite what I had said to Stephen, he was not wrong about the danger their weakness meant for us.

Turkish horsemen were through the gate and into the farmlands behind us.

"Might have to fight soon, Richard," Walt said, loping along with his axe in hand.

"Should we not head north?" Rob called. "Or south? Protection there? The Catalans guard the palace, no?"

Along the southern and northern edges of the peninsula, the confined streets between dense housing and churches and public buildings seemed to offer a way to fend off the cavalry.

"We cannot stop. The Catalans are finished, Rob. They will soon be surrounded with no way to escape. And if we do not reach a ship tonight, we shall never escape. We push on. Come on lads, you can do it, we'll find a ship home, shall we? Come on. On, on!"

We hobbled further toward the city proper while shouts and cries sounded behind us.

Eventually, we made it to a street lined with houses and from there I led my men north, towards the gates that led out to the harbours of the Golden Horn.

"Richard," Eva said, jogging up beside me, "you hope to find a ship to take us from the city, yes?"

"That is where the fleets are," I said.

"But the great chain has closed the way," she pointed out. "And already the Turks have their ships behind, in the Horn."

"The chain must be drawn in," I said. "Or broken."

She stared at me in disbelief. "How? Are we to do this

ourselves?" She indicated our shattered, limping company.

"If we have to."

Eva coughed and wiped blood from her eye. "Even if that were possible, the other half of the Turkish fleet is *beyond* the chain. Any ships attempting to flee will be boarded or sunk before they can get beyond the Acropolis Point and then we—"

I turned to her, stopping her with a hand on her shoulder. "Listen, Eva. I do not know what will happen. I do not have all the answers to your questions. All I know is that we must take a ship, tonight, to be free of this place. And I know that we shall not be the only ones who know this. We go to the docks. We find a ship. We do what we must to escape. Agreed?"

She took a deep breath, nodding at me as she let it out.

"Good," I said. "Let us do it."

The docks were chaos. Thousands of people swarmed there, looking for a way out. Some were Greek residents, some merchants and workers, others were foreign soldiers or their servants.

Of all the thousands of soldiers left alive, most of the militia had returned to protect their homes and their families. It would do them no good. They would be overwhelmed and killed, their homes looted, their wives and daughters raped, and the survivors taken as slaves. But the foreign soldiers had to either fight to the death, surrender, or flee. And they had nowhere to go but home and they were the ones fighting each other for access to the ships in the harbour. The many gates had been forced open and crowds pushed and shoved through, shouting and wailing at each other. Others called for calm but the panic could not be contained.

"There is an entire army here," Rob said. "If these fools had stood, the city would not have fallen."

"Why don't you explain that to them," Walt said. "I'm certain they would welcome your observations, sir."

"Come on, let us stay together," I said. "Tight together, everyone. Hold on to each other, protect our mortals. Rob, take up the rear, will you? See we do not lose any of our fellows in the crush."

Using our strength, we pushed through protesting soldiers and batted down any outraged hands who attempted to hinder us. We were armoured in steel and had immense strength and so we were irresistible. Salvation lay beyond in the water and I would not stop for anyone, even if he was a desperate Christian soldier looking to make his way home. The noise of the crowd filled my ears.

Pushing through the Neorion Gate, we came out to the docks ringing the harbour where a dozen ships were moored. The Golden Horn glittered in the light of dusk and the lights on the hundreds of ships on the water. Far to my left was the Turkish fleet, many of which assaulted the walls. In front, across the Horn, lay the Genoese town of Galata. Ships and small boats headed straight across the Horn toward it, while others came from there to the harbours to collect refugees and take them to relative safety.

Most of the moored ships around the harbour before me were taking on scores of desperate people and those would be no good for us. But one galley further up the arm of the harbour was defended by sailors with pikes who fended off those attempting to swarm the pontoon and board the ship.

"Venetian," I said to my men. "Do you see it? We shall make our way there."

"How?" Stephen asked. He was keeping very close to me at all times, which was sensible but irritating. I ignored him.

"With me, men, with me! Stay fast together, come on!"

I pushed forward through the crowd, drawing irate curses. When they saw that we were foreign mercenaries, some flinched away in fear and space opened around us so that we advanced swiftly. Some of those same people cursed us for abandoning our posts and betraying the city. That they were doing the very same thing perhaps had not occurred to them. In no time, I approached the galley I was aiming for. In front of me, an Italian man shouted at the sailors to let them on, shaking his fist at them. He had lost his helm but was otherwise very well armoured.

"What are they waiting for?" I asked the armoured man.

"We are Venetians," he replied. "They must take us, they must."

I grabbed him. "Why do they not?"

He sneered. "They wait for the Catalans. Bastard sailors care only about money." He raised his voice again. "We are your countrymen. We serve Cardinal Isidore! We are your brothers, you dirty bastards!"

"Come on," I said to my men and pushed through the angry men.

"Keep back," a Venetian sailor shouted at me in Italian. "Keep back, I say."

"We come from the Catalans," I said. "We come with a message."

"Lies!" the man next to me shouted. "He lies!"

I elbowed him in the face and he dropped down in a clatter of steel, out cold.

"I will give you their message, sir," I shouted. "I will give you the message from my friend, the Catalan commander Pere Julia, and then I shall go."

"Just you," their commander said, pointing to me.

I pushed forward with my hands up and palms open, slipping through the points of the spears they brandished.

"I was with the Catalans," I said to the man. "They were cut off at the Great Palace when the Turks broke through. The Catalans are certainly cut off and surrounded. None shall escape. None shall come here."

He scowled. "You lie."

"I do not. Besides, the Turks are through the walls at the Saint Romanus Gate which they held. They are likely within the city already." I jerked my thumb over my shoulder and the Venetian's eyes looked at the walls behind me. "At any moment, you shall see the enemy attacking the rear of this mob and then your ship will be swarmed and you will not leave at all."

He nodded and glanced at me, sneering. "So you are telling me to flee. Without my payment. Without my protection, should the ship be boarded."

I looked him in the eyes. "I will pay. I will bring my men. A score of knights, just as many squires, and as many servants again. But we must be gone before it is too late to do so."

He scoffed. "You will pay? What will you pay for your sixty men? I am awaiting the payment of five hundred Catalan mercenaries."

I turned and called to Stephen. "Let my man there in the Italian armour come forward and offer you our gold."

The commander nodded to his men and Stephen stepped up and pulled a heavy purse from his belt. With an unhappy look, he passed it over.

"All ecus," I said. "All gold."

He hefted it and was impressed, though he attempted to hide it. "Hardly what I am due."

"You will not get what you are due. The Catalans are dead or captured, I swear it to Christ. If not by now then certainly by morning. If you do not wish to take us, please return my gold and I shall seek another vessel. I see dozens ferrying men across to Galata. The Genoese know a good deal when they see one."

He snorted at my jibe as he hefted the bag. "Your men only. A score of knights you say?"

"Twenty-three soldiers and their squires, all experienced fighters, and those that serve us must come also."

With a last look at the crowds and the gate beyond, the Venetian nodded and took my hand. "My name is Alvise Diedo."

"Richard Ashbury."

"Get your companions onboard, Englishman."

We boarded quickly as the men on the dockside cursed and damned us all. Once we were through and onto the ship, they began to push off while men rowed us out onto the black waters of the harbour toward the fleet in the Golden Horn. The desperate soldiers on the dock surged forward and grabbed for the sides of the galley as it departed. Some were fended off by the sailors, falling into the lapping water.

"You said you had five hundred Catalans," I said to the master as we watched the scene in silence. "This boat would not hold even one hundred packed to the gills."

"That is my ship also," he said, pointing to a great three-masted cog out on the water, with a high sterncastle and forecastle. "And two more, beyond."

Silently, I thanked God.

"Was it true?" the master asked. "What you said about the Catalans?"

"I wish it were not," I said. "Pere Julia is a good man."

"They are all good men." He sighed, looking me up and down. "You were at the walls?"

"I was."

"They say the Emperor is dead. Did you see it?"

"I heard it also but I did not see. I believe he fled southward along the wall. Later, word spread as we ran that he had fallen. Whether it is true, I cannot say."

The master grunted. "Small fleet of Genoese ships by the Golden Gate at the south, leading into the Sea of Marmara. Going for them, I would wager. Should have stood and died for his city. What of Longo?"

"Wounded. His men drew him back and it caused the rout. He was alive long enough to order a full retreat, I heard the trumpets sound. Or perhaps one of his men gave the order. His men were taking him to a ship but we went on separate roads and I do not know where they went."

The master shook his head as he gazed back at the dark city.

"She has fallen, then. She has truly fallen."

His eyes glittered with tears.

"How shall you break through the Turkish fleet?" I asked him. "And before that, the great chain?"

"Word was that the Genoese in Galata would pull in the chain but it has not happened yet. I doubt the useless bastards shall do it, fearful as they are of breaking their oaths of neutrality. But if they do it, we shall be ready for the Turks. Their ships are weak, they cannot sail."

"I heard they hired Christian crews."

He smiled a little. "But we are Venetian."

We were transferred to the great cog, with its slab sides and square sails on the masts. Many of the Greek lords had sailed or were sailing across to Galata but everyone knew they could not stay there. The Genoese might have sworn to remain neutral but they had sent men to the defence of the walls and they were assisting in the evacuation of the city and so they would soon surrender to the Turks or have their gates broken and their people slaughtered. Through the swarming ships of all sizes in the Horn, word was passed that Longo had indeed survived and he was on one of the ships. Though he had failed in his duty, he was still loved by the Genoese, the Venetians, and the Greeks, and they were pleased to find he yet lived.

"I know you are all tired," I said to my men as we bobbed at anchor. They lay in heaps, half tangled with each other, on the deck of the cog, relieved to be away but afraid of what might come. "And we will take what rest and sustenance we can. But we must be prepared to fight once more. When the ship sails, we shall keep well away from the crew and we will not obstruct them in their work. But if a Turkish ship attempts to board us, we must be ready to repel them. Do you understand?"

They did and I left them to rest.

"I'd rather have died on my feet," Walt muttered beside me as we looked out at the burning city. "Than get sunk out here and drown beneath the waves."

Drowning was a great fear of my own but a leader must show confidence at such times. "We must have faith in our Venetian friends. They are the masters of these waves."

"If you say so."

The night drew on and the fleet signalled to each other by lamps and by whistles, bells, and trumpets and by shouting across the waters. Small boats were rowed between ships and gradually, some sort of plan was agreed upon. The darkness made it hard to see what was happening but soon our ship was underway. To the east, the great chain was broken by Genoese ships and in several groups the fleet of Christian survivors sailed out toward the Turks beyond the Horn.

There were hundreds of us, and the Venetian master had not been lying when he said their skill outweighed that of the enemy. Some of our ships fell to enemy assault. Arrows flew and guns fired, flashing and banging in the night. Men were killed and ships boarded, even sunk in collisions. My men were called to arm themselves and to stand ready many times through the night but the enemy ships were always avoided before they could close with us.

We made it through the strait and south into the Sea of

Marmara, and from there we forced our way through the Dardanelles into the Aegean. Once there, we had days out away from the coast and our small fleet aimed for Greece and the few free Venetian port cities that the Turks had allowed them to keep when they took Greece.

We spoke little during the journey. Even of what would happen next. The fighting had been hard enough but the defeat was far harder to bear.

The city was sacked for three days. Some quarters resisted the Turks for a time before surrendering but the Catalan mercenaries fought to the last man. The Turks looted homes but focused of course on the churches and monasteries, desecrating them with their heathenry and stealing their wealth. Constantinople was looted on a massive scale. The richest lords of the city and their families sought sanctuary in the Santa Sofia, hoping that the sanctity of that greatest of churches would save them. Instead, the vile Turks broke down the doors, raped the women on the floor of the holy church, and dragged the survivors off to be ransomed or sold into slavery or defiled until death.

Later, Mehmed rode into the city and into the Santa Sophia where he had the building converted into a mosque and held afternoon prayers that very day.

That was the Turkish way. They had stolen everything from the Byzantines by force. Stolen her cities and her towns, her fields and orchards. Stolen her sons for their Janissaries. And now they had stolen the most beautiful, the most magnificent building on earth and defiled it by worshipping their false god within.

Genoese Galata surrendered. The terms were negotiated by

William himself, no doubt because he spoke the language so well. The thought of William's red Janissary regiment forcing their way through the walls and into the city turned my stomach every time I recalled it. The fact that William had not fought alongside them enraged me further, but I did not know why.

In return for winning him the city, Sultan Mehmed made William his official Grand Vizier, the second most powerful man in the Turkish Empire.

"What now?" Eva finally asked me, days later as we approached Negroponte, on Euboea.

"What will William do?" Stephen said, when I did not answer. "Where will he strike next?"

"Where else is left now for him to conquer but to the north?" I replied, finally. "Whether he strikes at Serbia, Wallachia, Moldavia, Hungary, the line must be held."

"But how can we stop William?" Stephen said. "How can we stop his Janissaries?"

"You urged me for so long to build a great company of immortals but I resisted. For good reasons, I thought. And then we made our Company of Saint George into members of the Order of the White Dagger. I had hoped it would be enough."

"We know now that we need more," Stephen said. "More than two score. We need as many as William has. Five hundred at the least."

"And yet the problem remains. How can we find and support and supply so many? Already, I worry about the men we have."

He nodded, warily. "We would have to trust the men completely. We would need enormous amounts of mortal blood.

And it would need to be done in secret, lest we are challenged, declared enemies, outlaws, expelled from Christendom."

"All great challenges that must be overcome," I said. "I see it now, with my eyes clear and open. Because the only way we will ever stop William from conquering all of Christendom is with our own army of immortals."

7

Wallachia

1456

OF COURSE, CREATING AN ARMY OF IMMORTALS was more easily said than done. It was a clear goal but how we could accomplish such a thing was far from resolved.

It took months to make our way back to Hungary in safety, first by sea and then by land.

In Buda, the court was subdued and focused on internal issues. When we told our friends and contacts, whether merchants or knights, that we had been in Constantinople for the siege, few seemed interested in discussing it further. It was a matter that people already seemed to believe best forgotten, even though the implications were enormous. It was as though they could deny it had ever happened, if only it was never spoken of.

The Turks continued to reinforce the frontier. And all the Christian lands under Turkish authority continued to be subjected to the *devshirme*, the Blood Tax. Hunyadi had a report compiled by a group of monks who believed that fifteen or twenty-thousand Christian boys were being incorporated into the Janissaries every single year. Twenty thousand of our strongest boys, every year, taken as slaves and used against us. That says nothing of slaves taken from the Rus and other people of the north by the Golden Horde.

Our Albanian warlord Skanderbeg made a swift and secret visit to his allies in Naples to discuss the strategic implications of the loss of Constantinople and discussions were begun regarding a new crusade to retake the city. We long held out hope, for all of the years 1454, and 1455, but it came to nothing. In the meantime, I trained the survivors of our company and we sought new armour and weapons and supplies. Hunyadi was glad enough at my return to fund us once more so that we would be on hand, though he did not have much use for us. Still, we took the opportunity to regain our strength and improve our skill. The new immortals delighted in their new abilities and they gave me little trouble.

Eva and Stephen re-established contact with their agents and brought many to our company's house to provide regular reports of enemy activity.

By 1456, the Sultan had about ninety thousand soldiers in Edirne and a fleet of sixty ships at the mouth of the Danube. Agents provided word that the Turks were producing cannons in new foundries in Serbia, which would save them the time and effort needed to bring them up from Greece or Anatolia.

It became ever clearer the Turks meant to take Belgrade.

Swiftly, Vladislaus II the Voivode of Wallachia turned even further toward the Turks and was said to be making ever more promises to the Sultan. If Wallachia could not be brought to heel then it would soon fall, perhaps without a fight. More immediate a problem though was that Vladislaus had begun raiding across southern Transylvania with Turkish soldiers. This raiding tied down thousands of Hunyadi's best men who were guarding against this new Wallachian assault.

"But I need those men," Hunyadi said, after summoning me to his private chambers. I knew that it meant he had finally found a use for me and my company. "I need them for the defence of Belgrade. It is there that the Sultan's hammer blow will fall next."

"Why not remove Vladislaus now?" I asked. "You have known it needed to be done for a long time. But it cannot wait any further."

"You are more right than you know. Vladislaus has stirred up the people of Fogaras, encouraged them into a full rebellion against me. Against Hungary. They sent word that they are no longer my vassals but the vassals of Sultan Mehmed. This means they will throw themselves into the arms of the Turks when they arrive and so already we have a Transylvanian town lost to us and gained by the enemy. We cannot allow them to do this."

"So send an army, take back Fogaras and march over the mountains into Wallachia and be rid of Vladislaus."

"An army, Richard?" he shook his head. "I cannot take even more men from Serbia and send them into Wallachia. You have seen the country. Seen those mountains. You have fought in them. If Vladislaus refuses battle, which he will do if he has any sense, we could have ten thousand men tied up there for years. We do not have *time*."

I could not disagree with that. "But you have something in mind, or you would not have asked to speak to me."

Hunyadi sighed and gestured to a servant to bring us more wine. "You seemed to do well with young Vlad Dracula last time you were with him, in Transylvania. Are you on good terms?"

"I kept my men clear of him, truth be told. But I made my peace with him before I left for Constantinople and we parted on good terms, certainly."

"What did you think of his abilities?"

"We did not do any fighting and neither did he. But throughout the negotiations and during the journey from place to place, he seemed a perfectly steady young prince."

"Steady?" Hunyadi drank his wine and frowned. "Do you damn him with faint praise, sir?"

"Not at all. Young Dracula knew what he wanted, he told his men clearly what he expected, and they obeyed him. He knows how to lead."

"Good, yes. But you were not impressed?"

"It is not that I was unimpressed. He is young and untested. But most of all, I still wonder where his true loyalties lie. You wish to put him on the throne and so make a true ally of Wallachia again. But this is what we did ten years ago, and your man has turned to the Turks even more thoroughly than the old Vlad Dracul ever did."

He sighed and scratched his cheek. "And you fear I will make the same mistake again. It is certainly a possibility. But there seems to be a deep well of contempt in the young man's heart, reserved above all for the Turk."

"Perhaps he is deceiving you. Perhaps he has been their man ever since they released him. After all, why would they do so? I believe the Turks yet hold his younger brother, Radu. Is that still the case?"

Hunyadi made an unhappy growling sound in his throat. "It is. It appears that he is serving the Sultan in a military capacity."

"Perhaps they threaten to end Radu's life if Vlad does not do as they command."

"Do you have a brother, Richard?"

I swallowed. "Why do you ask?"

"I merely wondered what you might do for the life of a younger brother. How far you would go. What would it take for you to trade your honour as a prince and a knight, and a life as an independent ruler for that of a slave subordinate to the Turks? Would you do it to save the life of your brother?"

"You are speaking to a lowly and landless knight with no family, my lord. I have never had to consider such a question. But I take it you do not believe the threat to his brother's life would be enough to bind him in servitude to the Turks? Perhaps not. We cannot know what is in his heart. But you have asked me here and you speak to me of Wallachia and Vlad Dracula instead of the coming battle at Belgrade. And so I take it that you have decided to make your move with young Vlad? To place him on the throne?"

"No." Hunyadi drank off his wine and snapped his fingers for another. "I cannot place him there. He must take it for himself. But I will provide him with a small number of soldiers, as many as I can spare from the defence of Belgrade. Perhaps Dracula can make his way into Wallachia and overthrow the *voivode*, with the help my men and of loyal *boyars* who have been exiled by Vladislaus."

"How many men do you mean, my lord?"

"*Boyars?* Almost thirty, with their retinues. And I have secured the services of six hundred Hungarian mercenaries and five hundred more from Transylvania and Wallachia."

I laughed aloud. "You are sending, what, fifteen hundred men against the armies of Wallachia and the Turks he controls? They will be outnumbered ten to one. It is madness."

"Madness, yes," Hunyadi said, smiling. "And that is precisely why I thought of you."

∞

"We're doing what?" Walt said, after I explained it to them. He sat at my right hand at the top table and I looked down at him from where I stood before looking around at the rest of the men seated below me.

Our hall in Buda was large enough for the company to assemble. I had not recruited anyone to make up our numbers as I was concerned about a company of immortals and mortals mixing together. Certainly, the servants could not be trusted to hold their tongues about the nature of their masters and any new mercenaries would have to become members of the Order. Indeed, the Company of Saint George had become essentially synonymous with the Order of the White Dagger. The outside world saw us as a small but elite mercenary company retained by the Regent of Hungary and yet we knew ourselves to be the Order, committed to destroying William de Ferrers and all his evil, immortal followers.

Some of the men took time to understand what a fine line it was to thread between these two realities. Indeed, I struggled to do so myself every day.

"It might be done," I said. "Though it will be a challenge, I do not doubt it."

They all looked at one another and said nothing.

"What is in it for us?" Stephen said. "How does agreeing to win Vlad Dracula his kingdom help us make the immortal army we need to defeat William?"

I nodded and clasped my hands before me.

"If it works," I said, "and if we show ourselves to be indispensable, then we might find ourselves with a ruler in Dracula who can give us the sanctuary we need."

Rob rapped his knuckles on the table and pointed across the hall to Serban, sitting far away below the salt. "What do you say, Serban? What do you make of Vlad's chances?"

Old Serban dragged himself to his feet and glanced around the hall, all eyes turned to him. "It can certainly be done, my lord. It has been done before. The throne of Wallachia changes hands more often than a halfpenny strumpet."

Walt burst out laughing and banged the table and most of the men laughed with him.

"I take it you taught him that?" I asked Walt as he wiped his eyes. "Thank you, Serban, for sharing with us your expert local knowledge. That will be all from you."

Stephen cleared his throat. "Do you truly believe Vlad could be the ruler we need? He may be working for the Turks. He may be a weakling. He still may turn on you and have you killed because of his father."

"Yes," I agreed, clapping my hands together. "All that you say is true. But where else might we find our friendly ruler? So, before we conclude, are there any other objections to be made?"

"So," Stephen said, getting to his feet. "No matter what we say today, you have decided that we will ultimately agree to this mad scheme?"

"I have agreed already. Make your preparations. We return to Transylvania."

It was June 1456 when we slipped over the mountains from Transylvania and into Wallachia with our small, makeshift army. Those mountain peaks were black and jagged, with grey streaks and were inhumanly large and intimidating and entirely unscalable. On their flanks clung dense forests of pine trees so dark when in shadow that they seemed black as charcoal. The passes and valleys were prone to sudden changes in elevation, but they were often lush and green, whether with meadows grazed by hardy sheep and mad goats, or in broadleaf woods thick with herds of pigs. Below, the lands were crossed with rivers running from the mountains to the distant plains and on to feed the mighty Danube, sometimes becoming long, narrow, and spectacular lakes. In between was a wild land of forests of beech, oak, and elm in the lowlands, or pines and spruce and fur above.

Our leader, the young Vlad Dracula was in fine form. Whether with the exiled *boyars* or the mercenary captains, he was always at ease. His own men, young lords or sons of lords or other Wallachian adventurers who had thrown their lot in with him, clearly adored him and hung on his every word. Though he was often the shortest man in any group, he seemed to dominate it with his loud voice and sure gestures. The young prince was born to rule and had been raised in that very expectation. Despite his prolonged period of confinement in the lands of his enemies, he certainly appeared to believe in himself deeply.

The only man he was wary of was me.

Despite my presentation of his father's sword and dragon amulet, young Vlad kept his distance. At councils of war, though he was courteous enough and listened to my suggestions just as he did for others, with me he was always reserved.

"He does not favour me," I muttered to Walt as we left his tent a week after crossing the border.

"You cut off his dad's head," Walt said.

"There is that."

"Reckon he means to take yours?" Walt asked.

"I think it is a distinct possibility."

"Don't worry, Richard, I'll watch your back."

Vlad's plan relied on bringing as many of the *boyars* to his side as he could before open fighting began. Without wooing former allies of his father and enemies of Vladislaus, the attempt on the throne would be doomed to failure. With that in mind, we made for the fortress of Copăceni at the head of a severe valley in the north. Once our army filed into the valley and approached the fortress, Vlad took some of us up the final steep approach and there demanded to see the lord, a boyar named Bogdan.

At the gate, our horses were breathing heavily from the climb. I was at the rear of the party, with a few of my men to accompany me. The gatekeeper looked down on us and raised his voice, which echoed from the rocks and thick stone walls. "Who are you and why do you come here?"

I looked up at the dragon banner held aloft over our party and shook my head at the gatekeeper's absurd attempts at haughtiness.

"You know who we are," Dracula said, his voice projecting over the entire fortress. "Tell your lord I will speak with him."

"State your name," the gatekeeper said.

Vlad paused for half a moment before answering, the silence filled with his contempt for the stupidity of the question.

"I will not be kept waiting," Dracula replied.

The man hesitated, looked at the soldiers flanking him, and disappeared into the tower. We stood in silence on our horses.

It was not long before the gatekeeper reappeared. "You, my lord, and ten men. No more. And no weapons."

"Ten men it is," Dracula agreed. "But we shall keep our weapons. Open the gate."

The gatekeeper pursed his lips and his gloved fingers drummed on the parapet before he muttered to the man beside him, who hurried off. A few moments later the gate below creaked into life as it swung slowly inward.

"That was easy," Walt said, grinning. "We'll be camped in the valley tonight, then. Wonder if the lads might shoot a deer. Do you reckon there's boar in these woods?"

"Undoubtedly," Rob said, his tone miserable, staring at his stump.

Before he dismounted, Dracula called out the names of his men, commanding them to accompany him inside the fortress of Copăceni.

The tenth name he called was mine.

Caught off guard, I hesitated but swung down from my saddle.

"Do not do it," Rob muttered. "It may be a trap."

"Might be," I said, adjusting my clothes and slipping an extra knife up inside my doublet.

"This may *all* be theatre," Stephen said, hurrying forward and whispering. "This entire event."

"What do you mean?"

"It was rather easy to gain access to this supposed enemy stronghold, was it not? What if it was prearranged? What if the purpose was to separate you from your men?"

I turned to Serban. "What do you think?"

"I think at such times a man must flee," he said, shrugging. "Or go forward to meet his fate."

"Do you know something about this trap, Serban?" Stephen said, reaching for him. "Are you in on it? Are you a part of it? If you are, you will speak now, or I shall flay you myself."

Serban stared back, his wrinkled face filled with contempt and bitter amusement.

"Enough, Stephen," I said, smiling and patting him on the back. "Our Wallachian friends are looking."

"Be careful," Eva said. "And hurry up. They are waiting for you."

I winked at her and followed Dracula and his nine companions into the fortress. It was a small place but sturdy enough. Like so many such structures in those highlands, it was a stronghold where a lord could feel safe from raids and assassinations and other mischief started by his neighbouring lords, while ruling over the villages in his valley below.

There seemed to be no more than forty soldiers and as many servants. A hundred men and women in the entire place, mostly men.

We were escorted into the small, dark hall. A table and benches had been set in the centre of it while a fire burned in a surprisingly modern fireplace on the side.

At the head of the hall sat Lord Bogdan of Copăceni, a big man even seated in his chair, with wild eyes and a thick, greying moustache.

"So," Bogdan said, his voice gruff. "You have come. Sit at my table and take refreshment. Then I will hear your requests."

While we stood in a line at the rear, Dracula said nothing and strode the length of the hall toward the seated old boyar. He stopped an arm's span from him, looking down.

"You, Bogdan, have sworn to follow the false prince Vladislaus," Dracula said.

The boyar shifted in his seat, discomforted. "But of course. He is the Voivode of Wallachia."

"Not for long," Dracula said.

The boyar peered around Dracula, looking at his men for help, even at us. I glanced at Dracula's men, his bodyguards and exiled *boyars*. None moved to help Bogdan. Some were smiling.

"Come, let us drink," Bogdan said, attempting to take control of the situation. "Let us eat. Then we can discuss things."

"There is nothing to discuss," Dracula said.

The boyar coughed and shifted in his seat again. "Then why are you here?"

"To accept your apology," Dracula said.

"Apology?" The boyar snapped. "For what? I have done nothing to you."

"I have come to hear you beg forgiveness."

Bogdan's mouth gaped. "For what? I supported your father until they killed him. What else could I do then but support Vladislaus?"

Dracula half turned to the men behind him at the back of the hall. "These men went into exile rather than follow a false prince. And yet you did not. Why?"

Bogdan attempted a consolatory tone. "Let us eat."

"Why?"

He slapped his hands on the arms of his chair. "Why do you think, you upstart? I am a lord. This is my castle. This is my land. I rule it. They are my people. Give that up, for what? For the memory of my dead lord? His sons were in the claws of the Turks, I did not know if they would ever return. If you would return. What was I supposed to do?"

Vlad stared at him, unmoved. "I will accept your apology, once it is given."

"And what will you do if it is not?"

Dracula said nothing and I could not see his face. But the boyar could and his eyes opened wide and his skin turned white. He coughed again, before looking around at his men. Many shuffled with unease.

"Very well," the boyar said with his chin up. "Very well, then. I do here before witnesses say to you that—"

"On your knees," Dracula said.

Surely, it was too far.

The boyar stood. He was taller than Dracula but it somehow seemed as if he was still looking up at him.

"If you would step back, my lord," the boyar said. But Dracula did not move. The man smiled in discomfort and edged around the younger lord before dropping slowly to one knee. Now, Dracula was the one with his back to the lord's seat and the man before him appeared to be a supplicant in his own hall.

"I beg my lord to forgive me for following the false Voivode Vladislaus instead of taking myself into exile. I should have honoured my word. In the name of God, allow me to make amends."

Dracula held out his hand with his silver dragon ring and shining rubies. "You may swear fealty to me and follow me as I retake the throne of my ancestors."

The boyar took Dracula's hand in both of his and kissed the ring, swearing that he would do so.

"Very good," Dracula said, smiling and clapping his hands. "Now we may eat."

∞

In the sweltering heat of the valley, as June turned to July, we rode hard in pursuit of Vladislaus II and the last of his loyal men.

It had taken Vlad Dracula a mere four weeks, going from lord to lord, stronghold to stronghold, to gain the support of the majority of the Wallachian *boyars*. With his support fading away and even his Turkish troops drifting south back across the Danube into Rumelia, Vladislaus had seen what lay in store for him.

And so he ran from Târgovişte.

To me, it was a familiar feeling. Ten years before I had pursued Vlad II Dracul from the very same city, only this time my quarry had a greater start and he was not fleeing down into the plains and toward the Danube and to his friends the Turks but instead east across the valleys toward the last of the *boyars* who remained loyal to him.

We sweated and our horses gasped but we had to catch him before he could raise a spirited rebellion. If Wallachia descended into a civil war, even if Dracula won it would be weakened and open to invasion. A swift victory on the other hand would mean Wallachian troops and the mercenaries we had with us could all be directed to the vital defence of Belgrade.

And it was my company who had finally scared Vladislaus into full flight. If I could catch him and hand him over to Dracula, perhaps it would bring me such favour that I could approach him about our immortal army. Perhaps, at the least, it would start us down the road that would lead us to that place.

Just as I had years ago, I followed Serban once more, who proved to be an excellent rider. The rest of my company followed behind along the road. Miles behind, I expected Dracula himself and the core of his followers to be advancing as swiftly as they could.

It was late afternoon when we found them, stopped on the side of the road by a pond where they watered their horses and fed themselves with cold meats. We were surprised to come across them so suddenly but they were astonished at our unexpected arrival around a bend in the road. They rushed for their horses and half of them stood to fight while others took flight. Some that attempted to stop us were on horseback and others were on foot. Frightened horses without riders ran in panic. Without waiting for my men to come up beside me, I charged in amongst the enemy, killing one and knocking another from his saddle and charging through their line and on for Vladislaus. I recognised him by the crest upon his clothing and the excellence of his German armour and helm. With a glance over my shoulder I saw that some of my men were with me but not many, most having become entangled with the prince's men.

When I turned back to the road, my horse tossed his head and attempted to turn away, for Vladislaus and his men had turned and were starting to come back for their friends.

Gritting my teeth, I pulled my horse back onto the track and raked my spurs on him. My bloody sword raised high, I shouted a wordless cry and crashed through them, taking a blow on my shoulder from a warhammer that almost knocked me sideways. I cut at them, wheeling my horse around and around, fending off blows from all sides.

My company was outnumbered but Vladislaus and his men were outmatched. They were unable to conceive how much stronger we were than they and their misplaced confidence proved to be their undoing. We killed a great many of them and caught the rest. Out of sight of the survivors, a handful of the dying were drained of their blood and we finally stopped to take stock of our victory.

Rob and Walt grinned, for between them they held Prince Vladislaus. He was shaken and furious and behind his anger was a deep fear.

"Well done, men!" I cried. "You have unseated a prince, this day!"

We began escorting Vladislaus down the mountain and had reached a flatter section of the track where the river curved away to reveal a wide meadow on one side and the woods on the other.

Approaching us was a great mass of galloping horses.

"Line up!" Walt roared. "Defensive line here! Prisoners to the rear!"

"It is Dracula," I said.

"He got our message, then," Rob observed as Vlad Dracula's enormous column of horsemen came to a stop between the woods and the swift flowing river, spreading out into the meadows on either side with their long grass and array of red, purple, and white flowers.

"Bring up the prisoners," I called.

Vlad rode closer before throwing himself off and stepping away from his men into the open space between my company and his bodyguard.

When Vladislaus was brought forward to me, I took him by the arm and walked toward Dracula. We had removed his helm when we captured him, along with most of his expensive armour, and all could see who it was that I had beside me. Vladislaus glared at me once but then he had eyes only for Vlad.

The young would-be prince stepped forward. Dracula said nothing, his face cold and hard and his eyes glaring as they came together. He looked up at Vladislaus who sneered down.

"They told me you were a skilled knight," Vladislaus said. "But now I see that you are nothing but a little boy."

Dracula's face did not change, he simply stared into Vladislaus' eyes.

"What?" Vladislaus said, scoffing. "You think you can frighten me? I know I am to be executed. What can you frighten me with?"

I spoke up. "Your men burned his older brother to death, did they not? I wonder if that's how you will go? Or if they will remove your skin first?"

He glanced at me, angry. I laughed.

"No," Dracula said, the first word he had spoken. "No, you shall not be burned. Nor flayed."

Vladislaus looked down his long nose. "What is it to be, then?"

Dracula seemed not to have blinked at all. "You shall not be executed, Vladislaus."

The *voivode* scoffed but I saw hope kindle in his eyes. "Ransom, is it? A wise choice. You will earn for yourself a fortune, have no doubts about that."

Dracula did not smile but I saw that he was amused. "And who would pay this fortune for you? The *boyars* will raise a fortune for a man who cannot protect them and their people? Or do you mean that the Turks will pay for a king who cannot hold a kingdom?"

Vladislaus sneered. "There are many yet loyal to me."

Dracula shook his head. "There will be no ransom."

"What then?" Vladislaus snapped, unable to stand it a moment longer. "Not execution, not ransom. Then what?"

"It is to be combat, my lord," Dracula said, calmly. "You against me. To the death. Now."

Vladislaus looked at the men behind Dracula and then back to the young man. "Even if I win, I will lose."

Dracula raised his voice but still did not turn away from his enemy. "If Vladislaus defeats me in this fair trial of combat, you shall let him and his men go free. This is my command as your lord. Do you agree to honour it?"

They called out their assent. If it came to pass, I doubted they would honour their word. Still, it was enough to give Vladislaus hope and I understood later that it was as much a matter of Vlad's cruelty as it was his sense of honour.

Vladislaus was ordered to prepare himself and his surviving men were allowed to approach and dress him for combat, with his own armour and weapons. I was mildly annoyed because I had already claimed those fine items for myself and I was not about to have my men strip the dead man in front of his former subjects.

"You disapprove, Richard?" Vlad asked me as his squires strapped his armour on.

"I approve very much," I said. "It is always a pleasure to see young people embracing the old ways."

He smiled. "And you know about the old ways, do you?"

"A little."

"And yet you do not seem happy. Is it because I have not thanked you for catching him for me?"

"I have no need for words of thanks. It is the favour of the Voivode of Wallachia that I seek."

He stepped forward, scattering his surprised squires, and held out an armoured hand. I took it as he looked into my eyes.

"You have it, sir. We must talk, you and I. There is much to discuss."

"Then we shall do so," I replied, letting him go and pointing over my shoulder. "After you kill that bastard."

His eyes were mirthless as he nodded to the squire holding his helm. "It will not take long."

Eva came close to my side. "Walt and Rob are taking bets."

"I would not bet against our young lord, here."

"No? Do you not often say that in battle experience more often bests youth?"

I glanced at her. "I say no such thing."

She scoffed.

Fully armoured, the great lords stalked toward each other as the sun touched the rim of the ridge to the west, casting deep yellow light into the valley.

Dracula feinted an attack and Vladislaus covered himself, but it was clear he had not been deceived. Their blades clashed and they withdrew, feeling each other out for a few more moments until Vladislaus launched into a furious attack. Vladislaus was taller and his blade longer and he used his reach advantage to thrust at Dracula's face. The shorter man parried as he stepped back and back. But he was not in a blind panic and he did not retreat in a straight line, stepping and moving at oblique angles as he defended. Both men had been raised since early childhood to be great knights and had received superb instruction by experienced masters, and they had made it their business to practice throughout their lives since. Even when he had been a hostage of the Turks, he had received martial instruction.

But Vladislaus was taller and older and it became clear that he had the advantage, as slight as it was. Dracula's attacks came up short and it seemed to all watching that the combat was certain to end only one way. Certainly, Vladislaus had sensed it and he redoubled his efforts to break through Dracula's defence before exhaustion overcame him. After their sharp start, their movements had taken on the rhythmic state that one reaches when weariness begins to take hold. And there are few activities in life more wearying than prolonged armoured combat.

Vladislaus gave a sudden burst of speed and caught Dracula on his helm with a powerful blow, powerful enough to knock any mortal man from his senses. The watching crowd cried out.

But Dracula did not fall. Nor was he dazed, even for a moment. Instead, a change came over him. He stopped defending and instead attacked and all trace of weariness was quite suddenly gone. Indeed, he used his sword with one hand instead of two, almost casually, as he advanced on his tired opponent.

I realised then that the fight up to then had been all deceit on Dracula's part, feigning lesser skill than he had. It stunned Vladislaus, who began retreating in panic.

Dracula surged forward so quickly that he was almost a blur, and his sword whipped through the air, left and right, knocking away his enemy's sword and driving him to his knees with a flurry of blows. Eva grabbed my hand and squeezed it.

Advancing on his kneeling opponent, Dracula twisted the helm from Vladislaus' head and tossed it aside. The Voivode of Wallachia's eyes were wide, and his face and hair were soaked with sweat.

"Look at me," Dracula said, grasping Vladislaus' slick hair in his gauntleted fist and pulling the man's head back.

Just as Vladislaus opened his mouth to speak, Dracula lifted his sword hand high and drove the pommel down into the fallen man's face, breaking the bones of his cheeks and eyes. It was powerful enough to knock Vladislaus unconscious, as his raised hands fell limp. But Dracula held his head in position and brought the pommel down again and again, until the man's face was caved in and the insides pulped. When there was nothing left but a sucking hole, he pushed the dead man down and walked slowly back toward his horse.

The hundreds of watching men stood in silence for a long moment before one of his men cheered and then suddenly, they all were.

"Richard," Eva said, speaking rapidly. "Did you see? See the way he moved? The speed. Do you think—"

"Yes, I saw it," I said. "There is no doubt. Dracula is an immortal."

8

The Battle of Belgrade 1456

"I WOULD HAVE YOU STAY," DRACULA SAID as I prepared to mount my horse. All around us, the field swarmed with men and horses, assembled for the ride to the west. "You and your entire company."

"It would please me to stay," I said to Dracula, "and there is much to discuss. But there is not a moment to be lost. Belgrade must not fall."

"There is no doubt about that," he replied, shading his eyes with a hand and wincing. He wore a broad-brimmed black hat and gloves. I recalled that he had always been well covered when outside, especially in the bright summer sun. "I wish that I could fight also. There is little I would prefer in all the world than to fight a great battle against Mehmed. Alas, it shall have to wait. I cannot leave the land I have not yet completely won."

"I understand, my lord, and when we have smashed the Turk at Belgrade, I shall return."

"Do you think you shall?" Dracula replied.

"Return?"

"Smash the Turk. Hunyadi has not managed to do so yet. Not when it truly mattered."

"We must," I said. "If Belgrade falls, they will be across and into Hungary and from there, where can they not go?"

He nodded, his face unreadable. It was as though he did not care either way.

I hesitated. So many questions were on my mind but I could not ask them. Not yet. "What will you do now, my lord, if I may ask?"

"There are many men I must speak with. Wallachia must be put into good order. The traitors must be discovered and punished, and good men put in their place. I hope that you will return soon, with as many of my soldiers as possible. I need them. Wallachia needs them."

"You need them to return?" I asked. "Or do you need them to kill the Turks?"

Dracula's mouth twitched. "They have been poorly led in past years. My predecessors gave orders that they stay intact, no matter what. I have ordered these men to do their duty and kill twice their number in Turks, and to show Christendom that Wallachia is resolved to destroying the enemies of Christ. I will not have my people shamed once again."

"I am very glad to hear it, my lord."

"Come back, Richard."

He held out his hand and I took it.

"I will, my lord."

Dracula had already turned away to speak to his lords as I mounted and rode to my men, who sat watching me.

"Getting on rather well with the little bastard," Walt said, "aren't you, Richard?"

"I think he likes me," I said.

"He is luring you in with false courtesies," Stephen said. "So that he can catch you and kill you."

I tilted my head. "Thank you for your unique insight, Stephen, it had not occurred to me that one of William's immortals may mean me harm."

He blustered. "I simply meant that he will kill you the moment he has the chance and—"

"But he has had the chance," Eva said, cutting him off. "Many times. Something has stayed his hand. Perhaps he is not certain about Richard, or perhaps there is some other reason. Perhaps there is something he wishes to know before he acts. Or it may be that he wants you as an ally after all. Perhaps William has sent him with orders to win you over."

"Fat chance of that," Rob said. "Right, Richard?"

"We do not know what he wants," I said. "I do not know how much it matters. There may be an advantage in capturing him and questioning him about William before we kill him. And before we capture him and kill him, we must come up with a plan that does not lead to us all being slaughtered by an army of his men. But first, before all that, we must go to Belgrade. For all we know, the Turks have already reached it."

"We ride with Wallachian horsemen," Walt observed. "Many of them are the very same Wallachian horsemen that abandoned us at Varna."

"Yes," I said.

"And they deserted again at Kosovo."

"Many are the same men, certainly."

Walt nodded. "And these same lads are our allies now?"

"We are riding with them, that is all. When we reach Belgrade, Hunyadi will know not to trust these men." I thought of Dracula's earlier words. "Besides, they may not act as they have before."

My men were not convinced.

"What if they do not flee," Walt said, "but instead attack. Dracula is one of William's and he will have ordered these men to fall upon the Hungarians at just the right moment. Did that occur to you?"

"I will warn Hunyadi, do not fear. Until then, we must treat our companions with respect and courtesy. Understand?"

"Can I not just keep apart from them instead?" Walt grumbled.

"Once our business in Belgrade is finished, we must return here and capture and kill their new prince. We cannot make enemies amongst the soldiery before then, and so you will be courteous," I said, wagging a finger at him. "Like the knight you are. Come on."

∞

We marched first with the Hungarian and Transylvanian mercenaries from Wallachia across the plains to the Danube, crossing by boat, and then up into the mountains toward northern Serbia. The mercenaries knew they would be paid when they reached the Hungarian army at Belgrade but they also looked forward to the prospect of enormous quantities of loot, assuming of course that the Turks could be defeated.

We pushed hard and I drove my company faster than many of the others, gaining distance every day. The land was teeming with soldiers from all over, heading for Belgrade. There is no doubt that there were Turkish spies everywhere also, whether they were Anatolian, Bulgarian, Serbian, or Wallachian.

My company gained half a day and then a full day and soon we were one company out a day ahead of the mercenaries and the Wallachians a day behind them. It was no simple thing to cross from the plains of Wallachia into Serbia and the hills and valleys between the two seemed endless. It was a sparsely populated land but our guides knew their business and every day we rose early and stopped late. It was gruelling travel, especially for my mortal servants, but I dared not miss the battle. There was no doubt in my mind that William would be there and God alone knew what atrocities he could commit with his red-robed immortals. We could not face him directly, not yet, but we could not abandon our allies to face them alone, either.

Once we dropped down from the hills into the long, north-south valleys of Serbia, the going was far easier. We headed north, toward the Danube again, before crossing three wide, fertile plains as we headed west once more.

I grew up in hill country but where Derbyshire was rounded and filled with bright, verdant greens, and the rocks were warm, soft limestone and sandstone, Serbia was a land of all dark greens and the stone was jagged, hard and harsh, in deep greys and red-browns, and the soil thin and black. It seemed nowhere in the entire land was flat, other than their three valleys in the northeast, even as we followed the Danube for the final leg of the journey to the massive city that was our destination and our great hope for stopping the relentless advance of the Turks.

Belgrade was a Hungarian possession, but it remained to all intents a Serbian city. And the Serbs had, for once, decided to defy their Turkish overlords and were intent on defending the city. Indeed, they must have known that once Belgrade fell, there would be no Serbia left to resist the Turks at all.

The local Serbian population around the city had added to the number of defenders within it and the land all around had been well prepared by them for the siege. Defences had been dug, erected, and extended and fields of fire cleared for the cannons and gunners on the walls and towers. Indeed, Hunyadi had been lavishing vast sums on enhancing the defences at least since I had arrived in the region more than ten years earlier. But recently there had been a final surge in effort and the locals had been building the walls higher and stronger for months. Anything edible had been removed from the enemy's line of march, all the water sources poisoned, and bridges destroyed. It would not stop the Turks but it would not help them, either.

"Come on," I said every morning to my tired and aching men, "just a little further." Our guides were eager to get us into Serbia and they ranged ahead every day to ensure the way was clear. When we reached the city, they came back and urged me to bring just a small party ahead to see for ourselves what awaited us.

Belgrade sat nestled between the River Sava where it ran into the Danube and as we approached the peak of the highest point a few miles from the city, we were awed by the scale of the fortress on the horizon.

And yet the triple-walled fortress city was not what stilled our tongues. We had been avoiding Turkish patrols in the hills for days before we arrived and dreaded what we would find as we crept through the long grass to the top of a ridge.

"We are too late," Stephen muttered, looking out at the city close to the horizon where it sat at the confluence of two great rivers.

"Damn the bastards," Walt hissed.

The army of the Turks was arrayed before Belgrade, encamped in an arc completely cutting them off. Tens of thousands of soldiers, horses, and great artillery pieces, already intent on reducing the outer limit of the fortifications. On the wide Danube, an enormous Turkish fleet swarmed the waters. The tributary Sava River looked clear of Turkish vessels but still the city was close to being cut off. More wagons and groups of riders trailed from the south up to the camp, bringing supplies and more men.

Though camp fires burned in the Turkish camps and lines and lines of trenches and earthworks were thrown up between the army and the city, the walls were intact and there was no fighting going on.

"The city is untouched," I said. "We cannot have missed much."

Walt scowled. "How are we going to get in past that lot?"

Stephen laughed. "Well, I think it is clear that we shall not do so, Walt."

"What, then?" Walt said. "We going back to Wallachia?"

"William is down there," I said. "And the Sultan, too, do you see his banner there in the centre camp? His vast tents below them. We will not flee."

"Shall we camp in the hills, then?" Rob asked. "Sit and watch from afar, shall we? Move in when the fighting starts?"

"Patrols will find us before then," Walt said. "It'll take the Turks months to get in there. Look at the walls, by God. We should go north, cross the Danube, go into Hungary and back to Buda. I bet our good Regent is yet building his army, don't you? Reckon we should join it."

I scanned the river beyond, where it curled away into the horizon. There were no allied ships to be seen and no army on the banks. "Listen, Hunyadi knows just as well as anyone that a city, even one as well-fortified as this one, cannot resist these new cannons for long. Weeks or a month, perhaps. But they will blast away at the walls, like at Constantinople, and they will break through. Not in months but weeks and perhaps even days. Look how many cannons there are. A hundred? Three hundred?" They looked at me, waiting for the good news. "And that is why he was building an army which can bring the Turk to battle before that occurs."

Walt held his hand out to the scene before us. "And where is this army?"

"He will come now, right away. He will be here any day. Tomorrow. Soon. He knows he cannot leave Belgrade to its fate and so he will come. He has to."

"Remember that old Cardinal?" Rob said. "The one preaching for a crusade in Hungary before we left, commanding Christians to take up arms and come to the defence of the city."

"John of Capistrano," Eva said.

"That's the fellow. Perhaps they are coming also?"

I shook my head. "The only men who listened were peasants. They started assembling in southern Hungary but they had nought but slings and clubs, for God's sake. What do you think they will do against the Janissaries?"

Rob shrugged. "Better than nothing."

"Hunyadi is coming with the soldiers of Hungary but he is coming from the other side of the city. The other side of the siege, beyond the Sava. We must do two things. First, send word back to the mercenaries behind us and Wallachians behind them that if they come this way they will be seen due to their great numbers, and then they will be chased down by thousands of *sipahis* and defeated in a pointless battle. Secondly, once our message is sent, we must cross the Sava and join with Hunyadi's approaching army."

"Why not join the mercenaries behind us?" Stephen said.

"There are thousands of them and we would be safer in numbers if we force a crossing of the tributary."

"A small company like us can evade notice. Even if we are seen, no one will be overly concerned. If we are a force of a thousand or more, we will find ourselves run down by entire divisions of Turks. Their only hope of joining the battle is going around for miles or waiting in the east. It is up to them."

"They'll run," Walt predicted. "They'll just run."

"Perhaps we should, too," Stephen said. "This is too much. Too much."

"It would do us no harm to take a few days to ride around," Eva said.

"Longer we wait, the more dug in they'll be," Rob said. "Less chance of getting in at all."

"And I will say it again," Stephen snapped. "We need not fight every battle, especially when we are so likely to lose. William and the damned immortal Janissaries are there, I understand that. But approaching the city in these circumstances seems foolhardy at best."

Walt shrugged. "Might be all right."

"It is suicide!" Stephen said. "If we had any sense at all, we would flee and find another place to defend."

"After Belgrade," I said, "it will be Buda. After pacifying Hungary, it will be Vienna. And then where? Prague? Venice? If Venice, then Rome? We will not run. We will do our duty." I pointed due west across the rear of the great Turkish camps with their hundred thousand soldiers and tens of thousands of horses and servants spread across the plain. "We make our way there, to the banks of the Sava."

∞

We reached the Sava a few miles upstream from the city in the night, at a place where the tributary curved into a great bow shape. Our guides had made contact with Serbian spies, and they assured us there would be Hungarian forces ready to ferry us across. I did not know what to expect but we moved across the Turk's line of retreat to the water's edge as dusk fell. Enemy horsemen roamed the countryside all around and we were certainly spotted more than once but we moved quickly and were not challenged directly. No doubt, they assumed we were allies or too small an enemy force to be concerned with.

"We're in danger," Walt muttered as we huddled in the orchard on the outskirts of an abandoned village for our guides to return. "Sat here like a bag of plums, ain't we."

The residents had likely fled into the city days or weeks before the first Turks arrived and they or the enemy had later burned half of it to the ground for good measure. The obvious thing would have been to take shelter in the ruins but I did not like my men to be so confined, should enemy cavalry find us. The banks of the river were a stone's throw away and our position was sheltered by a rise on the landward side and I had positioned a few men up there to keep watch, and at our rear. Others kept an eye on the waters for the approach of the ships that would collect us. Our horses were nipping at the grass on the ground beneath the apple trees.

"The men are ready to repel an attack," I said. "And we shall be across the river before dawn."

"Balls, we will," Walt muttered. "We'll be sat here with our arses wet when the sun rises and an army of Turks is coming over that ridge down onto us."

"Then we will fight our way clear. Or we will die. What has got your gizzard, Walter?"

"Don't mind him, Richard," Rob said. "He wagered Serban we would make it inside the city before the Turks arrived."

"I would have thought you would welcome a quick death then, Walt, rather than part with your silver."

"We've been abandoned," Walt said. "Our damned guides have led us here and fled. Probably found a tub and rowed across to save themselves. Lying bastards, I'll skin them alive when I find them."

"They have not let us down so far." I raised my voice just a little. "Serban?"

"My lord?" he said, shuffling over.

"Do you trust our guides?"

He scratched his weathered face. "They are Serbians. They can be trusted only so far."

Walt scoffed. "There, you hear that? We have to run, now. Head south and see what's what."

"We shall wait."

As the night drew on, I could not contain my own fears. In frustration, I went out on foot toward the river to see what was happening. The moon's light was shaded by wisps of cloud and the wind whistled in my ears. The river was far wider than it had seemed at a distance, when I could compare it to the mighty Danube. Half of me had expected to be able to swim in, with our horses, should the boats not come, but looking at it close up I knew we would never make it across. Not even those of us who knew how to swim. Somewhere downstream along the bank, a grebe chattered its frantic, warbling trill and then a loon gave its long, mournful, two-tone wail. Further away, the loon's mate gave it's answering call which echoed across the water. It was eerie and unusual to hear them in the dead of night. I wondered if someone had disturbed them.

"You are afraid," Eva said, from just behind my shoulder, startling me.

"Good God, Eva," I snapped. "I am when you are creeping about like a bloody wraith, woman."

"You are deciding whether to wait longer or to take the men away."

"Walt is right," I said. "Being here at sunrise is too great a risk. It is a wide river but perhaps there is a ford upstream."

"The Sultan is five miles downstream."

"Closer than that, even."

"And William is very likely with him."

"With tens of thousands of soldiers and five hundred immortals guarding him, so do not suggest we attempt to steal through their ranks to slit William's throat. Believe me, Eva, if I thought it was possible, we would be attempting it."

"I was not going to suggest it. All I suggest is that perhaps your mind is focused upon your brother instead of the battle ahead."

"What do you mean?"

"The city is encircled by land and almost closed off by river. And you said it yourself, the Sultan has hundreds of cannon. Hundreds. Have you ever seen so many before? There are more here than at Constantinople, are there not? The city is doomed. And where is Hunyadi? Where are the Hungarians? Not even the crusader army of peasants has come."

"Hunyadi will be here."

"You like him as a man," Eva said. "You like him as a fellow old soldier."

"Speak plainly. You believe my judgement is clouded where Hunyadi is concerned? He has faced the Turks a hundred times and defeated them more times than he has lost. Who else can say such a thing?"

"He has done well. But he is old, now. His sons are taking their own commands. Hunyadi's losses have taken the shine off the man and the lords of Hungary, who have always been jealous, are asking what comes next."

I turned from the river and looked at her. "You think he will not come."

"Already at Easter, the Hungarian lords were refusing to answer his summons. You said it yourself, all the crusade could recruit was useless peasants. You must consider the fact that Hunyadi may not have an army to bring."

"He will come," I said. "Alone if he has to."

She did not reply. The loons had fallen silent and splashed out onto the dark river. Only the grebe still chattered, as if it was as nervous as I was.

"What would you have us do?" I asked.

"As you said. Go upstream, find a ford and head north until we can cross the Danube into Hungary."

"Abandon Belgrade?"

"Only so we may fight another day."

"You and Stephen are both pragmatic to a fault. Our Christian duty is to defend Christian lands from the infidel."

"Our duty is to defeat William. Our oath is to accomplish what no one else can."

"Perhaps—" I broke off at the sound of a large splash, staring out at the water and straining to hear it again. Whether it was a large fish jumping or a bird landing or something else, I could not say.

Eva said nothing, listening also.

Rob approached quickly, wading through the rustling tall grass behind me. "Riders approach," he hissed. "Heading into the village."

"Turks? How many?"

"Anatolian light horse," Rob whispered. "Two score, perhaps."

"We could kill them," Eva said. "And flee south."

"Not before some escaped and then we would be in a fighting retreat, looking for a ford and—"

I heard it again, only this time I was certain that it was not an animal.

"What is it?" Walt asked.

"Water slapping on wood," I said. "Oars. A boat. Something.

What can you see?"

They both peered out at the river, their eyes far better than mine at seeing into the darkness.

"It is boats," Eva whispered. "Galleys, heading for the bank. For the landing stage by the village."

"Ours? Or Turks?"

"I do not know."

Leading them back quickly to the rest of the men, I called Walt, Stephen, and Serban to join us.

"Turks in the village," I whispered. "Galleys coming to pick us up from there."

Eva and Rob shot me looks but I ignored them. We would have to assume the ships were meant for us rather than for the Turks. And if they were not, perhaps we would have to kill the crew and row ourselves across. Sometimes one simply has to act decisively and push through.

"Walt, take your half of the men around to the north. Rob, take your half to the edge here. Our cry shall be Belgrade. Let our boats know who we are, yes? Do not pursue any riders that flee. All that matters is that we board the galleys and get across the river. Questions?"

We mounted in the orchard and got our horses lined up ready to attack. The Anatolian's campfires in the ruined village suggested they were simply looking for a place to wait out their night patrol and I hoped that meant they were unprepared to defend themselves. I was determined to wait until Walt got his men in position on the far side of the village but it was impossible for so many men and horses to move in silence and the Turks were alerted to our approach.

A voice cried out a query.

"Hold the men until Walt attacks," I ordered Rob and kicked my horse forward. "Be ready."

"Good evening," I called out in a friendly tone in my best Arabic. "Peace be upon you!"

The closest man on watch shouted back in Turkish. Another man further away called a query and the guard rattled off something in reply.

"Do you speak Arabic?" I called, riding slowly forward into the space between two burned houses. Their roofs had burned away but the walls were solid. I was sure they could not see me very well out in the darkness.

The guard shouted something back and I caught both the surprised tone and the word *Arabiyah*.

"Yes, friends, I am a peaceful and humble merchant from Damascus. Could I share some of your food?" I asked, politely, riding my horse at a slow walk forward.

He came forward, drawing his sword and two more men hurried behind him both bearing their lances.

"You should tell your men that they should not be seated around staring into the fire in that manner," I said, keeping up my friendly tone. "They will not be able to see a thing when we attack."

They shouted at me to stop and I whipped out my sword and roared at them. "Belgrade!"

Raking my spurs to startle my tired horse into action, I charged into the first man, knocking him down. One of the two men froze in shock but the other rushed at me with his lance up and thrust it at my chest. I twisted and leaned in the saddle, the point missing me by an inch, and I cut the other man across the face, spilling his blood and drawing from him a terrific wail. I rode on into the centre of the village, shouting and slashing at anyone I came near, then I rode on through toward the river to draw some after me.

A great cry of *Belgrade!* went up as Walt's twenty-odd men attacked from the north and Rob's company came up behind me, shouting the name of the city.

We made short work of them, and Walt had found their horses before he attacked and so none got away. Still, we had raised an awful cry into the pre-dawn night and all suspected the enemy would be coming to investigate before long.

I hurried to the landing stage where the first galley waited. One of our Serbian guides jumped out and came forward, waving and grinning, very pleased with himself.

"Give him some silver, Stephen," I said, as the man beside him began speaking rapidly in Hungarian. "Give him a lot of silver."

"Come, you must come now, now!" he said. "Now, my lord. Before it is too late."

"We shall do just that," I said. "Where is the army? Where is Hunyadi."

"Coming, coming," the boatman said. "Yes, he is coming."

"When?"

"Soon, soon. Come, you must come. You are fifty men, yes?"

"With servants we are over a hundred," I replied.

He almost swooned, crossing himself repeatedly. "No, no, it cannot be done."

"It will be done. Do it well, and there is silver in it for you."

He eyed me, looking me up and down in the darkness. "You must hurry, we will have to use four boats."

"How many horses can you bring across?"

The man was horrified. "No, no, no. It cannot be. Men, yes. Horses, no."

"Get the men across first and then we will bring as many horses as we can."

"No!" he snapped. "Horses take too long. The Turks will shoot us from the banks. We must away."

"Just six horses then," I said. "I will pay much more."

He crossed his arms and stared at me. "No horses. Not one. You come now, come, come. Just men. Come."

We crossed in five boats, a score of men to each one with our gear piled in amongst us as the sun came up. I waited until the last so I could be certain that all would escape and said farewell to my fine horse.

"Hurry," Stephen said. "Leave the beast be."

"What a fine fellow you are," I said softly, holding his chestnut head in my hands and looking into one of his big, dark eyes. "You crossed mountains without complaint and you always fought well. You never hesitated and did everything I asked of you. I hope that your next master treats you well."

"Perhaps we should kill them?" Stephen said, behind me. "So that the Turks cannot make use them against us."

I turned and stared at him. "Get in the boat, Stephen."

By the time the sun came up, we were out on the river being rowed rapidly downstream toward the city. The galleys were part of a small fleet that yet plied the River Sava, though the Turks had two hundred warships on the Danube. Their fleet nestled behind an island in the mouth of the tributary where it flowed into the massive Danube. Commanding them was a lord I knew named Osvát and he had me brought across to his ship to speak to him. The walls of the castle and city were across the channel to the east and the smoke from the cannons and the campfires filled the air, along with the smell of a summer siege. The cannons sounded continually since dawn, unseen on the opposite side of the city.

"I doubted it was true," he said, taking my hand. "And yet here you are. How did you get by the Turks, Richard?"

"A handful of Serbians have guided us since we crossed the mountains and they helped us reach the river."

"My men believed they were lying and even I thought they must have been mistaken. Is it true you brought thousands of Wallachians with you? Where are they?"

"I expect they went back to Wallachia. There is no way through for a sizeable force and if they had stayed, they would have been destroyed. It is just us."

His face was grim. "Every man will make a difference. We are so low on soldiers. Did you make out their number from the east?"

"Perhaps ninety thousand. Rumelians on the Danube, Anatolians against the Sava there, and Janissaries and the Sultan's camp in the centre. Light horse on the flanks and rear but it seemed as though he has brought mostly infantry this time, in addition to the Janissaries, of which there were perhaps ten thousand."

He sighed. "That is what we have heard. Did you see the cannon?"

"If I had not seen them, I would not have believed it. We counted as many as three hundred, if you can believe it. And a great smoking workshop at the rear churning out smoke and casting even more cannon."

His face was ashen. "I have been praying that the Serbians were exaggerating the number. Three hundred cannon. Even those mighty walls will not stand such an assault for long."

"What of the Sultan's fleet?" I asked. "There were hundreds of ships but they were upstream, beyond the mouth of the Sava in the Danube."

"They are there to block reinforcements and supplies coming from Hungary to the city." He shook his head. "Turks with two hundred war galleys. Can you believe it?"

"And Hunyadi?" I asked. "He is coming?"

Osvát hesitated before answering, turning to look northwest as if he might see that very thing. When he spoke, his voice was sharp. "He is coming. We have had word. Hunyadi is coming."

"And yet you sound embittered, my lord."

He leaned on the side rail and spoke without turning. "They have abandoned him. Our great lords have not come. Our kingdom is on the eve of a terrible disaster, for neither with our own resources nor with the aid of the mercenaries we have engaged can we bring enough forces to cope with the Turk. Our only hope is that God will listen to our prayers and move the hearts of our treacherous princes to bring their fleets and men.

And yet so pressing is our peril that the delay of a day or even an hour may bring about such a defeat as shall make all Christendom weep for evermore."

"What of the crusaders?" I asked. "Led by Cardinal John of Capistrano?"

"They came down the Danube to meet Hunyadi. Ten thousand at least, camped miles up there with the Regent."

"Well, that is something to thank Christ for."

"Common men with sticks? There are thousands of them but what can they do? Even if they get into the city, all they can do is fetch water and rebuild walls and so on but as for fighting the Turks..." he trailed off.

We watched the horizon. "How is it that you are still here? You must have over twenty boats here."

"Forty," he said, smiling. "I have forty boats, most small but some as you see. The others are hidden in bays around the island, or pulled up on shore and some are patrolling, keeping watch. Yes, forty boats, thanks to Christ."

"But how has the Turkish fleet not assaulted you?"

"They do not wish to come under the guns on the walls. And I do not believe they know how many we are. We are hidden here behind the island. If they knew what a threat we were to their fleet, they would perhaps chance it."

"Well, then, I thank you for sending the galleys to pick us up. It was a risk to you. But can you now transport us to the opposite bank? I would like to take my men along the south bank of the Danube, find Hunyadi's army and join it for their assault on the enemy."

He turned, surprised. "The Turkish fleet holds the river and they have men on the banks, also. You will not make it through by land or by river. Hunyadi cannot bring his army by river, due to the Turkish blockade upstream."

"So he will march along the banks, to the Sava?" I said.

"And then I am to ferry them across. As many as I can before we are destroyed by the enemy fleet. I will get Hunyadi across at the least, if it is the last thing I do. With his leadership to inspire the men inside the walls, perhaps we will have a chance."

"You can get him inside the city?"

Osvát pointed to a landing stage at the base of the wall, right at the river. Large enough for three galleys to moor against at once, there was a short stair up to a small postern gate. "I can take your men across now, if you like."

There was no point in trapping my men further inside a doomed city. "No," I said. "With your permission, my men will serve on your fleet until Hunyadi arrives."

And if he does not, we shall have to flee.

"Glad to have you," Osvát said. "But if the city falls first, I am to evacuate as many as I can to the far bank. I shall have to disembark your men there first. Perhaps you can help escort them to Hungary?" He crossed himself. "But God will not allow that. Hunyadi will come. By one way or by another, Hunyadi will come." Osvát crossed himself again.

I hung my head. Through my own recklessness, I had brought my company, all of the Order of the White Dagger, into a trap from which there might be no escape.

∞

For two days, my company was distributed amongst the fleet where we manned the boats and we all waited anxiously for word of Hunyadi's army. As subtly as we could, my immortals consumed the blood of their servants without any of Osvát's men noticing. If they did, they said nothing about it. Perhaps they had bigger concerns. The cannons never ceased their firing and it seemed certain that Belgrade would be assaulted on the far side of the city at any moment. Smoke from fires and cannons and guns drifted over the walls and across the waters and birds wheeled overhead. What they made of it all, I could only wonder.

"I have been thinking," I muttered to Eva at the rail, leaning close to her. Like all of us, she stayed in her armour all day and she stank just as much as I did.

"Then times are desperate indeed," she quipped, looking across the Sava to the northwest, where we hoped every hour to see sign of Hunyadi's army.

"I have been thinking about your suggestion to sneak into William's tent at night and there assassinate him."

"Richard, I suggested no such thing. That was your notion, not mine."

"Well, whoever suggested it, I think the time has come to—"

"Wait," she said, grabbing my vambrace. "Christian riders."

From the opposite bank of the Sava, those riders pushed through the long grass and reeds to the water's edge and signalled to our fleet. Boats were sent to bring the men across to the island and finally to Osvát's boat. I made certain I was present when the message was delivered.

"My lord comes with every boat and every man that he can find," the messenger said, a fair Hungarian youth with ruddy cheeks and fluff on his cheeks. "When he attacks the Turkish fleet, he asks that you bring your fleet to attack their rear."

"Your lord?" I said. "Hunyadi?"

The messenger bowed. "Indeed, sir."

I looked at Osvát, who seemed astonished. "Hunyadi is going to attack the Turkish war galleys? By Almighty Christ. How many boats does he have?"

"Almost two hundred, my lord."

Excited, I could not hold my tongue. "That is as many as the Turks have, is it not?"

Osvát nodded but he turned to the messenger. "What manner of boats are these? They cannot all be warships?"

The young man's cheeks coloured, as if he were personally embarrassed. "Crafts of many kinds, my lord. Transports, galleys..." he trailed off. "Fishing vessels. Many kinds."

"Dear Christ," Osvát said, crossing himself.

"And the army is on the ships and we will fight our way through but there is also the army of the crusaders," the messenger said. "Lead by Cardinal John of Capistrano. They come in a great body of many thousands, keeping pace with the fleet as best they can."

"Many thousands of peasants with sharp sticks?" I said. "Just what we need."

The young man was offended by my cynicism. "They have taken the cross to fight for Christ, sir, and they are filled with His strength."

I bowed to the fellow. "I am sure they are."

Osvát nodded to himself, looking out at the waters. "Are you and your men to return?"

He shook his fair locks. "We barely made it through the Turkish patrols on our way here. Besides, there is no time. He comes now, my lord. We are to join you for the battle, sirs, if you will honour us so."

"No time? When will he assault the Turkish fleet?"

"Today, my lord."

Osvát, to his credit, smiled and took the young fellow's hand for a moment before turning to issue a stream of commands. Boats skirted off in all directions, taking messengers to the city and to other vessels in the fleet.

"I will drop you on the far shore, if you wish it," Osvát said. "So that you can go out to meet the force by land. Or I could send you into the city, perhaps, if there is time. But I would rather have your men fighting in my ships."

More than anything, I hated boats. I hated the sea most of all, with its impossibly high waves and the motion of the boats in it. But the Danube was a river like few others. As wide as a lake and endlessly long. Fighting on boats was as brutal and bloody a battle as one might find. Then again, I had done it before.

"Certainly, we shall join you."

Osvát stepped closer and lowered his voice. "We shall fight with all we are worth but it is likely that we shall fail to destroy their fleet and we will have to withdraw. But I mean to make a hole big enough, for long enough, for as much of Hunyadi's army as is possible to reach the city. If we can draw the Turks close to the city, perhaps they will break off and flee. Do you see?"

Damn. I wished I had thought about offering my services before knowing the plan.

"Very well. We shall do what we need to. I would fight with my closest men beside me, if you will send me to their galley."

"We will bring them here, no more than a dozen, and you will fight with me." Osvát grinned. "I have seen you and your men in battle."

It was not midday when the fighting started. Hunyadi's makeshift fleet came down the Danube flying flags and banging drums.

The Turkish fleet manoeuvred to face them and we edged out through the channel into the Danube behind them, trapping the enemy's war galleys between Hunyadi's larger, makeshift fleet and our smaller, well-equipped one of forty ships crewed with Hungarians and Serbians.

"You look unhappy, Serban," I said to him as we approached the enemy.

"I do not swim," he said.

"Then do not fall in," I said, and clapped him hard on the back. "Have you fought on ships before?"

"No," he admitted, shielding his eyes from the sun and pulling his hat down.

"The most important thing above all else is to keep your feet. Stay away from the sides as much as you can," I advised.

"Remember that boats move, sometimes drastically, even when they seem stable. And the decks are slippery, especially when the blood starts to be spilled. If you fall, roll away and keep moving as best you can. We will stay together, all of us, and fight as one."

Rob elbowed him. "Stick with me, Serban. I'll keep an eye out for you."

Serban glanced at Rob's stump and attempted to smile in thanks.

Our rowers heaved for all they were worth and the ships with sails made the most of the diagonal crosswinds. Still, it took us a long time to join the battle that had by that time already been raging for hours. As we approached the sound of guns firing grew and the shouting of the crews and soldiers filled the air. Arrows streamed in all directions and small cannons on the boats fired at each other.

It was like heading into hell.

Hunyadi's fleet may have been thrown together but there were some magnificent vessels that were a part of it. His flagship was the biggest of all the ships on the river by far and it poured fire from hand-gunners into the enemies on all sides. His ships were filled to the rails with archers, hand-gunners, and soldiers armed with pikes and halberds and axes but it was not his entire force.

On the southern bank were ten thousand men or more in a great swirling mass. I recognised banners from Transylvania that I knew belonged to horsemen. But most of the men were the peasant crusaders I had heard about, armed with slings, hunting bows, threshers and probably sharpened hoes and pointed sticks. They massed on the banks and shot arrows and slung stones and shot at the Turkish ships that came close to shore.

"The Turks are outmatched!" Osvát shouted in my ear as we approached, grasping my arm and shaking me. He turned to his crew. "Signal the fleet to spread out. We can trap them all. Kill them all. Let none escape! Christ be praised, the Turks are outmatched."

Their ships were pushed aside by ours and many were forced hard against the banks. There, the crusaders swarmed them and slaughtered them. One was swiftly set on fire and it went up like a demonic candle, burning hot and bright.

Osvát steered our ship into another galley that attempted to flee and crashed into it hard enough to throw us onto our knees. The Turkish galley was stuck with arrows and the side was covered in charred timber and soot where a fire had been put out. Wounded men lay in the bottom of it already but when our hulls ground against each other, they seemed keen enough for a fight.

"With me!" I shouted and led my companions across and down into their galley. My men made short work of the enemy and soon we got back on board our own vessel and looked for more prey.

Osvát cheered us and even Serban had a smile on his face.

We captured or destroyed at least a hundred and fifty of their fleet. By the end, they were burning their own immobilised ships before abandoning them so they would not fall into our hands. The remaining handful fled downstream, being peppered with shots from the walls and towers of Belgrade as they went.

The battle lasted many hours and the men were exhausted but were buoyed by the elation that victory brings. The way was clear now for Hunyadi's army to be ferried into the city by the docks on the Sava side, protected from the Sultan's army by the walls and mass of the city itself.

It was a relief of sorts to see my company through the postern gate and finally into Belgrade, where we had hoped to be for so many days.

And yet even while the river battle raged, the enemy cannon had not ceased their bombardment and we knew we would soon have another fight on our hands.

This time it would be a fight to save the city itself.

A week after the river battle and the outer walls of Belgrade were crumbling.

Our cannons would fire out at the Turks as often as they could, hoping to destroy an enemy cannon but often as not hitting Turkish earthworks or ploughing a useless furrow into the mud. There had been a giddy moment of joy days earlier when a cannon on the city's easternmost tower shot and killed the Beylerbey of Rumelia, striking him down, killing him, his horse and at least two of his servants. The damned fool had been inspecting the front lines of the siege within range of our guns, in broad daylight, flying his banners and gesticulating toward us as he no doubt propounded to his men on how the city would fall. It was a lucky shot, to be sure, but many in the city took it to be a sign from God and who was I to argue with that?

We certainly needed the victory, no matter how small it was. The city was as well prepared for a siege as it was possible to be. Indeed, it had been preparing for over a decade, for it was no secret that it would be so assaulted, and there were supplies enough to last months, even with twenty thousand extra mouths to feed with the arrival of Hunyadi's army and the crusaders. And with the river cleared, it meant more supplies could be brought in at will along with reinforcements. We knew we could therefore survive a siege indefinitely.

And the Sultan would know it, too.

The only way he could take Belgrade now was by direct assault and so we waited, day after day, night after night. Waited for the sudden assault by tens of thousands of veteran infantry on the outer walls of the city. The repairs on both the outer and inner curtain walls went on ceaselessly. Every breach was filled with rubble and shorn up by enormous timbers. When these were blown apart, they were built back up again, stronger than before.

"I made a mistake," I admitted to Eva as we stood on the steps of a church and watched the repairs from a distance, the air filled with smoke and dust and the shouts of the men rebuilding and the ringing of mallets and hammers. "I should never have brought us here. Especially after Constantinople. I have trapped us once more."

"Your reasoning was not faulty," she said. "But I sometimes do wonder..."

"What do you wonder?"

"You often make it so that you will have an impossible victory or death. When instead you would do better to wait and pick another battle. What is it to the likes of us if Hungary falls? Might we not in our long lives see a dozen kingdoms fall and another dozen rise in their place?"

"You sound like Priskos. As if mortal matters mean nothing."

"Not nothing. And yet we are so much more than they." She jerked her chin at the men toiling at the walls. The streets near the landward walls of the city were where the crusaders had been quartered, packed in with a dozen in each room and others sleeping huddled on the streets. Some were active in helping with the repairs while others seemed to do little but pray, while others lay slumped in alleys, drunk or sick. Our holy army.

"It is easy to feel contempt for the smallness of their lives," I said. "At the same time, I feel less than they are. They are natural, living, dying. Raising sons and daughters. While we... endure."

She lowered her voice and glanced around. "It is not too late to flee. We could go through the castle, down to the river. Take a boat."

"We cannot."

"No," she admitted. "No, we cannot."

The next day, in the full light of day, the enemy broke through,

The Turks assembled in their tens of thousands and charged the walls in waves. Our brave garrison poured down fire from cannon and the hand-gunners and crossbowmen shot as quickly as they could, and arrows flew into the advancing men but still they came on and assaulted the high breaches and the gates with ladders and ropes while others behind them shot back at our men on the battlements.

"We must stay out of it for as long as possible," I said to my company in our quarters near to the castle. "The mortals must do their work at the walls. We must save ourselves, where we can, for our true enemy."

Claudin raised his hand. "We will look like cowards, no?"

"No. We will stay close to Hunyadi and the other commanders. We must have patience. There will be fighting enough for all of us before all is said and done here. Now, bleed your servants and drink while you can."

Late in the day, the Turks breached the outer walls. The garrison and the mass of crusaders fell back in panic while the professional soldiers attempted to stem the tide in every street and courtyard. But the blind retreat was unstoppable. They swarmed by our position in their hundreds and ran across the drawbridge into the inner fortress where they hoped to be safe. And yet that drawbridge could not be closed before the pursuing Turks reached it. The Janissaries swarmed over the drawbridge into the fortress courtyard and they began slaughtering the crusaders, militia, and soldiers inside.

By the time we rushed to the fortress, the streets were so packed with panicked peasants that we could not get close to the enemies that had broken through.

"We are close to disaster!" Stephen shouted at me. "What do we do, Richard?"

"Guard this position," I commanded my men. "Walt, with me."

I pushed forward through the bodyguards and lords crowding

257

Hunyadi, meaning to discover what his plan was. If something drastic was not done, the city would be taken before sunrise the next day.

"We must secure the city walls," one of the lords shouted at Hunyadi.

"Yes," another cried. "We must assault the walls, my lord!"

"No," he shouted. "The Janissaries are enclosed within the inner fortress. We attack their rear, trap them within our fortress, and kill them to a man. They are the Sultan's best troops and we shall slaughter them all, then retake our outer walls. All of you, with me. Bring every man you can. God be with us."

I pushed back to my company and told them that we do as Hunyadi commanded.

"Are they the red bastards?" Garcia asked. "These Janissaries?"

"If they are, we will kill them."

We rushed through the panicked streets to the inner fortress, where there were so many Turkish infantry and white-robed Janissaries that they could not all fit inside the fortress and instead massed on the drawbridge, as if waiting their turn to kill our men. Our assault on their rear took them by surprise and they had no room to manoeuvre. Hunyadi's men killed them, cutting them down and stepping forward and killing the next man and the next but the approach to the fortress was so dense with enemies and they could not fly through them with ease. The flagstones underfoot ran slick with blood and the air was filled with the smell of it, along with the screams and shouts of the dying Turks.

Holding my company back behind the Hungarians, we finished off any survivors that writhed on the floor.

"No immortals!" Claudin shouted.

"Quiet, you fool," Walt snapped at him.

Soon, Hunyadi's men reached the edge of the drawbridge, slaughtering the men who stood shoulder to shoulder now. Beyond the drawbridge, still thousands more Janissaries attacked our men.

"Damn the bastards for this," I muttered, feeling a desire to throw myself at them.

"A fire!" someone shouted. "They set a fire!"

Smoke billowed up beneath the men on the bridge and then the yellow flames flickered behind and amongst the Janissaries.

"What is happening?" Rob asked.

"The Turks have fired the drawbridge," I said, raising my voice so my men and allies could hear.

"But they have cut off their means of escape," Jan said.

"And they kill their own men who stand on the bridge," Rob said.

The fires grew and many of the Janissaries on the bridge jumped thirty feet down into the dry moat below, breaking their legs and trapping themselves.

"They are burning the bridge so that we cannot save our people within. They trust their reinforcements outside the walls to come in and take the city."

"There is no other way into the fortress, now," Stephen said.

"Aye," Walt said. "Best go to the outer walls instead, Richard?"

"Wait," I said. "The entrance from the river into the city comes up through the fortress."

"From the boats?" Stephen said. "That is all very well but how do we get out of the city and reach the river in order to come in through the back door?"

"We shall fight our way clear of the city walls and get down to the river," I replied. "The defenders within the fortress will hold out long enough for us to do so and—"

"Richard!" Eva said, grabbing me by the armour and yanking me around to face her. Her eyes were wide and angry. "You do not have to do everything yourself. You said the mortals must do their work and we must save ourselves for our true enemy. So tell Hunyadi. He has thousands of men."

"Yes, yes," I said. "But can anyone do the job but us?"

She pulled my arm and shook it. "And when William's red Janissaries come marching through the streets, who here can do the job of stopping them?"

"Damn you, woman," I said. "Where is Hunyadi?"

It was a fight just to get close to the man but when I suggested he send a message to the fleet to assault the fortress from the Sava, he cut me off and began issuing orders for that very thing. Six lords or knights were given the task, along with their retinues and companies, to reach the river by different directions so that one at least would get through.

As they made off, Hunyadi glanced at me. "Something else, Richard?"

His helm was off and his cap beneath was soaked with sweat. Hunyadi looked old, the light of torches, lanterns, and the fire of the burning bridge picking out the deep lines in his grey face.

"Have the red Janissaries been sighted, my lord?" I asked. "Or the banner of Zaganos Pasha?"

He shook his head. "Ask Michael," he said, jerking his head and turning to command his men for the defence of the city.

Pushing through the soldiers, I made my way toward the banner of Michael Szilágyi, the commander of the fortress of Belgrade, a great lord, and the brother of Hunyadi's wife.

"My lord," I said, raising my voice and interrupting the knights speaking to him. "My lord, have the red Janissaries been seen within the walls?"

"Richard?" he looked me up and down. "Last I heard, the red-robed bastards are yet beyond both walls, outside the breaches, guarding the Sultan. I doubt we shall see them anywhere that the Sultan is not. Where is your company?"

"With me."

"The Turks are within the city walls but they have not broken through everywhere. We are holding them in every quarter. If we act *now*, we can get behind them and trap them inside before we slaughter them. I will take my men along the Danube wall before attacking their flank. Will you join us?"

If William's immortals were beyond the breaches, we would do well to keep them there lest they slaughter their way to victory. And Szilágyi's flanking attack would take me close to the red Janissaries' position.

"It would be an honour, my lord."

Szilágyi was a good leader and a competent commander. His lords liked him and the men trusted him and so when he marched off for the walls, he drew hundreds along behind him. A more cautious man would have waited until more precise orders were given and until more men had assembled, but there are times for caution and there are times to throw oneself into danger.

Our numbers overwhelmed the Rumelian infantry on the northern flank and we pushed on through the streets, spreading out where we could. The fighting at each juncture was hard but brief, and the Turks fled, in one company after another. It soon seemed that the battle had swung in our favour, for our men were filled with vigour and high spirits and the Rumelians and Anatolians were crumbling, their morale shattered. No soldier likes to find his enemy has gotten behind him but the Turks were taking to their heels before we could even reach them.

"Is it a ruse?" Stephen asked beside me after catching his breath. We watched two hundred well-armoured Rumelian soldiers pushing each other aside in an effort to get back to the breach in the outer wall. "Will our men be trapped and counter-attacked?"

"Perhaps," I said. "But it is difficult for ordinary soldiers to feign fear so effectively. They expected no resistance. They believed that breaking into the city would be like Constantinople all over again, and all the fighting they would need to do would be over wine jugs and women. Our resistance broke their spirit."

"The Red Janissaries have not yet engaged?"

"That seems to be the case."

"Why would he not throw them in now and push on to victory?"

"Even immortals can be killed, especially in narrow streets. Anyway, tonight's battle for the walls may be over but the enemy is not defeated. They will come again, tomorrow perhaps, and again until one of us is truly broken."

By sunrise, the fighting was essentially over. The Hungarians and Serbians had forced their way into the fortress and had slaughtered the Janissaries trapped within. After the killing had been going on for some time, Hunyadi and Szilágyi's men threw down a makeshift bridge over the remnants of the still-smouldering drawbridge, crossed the chasm and sent hundreds of heavily armoured men across. Caught between the two Christian forces, the Janissaries died in their thousands. The fortress ran with blood and the dawn air was filled with screams.

Watching from across the bridge, it turned my stomach to see it. The Janissaries were our enemies, it was true. They worshipped the God of the Mohammedans. But they were our own people by blood, our sons and brothers, and they should have been fighting beside us instead of dying beneath our blades.

But the job was done and done well.

It had been a close thing, perhaps, but the Serbian militia, the Hungarian peasant crusaders, the foreign mercenaries like me and my men, and the Hungarian lords and their retinues, had all held fast and so done their duty.

But the task was not yet done.

"I had hoped that they would pack up and leave," Walt said from the top of the city's inner wall walk when I joined him and the others in the morning. He yawned and rubbed his eyes, squinting at the light. "What did our great lords have to say?"

"As much as always," I replied as Eva passed me a jug of wine. I drank two great gulps and wished it was blood I was supping. Our squires stood ready with our helms but we were clad in the rest of our armour.

Beyond was the lower outer wall with its crumbling breaches. Outside of that was the enemy siege works and the huge camps themselves. Tens of thousands of men, ready and willing to come back and kill us. The crews for the hundreds of cannons were busy preparing their weapons for the day's bombardment.

Rob sat in shadow with his knees up and his back to the parapet wall, head back and eyes closed, snoring away like he was in a feather bed.

Walt followed my eyes and smiled. "You made him a knight, Richard, but he'll always be an archer at heart."

"What have they decided?" Eva asked.

I shrugged. "Repair the breaches, restock the powder and shot, and pray the Sultan does not come back again tonight."

Walt sighed and his head drooped. "These people lack boldness."

"It is true," Serban muttered. "They fear losing more than they long for victory."

"What did you say to them?" Eva asked.

"I politely suggested we might assemble every able man right now and drive the Turks from Christendom."

"Politely?" Eva repeated.

Walt snorted.

"I *was* polite," I snapped. "I even suggested a compromise. A limited sortie on the enemy lines to destroy their cannons." I pointed at them in the distance. "Perhaps they would then withdraw. No Janissaries, no cannons. It would be enough to force Sultan Mehmed to withdraw, surely."

"And our lords declined, I take it?" Stephen said, pulling the brim of his hat down. His eyes were yet wild. He had seen more of war than most mortal soldiers ever would and yet he never grew used to it.

"We would be outnumbered on the field. We risked more than we might gain. The battle would more likely be lost than won. The usual."

Walt slapped a hand on the parapet. "Bloody fools. They would rather sit here and die slowly than die like a man?"

Stephen smiled. "One suspects they would rather not die at all, Walt."

"It's no easy thing," Rob said from where he sat, his eyes yet closed and his head back. "Leaving the safety of these mighty stone walls. No easy thing to be bold. A man would have to be halfway mad to leave his castle to attack an army of barbarians beyond the gates. And you're right enough, Stephen. Most soldiers, lords especially, would rather victory be won by someone else so that they might live to fight another day."

"Truly spoken, brother." Walt grinned. "Shame we ain't got an army of madmen here instead of great lords, ain't it."

"But we do," I said, turning to look down into the city. "Come on."

We made our way through the city to the quarters of the Roman delegation, led by John of Capistrano.

He was a Franciscan friar and a powerful Catholic priest and cardinal, a friend of the Pope, no less, and he had at least a score of priests and monks trailing him wherever he went, along with dozens of servants and supplicants and desperate souls wishing to hand him some pathetic gift or to beg for his prayers. As such, he was never a difficult man to find but he was always difficult to get close to.

John of Capistrano was holding court in a large house in the north-eastern quarter, not far from where the cannons once more took up their bombardment of the walls. The streets were filthy with grime and it stank of wet shit everywhere.

A mass of crusaders pressed in close to the cardinal's house, hoping for sight or sound of their illustrious and beloved leader. Luckily, I have never minded pushing a gaggle of peasants and priests aside when it is called for.

"And who are you, my lord?" a fat monk asked, pushing his belly between me and the interior of the house. "And what might be your business?"

I leaned in close to his face and lowered my voice. "I am a soldier of Christ and my business is cutting the heads off Turks."

He furrowed his bushy brows. "If you have business with Brother John, I will take to him your message, my lord."

Pushing him aside, I stepped into the room where John of Capistrano was speaking, surrounded by monks and priests hanging on his every word. An old man with a bald head and masses of grey hair over his ears, he wore nothing grander than a plain monk's robe. But even had I not seen him before, I would have known which of the men in the room he was, for he had a commanding presence and a magnificent, booming voice.

"What is it?" he said, his Italian accent very strong, breaking off from his discussion. "What has happened?"

"Nothing, my lord," I said in French. "I merely came to speak with you."

He frowned and replied in kind. "I recognise you. Richard the Englishman, is it not? Do you mean me harm?"

"Harm? Why would I wish you harm, my lord?"

"I have heard the stories about you. The bloodthirsty slayer of Vlad Dracul. You have never been seen in a church. They say you drink your servant's blood."

Spreading my hands, I smiled. "It is all true. But I am a Christian, my lord, and more than anything I love Christ and pray daily for my salvation."

He snorted. "You have the smell of heresy about you, boy."

"Never, my lord."

"They say you are sympathetic to the Hussites," he said, his voice ringing from the walls of the small chamber. "And you enjoy the company of the Jew."

The meeting was not going as I had intended. "Perhaps someone heard me express admiration for the Hussites' ways in battle, which our own regent has emulated with great success. But I do not hold with their views. Indeed, I do not know what they are, precisely, only enough to know that I will not stand for such heresy."

In truth, much of what I had heard, especially with respect to indulgences, sounded rather appealing to me but I knew never to say such things in company. Whenever there were discussions on the matter, I held my tongue. But that is the way with heresies. Either one joins in wholeheartedly in condemnation or one is considered a sympathiser, which means one is a heretic also.

John of Capistrano lifted his chin. "So you do not deny enjoying the company of Jews?"

I sighed. "Of course, my lord, I hold the Jews in contempt, just as much as anyone. It is merely that myself and my companions often seek information about our enemies, the Turks. And as you know, the Jews are welcomed in those lands, travelling to do business whether mercantile or diplomatic. And many of these Jews will happily speak of the things they see, if your coin is good."

The great priest shook his head in disapproval, lifting a finger and taking a deep breath. "A good Christian would never commune with Jews, as you do, sir. A man of godly character could not stoop so low as that. And he who trusts the word of a Jew makes himself a fool before God and the world. No, no, I will not abase myself by conversing with a friend to Jews."

"We are hardly friendly with them," I snapped.

"Do you break bread with them? Do you share wine?"

I floundered, irritated at having to discuss such a pointless thing. "It is a transaction, no more. A trade. We purchase their words with coin and while we discuss—"

"You purchase *lies*," he said. "And I will not listen a moment longer to one who breaks bread with the murderers of Christ. Mind your tongue and begone from my sight, sir."

In the silence, the room resounded with his loud voice. Monks and priests stared at me while the greatest amongst them pointedly turned his back on me and began conversing with the man beside him.

I turned and pushed my way outside and through the crowd to my men.

"What happened?" Eva asked, aghast at my expression.

"I am not certain," I said.

"Is he willing to lead his men against the Turks?" Stephen asked.

"We did not reach a point in the discussion that allowed the question to be raised."

"What do you mean?" Stephen asked. "How could you not ask him?"

Ignoring him, I addressed Rob and Walt. "What do you think of the crusaders?"

"Keen as mustard," Walt said.

"They are stark raving mad," Rob said. "Which is what we want, of course."

"Serban?" I asked. "Do these men want to attack?"

Beneath his steel hat, his face was grim. "More than anything, they wish to strike a blow against the enemies of Christ."

Walt nodded. "Some of them keep trying to sneak out and have a go at the Turk all by themselves. You know, groups of young lads, that sort of thing."

"What about the rest of them?"

Rob gestured with his stump. "Speak to them yourself, Richard. They came here to drive the Turks from Christendom. After last night, with their mallets and clubs still bloody, they know for certain that God is with them. God wills this. There is no fear or doubt amongst them. Come on."

When it came to knowing the hearts of common folk, whether soldier or peasant, Rob was never wrong. And so it proved.

Men asked if I had seen their actions the night before or if it was time to make an attack on the enemy. Others stopped us to ask for advice on how to use this weapon or that, or what was the best way to kill a man in armour. Some wished to show me their knife or the spear they had taken from an enemy. A few men strutted about in pieces of armour they had stripped from corpses. Their mood was high indeed. And dangerously high, for we witnessed more than one angry argument and two fellows almost came to blows before their friends drew them apart.

"Won't take much," Walt said softly, raising his eyebrows.

"We would be sending them to their deaths," I replied. "All these fine people."

Rob held his nose. "These fine people have turned the streets into rivers of shit. It is no wonder they would rather be outside."

"It is what they want," Walt said. "We'd be sending them to glory."

"Not much glory dying in a ditch, Walt," I said, looking at the filthy people, some laughing and others clutching their bellies.

"There's glory in saving Christendom, though."

"Rob?"

He scratched his stump as he regarded the men, nodding to one or two who caught his eye. "We must all make sacrifices for our world. The order of things does maintain itself. Walls are nothing without the blood spilled to protect them."

I sighed. "It must be all of them, or it would be better for it to be none."

"Start the stone rolling and the mountainside will fall," Stephen said. "Where one peasant goes, the rest shall follow."

"How will they even know where to go?" Eva asked. "They will get bogged down out there, trapped, and destroyed. We will have gained nought but lost a great deal."

"It is as I said before," I replied, sighing. "They must be led."

"But John of Capistrano will not even speak to you."

"We shall lead them. Each of us."

Eva shook her head. "Richard, this is not—"

I placed my hands on her armoured shoulders. "You were quite right last night. There is no need to carry out such a task when there is another who will do it. I agree. But now there is only us."

She looked up at the sky. "Your heart's desire is to fight and so that is where your reason leads you."

"I would never argue with you, Eva," I said, drawing scorn from her and quiet laughter from the others. "But we can have victory today or defeat tomorrow. And I know what I chose."

She gave a small nod. "We should none of us get ourselves cut off from retreat back to the city, agreed?"

We all gave our assent.

"Rob, Walt, you find a group of angry young fellows and rile them up. Tell them to spread the word."

"What word?" Walt asked, frowning.

"What should we say, Richard?" Rob said.

"Men rarely wish to be the first but they will fight the devil to avoid being last. Tell them that we are attacking. No, tell them that the attack has begun. We must hurry or we shall miss the attack. And lead them out. The fighting will be desperate, disorganised. They will have to cross from ditch to ditch, killing the Turks hiding in their trenches and their holes. But we must push on and on. Serban? You take some men and find drums, trumpets, and go to the walls and make some noise. It need not be proper signals, just make it loud. Raise your voices and sing if you must. Stephen? Eva? You must go to Hunyadi and Szilágyi and tell them that the crusaders are not only attacking but they are *winning*. The crusaders are driving the Turks away. They are going to destroy the enemy cannons. But they must have support from the soldiers."

"But that may not be so," Stephen argued. "Even by the time we reach the lords."

"If you do not say it, Stephen, then it shall never be so. By speaking it, you will make it come true, do you understand?"

Walt grinned. "We done some foolish acts in our time, Richard, but this is—"

"None of that, Walter. Hurry now, let us gather our men, and then we shall stir these shit-stinking warriors into action."

The Hungarian crusaders were filled with their recent victory and they jumped into action. Few doubted the words we spoke, even the first of them who pushed their way up and across the breaches and down toward the enemy siege works while the cannons blasted the walls overhead. The stream of men turned into a torrent and soon there were hundreds and finally thousands of common folk wading their way over the churned mud toward the enemy lines.

Surprise was on our side. I doubt the Turks could believe what they were seeing at first. To them we would have looked like a mass of desperate civilians fleeing the city but if they had any doubts initially, we soon showed them our true intent. Forward positions with small cannons and hand-gunners were overrun with barely a shot being fired. Our crusaders ran gleefully through the trenches, battering any enemy who stood to fight. We swarmed each palisade or position and overwhelmed it before doing the same to the ones beside and behind it. Every time I looked back toward the city, our numbers had swelled further and there was a line of men all the way back to the walls.

Whether we lived or died depended on Hunyadi and Szilágyi. Would they abandon the fools who had attacked without orders or would they seize the opportunity?

A huge cheer spread through our men and at first I assumed the Sultan had fled or, more likely, Hunyadi had come. Instead, we discovered that the ancient priest John of Capistrano had come to join the attack. A while later I saw him, still wearing his monk's robe, swinging a bloody mace over his head into the skull of a cowering Turk while roaring some prayer.

Turkish cavalry finally came to attack, as I had dreaded, charging our flanks in a thundering of hooves and flashing blades.

We lost a lot of men but the crisscrossing earthworks now worked in our favour as the cavalry could not charge through them to kill our peasant soldiers. Still, they pushed slowly in between the lines of interconnecting trenches and palisades and did their bloody work more slowly. Our crusaders did not break, though. Far from it. They swarmed the slow or stationary cavalry

273

and killed the riders.

Finally, Szilágyi and Hunyadi led out their men against the entire Turkish line.

With their help, we pushed the Turks away from their cannon and because we now had professional gunners with us, we trained the enemy cannon on the enemy. Although the massive guns could only be turned with teams of men and horses, the smaller cannons were turned about or brought up and aimed toward the Turkish centre.

Where the Sultan was.

He yet had thousands of men defending his central position, not to mention William's immortal Janissaries but slowly we crushed or drove off both wings and the cannons opened up on the Sultan's men.

"We need to get to Hunyadi," I said to the men of my company. "Tell him not to engage the red Janissaries again. Let the cannons do the work."

"He knows by now," Walt said. "Surely to God, he knows."

"He may know," Rob said, jabbing his arm across the battlefield. "But someone should have told his men."

The Hungarians and Serbs made a series of assaults on the dwindling Turkish centre. But they broke themselves repeatedly on William's Janissaries who could not be pushed aside or broken, no matter how many charges crashed against them.

We went from gun to gun, begging those in charge of it to aim their fire at the small target of the Janissary formation. Kill those five hundred men, I would say, and we win the battle and save Christendom.

Some men agreed but most of the rest told me to mind my own business or said they were determined to kill the Sultan himself. Considering the unreliable accuracy of those guns, other than a lucky shot, there was little hope of that. But still, every artilleryman I ever met, from the earliest days down through the centuries, claimed he could shoot the cock off a gnat if only I would stop talking to him.

"Should we attack?" Rob asked, shouting over the noise of the cannons. "William and his men are there, deep in that formation."

"I cannot lead us into that death trap, Rob," I said. "Our new cannons may do the work for us."

"If not?" he said.

"We shall have to be content with a victory," I replied. "We must be patient."

Night fell and it was a dark one. The battle turned to skirmishes and those to withdrawals.

The Sultan took his remaining men away with him in the darkness, and William was gone with him.

Belgrade had been saved.

And yet there would be more casualties to come.

The Turks left behind a staggering amount of treasure and provisions in their abandoned camp.

Once the bodies were collected and burned and buried, the priests calculated that we had killed about twenty-five thousand Turks within or outside the walls of Belgrade. It was an incredible and unlikely victory.

Later, we found out that the Sultan had retreated to Sofia and then had several of his generals executed. Sadly, William was not one of them. He had done his job.

We would also hear that Pope Eugenius IV called the salvation of Belgrade the happiest event of his life.

And the battle was hardly over when the plague struck.

It was a camp sickness, brought about by fouled water and hundreds of thousands of people eating, drinking and shitting in proximity for weeks on end. We knew even in those days that bad water and rotten food caused sickness and we knew that stricken people spread their afflictions to others. But what could we do in such situations as sieges, when it was bad food or no food? Whenever armies camped in one place for long, many more people than usual would fall ill. But sometimes, as during that hot, wet summer in Belgrade, a terrible plague might appear. In this case, it was probably brought by the invading army and contracted by us when we killed them and looted their camp. Or perhaps the peasants brought it and spread it due to their filthy conditions in the city.

Whatever the cause, the crusaders died in their thousands, the Serbian residents died, mercenaries from all over died.

Janos Hunyadi died.

He was over sixty years old and had been leading vast campaigns for his entire adult life. After the pressures at Belgrade, he was weakened in spirit and in body. And the illness took hold of him mercilessly.

Before he succumbed, he sent for me. I was surprised, to say the least, and it was clear from the grave and displeased faces of his men that they felt the same.

"Do not tax him," Szilágyi said, grasping my arm. "Do not go within, Richard."

I stared at him for a moment and looked at his hand. He withdrew it and stepped back.

"You are afraid that he might die," I said, understanding his anger. "But he summoned me."

"Why?"

"I have no idea. You know, my lord, if you wish it you could bar me from entering and he will likely not live to voice his displeasure."

Szilágyi, shamed, nodded his head toward the door and I ducked inside. The room was hot and humid, with fabric over the shuttered windows and curtains around the bed and a crowd of people crammed within. His servants and physicians busied themselves and priests prayed.

"Sir Richard," his chamberlain said. "My lord is awake, come closer."

Hunyadi's face was pale and he stank of foul shit. A servant wiped his lips with a wet cloth and Hunyadi raised a hand to mine. I did not want to take it but I did. It was ice cold and sweaty.

"Richard," he said, his voice a whisper. "Protect Dracula."

"Dracula? My lord, he is dangerous." I lowered my voice. "More than you know."

Hunyadi shook his head. "He will save his people."

"Perhaps he will, or perhaps he will not."

"Do not abandon him. Help him. Secure the borders. Hold the enemy at Wallachia."

Dracula is an immortal and I will use him however I can before I cut off his head.

"I know, my lord. I know. All will be well."

Hunyadi's will was iron, and he survived for days after I last saw him. They moved him to Zenum and many hoped he would recover but his body and mind had been through too much and so passed the White Knight, Regent of Hungary and Christ's Champion, Janos Hunyadi.

Cardinal John of Capistrano died also, leaving the crusaders without a leader. The survivors made their way back home.

The Despot of Serbia George Branković, for so long a thorn in Hungary's side and latterly an unwilling ally, died also and Serbia fell into the chaos of a succession crisis. Even Mehmed II submitted a claim to the Serbian throne, his rights based on his Serbian stepmother but he had enough problems to deal with following his defeat and did not press seriously.

Skanderbeg, seizing the opportunity our victory provided, brought his men out of the mountains of Albania to raid the Turkish garrisons stationed in the lowlands.

Hungary turned into itself as they looked to a future without their great leader. Hunyadi's son Laszlo took command of Belgrade.

And I took my company back to Wallachia, and to the immortal *voivode* Vlad Dracula.

278

9

The Boyars

1 4 5 6 – 1 4 5 8

Dracula was formally elected by the high boyar council in August that year and confirmed by the metropolitan in the cathedral of Târgovişte with the title Prince Vlad, son of Vlad the Great, sovereign and ruler of Ungro-Wallachia and of the duchies of Fogaras and Amlas.

I half expected to be seized in the borderlands and every night our company slept in or near a new boyar stronghold on our way to Târgovişte I expected to be set upon in the darkness. And then when we reached that fine city, we set up our company camp in the great meadows to the west, alongside a few other mercenary companies and with the retinues of visiting dignitaries.

I wondered whether Vlad would send an army out to greet me. When his messenger came with word that the prince begged my presence, my men urged me not go.

The walls of the city were somewhat intimidating, I will admit. I had seen the citizens burn young Mircea alive years earlier, after burning his eyes out, and I had no friends within who would speak for me were I taken.

"Send us in, Richard," Walt said. "We will explore the city and decide on places we may flee to, or fight our way from, and points where we might escape the city. Then we will spread ourselves at various places, ready to act if things go against us. And then you can go in and speak to Dracula."

"Black Walter, when did you become so very sensible?" I quipped.

He shrugged. "Must have been sometime this last century."

"Well, it is good advice. Let us not rush straight at danger for once. Take as many men as you need, see what you can see, and return before dark."

The messenger was sent away with my apologies, explaining that I was fatigued from the long journey and would be well enough to call on the prince in a day or two, God willing.

While my men roamed the city, I had my servants clean and repair my armour and clothing. A few of them went into the city to purchase cloth and thread and clothes brushes and it was these men who came hurrying back across the field with word that Vlad Dracula himself was riding from the city with a hundred lords behind him.

"He has come for you," Eva suggested, before ordering her squire to fetch her armour.

"I do not think mail and plate will save us," I said to her as she ducked inside our tent.

"You should prepare yourself," she called in return.

"He could be going anywhere," I said but I saw the great party of riders now on the road and they turned from it onto the track through our great field. "Although it seems he is coming here."

His bodyguards and lords stayed far behind him and the prince rode up in his finery on a magnificent charger. I went forward from my tents to greet him.

"I see you are feeling better, Richard," Dracula called, smiling beneath his broad-brimmed hat. "That makes me so very glad."

"My lord," I said, smiling. "I did not expect such an informal and intimate greeting as this, considering that you are now the Prince of Wallachia in the eyes of God and of all men."

His expressed turned serious. "I do not think such close friends as we need be beholden to formality, Richard."

I bowed. "What an honour to be named friend by one such as you, my lord."

He seemed amused again, though he did not smile. "Indeed? Well, then, as a friend who feels honoured, I ask that you join me on our hunt today."

"Thank you, my lord, but I am much weakened by the weeks of riding and the hard-fought battle."

"Nonsense. I can see with my own eyes that you are as strong as a bull. Have them bring your horse. I shall insist if I have to, and I would really rather not do so."

I glanced at his waiting men. From the corner of my eye I saw Eva inside our tent with her sword drawn.

"It would be a pleasure, my lord," I said and bowed again for good measure.

While the grooms prepared my courser, I dressed as swiftly as I could.

"These clothes are suitable for riding," I said to my valet, "though they are not fine enough for noble and royal company."

"It's all you got, Richard," he said. "You want better, you got to buy better."

"Watch your tone," Eva warned him. "And Richard, I think your attire is the least of your worries, don't you?"

"Oh?" I said. "You think our prince means to have me murdered in the trees?"

"It would not be the first convenient hunting accident to befall a prince's enemy."

"I wish Walt and Rob were here," I said. "Or Garcia, Jan, or even Claudin."

"Take Serban," she said. "He did not go into the city with the others."

"That is something, I suppose, though an immortal would be better."

"You could take me?" she said. "And damn their judgments."

"That would be unnecessarily provocative. I will be well. All will be well."

"Do not placate me as though I am a child," she scowled. "I know full well this may be the last time I see you."

I crossed to her and looked into her worried eyes. "I mustn't keep our prince waiting." I bent to her and kissed her lips. There was nothing more to be said.

On the hunt, we rode down through the valley while the

hunting masters and dogs ranged ahead into the broadleaf woodlands. It was a good day for a pleasant ride.

"Not a bad day to die on, right, Serban?" I called to my Wallachian servant.

He scowled under his hat, hunched over in the saddle. "Too hot."

"You would rather die in winter? Come on, man, if they do turn on us I will ensure I give myself a glorious death. I will kill a score at least, what about you?"

Serban shook his head and muttered something about Englishmen I could not quite catch. "Death is not to be mocked."

"I do not truly believe the Prince will murder us today," I said. "He could have me executed in a dozen simpler ways. So, enjoy the ride. Perhaps we will scare up a deer or two."

"Not much deer in these parts no more."

I shook my head. "Serban, assuming we survive the day, you must do as agreed and find word of immortals in these lands. Any stories, any legends. Anything at all."

He did not meet my eye. "I will, my lord. I will."

Dracula sent word for me and I was escorted through the masses of horsemen until I rode beside the prince. A hundred men before us and a hundred behind but we were alone, side by side. The woodland was ancient but large sections had been cleared for timber, revealing distant mountain peaks over the tree tops. Crows cawed and hopped between the branches overhead as we crossed a wide clearing.

Dracula glanced at me from beneath his hat. "This sun does not bother you, Richard?"

"I love the feel of the sun on my skin," I said, grinning. "Do you not, my lord?"

He smiled back at me, his long moustache curling up with his lips. "In my youth, I delighted in Wallachian summers, whether in the mountains or on the plains. However, I was sent to Anatolia when I was a prisoner of the Turk. The sun is different there. Relentless and punishing. I learned to despise it."

And since you were turned, it burns your skin most frightfully, marking you as something not quite human.

"A terrible shame, my lord, for the summers of your land are delightful."

"Is it different in England? I hear the land of your birth is dark, and wet, and cold, all the year around."

"Indeed, no, my lord. The weather of England is perfection itself. The summers are warm and long, though rain falls at night so that the crops grow tall and strong every season. Spring comes early, with an abundance of rain to enrich the soil for planting, and the harvests are the most bountiful on earth. Our winters are cold but not deadly. If there is an Eden on earth, my lord, it is England."

He grunted in disbelief. "I have it on good authority that England is a deeply unpleasant land for civilised men."

"Oh? And from where did you hear such a thing?" I asked, suspecting that William had filled his ears with it.

He waved a hand dismissively in my direction. "I received an excellent education, as befitting a future prince. I learned many things about England, even though it is a distant and unimportant kingdom. Perhaps I shall journey there and see for myself if what I have learned is true."

I will kill you before you go causing mischief in my homeland.

"That would be a great honour for me and my people, though I fear you have much to occupy you here, at the moment."

He smiled again at that. "You are quite correct. Hunyadi is dead, and Hungary looks inward. Branković is dead and Serbia is without a leader. What do you believe Sultan Mehmed will do now?"

"Why would I know better than you, my lord?"

He smiled. "I would very much appreciate your advice, sir."

A wiser man than I could turn such situations in his favour. If I had the wits to do it, I could have given Dracula false advice in order to manipulate his actions or plant seeds which I could later harvest. I even had a distant, fantastical notion that I could turn him from loyalty to William to joining our cause in bringing his destruction.

But I was not a wise man and so I decided to speak the truth, as I saw it, and to advise him as if he were a mortal ruler.

"The Sultan will invade Serbia again, though he will not attack Belgrade. He has patience. Mehmed will slip into the rest of Serbia almost unopposed and his garrisons will embed themselves."

Dracula tilted his head. "What do you believe I should do about this?"

"Your western border with Serbia will become a possible line of attack from the Turks and so you are right to be concerned. But there is little you can do to stop it. If you move alone to push the Turks from Serbia, you will be invaded on your southern border. If I were you, my lord, I would ask the Hungarians what they intend to do about the Turkish threat."

He nodded noncommittally and said nothing for a while before casually asking another question. "What else needs to be done with regards to the Hungarians?"

"The west is not the only border you need be concerned about. You must understand what is planned for Transylvania, whether the lands will be properly protected by Hungarian armies or if the towns there will have to stand alone. And if they must defend themselves, how will they do so? Which of them, if any, are considering bowing down to the Turks to protect themselves?"

"How might I discover these things, Richard?"

I looked up at the distant mountains. "You would write to the mayors of each of the important towns of Transylvania and ask them explicitly. But you cannot be certain that what they say is honest and so your messengers will have to attempt to discover the truth by whatever means they can before they return with the message."

He pursed his full lips, seemingly amused by something. "What of my eastern border, Richard?"

To the east of Wallachia was Moldavia, which had traditionally been in vassalage to Poland, to the north. Its position, northeast of Wallachia and the Danube, had spared it from conquest by the Turks until about 1420 when the old Sultan Mehmed I had raided. And then Moldavia had turned inward to wage a series of civil wars in the 1430s and 1440s which Sultan Murad had taken advantage of by promoting one side over another. And by 1455, Peter III Aron had accepted Turkish suzerainty and agreed to pay tribute.

"Moldavia? I have little knowledge of it, my lord, other than to suspect that Peter III Aron should be removed by some means or other and your cousin Stephen should take his place on the throne. And Stephen is in favour with the Hungarians so it would draw Moldavia away from Poland and into the fight alongside Hungary and Wallachia against the Turks. Assuming you believe Stephen capable of resisting the Turks, of course."

He snapped his eyes to me. "What do you know of my cousin Stephen?"

"Nothing at all," I said. "I believe he is in Wallachia, however."

Dracula snorted a laugh. "He is with us on this very hunt, sir. At the front, with a bow and a spear and keen to bring down both stag and boar. He loves hunting and he loves war."

"I am sure that he does. And how many wars has he fought, my lord?"

Dracula whipped his bulging eyes to me. "Do you mock me, sir? Do you mock my cousin?"

"I would never presume to mock royalty, my lord. I merely wonder how a man can love something he has so little experience of."

Dracula held himself stiff in the saddle. "And yet a man may love women before he has ever had one for himself."

I laughed. "Very true, my lord."

We rode into shadow beneath ancient trees once more. "What would you recommend I do with regards to my *boyars*, Richard?"

I turned, surprised at his question. Asking me about foreign matters made some sense, as I had spent over a decade at the Hungarian court and travelling through Transylvania and latterly Serbia but Wallachian politics was almost entirely opaque to outsiders.

"I am afraid I know nothing of your *boyars*, my lord and so my advice can only be general. All princes should reward his most loyal and most capable men and all disloyalty and incompetence must be punished."

"Ah," he said. "What punishment would you recommend?"

"That would depend on the crime, my lord."

"And a severe crime would require a severe punishment, would you say?"

I wondered if I was being set up in some way. Dracula held himself with a stiffness that suggested suppression of some high emotion and I feared it may well be murderous rage. Was he leading me to condemn the guilty to a terribly punishment only for him to then accuse me of some such crime in turn?

"The punishment of crimes is surely established by the law?" I ventured. "And by custom."

He scowled. "The prince is the law."

That was very far from being the truth, as I had seen for myself when Dracula's father had attempted to have Hunyadi summarily executed only to be refused by his council of *boyars*. But I had no wish to argue the point so I held my tongue and we continued in silence.

"Much of what you say is true," Dracula said eventually. "I must discover what my enemies and allies intend. But it is imperative that my cousin Stephen takes Moldavia, for that shall be a new kingdom to join us in our struggle."

Yes but for Hungary or for the Turks?

"So you will lead your armies into Moldavia?"

"I would dearly like to do so but I have work here. Instead, I shall send six thousand horsemen with my cousin. With these men, he can take his throne, as I have taken mine."

"Forgive me, my lord, but will that not weaken your defence of Wallachia against Turkish incursion?"

"It will not. For I shall welcome the Sultan's emissaries and I shall agree to their demands."

"You will do what? My lord, you took the throne from a man who was too acquiescent with our enemies and yet you will now do the same?"

He lowered his head and glared at me. "I shall acquiesce only for as long as is necessary to strengthen my position and my kingdom."

It sounded like the justification a man makes to himself when he knows what he is doing is wrong. It is only this once, he says, lying to himself. It is for a good reason that I do this thing I know is wrong. All men do this, and women also, though for a peasant it may mean nothing more than encroaching on his neighbours' land, or for a merchant it may mean undercutting a partner, or for a woman it may be betraying the trust of a friend or her child. But for a prince, it might mean beggaring away his kingdom.

Whether it was that or whether Dracula was William's man, working for the Turks all along, I could not yet say.

"How will your lords react?"

"Those loyal to me shall react by demonstrating their loyalty."

"That is quite a test. You are asking your *boyars* to trust that you will not..."

"Not go the same way as my father? The father that you killed with your own hand?"

"Yes."

"You disapprove of paying tribute to purchase myself time?"

"What could possibly be worth the cost, my lord?"

"There are a great many *boyars* in Wallachia who care nothing for their people. They care nothing for their prince, nor for Christendom, nor for God above. They care only for themselves and so these men must be dealt with. I must have time to clear Wallachia of its rats. A prideful man would not stoop so low as giving in to the Turks but I consider my pride as nothing when compared to the continued existence of my people. I shall sacrifice my pride and my morality for them. And when my people are free and safe then I shall feel pride in myself once more. Do you understand?"

It sounded ominous to me. "I do not know."

"You will, in time. And I hope that you will help me."

"What would you have me do?"

Dracula hesitated, as if he was about to say more but stopped himself. "I would ask that you have patience and trust me for a while longer."

"Have patience? That has rarely been a virtue of mine."

"I find that hard to believe," he said, smiling and watching me.

"My lord, I am nothing more than the captain of a mercenary

company. If you will pay us, we will remain on hand."

Dracula smiled. "I am delighted to hear it. You will be right where I want you."

"You are a fool," Eva said.

Stephen nodded emphatically. "It is clear now that he is both an immortal of William and an agent of the Sultan. We must dispose of him immediately before he turns on us."

"Keep your damned voice down, Stephen," I said. We were meeting in our house in Târgovişte, in my bedchamber, without servants in attendance. It was as private as we could manage in that city but one never could know who might be listening. "It is hardly a surprise. We knew this would happen."

Earlier that day, Vlad Dracula had done as he had said, receiving the Sultan's emissaries at Târgovişte with extreme courtesy. I had expected Dracula to pay the annual tribute, and it was agreed at two thousand gold ducats, but then the Turks had demanded the resumption of the rights of access that Vladislaus II had given. That was the right of free passage through Wallachia for Turkish soldiers so that they could raid the rich towns of Transylvania. In exchange, the Sultan would recognise Dracula as the rightful ruler of Wallachia. This meant the Sultan would not seek to remove him or undermine him nor would he invade or raid his lands.

Dracula readily assented.

He did at least decline their offer to travel to Constantinople to make his obeisance to the Sultan in person but how much meaning that had we could not agree.

"And there is Moldavia to the east likewise rolling over without a fight," Eva said.

Stephen of Moldavia had taken the throne there with Wallachian support and so there was now a unified front of sorts but it seemed as though both kingdoms would simply continue to pathetically submit to the Turks.

"Can you really blame them?" Stephen had said. "By submitting, they hold on to their lives and their position. Why challenge the established order when it is that very order which keeps you where you are?"

"I do blame them," I said. "Not just the princes but the *boyars* of both kingdoms who allow it. It is weakness. It is treachery. They throw their people to the wolves so that they may sit in their palaces and pretend to be lords and kings."

"What now?" Eva asked.

Walt scoffed. "Obvious, ain't it? What we always said. Get close to our dear Prince Vlad and..." Walt drew his thumb across his neck. "And then we make off to some other likely kingdom and there attempt to make this immortal army."

"There is no likely kingdom left," I said. "And even if there were, we must first do as you suggest with the prince. It can be done, of course, but how shall we then escape this damned country? We will have ten thousand Wallachians after us."

Rob had a suggestion. "We wait until he journeys to the

lowlands, close to the Danube. We do him there, in the south, then we can reach the river by nightfall."

"And then what? Sail to the Black Sea? And then?"

Rob shrugged.

"Anyway," I said, "he never leaves the safety of the north. This is where his power is located and he stays clear of his enemies within the country."

"We need allies," Eva said. "Or at least one powerful boyar who will protect us after the deed is done and help us escape, perhaps into Transylvania."

"Dracula has his own possessions in Transylvania," Stephen said.

"Yes, who could we possibly trust enough there who could shelter us?" I asked.

Eva pursed her lips. "We shall have to make further enquiries while avoiding suspicion."

"Everyone here is suspicious of everyone else," Rob said. "It is a nest of snakes. I would not wish to trust any of them."

"What of the Germans?" Stephen said. "The Saxons have their towns all over and they almost all hate and fear Vlad. Perhaps they might be trusted? They are more civilised than these Wallachians after all."

"The Saxons here are merchants and craftsmen," I said, "how much can they be trusted?"

"We do not have very many choices."

"Very well, Stephen, perhaps you should develop your contacts with the Saxons. Eva, see what you can discover about any *boyars* who might be willing to see our prince meet his end.

But be subtle, for the love of God."

"We know what we are doing."

"I hope you do. A wrong move here may mean we have to fight our way through hundreds of miles of forests and hills. Get to work."

We stayed with Dracula's court wherever it went, and it rarely strayed far from the northern mountains. His family was from those parts and the bonds of decades and centuries of familial ties meant the people of the region were the most loyal of all his subjects. And the mountains would offer safety from assaults from any direction. He never strayed far from his Transylvanian possessions either.

Poenari Castle was his key fortress, located in the mountains on the Wallachian side of the border and the most defensible of all his fortresses. It was also a little way north of Curtea de Arges, the ecclesiastical capital of Wallachia which also held extensive political power and influence over the people. Dracula worked hard to make it so that the security and prosperity of the Wallachian church was increasingly tied to him personally.

The fortress at Poenari was at least a hundred years old, probably much older, but it had fallen to ruin when Dracula declared that he would bring it back into use. It was perched high on a steep rock precipice and its position alone made it almost impregnable. Dracula ordered it rebuilt grander and more modern than it had ever been.

In fact, he brought in highly skilled and very expensive engineers to do it. They started to construct five towers which were positioned so that when completed they would be able to provide crossfire on any section that might be assailed. The grand central tower was being built with stone reinforced by brick which was supposed to ensure it would withstand shots even from massive cannons. It was a long, slender fortress and when completed it would only need a hundred soldiers to defend it, as well as all the necessary servants. It was clear that Dracula meant to have a place that no one, whether king or sultan, *boyars* or Hungarians, and perhaps whether William or me, would be able to roust him out of.

By starting to rebuild this fortress, Dracula was in breach of his agreements with both the Hungarians and the Turks who prohibited him to construct any defensive works, lest he be seen as planning mischief.

"Does this building of fortresses and fortified monasteries mean you will be going to war again soon, my lord?" I asked him at a feast in the hall at Târgoviște. Many of the Wallachians muttered their disapproval at my impertinence. "But, my lords, I am a crusader and I wish only to know where best to fulfil my oaths."

Some cursed me openly.

"You are a mercenary and will go where there is payment to be had," one fat lord said, to much approval.

"Quite right," I said. "And will there be war here?"

"There will always be war here," another said.

Dracula would not answer me and he would not comment at all.

In fact, he avoided me and over the winter declined to offer me a formal post at his court or give me a task to complete. It was possible he believed I intended to assassinate him and yet he did not banish me and my company and he did not have me arrested. Instead, he sent word that he would have work for me and my men in spring and that I was to have patience. It would be work that we would be richly rewarded for, so he said. And I told my company that we would bide our time and receive a grand payday when the weather turned.

It was not just Poenari Castle that he began building. Down on the plains near the Danube, he began construction of new fortresses that he could garrison with his own men. It would mean extending his power into the lowlands and they would also provide much-needed revenues. One of the first that he founded was a fortress called Bucharest, at a place which was almost exactly where I had killed his father.

He also fortified a monastery called Snagov and built a line of minor forts right along the plain and the river.

And then in early spring he invited me to dine with him in his new hall in the almost-completed Poenari. There were over a thousand steps to climb on the path up to the first gate, and the men gleefully told me there were a thousand more up to the top of the central tower.

It was a small gathering of his closest men, the strongest and most capable soldiers loyal to him.

Even though the summons had said to encamp my company in the valley below, I had been allowed only a single valet to attend me into the fortress itself. Of course I chose Walt but even together we would have a hard fight if Dracula meant me harm.

"Do not go," Eva had urged. "Do not take the risk."

296

"There is no way forward without risk," I had replied. "I have been patient for months waiting to see what he would do next. Well, let us see."

"You seem on edge, Richard," Dracula said during the meal. These were his first words to me since I had arrived, the first to my face in months, and they drew laughter from his men.

"I am filled with longing, my lord."

He furrowed his brow. "Longing?"

"Longing to know why you asked me to join you, my lord. I can only assume that you have some task for me and my men and I am overjoyed at the prospect of action after so long a winter, doing little but training with the sword and in wrestling and other martial pursuits."

Vlad's long moustache twitched under his long nose. "Come up from down there, sir. Come here and sit at my side."

I moved to do just that and Walt came with me until Dracula waved him away. Walt's face clouded in warning but what could we do? He trudged back to his place below the salt and sat watching us from the corner of his eye, tense and ready to leap into action.

Dracula peered at me as I took the stool at his right hand, cold amusement on his face. "Do you know, Richard, that Wallachia has had twelve princes on the throne in the last forty years? That makes one prince for every three or four years. How long do you think I will last? Tell me, I wish you to answer."

"I shall pray that you last a lifetime, my lord."

He laughed, briefly. "You are a cleverer man than you seem, Richard. There is more to you than meets the eye, is there not?

Tell me now, who do you think might become *voivode* if I am killed?"

I shrugged, as if I had not given the matter much thought. "I suppose there is your younger brother, Radu, who has elected to stay with the Turks."

Dracula's eyes looked through me. "My beloved brother, yes. Such a delightful boy, so obedient and lovely to look upon. The Turks love him dearly, though I do not think he will find much favour with our *boyars*. They are a rough people, do you not think? Of course you do. Have you heard any talk of my father's other sons?"

I had, of course, but I pretended ignorance. "Others, my lord? I had no idea."

He smiled. "My father left a string of bastards behind him wherever he went. Some of them are still alive but they know enough to keep quiet, for now. If I am killed, they shall be brought out of their holes and one promoted over another by this boyar or that one. Such endless intrigue. We are a people at war with ourselves when our enemy is united behind the Sultan. How can we hope to win the war for Christendom when we cannot win this war over ourselves?"

It was an old point, made many times before but I sensed this time he had something specific in mind that he was alluding to. "My lord?"

He waved away my confusion.

"Certainly, you know that my greatest rival is the boyar Albu? Have you heard that his men call him Albu the Great? He pretends his name comes from his grand achievements but in truth it is because of his gross corpulence? Admittedly, he is powerful, but what has he achieved in his life that men would think him great, other than attempt to unseat me during my first few months on the throne? I shall tell you, he has maintained his private army and has ceaselessly agitated for my removal. What do you think I should do about this largest of my subjects, Richard?"

"Take your men to his fortress, besiege it, capture it, capture him, and cut off his head."

Dracula wagged a finger at me. "Good advice, Richard. You always have such good advice. But what if you could take him on the road, when he is travelling between one fortress and another, in order to build his conspiracy against me, what then?"

"You know he is moving?"

"My men captured one of his messengers. He did not give up his secrets easily but give them up he did. So, Richard, do you advise that I move against Albu the Great?"

Another test for me. Did he wish to test my cunning or did he believe that I was engaged in this conspiracy against him? I wanted Dracula to leave his castles so that I could potentially kill him myself and flee, so I knew I should certainly advise him to pursue this Lord Albu in person.

But if I said as much explicitly, it would reveal me for a fool or as a possible assassin.

"I have known lords to give their men false messages," I said, "in the hopes that they will be captured. Perhaps Albu the Fat has done this very thing as means to draw you out of your fortresses and into the open. Your ambush on him might become an ambush on you, my lord."

He grinned. "I am relieved that you are so wise, Richard. Yes indeed, we suspected a ruse but then we captured a messenger, quite by chance, from the boyar who Albu is meeting. This messenger did not even know why he had been told to repeat the name of a place near to Pârscov. But he was confirming the meeting place. And so we know where, and we know when, and it is good that you and your men are here because we must leave at first light if we are to spring the ambush in time." He leaned in closer. "You will help me to secure my throne, will you not, Richard?"

Dracula was leaving the safety of his fortress with a small number of men and travelling into hostile territory.

I knew I might never have a better opportunity to kill him.

"I will join you gladly, my lord."

We rode out, fewer than three hundred fighting men and our servants. Each servant, from groom to valet, and squire to page, was able to ride hard and keep discipline. The Prince of Wallachia disguised himself beneath clothing provided by his men and no man was to kneel or bow to him at any time, on pain of death, lest we give him away to someone observing from afar.

Killing Dracula was on my mind. I might have been able to kill him while he slept but just as likely was being caught in the act, either before or after. Perhaps my company could manage to kill all of Dracula's men, especially if we took them by surprise.

But still I wished to question him. How did he become an immortal, what was his task in Wallachia, and most importantly of all, what were William's plans?

There was time enough yet for a better opportunity to emerge and so I continued to wait and to play the part of an obedient mercenary.

We came in time to the place of ambush and disported ourselves amongst the trees and rocks in preparation for the party to come by. We waited one afternoon all the way until dark, and then an entire day where the only excitement was a partly-sprung ambush on a shepherd and his sons. They were detained, lest they give our position away. I expected Dracula would have them killed but instead he treated them as honoured guests, poured them wine from his own skin and asked them about their lives. It took the shepherd some time to answer fully, and he looked terrified for much of it but by the end him and his sons were smiling with their prince.

"Friends of yours, my lord?" I asked, partly in jest when he passed by my position near sundown. I sat leaning back against an oak. "The shepherds?"

"They are now," he said, seating himself on the fallen tree trunk across from me and leaning forward with his elbows on his knees.

"You mean to befriend every man in the kingdom one by one?" I said, making it clear that I was speaking lightly and meant no criticism.

He almost smiled. "You think it a ploy? To pretend to enjoy

the company of the peasant so that he will speak well of me to his fellows? I can see why a man as cunning as you would think that but no, that is not it. I do truly love my people. Not the *boyars*, though many are my good and dear friends, but the people who make this land. It is all but barbarous, this land of my blood, and would be so if not for the toil of the peasant who sculpts beauty and function from the wilderness by his labour. When I see my people going about their daily business, I am filled with joy and good cheer, for it is they who work the soil and they who make the land what it is. It is they who I mean to save from destruction."

"An interesting notion, my lord. Was this how your father felt, also?"

Dracula tilted his head, remembering. "In part, perhaps. It was never stated so clearly, not in my hearing, but he had a love for his people that caused him to make the choices he made, as poor as they were. But no, he did not instil this feeling in me. It was only after being kept away from my people for so long that I learned what it meant to be Wallachian. Every year, every month, every day, and every hour I was held by the Turks, I missed my homeland more. And all the while I was there, I believed it was freedom that I longed for. My homeland meant freedom and freedom is what every imprisoned man desires above all. But when I was free, I realised it was not freedom from bondage that I longed for, it was home itself. It was this, what we have before us now." He took the glove from one hand and dug his bare fingers down into the mulch between his feet, pulling out a handful of black, damp earth. "This, Richard. All of this. The sunlight blocked by dark green trees, filtering through to the pine needles underfoot, and this dark soil and the fast rivers cutting through the hills above and the wide, winding waters of the lowlands. And above all, my people. It is the people who make the land, the people who give it voice and soul and its heart. Not the *boyars*, even the loyal amongst them, and not the soldiers, though I love them also. No, it is the shepherds and the woodsmen and hunters and the peasants who make Wallachia and it is them who must be saved. They must be saved from the Turks, from the Hungarians, from the Catholics, and from the *boyars* who would see them fall to one or all of the aforementioned enemies." He wiped his hands on his woollen hose and put his glove back on. "Do you understand now, Richard?"

"I think I am beginning to," I said.

Was it true, I wondered, what he said about his land and his people, or was it meant to deceive me? And if it was true, did it not sound a little like the mad ramblings that William had spouted so many years ago, in Sherwood or was it my imagination?

And what did it say about me that I found his paternalistic affection for his people to be endearing, even a touch inspiring?

I could not risk asking my companions these questions, not when there were so many of Dracula's men around us. But I did not have to spend long alone with my thoughts.

It was the next morning when the ambush was sprung.

Albu the Great and his men rode hard and fast through the narrow defile, certainly aware of the danger such a path presented. But we were well prepared for their rapid passage. They were cut off at the front by a barricade and we moved to block the rear. A mere handful of Albu's followers escaped capture. Dracula's men, positioned amongst the trees and rocks of the slopes both sides of the track shot their arrows and guns down into the horsemen until those that survived surrendered.

"There you are, sir!" Dracula called out as he rode down to where Albu stood, bleeding from a wound to his head. "Albu the Gluttonous. How in the world did the bolts and shot miss your great girth, my lord? You must be blessed by God, dear Albu. Truly, you are blessed."

Amongst the fifty survivors was Albu and his entire family. Afraid to leave them unprotected, he had risked moving them to a better fortress only for his entire clan to be captured by us.

They were escorted to a close-cropped meadow near to a fortress called Bucov. Our prisoners were sullen and frightened, and it distressed me that Albu's children and nieces and nephews were as mistreated as their parents. And I was not the only one who felt that way.

"He ain't going to kill the little ones, is he?" Rob asked me during the journey.

"Of course not," I said, confidently. "Dracula was raised as a knight."

Outside of Bucov, Dracula assembled his men about the huge clearing which had dense trees on every side. Most of the servants and many of the soldiers were set to work felling tall pine saplings from those trees all around and trimming off the spindly branches. Other men dug a series of narrow, deep pits in rows.

Naive as I was, I believed they were working to prepare the materials for a palisade to keep the prisoners safe in overnight rather than keep them in Bucov itself.

Almost three hundred years old, having seen and done evil that would break the heart of any sane man, and still there was the remnants of innocence in me. But there was some evil, even then, that I had not yet seen.

Sheep shit was everywhere underfoot though the sheep and their shepherds were nowhere to be seen and I wondered idly if Dracula had not discovered the field through his discussion with the passing locals.

However he had found the secluded spot, once all was prepared, he assembled his men in an arc around the prisoners and declared that "Albu the Rotund" was a traitor and a friend to Turks.

"Lies!" Albu shouted over Dracula's speech. "You are the Turk, Vlad Dracula. You and your father before you. And your Turk brothers. It is you who are traitor! God knows it. All honest men know it."

Dracula stared at Albu with an unreadable expression on his face. It might have been anger but there was such coldness in the young man that it was difficult to be certain.

"For your crimes, Albu the Bloated, I sentence you and your family to suffer death by means of impalement."

The women in the party began wailing and Albu and his brothers cried out, begging that their children be spared. If not the sons, then the daughters at least.

"I am merciful," Dracula said, holding up his hands. "All daughters present who have less than twelve years shall be spared."

There were but two who met this criteria and they were carried off from their wailing mothers by rough-handed soldiers. There were four young boys and three older girls who were not so lucky as that. Albu's entire family were trussed up and some or all of their clothing removed.

"We have to stop this," Rob said, appalled.

Stephen crossed himself and mumbled endless prayers. Eva took my hand and turned her back on the scene.

"Ain't right," Walt muttered. "God knows, this ain't bloody right."

I nodded but I knew there was nothing that could be done.

The prisoners were impaled through their backsides. Each person writhing and screaming in agony as the sharpened stakes penetrated deeper and deeper into their bodies. One by one, they were heaved upright and the bases dropped into pits so that the impaled body was held aloft. Many were already dead or unconscious by that point but others remained alive, if it could be called living. They writhed in mindless agonies, causing their bodies to slide down the poles and the points to work their way deeper inside them until the tips travelled through the guts and into the chest causing the victim to suffocate or burst their heart.

The Wallachian soldiers did their work grimly but without hesitation, even with the children. And grim though they were, they took great pride and pleasure in the occasions when a stake could be forced through a body to emerge through the mouth so that they resembled a pig being roasted vertically.

Dracula appeared, throughout the entire event, to be almost uninterested in what he was witnessing.

Albu was saved until last, so that he witnessed the appalling death of his entire family, his entire clan, and would know that he had brought his line to an end by his folly. He cursed and growled at Dracula, his tears all shed and his throat ragged from wailing.

"Make sure his stake is sturdy enough," Dracula quipped to his men. Most were too appalled by their own actions to even pretend to find it amusing but there were plenty still who grinned and jeered at the broken man. For they had prepared a longer, and wider stake for Albu than for any of the others. Holding him down, they smeared blood from his wife onto the sharpened point of the stake to make it penetrate him more easily, and they prepared the way by first stabbing his arse with a spear to split him open wider. His screams of agony and rage were the only sound while Dracula's men worked the timber deeper into him, three grim soldiers twisting and heaving the stake in unison until Albu, mercifully, fell silent.

When they heaved him upright, he was the tallest of all the bodies. The weight of his body caused it to slide further down. Not fast enough for the soldiers, who pulled on his ankles until the point emerged from Albu's mouth, ripping off his jaw. They were proud of their precision and shook hands.

Even to the end, Vlad seemed entirely unaffected by the horrors he had witnessed.

Once Albu was dead, Dracula ordered the bodies cut down and burned, and the remains buried.

"Why?" I managed to ask the prince before we set off for Târgoviște. "Why perform such an appalling spectacle at all if it is to remain a secret?"

"It was to ensure that Albu suffered as much as a man can

suffer for his betrayal. It was also necessary to spread fear amongst my enemies, for the tale shall certainly be told to all in time. You think my men, yours, and our servants will hold their tongues about this? And finally, simply, my men needed the practice."

"What practice? You mean impalement practice? What are you planning, my lord?"

He smiled, though there was no mirth, nor even pleasure, in it. "Come, Richard, we must hurry home. It is almost time for Easter, and we cannot miss the festivities."

∞

The Easter celebrations were lavish and rather joyful. Vlad had invited more than two hundred of the *boyars* to the palace, along with their families, and a great and delightful time was had by all. I was honoured with a high place, though there were so many nobles in attendance. Not just *boyars* from across the country but leading citizens from Târgoviște were invited also.

"I am sorry that you were witness to the recent unpleasantness in the woods, Richard," Vlad said after I was invited to sit by him at the end of the meal. "Do you understand why it was necessary?"

Unpleasantness, I thought, recalling the screams. "In part, my lord," I said. "Though there is some of it that I wish I had not seen."

"Come, Richard, you must have seen worse things than that in your time." He peered at me, his look loaded with significance.

"You mean in my time as a mercenary?"

"But of course, Richard. What else could I mean?" He drank from his wine, looking over his goblet at me with his dark, bulging eyes. "You do understand that ruthlessness is a most desirable trait in a prince, do you not?"

"I understand that a king must be the dispenser of justice in his kingdom."

"Ah, so you disapprove? How interesting." He frowned, not in displeasure but in what seemed to be genuine curiosity. "How is it that you have retained such squeamishness over your long life when your older brother has embraced all aspects of personal and political tyranny?"

I froze, preparing to grab one of the knives at my belt or within in my sleeve.

Dracula glanced at me just for a moment, as if we were good friends having a pleasant conversation.

"So it is true," I said. "William gave you the Gift of his blood. And in return you will give him Wallachia."

Dracula bent his head and looked at me through his thick, raised eyebrows. "You have misjudged me, sir. Sorely misjudged me." He sat upright and clapped his hands before rubbing them together. "We must, of course, discuss this further, Richard, but would you be so kind as to excuse me for a few moments? I must speak briefly to my honoured guests."

He got to his feet, and I made ready to fight off any assault. But none came. Instead, Vlad nodded at his seneschal who raised his voice and roared for silence.

It took mere moments for the conversation in the hall to die away into nothing while all eyes turned to Vlad III Dracula, who smiled and raised his hands, palms up, in a gesture of welcome.

"My comrades, my brothers, my friends. Once more, I thank you for honouring me with your presence on this most holy day of celebration. This feast of feasts, celebration of celebrations, is a joyous occasion on which we praise Christ for all eternity. Christ is risen from the dead, trampling down death by death, and upon those in the tombs, bestowing life. And so it is that Wallachia rises once more into greatness. My friends, it has been a trying time for our people. You have known such disruption, from the times of our fathers and our grandfathers."

Vlad picked out an old man and pointed at him with a smile. "Michael, my lord of Giurgiu, you are as venerable as many here." Vlad glanced at me before smiling broadly at Michael of Giurgiu once more. "Barring perhaps one or two exceptions. Tell me, my lord, how many Princes of Wallachia have you known in your life?"

The old man shifted in his seat. "Difficult to say, my lord. Seems at times like it may be thirty of them." He finished with a grin and many in the hall laughed lightly.

I glanced at Vlad, but he laughed also. "You would have to be two hundred years old for it to be thirty, my lord, but you are not wrong in spirit." Still smiling, Dracula picked out another older man on the other side of the hall. "Alexander? What say you? How many princes have you served?"

This old man did not smile and he his eyes were dangerous. "In my lifetime, perhaps ten or so. My lord."

Dracula clapped his hands, grinning. "You are close to the

truth, Alexander, very close, but it is in fact more than ten. Even the youngest of the lords here have likely known seven princes. Tell me, my lords, how do you explain the fact that you have had so many princes in your land?"

Vlad looked around the silent hall, while the smile on his face died away. The smiles on the faces of the *boyars* died away, also.

"As I see that you are all too afraid to speak, I shall tell you," Dracula said, his voice hardening. "The cause is entirely due to your shameful intrigues."

The lords protested, while their sons and their wives looked from man to man, worried about the sudden turn of events.

"No longer!" Vlad roared, his voice filling the hall like thunder, silencing hundreds of people. Dracula looked around the room, fixing man after man with his bulging eyes. "For the sake of my kingdom and of the people of Wallachia, I sentence every person here to death."

The soldiers must have been waiting at every entrance around the hall for they filed in at that moment from all directions and surrounded the *boyars* and townsfolk. A number of the *boyars*, unarmed though they were, attempted to fight the soldiers but these great lords were immediately murdered by spears and axes, bringing screams of terror and outrage from their women. Soon enough, the lords held their wives and children close while the soldiers escorted them from the hall.

"Come," Vlad said to me, still as a cat before it pounces and yet raging with cold fire behind his wild eyes. "You must bear witness to this, also, Richard."

There were close to a thousand prisoners in all, including the wives and children who had not attended the feast but who had been dragged from their lodgings throughout Târgoviște. All were rounded up and marched through the city and out of the gate to the assembly fields before the walls and beyond the suburbs.

When I reached the top of the wall and looked out over the battlements, it was just as I had dreaded. A thousand great stakes, twenty feet long or more, had been prepared and without fanfare or ceremony, Dracula's soldiers began impaling the great lords, their wives, and their children.

Just as I had witnessed in the clearing near Bucov, they were partially or entirely stripped and held down. Many were split first by sword, spear, or knife, and then the sharpened stakes were pushed within while the victim was held in place by up to four men, one on each limb. I noted that the points of the stakes were being smeared with white lard or oil to facilitate the ease of passage. The sheer mundane practicality of it filled me with revulsion and I wanted to turn away but I could not.

The wailing and screaming that filled the air was unbearable. Others around me walked away, and others stood watching but with their hands over their ears. One of Dracula's veteran bodyguards, sturdily built and old enough to be a grandfather, loomed nearby with tears streaming into his moustache.

Worst of all was the silent terror and confusion on the faces of the children and their mothers' futile attempts to shield their eyes and ears from the fate that awaited them.

Beside me on the wall, Vlad watched the scene wordlessly, and with a complete lack of expression on his face.

"You spared the youngest children before," I managed to say

to Dracula. "You must do so again."

It seemed to amuse him. "You are truly unlike your brother. That is good, Richard. He said that you were yet limited by archaic and idealistic notions of morality instilled in you by hypocritical mortals centuries ago but I assumed that was down to William's rhetorical tendencies toward hyperbole. And so, I will admit to being surprised to see it in action. But it pleases me to see I was wrong. Yes, you are different indeed."

"The children, Vlad."

He sighed. "Very well." Dracula turned to his seneschal. The man's face was ashen and he had vomit on his embroidered silk doublet. "Have the children under ten years of age separated. Chain them, one to the other, in view of their parents. Tell them that their youngest sons and daughters will be used as labourers on my new castle. They shall be slaves until they die from the work. Ensure each man knows that despite this act of mercy, his line is ended. Do this now."

The seneschal bowed and hurried away.

Below, there were dozens and then hundreds of dying bodies hoisted aloft and fixed in place. The sounds of men begging for the lives of their sons and the screams of women and the stench of blood and shit aroused in me the most profound horror I have ever felt.

"You think me a monster," Vlad said quietly from beside me.

"This *is* monstrous," I said, slapping the top of the crenel in frustration. "The *boyars* and their eldest sons, I can understand, but their wives and daughters? They should not be made to suffer this."

"You are at liberty to feel outrage at my actions because you are a knight," Vlad said.

"So are you!" I snapped.

"I was raised to be a prince," he said, speaking so softly it was difficult to hear his words over the screams. "And now I am the ruler of Wallachia. I cannot afford the sensibilities of knights, nor commoners, or *boyars*."

"Kings are not above God," I said. "And God says what is just."

"Oh? I thought you said that law and custom are paramount?"

"And what does your law and custom say about this?" I said, jabbing my finger at the carnage.

He turned and looked at me with those bulging, dark eyes. He seemed utterly calm and entirely unaffected by the unfolding scene of inhuman horror beyond his walls. "When the laws of the land are leading your people to destruction, it is time that those laws be changed, is it not?"

I had no answer for him. But I did have questions.

"How then does this act help to save your people?"

"I shall kill every Turk in the world and every man who stands in my way." He nodded at the dead and dying.

"Every man, and his family?"

"Precisely this."

The sheer barbarity of it, the totality of it, was stunning to me. His unwavering certainty, his seeming lack of guilt or shame for the acts of slaughter he had instigated, was breath-taking. He reminded me of my brother.

Vlad stayed to watch until most of his victims were dead and then he turned to the men around us. "You may all return to the hall where we shall complete our feasting. The cooks have prepared an array of fried pastries, marzipan cakes, and sweet custard. I shall undertake a brief perambulation about the walls and join you shortly, my friends."

Dracula walked away along the walls with his bodyguards, as if the air was pleasant to take in, and his remaining companions left for the castle.

I stayed on the wall and watched until every person had taken their last breath and still I watched as the flocks of crows came swarming onto the bodies from the darkening sky. Watched as they feasted on the eyes and entrails of the people who had earlier been feasting themselves.

"That's that, then, Richard," Walt muttered at my shoulder. "We'll have to kill him now and be done with it."

"Not yet," I said, watching a crow stabbing its mighty black beak into the wound around a neck where the stake had emerged on its passage through the victim's body. A long piece of skin stretched impossibly before it snapped and the crow gulped it down.

"He returns," Walt mumbled, covering his mouth. "We can do it now and flee."

I placed two fingers on Walt's sword arm and watched as Dracula returned from his tour around the walls of Târgoviște. "Richard, you are still here. If I had not been told so much about you, I would have thought you were revelling in this scene. But that is not it at all, is it?"

"Is it not?" I said, aware that Walt was like a coiled snake beside me.

Dracula took up position beside me, leaning on the crenel and looking out through the battlements to the scene of death that he had wrought. His flank was exposed to me and I knew I could run my dagger into his kidneys, force him down onto his chest across the parapet and strike his head from his shoulders before his bodyguards could reach me.

"William told me that you were prone to melancholia, brought about by a surfeit of personal responsibility and a desire to do penance for the sins of yourself and all of mankind, combined with the guilt of never carrying out said penance on account on your choleric nature."

"Utter nonsense," I snapped. "What is he now, a physician or a priest?"

"He is a demon, Richard," Dracula said, speaking softly. "A demon that walks the earth in the form of a man. You think me evil for my actions here today? I did this evil only because I must overcome the greater evil of another."

"Overcome?"

"I need your help, sir," he said. "I cannot do it alone."

"Do what, Vlad?"

Dracula stood and looked up at me, his face in shadow. "I will kill him, Richard. If it is the last thing I do, I shall kill my maker, William de Ferrers."

10

Vlad and William

1458

IT WAS AFTER DRACULA MASSACRED THE *BOYARS* at Târgovişte that people began calling him Vlad *Ţepeş* which meant Impaler in the Wallachian tongue.

The children of the *boyars* were indeed spared impalement. Instead, they were manacled and chained together in a horrific procession and were marched, hard, for two days up the River to the construction site of Poenari Castle. Those children were made to carry bricks up the dangerous slopes and steps to build the towers and the walls, and one by one they were worked to their eventual deaths through exhaustion and accidents.

With the massacre of their parents, the core of the ancient boyar class of Wallachia was smashed. Even many of those of the old families who had been spared an invitation to the feast decided to flee to Transylvania. Some even fled to the Turks, which certainly lent weight to Dracula's argument that the *boyars* were infested with traitors.

All the deaths and voluntary exiles meant that enormous tracts of land were now in need of new lords and Dracula offered those confiscated domains to new men, many of whom were of astonishingly low birth. It was quite clever of him to do so because those commoners now owed everything to their prince and their fortune was tied entirely to his fate.

He also set about rearranging his state and created a new body to be set above the grand council of the *boyars*, called the *arma*. In theory, the *arma* was designed to administer and carry out the policies decided by the grand council of *boyars* but everyone understood that it in fact would simply do the bidding of the prince.

The *arma* was set above the *boyars*, who had never had anyone above them before other than the prince himself. The *arma* was made up from many of the new, loyal *boyars* but Dracula installed other men also, such as peasants elevated to officers in his new army and even a handful of foreign mercenaries.

In fact, he named me as a member of the *arma*. My duties would be to attend these meetings and offer my opinion on matters and to then carry out the tasks assigned to me.

It was not only the civil administration of the state that Dracula set about reforming. He needed to pay swift and drastic attention to the organisation of the army, such as it was, and so he created an officer class called the *viteji*. The *viteji* were drawn from the free peasants who had proved themselves extremely capable in battle and they were intended to form a leadership role over the peasantry who the prince intended to call to war.

"You have been busy, my lord," I said to Dracula as we rode away from his latest batch of *viteji* who were undergoing military training in the valley beneath Poenari Castle.

"Not busy enough. We have much work to do and I cannot wait any longer."

Our horses walked at a steady pace along the track. It was a warm day and Vlad had spent it all sweating in his fine clothes, giving a steady stream of observations and orders to the men organising the training of his new officers. He knew precisely what he wanted. Efficiency, consistency, and obedience.

"You wish to rush to make war on the Turks?"

"We are not yet ready for that. No, there are more enemies within my borders who require bringing to heel before we can turn our attention to our common foe."

"Who?" I asked.

He frowned at my tone. "You will hear when I am ready to speak of it."

Vlad cultivated an air of supreme confidence and calmness, especially in physical confrontations and when arguing with another. But I had seen his mask slip when he was defied. I sensed also that he was more unsure of himself around me than he wanted to let on. I decided to push him by allowing more of my true self to come out. I was his superior in arms, in years, in ability, in strength. We had continued to play our parts in the days since his admission that he wanted to kill William but I could not wait patiently for ever to know more. I wanted to hear it now.

"You must tell me about William, Vlad," I said. "It is time. You have avoided the question long enough."

He scowled. "You cannot speak to me in that manner. Do you forget that I am a prince?"

I shrugged and spoke lightly. "Do you forget who I am, my lord?"

Vlad scoffed. "And who are you, Richard?"

"I am pretending to be a mercenary who is pretending to be a crusader. But you know who I am. You know what I am. And I want to know what my brother told you about me."

Dracula almost smiled. "Everywhere I go there are ears listening. We shall make our way to a paddock in the next village."

"A paddock?"

"I would very much like to test my skill against yours, Richard. And I shall not ask your permission, for I am the prince and you are one of my loyal men, are you not?"

I did not answer him, and he seemed content to let his jibe rest.

The village ahead was disbursed over half the width of the valley, on either side of the river. Each house had a large kitchen garden and pens for pigs, which were numerous, and tethered goats that stared at us as we rode by.

The villagers came in across the fields where they worked and out of their small houses as our party approached, calling out praise and blessings to Vlad Dracula. He smiled and blessed them in turn, flicking small coins to this man or that who caught them out of the air or stooped, laughing, to pick them out of the dust. The chief man of the village escorted us to his house, bowing repeatedly and babbling constantly until his wife shushed him and drove him into the house.

"He fought with me years ago when I was with my cousin Stephen in Moldavia. A good soldier, though getting a little long in the tooth to serve in the *viteji*."

"Oh? I would have thought experienced older men were a good counter to the young ones. If you breed two hot-blooded horses you may find yourself on an uncontrollable beast. Sometimes it is better to temper the hot blood with the cool and so steady the animal."

"Perhaps you are right. And if he cannot keep up with our pace, I can always have him dismissed. I shall speak with him once we are done."

The man's servants led the sturdy ponies out of their paddock and away toward the village.

Vlad declined the offered wine and food but did so with politeness. The man and his wife went away smiling at each other while I opened the paddock gate. Their children peered out of the open door, their eyes wide and round.

The bodyguards and servants distributed themselves around the village, accepting offered food and drink, while Vlad's squires provided wooden practice swords to each of us before retiring to beyond the wooden perimeter of the paddock and closing the gate.

"It has been some time since I used one of these," Vlad said, hefting his wooden weapon.

"Oh? I ensure my men utilise them regularly. There is nothing quite like being thumped by a length of timber to let you know you made a mistake."

"Not as true to life as using blunted swords," Vlad replied. "And I often use sharpened blades when I spar with my men. It adds true danger to one's practice that cannot be achieved through these sticks."

I shrugged. "When training in full armour, I might agree but otherwise a man will always pull his cuts a little short for fear of hurting his opponent."

Vlad smirked. "Not my men."

"Yes, your men," I said. "Especially your men. Your men most of all. If they killed you in practice it would mean their death and so they are careful to fight below their true abilities. You do yourself a disservice by using sharp weapons. Perhaps you are not as skilled as you believe yourself to be."

He narrowed his eyes. "I do not think so."

I shrugged again, as I had no care either way. "We shall see."

"Keep away!" Vlad snapped at two of his men who had drifted to the edge of the paddock to watch us. "I do not perform for your entertainment, you dogs. Turn your backs and move away."

They did as they were ordered, slumping off chastened.

He was irritated by my tone, I am sure, as no one had spoken to him with anything but deference for years. Perhaps it reminded him of his past, when he had been no more than a hostage. Perhaps my tone reminded him of my brother. I decided to push him further and the next time I spoke, I used French. He spoke it perfectly, but it was another passively aggressive way to anger him.

"Your bodyguards are afraid you will be hurt but they are too afraid of your wrath to tell you so. That is a mistake. A lord needs men courageous enough to draw their master back from acts that are a danger to him."

"Enough talk," Vlad said and lunged at me.

He was quick but after my gentle goading I had fully expected him to make a sudden attack.

Instead of feeling out my ability by a series of noncommittal exchanges, he instead continued to advance and attack with a flurry of cuts, feints, thrusts from all angles, changing directions and speed as he did so.

Our wooden blades clacked at a furious rhythm and our shoes stomped on the dry, short-clipped grass underfoot.

There were many styles of swordplay and it varied from place to place, with one kingdom adopting a certain style while a neighbour would develop another. Different masters had their own methods and practices which they would teach and this one or that would find favour with a monarch or with a series of powerful lords and their influence would spread across regions and down generations. And the practice had changed over the centuries as weapons and armour developed. Some men still liked to use shields or bucklers in practice or on the field but most that fought in plate armour had little use for them and so two-handed swords and polearms had become standard. As experience developed down through the years, certain tricks and their counters were developed and became established and new ones were introduced until duelling and sword practice had taken on a sophistication it had not had in my youth.

But I had kept up with it all. It was my business and my life depended on it. Indeed, it could not be avoided. My lifespan meant I was more experienced than any mortal man and most of the immortal ones also and my strength and speed meant I was essentially unbeatable in a one-on-one duel.

And yet there were gifted fighters. Men who were born with natural abilities beyond their fellows, who excelled at their chosen martial art, whether it be jousting, or sword and buckler, or spear fighting. Amongst many thousands of professional soldiers, I would find one every now and then who was a true master.

To my surprise, Vlad III Dracula was one such man.

I had seen his exceptional horsemanship on display before, and indeed he was known for it, and I had seen him thrash Vladislaus in a duel to the death. But I had not known what skill he possessed in the sword.

He came at me with such expertise that I had to leap out of my sense of complacency to avoid being thrashed by him. And when I stepped up my defence, he likewise adjusted and improved his attacks. Again and again, I moved to shut him down and he ramped up his skill and speed.

It was clear that he meant to beat me. With everything that he had. And yet his expression remained impassive, even when he began taking heaving breaths and the sweat streamed down his face, sticking his sodden black hair to his forehead.

His wooden sword snapped above the handle, sending the blade part spinning through the air so far that it landed beyond the paddock, causing the bodyguards there to duck as it bounced between them.

We stood, breathing heavily, with scores of Dracula's men staring at us from two sides of the paddock.

Vlad straightened up and lifted his hat. After wiping the sweat from his face he clamped it down on his head again and looked at me through his thick eyebrows.

"You are almost as fast as your brother."

Almost.

"You fought William?"

"Could you have beaten me?"

"Yes."

"Easily?"

"You are as gifted a swordsman as I ever met. But yes." He stared at me, still breathing hard. "You should not feel too disheartened, Vlad. How old are you?"

"I have almost thirty years."

"And I have almost three hundred."

He jabbed the broken stump of his sword toward me. "Perhaps in three hundred years, I shall have you."

I smiled. The courtly thing to do would have been to accept his attempt at saving face. "In three hundred years, Vlad, I shall be six hundred years old and you still will not beat me."

He scoffed. "Perhaps you will be dead. And then I will be the greatest swordsman."

"Perhaps I will be. But then we would never know who was the best, would we?"

Vlad tossed his broken sword to the side and turned back to his watching men. "Attend to your duties. I will not repeat my order again."

I could see why they had drifted over, in spite of themselves. The sounds of the fight must have drawn glances and the speed of our movements must have moved their feet close out of astonishment.

"Have you told your men what you are?" I asked.

"Do you take me for a fool?"

"You are their prince. They have sworn themselves to you. They have committed mass impalements for you."

"Not enough. They must do more and so I cannot afford doubt from them. Look at yourself, Richard. Ever since you came to Hungary, years ago, there have been rumours about blood drinking where you and your closest companions are concerned."

I shrugged. "We used to make extraordinary efforts to conceal it. Once, when I was in the east many years ago, I used only mute slaves who could not tell others about our bloodletting. They were rather difficult to procure. One slaver was particularly adept at procuring these mutes and after a while it became clear he was cutting out their tongues before selling them to us in order to raise the price. Later, we brought in servants from foreign lands who did not speak the local languages but you can imagine the difficulties that brought as far as their duties were concerned. Soon, we would change any servant we suspected of spreading the tales. But servants talk. They always talk. And word always gets out."

"And you have them killed?"

"Why? When one or two in the next batch would talk, also. Word always gets out, Vlad. No matter what we tried, there would always be the rumours of our bloodletting and what we did with the blood we took. Blood magic, dark magic, communing with the Devil."

"And blood drinking."

"Of course. What secret does any man hold alone who has servants in his house? In London, our house was often swamped in rumour. Some merchants would stop doing business with us or one or more of us might be expelled from a guild."

"I would have such men killed. Quietly, of course."

"That is one way. But pay a man a few coins and it is often enough to buy his silence. Or there are other secrets he might hold himself that he does not wish to be made public. We grew rather adept at bringing powerful men into our net and using them to discover even more secrets."

"You have been doing the same here," Vlad said. "Your man named Stephen and the woman who shares your bed. They are drinkers of your blood also? They have been made by you into one such as I am."

I considered holding back, suspecting that he was seeking to extract information that he intended to use against us. But sometimes one must throw away caution and embrace uncertainty.

"What did my brother tell you?"

"That you have a small and pathetic company of useless commoners that you drag behind you through the centuries."

How does William know that? He has not seen me for two hundred years.

I smiled. "Ah, you truly have spoken to him. Please, Vlad. Will you tell me about it?"

He stared through me and then up at the wooded hills, the rocky peaks and the blue sky beyond, shielding his eyes. Vlad nodded slowly, almost absentmindedly, and ambled to the far edge of the paddock which looked out at a field of green wheat and the river beyond. I followed and watched him from the corner of my eye as he locked the fingers of both hands together, rested his forearms on the top of the paddock fence and leaned on it. Were it not for his ornate clothing and muscular build, he would have looked for all the world like a peasant surveying his land.

"We were young when he first came to us. My brother Radu and I were almost alone there. The servants sent over with us had been stripped away, one by one, for spurious reasons. We were instructed in Turkish and Arabic. Taught to ride their horses, in their saddles. We ate their food and listened to sermons about their Prophet and their God. And then he came to us, big and loud and filled with movement and passions, speaking French and Latin and Greek, to talk about Christ and knights and jousting and bedding beautiful women. He brought us gifts of familiar horses and the saddles in which we had first learned to ride. This food makes me sick, he would say, come and dine with me and we will eat stews with sausages of pork. But do not tell the Turks about this, for such things go against their law and their God, it is a special thing just for us good Christians who are alone together in this strange land."

"He has always been a snake."

"It is so clear now that it shames me. How easy it was for him to make us love him. As easy as breathing. Mere child's play. But we were children and we were so desperate for home and for our father and so, yes, we loved him. Rejoicing at his visits. When he was absent it was as though we simply counted the days until the sudden brightness and joy of his presence."

"You are not the first he has charmed."

"Charm, yes. We were enchanted by him. And yet I knew something was wrong with him. The servants, the guards, our instructors and tutors, the behaviour of every other man changed when in his presence and it took some time before I recognised it for what it was. Fear. I rationalised that they were fearful of his power as a pasha of the Sultan but in fact it was something deeper than that, something deep inside them. It was terror. A terror one might feel when trapped in a cage with a hungry lion. Or the terror of finding yourself before God with a heart full of unrepentant sin. And I noticed that Zaganos Pasha enjoyed their terror. Revelled in it. He was amused by it and would draw it out further by engaging them in conversation."

"It frightened you."

"No. By God, no. I wanted that for myself. I wanted men to shiver as I passed them in the hall. I wanted soldiers to shake so hard when I addressed them that they dropped their spears and fumbled to pick them up again. But Radu is not like me. His enchantment turned to fear when William revealed his true nature."

"He told you of his immortality?"

"Later, yes. Before then, he turned his attention on Radu by humiliating him in public whenever he committed the slightest error. William would instruct him in the sword in good humour until Radu made an error, at which point William would strip him and whip his bare legs bloody, all the while proclaiming him to be entirely without merit. And at night, in private, William would come to him and whisper sweet words and embrace him and cover his hair with kisses."

"By God. He forced himself upon him?"

"Forced, perhaps or manipulated my brother into allowing it or even desiring it. I do not know for certain. Radu, in his shame, would not speak of it nor hear it spoken of. Whatever perverse delights he felt, it became clear later that William was in fact preparing Radu for Mehmed."

"I do not understand."

"Sultan Mehmed lies with many women. It is his duty to get sons on them. But his passion has always been for young men and the older sorts of boys. You see, my brother was always fine featured. It was often said that his face was more beautiful than that of a ripe young woman, with skin as smooth as silk, his limbs elegantly proportioned and supple as an almond sapling. Grown women and girls fell in love with Radu on sight but he was not allowed to go to them. Instead, William first made Radu his own, body and soul, and then sent him into the tent of Mehmed to win his heart."

"To spy on Mehmed?"

"To fill Mehmed's head with whatever William wanted, I suspect. Men are uniquely vulnerable when sated in the dark of the night, do you not think? It helped to secure William's place by Mehmed's side when old Murad died."

"William had been advising a succession of Sultans already before Murad."

"Yes and each time the transition between one lord and another was the most dangerous time for him, threatening to undo everything that he had done before."

"He told you this?"

Dracula took a deep breath and turned away from the scene before us to look back at the village where his men lounged and laughed in the sun. "I attempted to help Radu. I urged him to resist, to fight every time, every night, to fight even if it meant his death. That is what I did to survive. When William attempted to discipline me in public, I would harangue him in turn and call him a traitor to his people and a pathetic servant who should bow down to me, who was of royal birth." Vlad smiled to himself at the memory. "Sometimes he would make a joke of it. Other times he would strike me or beat me badly. But next time I just fought all the harder, even when William crushed the bones of my sword hand in his fist. Even when he broke my ribs one day and my jaw the next, still I fought. Radu would not. Or could not. He was younger, of course, and weaker in his heart. Always. And so I gave him up. He would not save himself and so I would not save him. How can one respect a man who does not respect himself? His weakness was contemptible."

"Not all men will choose death over subjugation."

Vlad replied without hesitation. "All true men would certainly choose death over dishonour. Only the slave chooses slavery over death. All slaves have chosen their slavery."

"Is it not better at times to live so that one may take revenge?"

"If one chooses that path, he must know that he will never be whole again. He will never be a true lord."

"Forgive me but how is that you then continued to live amongst your enemies?"

"I was a prisoner, not a slave. I was never subservient and all recognised me as a king."

"They intended for you to become their king. A client king, subject to the Sultan."

"They did. But always I knew I would fight them to the death rather than kneel and call them lord. And I wanted William's power in order to free my people."

"His power to fill men with terror?"

"That, and the terrible power of his limbs. When I witnessed him tear a man's throat out with his bare hands and bathe his face in the blood, I knew that he possessed a great magic. It was unnatural. Perhaps evil. And I wanted it."

"And you got it. How?"

Vlad looked pained and glanced at the sky. "It grows late. We shall return to Poenari and feast."

I wanted desperately to know it all but I knew it would be a difficult thing for him to speak of. No doubt, Vlad wanted time to compose himself and to fortify his heart with wine. And as impatient as I was, I wanted that too.

"I will see you there, my lord," I said.

When I walked back toward my horse, Rob strode over with a stiffness to his hunched shoulders that told me had important news to impart. What it might be, I could not imagine.

"Richard," he said, keeping his voice low. "There's a woman in this village. A very interesting woman. You should speak with her."

"Oh?" I said. "Pretty, is she?"

He sighed. "Please, follow me."

∞

The house was tiny, out away at the edge of the village and with a small patch of woodland behind it. With a steep thatched roof and a stone wall around the lower course and plastered wattle and daube walls above, the neat garden was surrounded by a hazel fence.

Walt and Eva lounged beside the open door on a low, stone bench. Both sipped on a cup of something.

"What is this?" I asked them as I approached.

"Rob made a friend," Walt said. "But we can't understand a word she's saying."

"Why do we need to understand what she is saying? Who is she?"

Stephen stomped from the door with a scowl on his face. "She is a hardnosed old crone and we are wasting our time, Rob. She knows nothing at all."

From inside the house came the sounds of someone banging around.

"She knows," Rob said. "If only we could understand what she was saying."

"Did you find Serban?" Eva asked.

"You know what he's like," Walt said. "Workshy old bastard sleeping it off somewhere."

"Richard speaks the Roman tongue like a native," Rob said.

"He can question her."

"Will one of you fools tell me what is happening here?"

An old woman appeared in the doorway. Her hair was tucked under a scarf, and she wore a vividly white shirt beneath a sort of embroidered waistcoat and a long, plain skirt down to her shoes. She scowled up at me and threw up her hands.

"So, you have come? What is wrong with you that you send these fools to me to ask their foolish questions when they will not listen to the answers? Well, I suppose you had better come inside, if you must." She held up a bony finger. "I warn you. If you try to take my blood, or turn me into a *strigoi*, I shall cut off your head, do you understand?"

I dragged my eyes from her outstretched finger and looked into her dark eyes. "I understand, good woman."

She scoffed and disappeared into the darkness.

"You could understand her fully?" Rob said.

"Of course," I said. "You speak the same tongue as she does well enough. And Wallachian is almost the same language as Italian, which you speak like a native. It is not so far away from Latin. What is wrong with you lot?"

"But her accent is so strong to be indecipherable," Eva said. "And there are the peculiar words these mountain folk use."

"She refuses to speak slower," Walt said. "Just won't bloody do it."

"You are all hopeless," I said, ducking to pass through the doorway into the dark house.

I took off my hat as I entered, only to find myself whipped across the face by a great bunch of dried herbs.

"What are you doing?" I said, fending off the next blow from the old woman.

She clucked her tongue and thrashed me on the hand and arm, then on my body, sending pieces of dried plant matter into the air and onto my clothes. She muttered some sort of spell or prayer under her breath as she did so. Apparently satisfied for a moment, she threw down her bunch of herbs onto the table and grabbed a head of garlic which she crushed together in both of her hands and held up to my face, muttering the spell once more. The pungent smell filled my nose and I moved away, wafting at the stink.

"Aha!" she said, "you are *strigoi*. I knew it. The herbs do not lie."

"Are you finished?" I said, looking around the room. Her house was a single room, with a table, a fire place, a sideboard, a bed, and not much else. It was spartan to say the least, but it was impeccably clean.

"No!" she said, fishing something out from beneath her waistcoat. "Not finished."

She whipped out a small crucifix on a leather thong and dangled it before me. "Take this iron into your hand and close your fist about it."

I sighed and did as she commanded, holding the simple little thing in my closed hand. "Is something supposed to happen?" I asked.

Eyeing me warily, she sidled over to her table and took a seat on one of the benches. "You will hold the iron cross in your hand until you leave, do you understand?"

"Fine, fine," I said. "May I sit?"

She nodded and indicated the bench across from her. On the table was a jug and two cups. Crudely made but with a blue bird upon the jug and a pattern in the Greek style on the cups.

"My friends asked me to come here to speak with you," I said, looking at the herbs on the table and still smelling the crushed garlic. Amongst the bunch of dried herbs I recognised the yellow flowers of wolf's bane and the leaves of belladonna. "And I can well imagine what it is that they wish for us to speak about." She watched me closely and said nothing. "My name is Richard."

"I will not tell you my name."

"Another method of protection against evil?" I asked but she only glared. "Thank you for welcoming me into your home. That was quite a welcome. Do you do the same for all of your guests?"

She grunted. "Only the ones that are dead."

"Dead? My dear woman, I am not dead."

"Perhaps," she said.

"Do you receive a lot of dead visitors?"

"Not as often as I would wish," she said, speaking quietly.

I sighed, hearing my friends muttering outside in muted conversation. A bee flew in through the window, flew around the room in one quick circuit and then flew out again. It seemed increasingly plausible that the old woman was not in the full possession of her wits but Rob had summoned me for a reason and he was not a man prone to flights of fancy.

"Do you know stories of immortal people? Those that live forever, and who are very strong, and who drink blood?" I watched her for a response as I spoke but her scowl did not waver.

336

Her brown eyes were so dark they were almost black and her eyebrows knitted almost together above her axe-blade of a nose. But it was not an unpleasant face for all that. "You seem to know spells and herb craft to ward yourself against them. Can it be that you think me and my men are immortals? Surely, if you truly thought that was the case, you would not have let us in. So, what can you tell me?"

She lifted her small, pointed chin to look down that nose at me. "I know that you are one of great power. I see it in your eyes." She jabbed a crooked finger at the doorway. "And I know that your friends are the lesser creatures. Yes, yes, I know this. Do not deny it."

"What do you know of it?"

"Why do you ask what you already know?"

I tapped my fingers on the table, smiling at her scowl. "Well, how about this, then? Would you tell me how you know about these people? What tales you have heard."

"Oh," she said, waving her hand in the air. "Everyone knows. Everyone. The tales are told to all children."

"What are these tales?"

She reached forward and poured a cup of water for me and filled her own before drinking from it. "I was born in the west. By the Iron Gates. There were stories about the *strigoi* and I knew they were true because my mother and father never lied to me. But I never expected to see one." She took a drink of her water and I noted her hand was shaking. "My husband was from here. He came with his father across the hills many times with their wool and it was a good match. My husband was a good man. A

337

good man. We lived well. We had a daughter and I was going to have a son but he died. One summer, a man came through, claiming to be an apothecary but he had little enough to sell and we thought him nothing but a vagrant. He had a monk with him, though, so we thought he must be right enough. The vagrant asked if he could collect leeches from the pond and we saw no harm in it and both men were put up by the blacksmith and his wife." She stopped to cross herself and then she stared past me to the open door and the colourful, sunlit world beyond.

"They were blood drinkers?" I prompted. "The leech-collector and the monk?"

She glanced at me, seeming surprised I was there for a moment before nodding and continuing. "In the morning, Rab and Maria were found dead. Their children found them, both their throats torn and bloody. Both drained of the blood."

"And the vagrant and the monk?"

The woman nodded. "Gone." She sighed. "So we thought."

"They came back?"

"They never left. I do not know where they went in the day but at night, they came and they killed us. We barred our doors and we listened to them outside, knocking on the door and the shutters and laughing. Some nights would pass and everyone would be safe in the morning. But every two or three days, another would be found dead. I picked and hung herbs. We made crucifixes and placed them around. At night, we prayed together over our child. My husband wanted to fight them. He said he knew how to kill them." She peered at me sidelong.

"How does one kill them?"

"Iron."

I lifted my fist up. "Held in the hand?"

She scoffed. "That merely traps them. To kill them, you must drive a rod of iron through their heart. Or elsewise cut off their heads."

"Yes, I find cutting off the heads to be the best method."

"You mock me," she said, planting her hands on the table and getting to her feet.

"I do not," I said, with sincerity. "The iron rod, I had not heard of before. Please, do go on."

Warily, she sat down. "My husband said that was why they had killed Rab first. He was the blacksmith. And my husband went there to find iron with which to kill the *strigoi*. But it was all gone. They had taken it all. Hidden it. Buried it. There was nothing else for it, he said. He would not wait around until we were killed. He would take the ploughman's riding horse and ride down to Arges. If he left at dawn, he could be back with soldiers by nightfall."

"Then what happened?"

"He did not return. They came for me that night. They hammered on my door and my window, they attacked the thatch. My girl, she cried and wailed. But my husband had strengthened the house everywhere. New timber across there, and there, do you see?" She pointed up at the roof above. Instead of the underside of thatch showing, the inside was lined with sturdy planks. The shutters and the inside of the door were likewise crossed with old oak an inch thick. "They cursed me. They said they had my husband and they were going to kill him slowly and then they would come back for me."

"And then?"

"They did not return. I never saw them again. I raised my daughter alone. She lives in Domnesti now, with her family. She visits me, sometimes, but her leg is bad."

"You never saw them again? Why did they leave?"

She looked at me. "Who can say?"

I had the sense she knew something more but was hesitant. "Is there anyone else in the village who might know?"

She smiled with genuine amusement and just for a moment I had a glimpse of her as she might have been in her youth, before grief and loneliness had taken her. "All who survived the *strigoi* are now dead. Their grandchildren or new people live here now. They all think me mad. Even my daughter. It was the Turks that raided the village, mother, she would say. The Turks or the Serbs. My baby, who I covered with my body and prayed over while those blood drinkers shook my house, my dear girl grew up to be a fool. But that is what happens when a girl grows up without a father. I beat her as best I could but it takes a man to do it properly." She waved her hand in the air, as if she could chop away the words she had spoken.

"Why did you tell me this?" I said. "Why did you speak to my friend Robert about it?"

"Would you pour me some more water, sir?"

"There is none in the jug, my dear woman," I said.

"The pail," she said, gesturing at the sideboard behind her, a high bench along the wall where she prepared her meals below shelves with her pottery and utensils. A bucket sat on one end. "Fill it for me."

Putting down the iron crucifix on the bench, I dipped the jug into the water in the bucket and poured the woman a glass of water. She nodded her thanks and sipped at it while I took my seat opposite her.

"You are a great lord," she said. "A soldier for the new prince."

"I am."

"You command those blood drinkers outside?"

"What makes you call them that?"

"I know it. I can see it in you. In all of you."

"That is not possible."

She smiled and pointed through her doorway. "I saw him. Your man, the one handed soldier, he had his servant bleed into a bowl, behind my cow shed."

I looked out at the ruined shack beyond the woman's garden. "Our servants are bled regularly for their own health. The most sanguine of them require it or else they forget their duties. That is all."

Lifting her gnarled hand, she pointed at me again. "You, sir, are a liar. And I do not converse with liars."

"Very well. You have it right enough. My men must drink blood to stay alive and in good health. But we do not kill innocents. The blood of the living, freely given, sustains us."

She nodded but was not completely placated. "You deny that you are *strigoi* also?"

"I do not require blood. But I am ageless, yes. What is this word that you use? *Strigoi*? What is its meaning?"

"Meaning? It is what you are. You and your men. And it is what those men that came were. And it is what my husband became."

"Your husband? He was not taken on the road as you said?"

She closed her eyes as she spoke, her voice little more than a whisper. "He was taken, yes. Taken, and bled. Taken away. But not killed. He was turned. He became *strigoi*."

My heart began to race. "How do you know this?"

"I thought he was dead. For so long, he was dead. More than ten years, he was dead. But one morning, as the sun rose behind the mountain, I saw him in the trees behind the house. I ran after him but I could not find him. My daughter said it was madness taking me. My friend Anca said it was his ghost and that I had to pour a line of salt across my door and window so he could not enter at night. I told her that I wanted his ghost to enter at night and then she called me mad also, the fat old cow. She is dead now. But my husband returned. I saw him and this time he did not run. I expected him to turn to smoke when I embraced him but he did not. He was real! Solid as this." She slapped the table top with her palm and closed her eyes as she breathed in a great, happy breath. "Ah, my husband. To feel him again. I wept like a girl."

She sat, lost in the memory, a smile on her thin lips.

"Where had he been?"

The woman was irritated that I had intruded on her thoughts. "Some things he told me, others he did not."

"Where is he now?"

"Gone. Never to return. Why would he return to an old woman like me? In the years since, I have prayed and I have asked travellers for stories of the *strigoi*. I hear things. I hear that you are

342

looking for these things, also."

"You heard I was looking for *strigoi*?"

"A man who serves a foreign soldier lord has been seen here and there, asking for stories of *strigoi*. He has never come here but when I saw your man, I knew it was you. And so I sent for you. Your men are fools. And you have a woman who dresses like a man? You are *strigoi* but I see now, you are not evil. You are like my dear Petru. Cursed for eternity but not evil. And so I tell you this story, which you have sought, and in return, you will send Petru to watch over his daughter and grandchildren in Domnesti."

"But I do not know your husband. If I find him... I will tell him what you have said. But I fear yours is the first story of the *strigoi* that I have heard and I have been searching for years. I had begun to doubt if there were any stories to hear."

"There are many stories. Many thousands. But none that you shall hear. None but mine."

"Why should I not hear them?"

"You are an outsider. We cannot speak of such things to foreigners."

"You did."

"But I want something."

"Everybody wants something."

"Not us. Not Wallachians. All we want is for you to go. You, the Turks, the Hungarians, the Serbs. All we want for us to be happy is your absence. Alas, you all want our land and you want us dead or enslaved. No, none shall tell you these stories. None but the monks."

That caught me off guard. "The monks? What monks?"

"In the south, there is a lake called Snagov. And there is a village there, called Snagov. And there on the lake there is a monastery named Snagov. The monks, they know. They collect the stories, also."

"Stories of *strigoi*?"

"They will tell you the stories and then you will find Petru and tell him to watch over our family. No matter what else he has sworn, he must do his duty to his family. You tell him. Now, you must go." She held out her hand. "Return to me my cross."

"I left it beside your pail when I filled your water."

She scowled and snatched up her bunch of dried herbs and thrashed against my back as I left, before slamming her door behind me.

My men stopped halfway through their conversation to stare.

"Always ends the same way, don't it, Richard," Walt said. "You and women."

"Actually, it went rather—"

The window shutters slammed closed.

"What did she say?" Eva asked as we walked back toward the village.

"It turns out that Serban has not been so useless after all. His questions somehow reached her and then today she saw Rob bleeding a servant in secret."

"Robert," Eva scolded, "for the love of Christ, you have to be more careful."

"How was I supposed to know anyone was looking?" Rob said.

"It matters not. Anyway, she claimed that she somehow knew

us for immortals on sight."

Walt scoffed. "How?"

"She did not say. But she wants me to find her husband, who was turned into an immortal decades ago, in this very village."

"We been looking for years," Rob said. "Did she say where to look?"

"Yes. A place where they have collected the stories of immortals. A monastery named Snagov, in the south."

Rob whistled. "Fancy that."

"Well, then," Walt said. "What are we waiting for?"

"Patience," I said, looking up the valley at the mountain peaks. "The monastery will wait. First, I must finish my business with Vlad Dracula."

∞

"Your forces are growing in strength," I said to Vlad later as the wine flowed in the cramped hall at Poenari.

The towers were still being built but the central keep had been largely completed and that was where we had dined. It was barely large enough to feast two score men but that was about all who could garrison the entire fortress, as small and incomplete as it was. In time, a separate hall would be constructed in the narrow space between the walls but for now, only his closest companions could join him at the top of the mountain, while the rest of his men, and mine, stayed in the camp below where the workmen and soldiers slept and ate, and fought when they were drunk.

I could well understand Vlad's preoccupation with Poenari. His life had been in a state of constant change. As a child, he had been sent to Târgovişte to begin his training as a knight, only for it to be interrupted when he was sent first to the Turk's capital Edirne and then on to a succession of palaces and country estates in Anatolia, surrounded by enemies and assaulted by my brother. When freed by the Turks he had been unable to return to Wallachia which was controlled by his enemies, and so he had fled to Moldavia with his cousin Stephen only for them both to be forced into Hungary by intrigues in Moldavia. The boy and the man had never had a home to call his own, had never known true security or stability.

Târgovişte was not safe, not even the castle within the city. The Saxon and Wallachian merchant burghers of the city had turned on Vlad's father, executed his brother, and forced the elder Vlad to flee. The young Vlad Dracula could never have forgotten that.

And so he had built himself a modern fortress on the highest, most inaccessible mountain ridge in his kingdom, far from the border with the Turks. And although the Transylvanian border was close, that border was with the Duchy of Fogaras, which was in fact a vassal land under Vlad's personal possession.

If his enemies, internal and external, ever pushed him then it would be to Poenari that Vlad would turn.

Watching him feasting with his men that night, I saw him converse more than I had at any other place. He even laughed aloud once or twice. If I had not been paying close attention, then

I might have assumed that he was drinking more wine than he customarily did but in fact he hardly seemed to drink much at all. He seemed simply to be a lord at home with his men.

I took a chance and moved from my place to sit beside him.

"Earlier, my lord, we were about to speak of William."

It was not a company of men that enjoyed carousing and conversations had quieted as the hour grew late. Vlad glanced around to see if anyone was listening. If they were, they gave no indication of it.

"I imagined, Richard, that you would wish to speak of such things where others cannot hear it."

"These are your men. Your chosen men, who will gladly die for you. I wonder how many of them know about the blood."

A couple of them glanced at me and then at Vlad.

"Not all know," Vlad said, slowly. "And not all who know fully understand."

"If you are going to defeat William then perhaps it is time that they be made to understand."

His eyes narrowed as he regarded me. "Perhaps."

"You said that you sought William's power. Clearly, he gave it to you. Why?"

Some of them were paying attention now, and Vlad thought for a while before answering.

"The day I witnessed him tear a soldier's throat out and drink the blood, I was surprised by it. It was a brutal act and a demonstration of inhuman strength, the way he held the man, in heavy mail armour, aloft with one hand as if it were nothing. But the others around us responded not at all. Some wore the hint of a smile. And yet it was as if nothing was out of the ordinary."

"They were immortals also."

"Some, certainly. Others were hoping to become so. Under Murad, William had become a lord with great wealth with many estates but every other noble Turk viewed him with suspicion or loathing and they sent assassins with some regularity. William dared not make himself too powerful without the total and complete backing of the Sultan or else he might find himself surrounded by a dozen armies. Even if he escaped such an assault, he would be outlawed and all his work undone. And so he kept the number of his true followers quite small at this time. How many they were, I never discovered."

"He told you all this?"

"When I told him I wanted his power, he laughed and said I would never be worthy. I knew it was a challenge. That he wanted me to prove myself. And so I did whatever I needed to in order to gain his favour."

"Such as?"

"He told me he could never give the sacred Gift to one who had never killed a man. And so I snatched the knife from William's belt and cut the throat of the slave serving our sherbet. His blood soaked into the ice while he died, glaring at me and trying to keep the blood in with his hands."

"I wager William was pleased."

"He sneered and said a child murdering a servant was contemptible. He needed soldiers not cowards. And so I waited until I was training in the sword with a soldier I believed I could beat. William was not there but I said to the instructor that I intended to kill him in the next exchange and that he should attempt to do the same to me. He did not believe me until I wounded him across the face and then he did indeed fight for his life. He very nearly took mine. When I came to myself, many days later, William was there. It was then that he began to instruct me in his ways."

"Ways of fighting?"

"In part. But it was more to do with his ways of moving through the world. His cunning methods for manipulating societies that he had learned in the East amongst the people of Cathay. Particularly, he said, he had grown too powerful and had fought to keep his position. He spoke of successions of weak kings that proved incapable of defending themselves and securing their kingdom. And so he had been determined to make the Turks into a powerful empire while keeping himself in the shadows, coming into the light when he needed to and fading away if that was in the best interests of the great plan."

"Which is?"

"Do you not know, Richard?"

"To rule," I said. "To conquer a land and to rule it as a king."

Vlad nodded. "But not just any land. He expects that all Christendom will serve him. And he will rule as a king like no other. He will be worshipped as though he is an angel descended to Earth, as though he is a pagan god in human form, immortal and all-powerful."

"He told you this?"

"After he gave me the sacred Gift of his immortal blood. He believes that it ties a man's soul to his. Why would he not tell me this?"

"He believes those that ingest his blood become tied to him? Through magical means?"

Vlad took a sip of wine. "Is that not how your followers are tied to you?"

Walt had not even been turned by my blood but by the blood of a son of Priskos. And he had been always the most loyal man to ever serve me.

"No. I do not believe so."

"Then why are they loyal?"

"My closest companions are my friends. My brothers. Why do your friends follow you, my lord? I do my duty. They do theirs. That is all."

"In many ways, you remind me of William. And in others, you seem to be his opposite. An anti-William."

"Well," I said. "Quite. And were you ever his man? Magically or otherwise?"

"His words have a strange power. His eyes seem to posess a kind of magic. I will not say that I felt no temptation to join his cause, in spite of myself. God knows, I felt the pull of that magic for years. But always in my heart, buried deep, I held on to my hatred of him."

"And he never suspected?"

"He suspected everyone. Always. Unrelenting, he was suspicious. We had been friends and companions for years and I had sworn to obey him and had done many crimes, committed many sins, all for him, when one day I held his gaze a moment too long and allowed a spark of hatred out of my soul and into my eyes. Up until that moment, it had been hidden and I had not known it was coming and no mortal man would have seen it. But he seized me and beat me and had his men carry me away and strap me to a rack. He pulled the levers himself, all the while saying I should admit to my treachery and he would end my life. He cut me and bled me and fed me blood to keep me alive so he could inflict more pain. It was some weeks before he was satisfied."

From the corner of my eye, I saw some of his men cross themselves.

"And after that William trusted you again?"

Dracula affected William's tone and accent and wagged a finger as he spoke. "You are lucky that you are so useful, my dear Vlad, or else you would have found yourself returning to Wallachia without a head. I have killed better men than you for less. But you will give me a kingdom and so you will live in gratitude for the life I have allowed you."

"One way to inspire loyalty is to kill all those around you who do not demonstrate obedience," I said. "Personally, I would prefer to inspire fidelity."

Vlad snorted. "He had much to say about you."

"He did?"

"Especially after you killed my father."

I glanced at the men around us, all listening intently to every word. They looked back at me, their faces impassive and unreadable in the lamplight of the hall.

"He wished to loose you against me," I said. "Use you as a weapon to destroy me."

"I think he was delighted to be able to relay it to me. We both share an enemy now, my dear Vlad. My brother Richard stands in our way. We shall kill him together. Draw him close, pretend to be his friend and isolate him. He is nothing without his companions. Richard is witless, quick to anger, impatient as a child, and filled with mad passions. Never fight him. Be his friend and then betray him."

My heart racing, I looked again at the men around the hall. They were all armed in one way or another.

"Good advice," I said, shrugging.

"It was," Vlad said. "The only allies you have in my fortress are two mortal servants to attend to you. And even they are not here."

"But I have you," I said. "My friend and ally, Vlad Dracula."

"Yes," he said, smiling at last. "You do. William is truly my enemy and you have proved yourself to be a friend. More importantly, you are a good Christian who has fought for years to keep the Turk at bay and so you are a friend to all Wallachians."

I let out a sigh and drank off my wine. "So you played along, no matter the cost, for years. And when the Turks released you, they believed you to be theirs. Do they believe it still?"

"I think that they do, yes."

"But you mean to fight. And you mean to defeat William?"

"I do."

"How?"

"He is more powerful than ever. His Blood Janissaries might be impossible to stop. But if I can draw William in, draw him close and away from his men, I mean to surround him and kill him."

"And how will you do that?"

"Sometimes I imagine filling him with arrows, other times having a hundred hand-gunners shoot him at once, or to blast him in half with a cannon. Whatever is left, I shall cut into pieces and burn."

"A very pleasant fantasy, I am sure. But how will you isolate him from his... Blood Janissaries, as you called them?"

Vlad glanced at his men. "I wondered if you might consider using yourself as a lure? If he knows where you are, I believe his hatred for you is so strong that he would come for you in person."

"And how do you propose to do that?"

"Send men with messages through Turkish territory and have them captured and—"

"That trick may work on a boyar but William would not fall for it."

"Well, then, there are many ways in which—"

"I have a far better idea," I said. "William has his immortal Janissaries. The red robed Blood Janissaries. As you say, they will prove almost impossible for mortal men to overcome and I am certain William will never leave their protection. That is why he created them, I assume."

"He made a personal army that is loyal to him. My intention is to avoid them and to kill William directly. To cut off the head of the snake. After that, they will be unable to replace their numbers and so I can grind them away into dust."

"We cannot isolate William from those men. We will have to go through them to get to him."

"But if, as you said yourself, they cannot be overcome then—"

"Not by mortal men. What about by immortal ones?"

"Your men? How many is your company? Twenty-five soldiers? You are outnumbered, sir."

"My immortal men, yes. And me and you, also." I glanced around the hall. "And your men."

"What do you mean, my men? I have no immortal men."

"Ah, yes. But I could make you some, Vlad. If you wished. I could make you five hundred of them. I could make us an immortal army of our own."

1 1

The Saxons

1 4 6 1

"REPEAT AFTER ME. I SWEAR TO SERVE Richard Ashbury from this day until the day of my death. I swear to obey him in all things and to obey the orders of his captains without question. With the strength of my arm, I will fight the enemies of Wallachia without flinching or fleeing and with the strength of my heart I will protect the people of Wallachia with unwavering fidelity. Together with my brothers, we serve the Voivode of Wallachia Vlad III Dracula against his enemies, wherever they are found. I swear also to take no wife, to have no sons and no daughters, and to have no father but my lord and to have no brother but my brothers of the *sluji*. All this I swear in the name of Christ."

I released the young man's hands and took one step to the side while Vlad Dracula took my place, holding the dragon amulet in one hand and his father's dragon sword in the other. The young man leaned forward to kiss the amulet and the hilt of the sword. Walt and Rob helped him to his feet and led him to the Blood Altar, a stone table at the top of the hall. Wearing no more than his undershirt, he shook in the cold air. No doubt, he was also terrified. Many of them were when it came time to be initiated into the blood brotherhood of the *sluji*. Over three hundred of the men who would soon be his brothers stood in the hall, silently watching.

Dracula had chosen to name our new immortal army the *sluji* which was a word that meant "to serve" and was meant to emphasise that our blood brothers were sacrificing their mortal lives for their prince and their people. The true nature of the *sluji* was hidden from outsiders, even most of the men close to Vlad. To everyone else, we were a special bodyguard, loyal to Vlad with foreign mercenary officers, namely me, my close companions, and the immortals of the Company of Saint George.

The young initiate lay on the altar. Walt sliced an incision on both of the initiate's wrists and his blood flowed into bowls. The bowls were taken when almost filled and passed amongst the watching blood brothers, who each took a drink and passed it on to the man beside him. There were many bowls of blood in a man's body.

Those chosen for the *sluji* knew that they were giving up their families and their chance of ever fathering a child again. Most of the volunteers we chose were peasants but all had proven themselves in one way or another to be competent or courageous in battle, or at least in training.

It had taken a lot of arguing to reach agreement about the immortal army. Vlad had argued that they should be loyal to him. I had refused to make any man an immortal who was not personally loyal to me, which Vlad could not agree to. Eventually, we came to a compromise of sorts. The *sluji* swore loyalty to me but they would only fight the enemies of Wallachia. I could never order them to England and expect them to follow me. And I could never order them to fight against Vlad or his allies. All the initiates understood that.

The newest man was so drained of blood that his eyes were clouding and his eyelids fluttering. Taking a knife, I cut my own wrist and held it to his mouth. He knew to drink quickly and so he did, grasping my arm in both hands and sucking the blood from my wound. When he had a bellyful, he fell back, unconscious.

My companions had argued that I could make no concessions as far as loyalty was concerned. They feared that Vlad would work to subvert my authority and take command using his rights and power as their royal lord. And the immortal knights and men-at-arms in the Company of Saint George had argued against adding so many men of one nation to our number, lest they turn against us. They were also contemptuous of the new men's abilities. I assured my men that this was a new venture, separate from the company that they had earlier joined. They were placated by being granted positions of authority in the *sluji*, with responsibility for first training and then leading the men in battle. Along with an accompanying increase in pay. They found the terms acceptable.

The young man was carried away to the quarters behind the

hall, where he would either die in his sleep or rise an immortal brother of the *sluji*. I drank a bowl of his blood to replenish that which I had lost and came forward to meet the next initiate, who came forward and knelt.

"Repeat after me."

While we made more immortals and trained them to fight as an army, Vlad was also busy.

He drew as much personal power to himself as was possible. He became a most generous patron of the Orthodox Church, granting tax immunities and other privileges to monasteries and built new church buildings and extended old ones. In return, he expected and received both submission to his will and passionate support from the pulpit. Vlad needed the peasantry to believe in him, in his vision for Wallachia and he knew it was going to be a hard fight. Peasants must be told something in the simplest terms and for them to retain it they must be told repeatedly and so the priests of the Church explained to their flock that the changes Vlad was making was in their interests and to trust in their prince as they trusted in the Lord.

In fact, the sermons that were preached were perfectly truthful. As the boyar class was weakened, the peasants and the Church gained power.

Vlad especially favoured a monastery at Comana which he founded himself and filled with loyal monks. The Catholic Church had long been exerting its own influence in Wallachia, especially since the recent crusades, and Vlad had many of these Catholics thrown out of his lands before replacing them with Orthodox appointees. I heard that several obstinate Catholic priests and abbots were impaled.

"It is evil," Stephen said to me, when this news reached us in the north. "He does great evil."

"He is making these lands his own, Stephen. All will be loyal to the Voivode of Wallachia. No divisions anywhere that can be exploited. This is just as you wanted."

"Under the Hungarians," he replied, as if I were a simpleton. "Under Catholic Hungarians, not barbarian eastern heresy."

"What else could we do?" I asked. "Beggars cannot choose their benefactors, Stephen."

"Please, Richard, do not let *axioma* dictate our actions."

"Come, come, Stephen. You know as well as I do that no man ought to look a gift horse in the mouth."

He tutted and huffed but we were certainly not about to challenge Vlad on his opposition to Catholic priests when it was Christendom itself at stake should we fail in our military duty.

"There will be no schism to heal," I said, at least a dozen times, "if we all live under the Turkish yoke."

All the while, Hungary continued its internal strife. Back in 1456, the young King Ladislaus V of Hungary had come to post-siege Belgrade which was under the command of Ladislaus Hunyadi, Janos' eldest son. The Habsburg-allied lords who controlled the King of Hungary were the enemies of the Hunyadi and no doubt meant to remove the commander of Belgrade from his position. And so Ladislaus Hunyadi seized the king and killed his ally Count Celje in the ensuing row. Capturing his own king was a bold move by young Hunyadi and he only released him after receiving assurances that the king would take no action in retaliation.

The king lied.

He arrested and then executed the eldest son of Janos Hunyadi and took prisoner the younger son, Mattias Corvinus. Michael Szilágyi, the elder Hunyadi's brother in law and the boys' uncle, rebelled against the King.

Szilágyi was an able commander and many were ready to follow him. God alone knows what a civil war would have done to Hungary but then King Ladislaus V died. He left no heir and the crown was once again up for grabs.

Wasting no time, Michael Szilágyi brought fifteen thousand soldiers to Buda and with such a force present, convinced a council of nobles to elect Mattias Corvinus Hunyadi, son of Janos Hunyadi, as King of Hungary.

Having a Hunyadi on the throne of Hungary was a good thing for us. Now, we did not know Mattias, but both Vlad and I had been supporters of his father and so we hoped and expected that we would be favoured in Wallachia's looming conflict with the Sultan.

But we did not realise just how difficult it was for Mattias to do anything but fight tooth and nail for his crown and for the true authority to wield his power. The first years of his reign were spent attempting to throw off the control of his uncle Michael Szilágyi.

And later, Mattias seemed almost uninterested in the wars on his south-eastern borders, preferring to focus on the struggles for dominance in central Europe. In fact, he did nothing to prevent the extinction of Serbia as a separate entity from Turkish Rumelia and clearly viewed Belgrade and the Danube-Sava junction as the natural defence line he would hold against the Turks.

In Wallachia, we were beyond that line.

Young Mattias Corvinus Hunyadi looked to the German elements within his lands for support and this included the enormously wealthy Saxon merchant colony towns of Transylvania and along the Wallachian border. Whereas his guardian Szilágyi looked for support from vassal lords.

Dracula was long a friend to Szilágyi. In fact, he admired the man greatly. When Dracula had been under Hunyadi, Szilágyi had shown him great friendship, helping him with words in ears and even with gifts of gold and men and such favour was not soon forgotten.

So when Szilágyi asked Dracula to help him with a rebellious Saxon town, Vlad readily agreed. He assembled a small but powerful force and we rode into north-eastern Transylvania to the town of Bistri.

"Bring the *sluji*," Vlad commanded me. "We will see what they can do."

"They are not at full strength," I replied, "and we have so much training to do before they will be battle ready."

"Bah!" Vlad said. "There will be no battle. We will raid. We will threaten. They will capitulate. This will be no more than another form of training."

Still, there was much to prepare, even for a short campaign close to home. We had to procure the horses, the servants, wagons, tents, and other equipment needed to maintain a force of almost five hundred fighting men. And immortal ones at that.

The experience of my mercenary captains was invaluable, however, and we were ready to march in time and joined Dracula's other forces as we made for Transylvania.

"We have long tolerated the Saxons in our lands," Vlad said as we rode through the mountains. "This rebellious town of Bistri is one such colony. Their forefathers were invited to settle in our mountains and ever since we have allowed them to prosper. It cannot be denied that they generate a significant amount of revenue through their trading and the making and selling of goods. Some of these towns were swift to support me against Vladislaus, although it is clear that they make decisions based on mercantile reasons rather than for honour and duty. For they honour only themselves and are not tied to our land the way our own people are. There is one town, you know Brasov, yes? Of course you do. The townsmen of Brasov were especially generous in their support of me and so I had to respond in kind. When I wrote to them that they were honest men, brothers, friends, and sincere neighbours, they knew my true meaning."

"It was more than empty flattery?"

"How can mercantile men ever be honest? How can they ever be brothers to those so different to them as we Wallachians are from Saxons? How can they be sincere neighbours when both they and us know they do not truly belong in our lands?"

"How did they take your jibe?"

"They will have taken it for what it was. A warning."

Not only was Vlad keen to put the Saxons in their place for Szilágyi, and to see the *sluji* in action, it was an opportunity to exercise his own men and to test the skills they had been training.

His army was small and new and he had to find out what already functioned well and what did not.

Bistri was well-fortified and that was no doubt one reason they felt they could defy Szilágyi and refuse to send him the requested revenue.

"The *sluji* can assault it immediately," I said to Vlad. "We can cross the outer works at a run, throw up ladders, storm the walls and open the gates for the rest of the men."

Vlad smiled. "That would be a sight to see, Richard. But our Saxon friends and our own men would certainly see the somewhat more than human nature of your soldiers. And we should do our best to avoid that, for as long as we can. Besides, there is no need. My boys can do the job almost as well. Bistri is nothing."

He was not wrong. The Wallachian cannons blasted holes in the town gate and the hand-gunners and crossbowmen kept the town militia ducking down behind the battlements while infantry rushed forward to assault the walls and the gatehouse. It took no more than that. Our soldiers soon penetrated the defences and looted and burned the town.

All the while, I stood and watched from a safe distance. Before the sack was completed, the ringleaders of the rebellion fled to the larger Saxon towns of Brasov and Sibiu and Vlad was content to let them go.

"We do not need to exterminate them," he said. "Our point is made."

"What is your point?" I asked Vlad.

He laughed. "It is that the Germans are guests in Transylvania and Wallachia, no matter how many generations they have been here. Do not rebel against our good will or you see what will occur."

In Buda, Michael Szilágyi was delighted with Vlad's swift work of retribution and rewarded him with a castle dominating the Borgo Pass. Having made his point, Vlad led us all back home and we called it an informative exercise. Adjustments were made to the organisation of the soldiers and the supply train and I continued to recruit and train the *sluji*.

But Vlad Dracula had stirred up a great mass of ill-feeling amongst the Saxon colonies in Transylvania. The German cities came together in rebellion and the royal captain general of Transylvania, Count Oswold Rozgony, threw his support behind the league.

The burghers of Brasov moved to materially support Vlad's great boyar enemies the Danesti. They were a dynasty long in opposition to Vlad's ancestors and they saw themselves as rightful rulers of Wallachia.

They began a campaign of subversion within Wallachia against Vlad III Dracula. They spread whispers that Dracula was in fact sworn in vassalage to Sultan Mehmed II and always had been. They sent men out to spread tales that Dracula was lying about his opposition to the Turks.

"Damn the bastards of Brasov," Vlad said when he came through and stopped to inspect the *sluji*. "Always those Saxon dogs have been ungrateful, disloyal, and treacherous. Have you heard what lies they are spreading? Have you?"

"I have," I said.

The most effective slander has the ring of truth to it and for years Wallachia had been in vassalage to the Turks. It was undeniable as the effects of that vassalage had been felt by every family in the kingdom. After all, the payments required under the terms of vassalage were calculated by Janissary tax collectors who went from place to place in the country, assessing the plenty or scarcity so that the rulers could not deceive their overlord the Sultan with regards to what was available. The taxes were paid in coinage and silver but also in livestock and in grain, supplied by the hardworking peasants to their lords and thence to the Turks. The Wallachian lowlands were so productive that the Turks viewed their northern vassal in large part as a vast granary which could be relied on to provide enormous quantities of grain that would feed its armies on campaign.

There was of course the *devshirme*, the Blood Tax, in which thousands of healthy boys were dragged from their homes and turned into Turkish slaves. Wallachians were a hearty and wily people who made the Sultan reliable soldiers and able administrators.

No matter what the rumours said about Vlad's subservience, the truth was that in 1459 Dracula refused to pay the tribute to Sultan Mehmed II. That act would bring the wrath of the Turks down upon us from the south and it was at that moment that the Saxons began stirring up open rebellion in the north.

Up until that Saxon rebellion, I had never seen him express much in the way of anger. But when he was told of the accusations spreading amongst his people, Dracula threw an ancient oak table across his hall with force enough to shatter it, sending jagged boards flying back to where his men stood. While they ducked and cringed, Vlad stood unflinching with the crushed letter in his gloved fist.

"What else?" Vlad asked his messenger, a new boyar raised up from the peasantry and granted lands on the Transylvanian border.

The young man who had conveyed the message got back to his feet and stopped shielding his head with his arms. "Dan III, brother of Vladislaus II the former prince, has established himself in Brasov," the man said, clearing his throat. "He has claimed the throne of Wallachia for himself and was elected as such by a group of Danesti *boyars* and other lords who fled from you or who you banished when you took your throne, my lord."

"He calls himself *voivode*? And these landless, illegitimate *boyars* claim to have elected him?" Vlad spoke with his voice level. "Do you have word of Sibiu, Alexander?"

Another lord stepped forward and bowed. "I have word, my prince, of a man who claims to be the son of your father, and half-brother to you. All lies, I am sure. He calls himself Vlad the Monk."

"He is my half-brother, of that I have no doubt. My father was not shy about spreading his seed. He is called Vlad the Monk because he was squirrelled away in a monastery so that he would be out of sight until he came of age. He has been stirring up trouble ever since. What does he have to do with the town of Sibiu?"

"The Monk has based himself at Sibiu, my lord, and they have granted him great sums of money with which to raise forces. He likewise has exiled *boyars* at his side."

Vlad's lip curled beneath his thick moustache. "A bold move for the burghers of Sibiu. I would have expected them to follow their brothers in Brasov, not go against them."

"I believe Vlad the Monk has promised to extend the trade rights of Sibiu and the towns allied with it."

"Those money grabbing fools. I already extended their rights when I took the throne and now they want more? And are willing to rebel in order to get it? Do they not fear my displeasure, Alexander?"

His face pale, the man bowed. "I cannot say, my lord."

Vlad pursed his full lips and glanced around at me. "It seems that we must put down two rival factions and two rival rebellions. Is there anything else?"

A new man stepped forward and fell to one knee before his prince. "My lord, I have had word only this morning from one of my sons that a third candidate for your throne has declared himself. I do not know much but it is another one of the Danesti clan. A son of Dan II, named Basarab Laiot."

Vlad raised his eyebrows and scoffed. "And who is backing this Basarab Laiot, who is the son of my father's great enemy?"

"I do not know, my lord. All I know is that he made a series of promises to *boyars* in Wallachia and Transylvania and he has promised great things for certain Saxon towns."

Dracula thanked the man and looked around at his lords, one after the other. "Is that all? Or are there any other of my father's enemies or offspring in open rebellion?" His men shuffled their feet and glanced sidelong at each other. "Just three, is it? Well, three is enough, do you not think? It is clear that our enemies mean to overwhelm us with problems. While I attack one, the other will come in behind me and assault my lands or attempt to pin me between them. But we shall do nothing so foolish as that."

Vlad broke off, looking up at the arches of the vaulted ceiling above.

"Shall we assemble the army, my lord?" one of his men said, as if prompting his overwhelmed prince.

"In time, certainly," Vlad said, looking down again and searching the faces of every one of us present. "But this is a war on many fronts. Their claims that I am a Turkish lackey must be countered by the truth. And we shall move first of all to strike them in their most precious, most sensitive, most beloved parts." He smiled, cupping a hand down low before him. "Their purses."

If I had been a prince, I would have gone to war. My armies would have smashed my enemies one after the other. But Vlad had been raised to consider statecraft and had studied cunning under no less a tutor than William de Ferrers.

He countered his enemies with writ and with sanction, with declarations and proclamations. Vlad withdrew all previously awarded protections for trade for the Saxon towns and encouraged Wallachian merchants with highly favourable tariffs. He imposed exceedingly disadvantageous terms on all Saxon merchants in his lands. There were many declarations issued, one of which required them to entirely unpack their wagons for inspection by Wallachian officers and merchants at Târgovişte. Every time I passed by, there were Saxons complaining and arguing with the officials while their produce was spread across the square being poked and ruined by grinning Wallachian customs officers. The Saxons were forced to sell to Wallachian merchants at far lower prices than they could have received further along the trade routes.

All his economic warfare frustrated the Saxons and reduced their revenues enormously, while boosting Vlad's. It also meant that the entire Wallachian merchant and artisan class became besotted with their new prince and he had swiftly won the loyalty of another caste in his nation.

The Saxon merchants of course did everything that they possibly could to avoid Vlad's newly empowered customs officials and so Vlad had a perfectly legal cause to bring them and their cities to heel.

"Now it is time, Richard," Vlad said to me one morning as I entered his hall. "We shall put the *sluji* to good use at last."

"Against the Saxons?" I said. "I would much rather take them south to raid across the Danube to kill Turks. That is why we made them."

Vlad scowled. "In fact, Richard, we created them to kill William's Blood Janissaries. Not ordinary Turks."

I sighed. "They are not yet battle hardened. They need honing further before facing William's men on the field."

"Well then," Vlad said, spreading his arms. "What difference does it make if they kill Saxons or Turks? Both are the enemies of Wallachia. Both are the enemies of Vlad Dracula. Anyway, Richard, by this rebellion the Saxons know they weaken a Christian kingdom in the face of the Turk. By rebelling against me they are working in concert with the Turk, if not in full collusion with him. It is a good and proper thing for a commander to test his men before throwing them into battle, yes. The *sluji* have trained together and now we will see how well they fight together? We must know. And these are the only battles they will see before Mehmed and William come. And come they will."

I knew that Eva and the others would disagree with our immortals being used to attack Christians but nothing Vlad said was incorrect. It was one thing to see them march and camp and deploy but we had to see the *sluji* in action to be confident in them. And anyway, the Germans could be bloody well damned for their treachery, as far as I was concerned.

"Very well."

And so we put the *sluji* to the test.

∞

Both the towns of Sibiu and Brasov deserved to be punished. They were the most Saxon of districts in Transylvania and they were also within the duchies of Fogaras and Amlas, which were possessions of the Prince of Wallachia. And so Vlad was in his rights to order Sibiu to give up its support for Vlad the Monk and Brasov was formally instructed that they were harbouring a traitor to the crown in Dan III.

Neither city so much as sent a letter of response to Vlad's demands.

While a light rain fell beneath a low grey sky, I approached the assembly field outside of Târgoviște leading my five hundred mounted *sluji* as well as the servants who would provide their blood and all other logistical support. There were hundreds of horsemen present but there was not the army I had expected to see.

Vlad had brought his bodyguard and a small number of *boyars* and their own retinues.

"Where are the cannons?" I asked Vlad, riding to him. "Where are the infantry?"

"Cannons, Richard?" Vlad asked, innocently, while his men laughed. "Infantry?"

I came close enough to him to drop my voice. "You want to take these towns, do you not? How do you expect to do it quickly without destroying the walls or storming them? If you expect my men to storm the walls of these wealthy places, one after the other, I will lose scores at least and possibly hundreds. You will throw away all I have built with the *sluji* if you mean to do such a thing."

"You fear I mean to overrule your command of your men, Richard?" he asked. "Do you worry that I will command them and they will obey?"

I was confused and caught off-guard because that had not even occurred to me. The fact that he jumped right to that raised my hackles and I was about to tell him he was welcome to try when he smiled.

"I jest, Richard, I jest. No, you are quite right, of course. I do not have time to make a siege of these places, one after the other. While I am in one place, the other will run riot. No, no. We will simply destroy their *lands* instead. Each town has a dominion filled with productive villages. Well, we will burn every village and drive off all their people. All the merchants we find shall be killed, of course. Soon enough, the towns will capitulate. And if they do not, well, my dear friend Michael Szilágyi has given his word that he will bring his army down upon them with all the cannons and infantry that we might possibly need. Either way, the Saxons will give up before they are conquered. All they care about is money. Shall we depart?"

Our cavalry force moved swiftly across the mountains in spring 1458, passing by the Turno Ro, the Red Tower, which the Wallachians swore was stained red due to the blood of all the Turks who had bled upon its walls in their futile attempts to take it. Absurd, of course, but they seemed to believe it. Our destination was the valley of the River Hirtibaciu. These were the lands of Saxons who continued to support Vlad the Monk and so the people there were rebels. Their punishment would be death.

"We must not do this," Eva said when we were about to order the men into the valley. "We did not make this brotherhood of blood to make war on the innocent."

"They are not innocent. They are rebels."

"Do not be so pig-headed," she muttered. "You know this is wrong."

"Very well, this is wrong," I snapped, speaking quietly so that no one would know I was arguing with my woman. "But this is the path we are on. This path leads to William's head on a spike and so it is our path."

"Unleashing our men on women and children?"

"I will order them to leave the women and children unharmed," I said.

She scoffed and walked away, because of course such a thing was absurd. Even so, I ordered the men to spare the lives of the women and to let the children flee.

"This will spread panic," I said, projecting my voice over them all. "And send hungry mouths to Sibiu, which will cause them to surrender."

The *sluji* broke off into companies, each commanded by a captain. Walt and Rob took the strongest, the steadiest of them in their companies. Claudin, Garcia, and Jan, took the rest. They knew their business and the *sluji* brought fire and death to the villages of the valley. The men they found were killed. Some of my men delighted in making spectacles of it, forcing their kin to watch as their menfolk were executed, sometimes in artful ways.

Rob made sure to protect the children at least, as best as he could, but even he struggled to keep the women from being violated. One might as well attempt to stop a white-topped wave from reaching a rocky shore. Such is the way of war. Everything a man does must be to make his own people strong so that war does not descend on his lands.

Thus, the valley of Hirtibaciu was turned to a smouldering ruin. Without resting, we moved on to the lands around the town of Brasov.

First, we destroyed the village of Bod. The houses were burned, as were the fields and the trees, and the waters were poisoned with corpses. Everyone was killed, other than a handful who were taken prison so that they could be publicly executed back at Târgoviște.

The village of Talme we also burned to the ground and every

person slaughtered.

Any Saxon merchants who were captured attempting to flee the area were tortured before they were killed. At Birsei, a community of six hundred merchants were captured trying to force their way clear of our encirclement. They had banded together in hopes of overcoming us. But they were merchants and we were soldiers.

"Do you know," Vlad said, his voice ringing out over them. They were tied up, on their knees, in a great mass. Many were bruised and bleeding and most had ropes around their necks tying them one to the other lest they attempt to flee again. "Do you know that I have promised to impale every Saxon merchant I find in these lands?"

The wind was the only answer. Somewhere, a man groaned in agony, physical or spiritual, and many of Vlad's men laughed.

"Why is it then that you would stay?" Vlad asked them. "Can it be that you do not fear impalement?"

Again, they hung their heads.

Stephen cursed under his breath beside me. Even Serban looked sickened.

"Where is Eva?" I asked him.

Serban did not look at me. "I think the mistress would not wish to see more men put on sticks," he said.

"She ain't the only one," Walt muttered.

"Impalement does not seem to frighten the Saxons overly much," Vlad called to his men, as if he was astonished. "I think we must try other methods. Have them boiled."

When it was clear that the prince was not joking, great

cauldrons were brought from the kitchens of grand houses, fires were lit, and one or two bound men at a time were dumped into the boiling water. The fires had to be built high and hot and hundreds of men brought wood for the fires for hours on end. Every so often the executions would have to be stopped while masses of boiled skin were scraped from where it accumulated on the sides of the cauldrons. The screams of the dying were nothing when compared to the sobbing and begging of the Saxons who lay shivering on the ground watching their friends boiling to death before them. It was hard work for the Wallachians, but their prince had set them the task and they were committed to seeing it done. At the end, a couple of dozen merchants were released before their time was up.

"In my great mercy, I have decided to grant your freedom," Vlad pronounced. "You fortunate fellows will return to your homelands. If any of my men lay eyes on you again, you shall suffer a fate worse than the one you have just avoided."

It was not mercy of course. Vlad wanted the tale to spread to the other towns. And spread it did, not just to the Saxons of Transylvania but to all German-speaking peoples and beyond. The tales of Vlad's bloodthirsty depravity had begun.

As promised, Michael Szilágyi brought his forces down from Hungary and besieged Sibiu in October 1458 and though he did not take it, the Saxons towns as one agreed to come to the negotiating table.

Just as Dracula had predicted.

The murder and terror we had inflicted had shaken their resolve and the Saxon rebels gave in. In November, the burghers of Brasov agreed to surrender the would-be prince Dan III and his supporters to Vlad Dracula. They even agreed to pay Szilágyi ten thousand florins in restitution for the revenues they had withdrawn from Hungary. In return, they would have their previous commercial rights and privileges restored.

And all was well. Vlad congratulated all of us on a campaign of terror well waged. The *sluji* had done their part superbly, following the orders of their captains. They had drunk the blood of their enemies only when no mortals could bear witness and they now felt themselves blooded as a company. When we returned to the valley of Poenari, I told them I was proud of them and that with peace on our northern border, we would soon face their true enemies the Turks in battle.

Sadly, that was not to be. Not yet.

King Mattias Corvinus Hunyadi was not his father. He was far more ruthless and far less honourable. The king was displeased at the way the rebellion had been handled. Indeed, he was furious at the amount of blood that had been spilled and he felt that the terror we caused had blackened his name by association. In order to distance himself from the massacres, he had Szilágyi captured and imprisoned and it was clear to all parties that everything Szilágyi had agreed in the negotiations no longer had value.

Even more astonishing for us, for Vlad Dracula, was the King Mattias Corvinus declared his support for the rebel Dan III.

"It is all falling apart already," Stephen said when we heard. "Corvinus hates Dracula."

We were in our camp, seated around a table in my tent. The company busied itself outside while we discussed what it might mean for us.

"He fears him," I said, nodding. "Fears his resolve."

"We should all fear his resolve," Stephen replied. "What happens to us, to the *sluji*, if Vlad is overthrown? With the King of Hungary for an enemy, with a replacement prince in his pocket, surely it is all but certain."

"Keep your voices down," Eva snapped.

"The treaty with the Saxons is finished," Stephen said, leaning forward. "And so we are at war with Brasov again when it is the Turks we are here to fight. We have our immortal army, but they are being squandered on these ridiculous dynastic squabbles. We wanted a king who was strong. And now we have Vlad who is still unable to suppress his nobles or his other vassals despite the evil he wreaks and what is more we find that the King of Hungary is favouring a new prince for Wallachia."

"These people are mad," Walt said. "No offence, Serban."

Serban looked up from his position guarding the entrance to the tent and looked away again.

"Do you doubt that Vlad will emerge victorious?" I asked them. "Even without our help, I would not doubt him."

"He is a perfectly capable soldier," Stephen said. "But with so many enemies how can he ever—"

"He is more than capable, Stephen," I said, surprised at the fervour with which I found myself speaking. "He is decisive and he leads his men well, whether peasant or lord. He knows how men think. His own and his enemy's. We are committed, now. We cannot abandon the *sluji* here and I fear that they would not follow me away from Wallachia. Not without Vlad's permission at least. Not yet. We must make it so that Vlad emerges victorious. That is our path to throwing the *sluji* against the Blood Janissaries."

"Everything you say is true," Rob said. "But this way of waging war does not bring glory. Only blood."

"Well then that is lucky for us," I said. "For blood is what we need."

They were not amused, and I could not blame them. It did not get any better and indeed, it grew to be far worse.

Early in the year, we raided the valley of the River Prahova, destroying the villages there which belonged to Brasov. We burned crops and killed everyone in our path. We reached Brasov swiftly, and they were not expecting us for many days yet. Much of the town lay outside its walls, having grown through its success so that many homes, large and small, lined the roads toward the town.

Unprotected by a wall, we smashed our way right into those suburbs and captured hundreds of residents.

Outside the walls of Brasov, Vlad ordered the prisoners be impaled.

They were raised aloft in their hundreds, writhing and screaming in full sight of the residents lining the walls. Those residents were the friends, business partners, and family, of the prisoners dying upon the stakes outside. On the walls, they screamed and begged and hurled insults, wailing as they watched their kin dying in the most horrific way imaginable.

Even the veterans of my Company of Saint George quailed at the sight and the sound of it and most of them walked away. But

I could not. The sheer horror of it was breath-taking. In all my years, all I could recall that was the like of it was the massacres of the Mongols. They had dreamed up satanic punishments for their conquered foes but they were a savage, barbarian people. To see Christians killing Christians in such a fashion was a fresh horror that stunned me.

"Astonishing," Stephen muttered, for he alone had stayed to watch. "Truly astonishing."

"You sound almost as though you admire him for this," I said.

"Do you not?" Stephen replied, not looking at me.

"Admire him? It is monstrous."

"Precisely," Stephen said. "Who could bring himself to do this? I could not. I could never. Never. Could you, Richard?"

"No."

"Do you think William could? Of course, I am sure that he could. It is the sheer will of it, do you not think? The sheer will that is to be admired."

"Keep your damned voice down, Stephen."

In response to the wailing and the begging from the residents of Brasov, Vlad had a large trestle set up in amongst the dying people around and above him. There, he was served a hearty breakfast and he tucked into sausage and cheese and bread with gusto. While the citizens of Brasov watched from the walls, he had a man's throat cut and the blood caught in a bowl. This was brought to him and he delighted in dipping his bread into it with every mouthful.

"By God, it is true," Eva said, coming up beside me. "Serban said Vlad was drinking blood in full view of everyone. I did not believe him."

I looked around and Serban was there beside Eva his face a mask of anguish. "No one will know what it means," I said. "He is merely dipping his bread in the blood. It is a display of barbarity. Meant to break the will of Brasov."

"He's a madman," Eva said.

Eventually, a quaking messenger was sent out under a flag of truce, while he covered his mouth to stop himself from vomiting or perhaps to block to reek of blood and ripped bowels.

"You bring word of your unconditional surrender?" Vlad asked, still eating.

The man's eyes were rimmed red and his gaze kept wandering up to the dead men and women all around him. "Prince Dan is not in Brasov."

One of Vlad's lords stiffened. "Address your lord properly, or you shall join these men in the sky, you fat Saxon pig."

He bowed and spoke again, shaking like a leaf. "Forgive me, My Lord Prince. It is just that..." he swallowed and tried again. "My lords the elders of Brasov send word that the rebel who names himself Dan III, left our city ten days ago. Neither he, nor his men, nor his soldiers, are within our walls or within our lands."

"If you are lying, then your entire city shall suffer this same fate." Vlad gestured above him.

"It is no lie. My Lord."

"Then tell me. Where is he?"

The messenger fell to his knees and vomited onto the ground. "Please, my lord, have mercy."

Vlad put down his piece of cheese and got to his feet. He strode across to the man sobbing over his own vomit, pulled his sword from the scabbard and used it to lift the man's quivering chin up. "Where is the traitor?"

"He... he... he has invaded Wallachia!"

It was true. Unbeknownst to any of us, or Vlad's agents, Dan III had moved decisively to invade Wallachia while we were moving on Brasov. It seemed that there were traitors yet in Vlad's army, or at least that Dan had been incredibly lucky in his timing. Either way, he had got into Wallachia behind us and he had begun his campaign of insurrection. He intended to do just what every would-be Prince of Wallachia had to do in order to gain the throne. He had to get assurances from *boyars* one by one.

I expected Vlad to be furious. I thought that he would rage and order his men to find what traitor had sold him out.

Instead of fire, though, he was ice. After Brasov was subdued, Vlad turned our army around and led us straight into Wallachia. If Dan had been counting on us besieging Brasov for weeks and months, allowing him free reign behind our backs, he was sorely mistaken. Due to Vlad's atrocity outside the walls, Brasov had fallen immediately and so Dan was shocked at our sudden appearance at his rear.

We caught up with him in April 1460 and defeated his small army before he could do too much mischief. It was not much of a battle. He was outnumbered and outclassed and I led the *sluji* on a wide manoeuvre around his rear, falling upon him when he was already engaged with Vlad's forces.

His men surrendered at once, throwing down their weapons.

Before the assembled *sluji* and the rest of Vlad's bodyguard and leading *boyars*, Dan III was brought forward. Dracula had ordered a proper grave to be dug and Dan was made to stand before it.

"What is this farce?" Dan said, shaking with rage. "You inhuman monster. Do you expect me to grovel in fear? Just kill me and be done with it."

"You misunderstand, sir," Vlad said, speaking loudly so that all could hear. "You see, you are already dead. Yes, you see, you died when you thought you could rise against me. This is simply your funeral."

Vlad nodded to a black-robed priest who stepped forward and proceeded to recite the funeral for Dan III while he stood bound before his own grave.

When the ceremony was completed, the priest hurried back and Vlad Dracula stepped up to Dan III, drew his sword and cut off the man's head in a single, effortless stroke.

It was masterfully done. Dan's body and head both tumbled into the grave.

"Now," said Vlad, turning to us. "Let us find my brother Vlad the Monk, shall we?"

We continued to plunder the Saxon lands and refused to make lasting peace with any of them until Vlad the Monk was captured. We hoped that the Saxons would collectively find the Monk and give him up but they seemed set against us. One could hardly blame them. We raided their lands all of the summer of 1460, taking their wealth and their people. Prisoners divulged that Vlad the Monk was in hiding in the Duchy of Amlas and so we burned the town of Amlas and impaled the citizens, after forcing a priest to lead them all in a repulsive procession to the site of their execution. My *sluji* burned and killed through half of the duchy and eventually everyone in the city and many in the villages were killed by one means or another.

How many it was that died, I do not know. Thousands, certainly. And the town of Amlas was so reduced that it never recovered.

It was disheartening.

"We waste our efforts against these people," I said to Vlad in the smoking ruins. "Anyone can slaughter peasants and merchants. The *sluji* was meant for greater things."

He turned his bulging eyes to me. "My enemies must be destroyed."

I gestured around us. "I think they have been."

"Not enough," he snapped. "They resist, in their hearts if not in their actions."

"Would you expect any less? You say they do not truly belong in your lands and that is true, of course. But then you still expect them to come to heel. They are not Wallachian. They know it as well as you do. You are a foreign ruler to them and always will be. You can never trust the Saxons but while they yet live and their cities still stand, will you not let them make peace? And then we can turn our efforts against the true enemy."

"I will have their obedience."

"Let them offer it. Let them offer some terms, at least. Everyone in Christendom knows they have been beaten."

Mattias Corvinus acted as peacemaker, ironically, as it was his endorsement of Dan III that had encouraged the Saxons into open rebellion. But with his mediation, accommodation was reached. Commercial privileges were returned, which is all the mercantile people really care about. And for their part, the Saxons agreed to pay an annual fee large enough to maintain an army of four thousand mercenaries who would be employed against the Turks.

Thus strengthened, we could turn our soldiers south again.

1 2

Ottoman Invasion

1 4 6 2

"DID YOU HEAR WHAT he's gone and done now?" Walt whispered.

We stood in Vlad Dracula's great hall in Târgoviște along with hundreds of *boyars*, burghers, monks, priests, and soldiers milling around waiting for the prince to arrive. Their muttering filled the air to the rafters.

"I do not know," I replied. "What has he done?"

"You heard about him going around and capturing all the beggars in Wallachia? All the beggars and the vagabonds. And he's had them executed."

"I heard. My heart does not bleed for the wastrels."

Walt nodded and smiled in greeting at a soldier who had

called out in salutation. "And did you hear that he had all the beggars rounded up and brought to a vast tent where they were served a mighty feast? And while they were eating, your man Vlad ordered that they be burned alive. See, he had the stools and benches soaked in oil, and the cloths upon the tables also, and when the order was given the whole lot of them, hundreds of the blighters, all went up like a bonfire."

I scoffed. "If that had happened, Walt, I would have heard about it."

"You don't want to hear, that's your problem, Richard. You have closed your ears to the truth of your friend."

"Nonsense."

"Did you hear what he done to that gypsy leader not a week last Tuesday?"

"No."

Walt shifted closer. "Well, what he done was, he had the leader of this clan of gypsies boiled alive while his whole clan watched. See, his flesh was boiled all nice and so Vlad had the leader carved up into little pieces while his people, what was in irons, watched and despaired. And then, this is the worst part of the tale, so listen well, then he had pieces of the flesh forced into the mouths of every one of the gypsy clan. Force fed them their own lord and father, imagine that."

I looked at him. "Where did you hear this?"

"One of Vlad's lads, you know Michael One-Eye? He split that Saxon in two with his poleaxe outside Amlas."

"I believe I do recall the fellow. He was there?"

"He swears it upon his mothers grave and all that is holy that his cousin Pepu was there."

I chuckled. "Well, there you have it then. It did not happen."

"Michael told me Vlad done a speech to the peasants who was watching. He said to them, he said, these men live off the sweat of others, so they are useless to humanity. Their lives are but a form of thievery. In fact, says Vlad, in fact the masked robber in the forest demands your purse but if you are quicker with your hand and more vigorous than he you can escape from him. But these vagabonds take your belongings gradually by their begging but still they take more. They are worse than robbers. I will see to it, Vlad says, that such men are eradicated from my land. And then he had the lot of them killed."

I grunted. "That does sound like something he would say."

Walt smiled, pleased with himself. "Told you so."

"Silence now. The envoys are here."

We knew that Sultan Mehmed and William's policy of conquest was now to conquer across the Danube and secure at least the lowlands of Wallachia and the lower Danube all the way to the delta where it ran into the Black Sea. That part of the river was controlled by Vlad's cousin Stephen in Moldavia.

Indeed, it was clear to all Christendom where the hammer blow would next fall.

The Turks would next attempt the conquest of Wallachia or Moldavia. Or both.

Pope Pius II called a congress of all Christian princes at Mantua for the necessary crusade. He even tried to create a new military order of knights, bearing the name of Our Lady of Bethlehem, who would be dedicated to waging war on the Turks while based on the island of Lemnos. But the Pope's congress and his new order were born lame. Nothing came of the new order and it was quietly dropped, no doubt embarrassing the Pope. Worse, almost no kingdoms answered the call to take the cross.

It was no longer surprising to me that Christendom could not be relied upon. In England, the great lords loyal to Lancaster or York were fighting over the Crown. The French were pouting about a decision the Pope had made to favour Aragon's suggestion for the throne of Naples rather than the pretender put forward by the House of Anjou. The Holy Roman Emperor Frederick III decided to taunt the Pope by sending Gregory of Heimburg as his representative, a man who had been excommunicated. The Holy Roman Empire was moving ever closer toward open defiance of Rome and Gregory was apparently openly hostile to the Pope in person during the congress. Ultimately, he promised to send thirty thousand infantry and ten thousand cavalry to the Danube in support of the crusade, which would have been a magnificent force to have on the frontier. In fact, though, Gregory never even attempted to raise them and the whole thing was no doubt simply an overt snub for Pope Pius II.

Poland, too, was engaged in its protracted conflict against the Teutonic Knights and even commanded Moldavia, her traditional vassal, to avoid conflict. The Albanians, isolated and threatened as they were, had secured a three-year truce with Mehmed II and they refused to break it, preferring to stay on the sidelines. It was short-sighted, for they would soon fall utterly before the Turks but mortal men act almost always in their immediate interest rather than doing what is best for their nation.

In an act of complete desperation, Pope Pius II sent a monk named Fra Ludovico da Bologna halfway across the world to the east of the Turks territories. There, he urged the Mohammedan states in the far east of Anatolia to attack the Turks and so open up two fronts at once, drawing away their strength from both.

I imagine that Fra Ludovico da Bologna was met with the same response wherever he went. Something along the lines of *what do you think we have been trying to do for a hundred years, infidel?*

Pope Pius was certainly being industrious, although some would say he was being desperate. He travelled to Ancona on Italy's east coast and declared he would lead the crusade in person but no one flocked to join him. It was certainly desperation that caused him to write to Sultan Mehmed II in an attempt to convert him to Catholicism.

I imagine William laughing down to his belly when he read that letter.

It was all rather pathetic. All it did was signal to our enemies that we were weak and disunited and desperate. They could scent our blood more than ever.

But Vlad Dracula responded to the Pope's call.

He was committed to destroying the Turks and all Mohammedans. As his father before him, Vlad was a member of the Order of the Dragon.

So few were with us.

Michael Szilágyi was one of the few good and honourable men left in the Balkans and he swore he would wage war against the enemy. But Szilágyi made a fundamental error. He was carrying out forward reconnaissance in Bulgaria in preparation for the invasion we knew was coming. But he failed to take the proper precautions despite being in enemy territory and he was captured.

This great man had not long previously been in effect Regent of Hungary and had by his actions secured the crown for his nephew. But the Turks captured him and took him to Constantinople and was passed over to Zaganos Pasha; my dearest brother. There, William tortured him mercilessly for information about Hungary's military preparations and the state of specific defences.

How much Michael Szilágyi gave up, I do not know.

But what I do know is that William had my friend and Vlad's mentor sawn in half.

Soon after, a large party of Turkish envoys arrived from Constantinople. Vlad made them wait for days for an audience which was a deliberate and obvious snub. Many townsfolk in Târgovişte were made nervous by the presence of the increasingly agitated envoys, knowing as they did that any provocation made it more likely that war would begin. The soldiers and leaders amongst them, though, knew that war was inevitable. The only question was when it would begin.

Finally, Vlad had them brought to the castle and he awaited them in his hall in all his finery. The Turks were irritated by the sneering soldiers who escorted them so closely that they at times dragged the envoys by the arms. When they protested, the soldiers laughed and mocked them.

But on they came in their colourful robes and great headdresses of wound cloth with jewels set over the forehead.

When they bowed before Vlad III Dracula, then, their blood

was up. The audience of *boyars* and burghers was clearly hostile and the envoys frowned and huffed to be so disrespected. Even the priests scowled at them.

"Not a happy bunch of lads, are they," Walt whispered.

"He means to send them back to Mehmed fully insulted."

Walt shrugged. "Good for a laugh, I suppose."

"It is an act of defiance. To shake his enemy and to show his men that he does not fear the Sultan. Hush, now."

The Turks made their introductions and bowed. "I thank you, my lord Vlad, Prince of Wallachia, for welcoming us to—"

"What is the meaning of this?" Vlad said, his voice overwhelming them and silencing every murmur in the hall.

The envoy broke off and traded glances with his fellows. "My lord? I am afraid I do not understand—"

"How is it that you come to me so attired?"

The envoy looked down at his robes. "My lord, this is the clothing commonly worn by my—"

"Look around you, Turk." Vlad commanded. "Look at the men in my hall. What do you see?"

All of the envoys looked at the hundreds of lords and soldiers and priests all around them, glaring in hatred. "I see the great and noble lords of Wallachia and no doubt of other Christian lands who serve—"

"What do you see upon their heads?"

He looked startled for a moment before recovering. "My lord," he said and bowed. "At your court and at the courts of Christian monarchs, it is the custom for your people to bare their heads when addressing their king, their prince, as a sign of respect. And yet it is the custom of the Turks to wear such turbans as you see us wearing before you as our own form of respect. For us to remove our turbans would be signifying that we disrespected you and this of course we could never dream of doing, my lord."

Vlad stared at him and allowed a heavy silence to descend once more. "Where are you, envoy of the Sultan?"

"My lord? We are in your fine hall, my lord. In the magnificent city of Târgoviște."

Vlad nodded slowly and wagged a finger once at the envoy. "Indeed, sir. Indeed, you are. And so would you not wish to follow our customs when in our lands?"

The envoy swallowed and bowed again. "I wish that I could, my lord, but as you know I am merely the servant of my master and he has bidden me to wear the attire you see before you. I cannot remove a piece of it without his command."

Vlad frowned, tilting his head as if confused. "So, you refuse to remove this hat?"

"It is not a hat, my lord, it is... that is to say, it breaks my heart but it cannot be removed without offending my master, the Sultan Mehmed II."

"In that case, my friends, I cannot allow you to offend your master. I cannot allow you to remove your hats. Not ever, for the rest of your lives. Would that be acceptable?"

The envoy hesitated, sensing a trap. "I... yes, my lord. I am most thankful for your courteous understanding in this matter."

Vlad clapped his hands once. "Wonderful." He gestured to the captain of his guards who came forward with his fist clasped around some sort of bundle in one hand and hefting an iron hammer in the other. "And to help you to keep your hats on your heads, we shall hammer them into place with these iron nails."

The envoys were confused and then they attempted to flee and then to fight. But they were seized by the soldiers and forced onto their knees. One by one, great iron nails ten inches in length were driven through the turbans and into the men's skulls. Some of them died or at least collapsed immediately but others continued screaming and begging, despite the iron in their brains. However, those men were also not long for the world.

"Take the bodies to their servants and send them back to Constantinople," Vlad commanded. "Along with my warm regards."

"Did you see that?" Walt said in my ear, chuckling. "He must have had those nails and hammer ready the whole time. Whatever anyone says about him, you can't say he doesn't have a knack for a good jest."

Most of the hall emptied temporarily and wine was served to the guests out in the courtyard below while the hall was decked with tables and benches ready for a feast. But Dracula stayed by his throne and called me to him as the work went on around us.

"Was that for Szilágyi?" I asked.

"Hardly. When I have Mehmed and William as my prisoner, and both are tortured for weeks before being sawn in half while they scream for their mothers, then we shall say that it was for dear Michael. This was…" Vlad shrugged. "A playful taunt. No more."

"You hope to move him to attack sooner than he wishes?"

"Not through insults, he is too hard of heart to be moved by such petty things. If we can draw him close by military means, then perhaps we can get him to move this year, before his full force is readied."

"And you have a notion of how to do that?"

Vlad brushed a finger along his moustache. "You know about the raids across the Danube?"

I nodded. "The *razzia* parties grow bold. They are taking plunder, which we cannot afford, and killing the men and ravishing the women to death but they are taking children now, also."

"Taking them for the slave markets in Constantinople. I have lost too many people along the river and I will not lose any more. The *boyars* are doing their best but they cannot guard against all incursions. Every time they arrive, it is too late."

"I am sure we could do something to help," I said.

"It is not only the raids but they are certainly testing the defences. They want to take every fort on the river before they launch their invasion."

"You want us to hold the fortresses? I am not certain the *sluji* will make good garrison troops."

"I do not want to hold them. Not all of them. I am of a mind to allow some to fall but to fight for others."

"So that Mehmed comes across where we want him to."

"And you know where, Richard. Can you be ready by tomorrow?"

"I will go now."

Vlad smiled. "There are not many men who would rather ride to war than feast with his friends."

I bowed. "My Lord Prince, I will feast on the blood of Turks."

Throughout 1461, we threw back many raids and in our turn raided enemy camps. The *sluji* were swiftly learning to fight together, and together we drank the blood of many Turks. The villages and fortresses by the Danube saw us as saviours, despite it becoming common knowledge that we killed our prisoners and sucked the blood of the dying from their very wounds. All the people knew we were fighting for them and so it did not matter what we were said to be doing to their enemies.

Despite our best efforts, we were only so many and we could only be a certain number of places at once. I requested that Dracula send more soldiers to help us but he wanted them, the peasant army that they were, to undergo further training together before the true invasion began.

The most important and greatest of all Wallachian fortresses on the Danube was Giurgiu. It was situated amid mud-flats and marshes on the left bank of the Danube where it swerves north for a stretch. There were many islands in the river there which made it easier to cross, and the land to the north produced enormous quantities of grain so it was a vital point in the defences. The fortress being surrounded by marsh made it difficult to assault from the land but the Turks swarmed the walls from the riverside and took it.

They held it for close to a year and Vlad said he was content for them to hold it, for he was not going to waste men on a frontal assault. As important as it was, I was likewise not going to waste any of my *sluji* when it was likely to continue to be fought over anyway.

And so, as much as it rankled, I let it be.

During that year, I captured and questioned hundreds of men before I killed them and they gave up as much as they knew. Often I would start the same way.

"What can you tell me that might save your life?"

It is remarkable the things that men say at such times. Almost always what they said was useless but I asked all the same.

One man, in the very depths of a freezing winter, gave me far more than most.

"An ambush!" he screamed. He was a captain of some importance, as evidenced by his clothes and his fluent Greek.

"What ambush? Our ambush of your men? Is that all you have? Very well." I placed the edge of my knife on his throat. He had a bulging Adam's apple and I poked at it.

"Vlad Dracula!"

I moved my blade away a fraction. "Say that again?"

He gulped, shifting so that his knees crunched the ice on the frozen ground. "An ambush on Vlad Dracula, my lord."

I put the blade under his chin and lifted his face up. "A likely story." I leaned down. "Where? When?"

"At Giurgiu!"

"He's not in Giurgiu, you damned fool. The Turks have Giurgiu."

He held up his hands. "That's true, yes, but Dracula is coming to Giurgiu. And before he gets there, in the woods in the north by the marshes, he is to be ambushed and killed."

"Why would he go to Giurgiu? In the depths of winter at that. Why would he risk his life in such a fashion? It is absurd."

"I do not know. All I know is, he is coming there. There will be a Wallachian bodyguard of a hundred men and so we needed to be at least twice that number."

Behind the man, Rob shrugged.

"You have less than a hundred here," I said.

"Yes, it was to be my men, many Turks from Anatolia, a company of Bulgarians and some other Greeks who serve Hamza Pasha."

"When?"

"Soon. Dracula has already left Târgovişte, so they say."

Rob waved Walt over to listen.

I leaned down. "If you are lying to me then I promise that your death will be long and dreadful. Admit that this was all a lie now and I will end you swiftly."

He swallowed. "It is the truth, I swear it."

"We shall see. Bind him and bring him. Drink the rest."

"Bring him where?"

"The road to Târgovişte."

We intercepted Vlad Dracula's company about twenty miles north of Giurgiu where Vlad was building a monastery at a place called Comana. Being so close to the Danube, it needed to be heavily fortified against raids and it looked more like a castle than a house of prayer. The building work was far further along than the previous time I had seen it and the great walls were almost completed. I had most of the *sluji* keep back out of sight and went up with just a handful of my men at first light. Dracula's bodyguards were alert to any danger and I was escorted inside.

"Where is the prince?" I asked them when I was through the monastery gates.

"Preparing to depart, my lord," the senior soldier said, blowing warmth into his hands. "He is eating in the refectory with Catavolinos."

"With who? And what in the world are you doing bringing the prince so far south?"

Vlad's bodyguard scowled, though it was not me. "Thomas Catavolinos, a Greek in the service of Hamza Pasha. There is to be a negotiation to avoid the coming war. Or delay it, at least, while we grow stronger. Hamza Pasha was due to come to Târgoviște but he sent this Catavolinos instead and the meeting place was changed to Giurgiu."

"But why would you let him risk himself by coming to the Danube?"

"He is our prince. We do as he commands."

"You men are supposed to protect him. Even from himself. Remember that. Take me to him."

Vlad's soldiers outnumbered the monks at least ten to one, crowding every corner of the monastery. But the refectory was empty other than Vlad's bodyguards, a handful of servants, and the prince and his guest. It was mercifully warm inside.

The Greek named Thomas Catavolinos was a sophisticated and charming gentleman who smiled ingratiatingly and made it

398

clear how truly delighted he was to be able to make my acquaintance. I told him the pleasure was entirely mine and begged he allow me to speak to my lord for just a few brief moments. Catavolinos bowed and said he would be delighted to take a stroll around the remarkable walls.

The moment he was gone, I turned on Dracula. "What in the name of God are you doing?"

"Good morning, Richard," Vlad said, chewing on a piece of bread. "This is a pleasant surprise."

"Why are you here, Vlad?"

He frowned as he leaned back. "I believe I should be asking you that question. Why are you not on the Danube?"

"It is a day's ride away. The real question is why are you so close to it? Why are you riding into a fortress on the river that is held by the Turks? Have you lost your mind?"

Vlad's moustache twitched. "There is no danger that I cannot overcome."

"Did you not expect a trap?"

He shrugged. "Of course. But I have a hundred of my best men."

"Do you not know that they would send a thousand? In order to kill you they would send ten thousand and you feel safe with a hundred? You would blunder inside Giurgiu and never come out."

Vlad lifted his chin and looked along his long nose at me. "Do not think me a fool. I would not enter the walls. It was my condition that Hamza Pasha meet me outside the fortress and so I shall be free to flee if there is danger."

"You will not reach Giurgiu."

He stopped eating. "What do you know?"

"I have a man. A Greek captain who was to be one of the men leading the ambush. Just north of Giurgiu before the ground becomes a marsh, there is a woodland."

"I know it. The garrison cut wood for fuel there. It is dark and dense, even in winter, as it is a pine woodland but they could not hide ten thousand men there, Richard."

"At least two hundred will attack from all sides. There could be as many as five hundred, if they lay in the marshes also."

He nodded and began picking at his food again. "Where are the *sluji*?"

"With me. Here. Unseen to the south."

"Can you get close to the Giurgiu woodland? Unseen?"

"Not in daylight. After sunset, certainly."

"Then I will delay here. The food has produced in me a sickness and I will only be able to travel at first light tomorrow. I shall ask Thomas Catavolinos to send my apologies ahead later and then I shall see you on the road to Giurgiu tomorrow."

"You mean to spring the trap yourself? That is not necessary."

"I am the Prince of Wallachia. It is necessary."

It was a test of our men that they maintain discipline throughout the approach to the woodland. It was a cold and wet night and they were sodden and freezing as they crept with me through the marsh, walking where we could on top of the thick ice that had formed on top but just as often crashing through it. We hid ourselves behind tussocks of frozen grass and stands of bare bushes and waited in silence for sunrise. In truth, I doubted we would make it until the prince's party arrived. I was certain one of the Turks would wander close to relieve himself and discover us but even if that happened I thought we could fight our way through them. Even if they were five hundred. I left half our men beyond the marsh with our horses, in case we needed to flee or pursue an enemy and hoped that my remaining two hundred and fifty immortals were strong enough.

But Vlad came along the road early, their horses surrounded by a cloud of steam illuminated by the morning sun. Even after his earlier bravado, he was sensible enough to wait beyond the wood and send most of his bodyguard in ahead while keeping the Greek Catavolinos back with him.

As the Wallachian riders disappeared into the darkness of the pine trees, I heard Walt and Rob whistling like birds, prompting me to order our men to attack. But I wanted to ensure no enemy escaped.

I whistled back.

Not yet.

When the sound of fighting started, I called out the order and rushed through the icy bog. As I stood, I realised that ice had formed around my legs and flanks and it shattered as I strode forward. All around me, the *sluji* emerged from behind tussocks and long grass and bushes and we swarmed over the ice toward the woodland. The cold and wet Greek, Turkish and Bulgarian infantry were trying to break the fresh, mounted Wallachians but they were biding their time as more of their men got into position.

My men came up quickly and cut the enemy to pieces. We cried the name of Vlad Dracula and the Bulgarians were so surprised they tried to surrender but we killed most of them without hesitation. The Greeks instead tried to flee but they were intercepted by my men and cut down by the Wallachian bodyguard.

When Vlad came up, he had Catavolinos bound to a horse.

"It was done well, men!" Vlad shouted beneath the trees. "I am proud of you all. Now, we shall go on to Giurgiu."

I strode toward him, still damp and shivering despite my exertion. "What do you mean to do?"

Vlad ignored me for a moment and called to his men. "Find the biggest Turk you can and strip his armour." Vlad turned back to me. "How is your Turkish coming along?"

"Still not as good as my Arabic. Why?"

Vlad grinned.

It was not long before I sat on a horse beside Vlad before the vast gatehouse of the fortress of Giurgiu. It was a massive, squat castle covering the only section of dry land for a mile in any direction, barring the road. Beyond the fortress, the great Danube was a sheet of white ice and beyond that was Turkish Rumelia which had once been Bulgaria.

Behind us, almost fifty of our men sat with their shoulders hunched and heads down in ill-fitting Turkish armour. In our midst, we had a cluster of Wallachian prisoners, including one wearing Vlad Dracula's fine clothes.

Vlad called out to the men on the battlements in perfect Turkish. "Open the gates, you fools!"

"Who are you?" the guards shouted.

Even Vlad's audible scoff had a Turkish ring to it. "Who do

you think we are, you damned idiots. Tell Hamza Pasha we have Vlad Dracula."

"Where?"

"See for yourselves? He is here, the treacherous dog!" Vlad said, gesturing at the soldier dressed up in his clothing. "And hurry, would you. We have a hundred Wallachian bastards chasing us."

"Praise God!" The guard said, and they were all smiles behind their beards. "You must wait there for us to—"

Vlad's friendly tone shifted at once. "I shall not wait! I have ended the war! The Sultan will thank me himself, *inshallah*, and you will be praised also, my friend, for doing your duty. But if you do not open this gate at once you shall be executed, this I swear. What is your name? Tell me your name, immediately."

There was a sudden commotion above and their hands pointed behind us. I turned and although I could not see what the guards on the walls were pointing at, I knew what it was. A hundred Wallachian horsemen galloping from the distant woodland towards Giurgiu along the road.

"Quickly!" the guards in the gatehouse called to us. "The enemy approaches. Inside, quickly."

The gates swung open.

Before we rode in, Vlad turned to me and winked, a crooked smile beneath his long moustache. I had to lower my head to hide my own smile from the men on the walls above.

Our first task was to capture the gatehouse and hold open the outer gate and the inner gate. While we held open the gates, the poor Turks on guard were silenced forever and it did not take long for our Wallachian companions to come charging up to the fortress. We allowed them to charge right on in and then we closed the gates and followed the sound of the screams.

Once inside, we set about killing and capturing every damned Turk in the fortress. They did not understand what was happening and panic spread through the garrison. There was hardly any resistance at all and none of it was organised. Our men swarmed into every pocket of the fortress and dragged out those that attempted to hide in storerooms and under floors.

Giurgiu was a Wallachian fortress and the soldiers saw the Turkish presence as an infestation and as a personal affront. The Turks could not surrender fast enough and though we killed many, we still took a thousand of them prisoner. Most importantly of all, the treacherous Hamza Pasha was captured, and we ensured that he and Catavolinos were kept safe from the rampaging Wallachians.

Walt laughed to see it. We sat on our horses in the courtyard as the Wallachians took their revenge. "You remember capturing a castle with such ease before?"

"Never," said Rob.

"I am sure I must have done," I said.

"What a bunch of gooseberries, Richard," Walt said. "Never was a fortress so swiftly taken as this, not never. Got to hand it to your boy, Dracula don't muck about."

"There he is now," I said. "Come on."

I rode toward Vlad as he was issuing orders to his captains. The valuable prisoners were bound and bloody on the floor.

"You shall march these men to Târgovişte," Vlad said,

pointing his bloody sword down at them, "and there impale them outside the walls. The longest of stakes shall be reserved for you, Hamza, and you, Catavolinos. I will see your rotting corpses there when I return."

"You are not going with them?" I asked.

Vlad turned and laughed, ejecting a great plume of steam. "The Danube is frozen, Richard! We can cross it at will. I shall send for thousands of horsemen and together we shall raid Bulgaria until the spring thaw."

"What shall we accomplish?" I asked. "William is coming with an army large enough to conquer your kingdom. We should rest the men through the winter."

"The Turk has ravaged our border and so we will ravage his. We shall weaken him and only grow in strength. Let Mehmed come. Let Zaganos Pasha bring his Janissaries. We shall reduce every point of strength on the border. Every point. God is with us and so we shall begin."

I turned to my men, who shrugged.

"Who wants to be warm, anyway?" Walt muttered.

It was as Vlad said. We crossed and re-crossed the great river at a hundred points along its length. We surprised the Turks at every point, from Serbia all the way to the delta on the border of Moldavia. We broke into smaller companies for certain raids so that we could strike at a dozen places at once. When we needed to attack a larger enemy position we assembled more of our number so that we always had the upper hand. We lived off the land, taking what we needed from the villages and fortresses that we attacked and burned. The damage we wrought in a single winter was remarkable.

In order to keep a tally of those killed, Vlad ordered that heads or at least noses and ears be cut off and counted. Our soldiers competed to outdo each other in how many noses and ears they could collect.

In February, we came together back at Giurgiu and took stock of the destruction.

"It is time that we informed our overlord Mattias Corvinus of these matters," Vlad said in the great hall after hearing twenty reports. "Are you ready to take a letter? It is to say the following. I, Vlad III Dracula, have killed men and women, both young and old, who lived at Oblucitza and Novoselo where the Danube flows into the sea, up to Rahova which is near Chilia, from the lower Danube up to such places as Samovit and Ghighen. It is a fact that I have killed... how many was it?"

A clerk referred to the tally he had earlier recorded and cleared his throat before answering. "Twenty-three thousand, eight hundred and eighty-four, my lord."

"I have killed that number of Turks and Bulgars, but this is not counting those that we burned inside their homes and those whose heads were not struck off by my men. Thus, Your Highness should know that I have broken peace with Mehmed II. That is all, add no more, do not include any of your niceties. Have it taken at once to Buda."

We hoped that we had done enough damage to delay the invasion or at least hinder it. Most of all, Vlad had scored a moral victory over our enemies by striking the first blow and it was a victory that had to be answered. We knew by then that Mehmed and William were in Greece, engaged in reducing Corinth but he sent another wazir, Mahmud, to conduct a raid in force across the river.

They had almost twenty thousand men and they struck first the port of Brila on our side of the Danube. We brought the army down and trailed them, looking for a good place to intercept. All the while the Turks marched and looted through the lowlands, repaying our winter raids.

"We must stop them," I said, watching smoke rise above the trees in the distance. "What was all of this for if not to stop precisely this?"

"Have patience, Richard," Vlad said. "I knew my people would bleed. We shall destroy them utterly but it must be at the right moment."

"But we could drive them off now," I said. "We have enough men for that."

"I do not wish to drive them off. The entire army must be destroyed."

Whispering to Eva in the dark, I said that Dracula would not listen to reason. "He wants nothing less than a stunning victory."

"He is vain," Eva muttered. "He says he will abase himself, suffer any ignominy, for the sake of his people. But he is a man like William at heart, who seeks greatness at the expense of decency and virtue. Greatness no matter the cost."

"What if he seeks greatness through the preservation of his people?"

Eva sighed. "When those come into conflict, which will he seek more?"

"You think he will choose himself over his people?"

"I think you should go to sleep."

Vlad waited and waited. And then, when it was almost too late, he ordered us into battle. In fact, it was only as the Turkish army of Wazir Mahmud headed back to cross the Danube at Brila that we finally launched the crushing assault Vlad had been planning for.

The Turks were loaded with Wallachian prisoners that they would make into slaves, along with tons of stolen food, wine, gold, weapons and everything they could carry on wagon and horse. Drunk on their riches, they camped by the river and prepared to ferry their piles of booty across.

It was there that Dracula got his stunning victory. We killed ten thousand Turks in that battle, shattering their army utterly.

And then in May 1462 we heard that Zaganos Pasha and Sultan Mehmed were coming.

The Turks needed their vast fleet on the Danube in order to supply and support their army and enable the crossing of the men and horses from Bulgaria and so to hinder them we had destroyed the ports along the river and deployed our men in certain strong garrisons. All our efforts then were turned toward discovering where the crossing would be made. We baited our traps by leaving certain regions lightly defended but William was cunning when it came to such things. We did not even know if they would cross in one place or divide to cross at multiple points and either join up or launch a series of smaller armies. Each one still might be larger than the entire Wallachian army all together.

Keeping up with the enemy troop movements on the other side certainly stressed our captains on the river but it had to be done. We needed to be able to respond quickly to the invasion in order to have a hope of stopping it before it reached Târgoviște.

We soon had word from our agents and spies that the Turks were bringing close to a hundred thousand men. This was as large an army as they could ever realistically supply in the field and so it showed Mehmed was determined to conquer Wallachia once and for all. It was as large as the army he had brought to Varna, to Kosovo, and to Belgrade and in all those places it had taken all the might of Hungary and her allies to fight the Turks to a standstill.

This time, Wallachia would stand alone.

The Turks had sixty thousand core soldiers with at least thirty thousand auxiliary forces including Bulgarians, Serbians and Anatolian *akinje* marauders. Of great concern was the hundred and twenty cannons that they would bring to the field.

Dracula did his utmost to bring allies to fight with us. For a time, we hoped the Venetians would send forces but nothing came of it in the end. No matter how many messengers we dispatched, Mattias Corvinus would send no one to aid us. Instead, he was facing off against Frederick III in the north and so it seemed he was happy enough for Christendom to lose another kingdom.

All we had was what Wallachia could provide.

The mass levy of Wallachian peasantry produced a rather motley army. Many were just boys, though they called themselves young men, and the elder of them were often bent-backed from their years spent tilling their fields. But the men knew their country and, in the woodlands and marshes and mountains of Wallachia, they were at home. And what is more, Dracula's *viteji*, his new officer class, had been recruited from these very same men and they knew their people, just as the people knew the land.

It was not just the country peasants but the townsmen also who were called up to fight. These fellows were the ones trained in the mass use of the hand-guns, as well as in the use of the precious few war wagons and cannons that we had available.

When the recruiters had gone out to find every able-bodied man and boy, many had come back with women also. These were not turned away and indeed many of them demonstrated their ability to shoot crossbows and even hand-guns and drive wagons. Most in fact acted as ammunition carriers and loaders for their husbands or sons but I saw plenty of women fighting in a murderous rage amongst their menfolk in the battles to come. Sadly, I saw some dead and injured, also. Women are sometimes driven to defend their homelands and they are brave to do so in spite of being weak in body. But it is always a tragedy when a people are forced into such positions and there is not a Christian man who has lived that enjoyed seeing a woman fight. They are the most precious thing in all the world and when they feel the need to take up arms then one knows her men folk have already failed in their duty.

410

Including women and children, our army numbered a mere thirty thousand.

Of those, we had about ten thousand cavalry, who were mostly experienced soldiers that knew their business. These men were well armed and wore lamellar and mail and their lords and their retinue were clad in plate armour.

And of course we had the *sluji*. Everyone in the army knew that if things were falling apart they were to rally around their prince, his bodyguard and the *sluji*.

As well as all this we had our very light cavalry, who were excellent riders with their wits about them riding fast horses. These men conducted lightning raids when opportunity presented itself but mainly served as our reconnaissance and messenger force.

With any army, it is necessary to be supported by thousands of servants to clean and mend and cook and support the soldiers in every way and in this we were blessed to have the entire nation of Wallachia behind us.

The old boyar families on the other hand completely abandoned Dracula and their own people and fled into the mountains. There is no doubt that they believed we would be destroyed and when we were they planned to come down from Transylvania and pledge allegiance to the Sultan and take up whatever positions they could under their new masters. Such men are so far beyond contempt that it is impossible to find a suitable punishment. I prayed that in time they would at least find themselves duly impaled.

But only if we beat an army three times our size made up of

veteran soldiers.

They came at us in two parts.

First they were sighted at Vidin. Mehmed came up the river by ship in the hopes of traversing the River Olt so they could strike deep into Wallachia and directly at Târgovişte.

And another detachment came to force a crossing from Philipopolis in Bulgaria which would cover the first army's flank.

We were waiting for them.

The Turkish advance force tried to send men to the northern bank but we came out quickly from the woodland, took up firing positions and blasted them with our hand-gunners and crossbowman.

When the Turks fell back, we also retreated into the trees.

I expected that they would come again the next day but they were willing to be patient and instead moved their forces to Turnu. We had burned it the year before but our scouts had watched the Turks carefully rebuilding it and so knew it was a likely crossing point.

It was the dark of the night when they came in force.

We fought with everything we had but trying to organise peasants into effective night fighting units was harder than I could have imagined. Even so, it was the cannons that did it. Dozens of them fired through the night, their flashes lighting up the darkness and the cannonballs crashing into our positions across the river. Men and horses were killed and the living were panicked. We could not hold where we were and so we fell back, enabling even more of their boats across.

They even brought light cannons across with them and they

dug in on our side of the riverbank. Our cavalry did their best to break them and drive them back into the river, charging repeatedly down on them, but the Turks had so many troops that no matter how many we killed, the men behind them continued digging defensive ditches until finally our horsemen could not approach the cannons.

Our war wagons had a commanding position above the landing area and our hand-gunners fired from the backs of them over and over, killing hundreds of Turks and wounding more.

More and more barges came across and we simply could not hold them. When morning came we counted seventy barges ferrying Janissaries across. Still, we attempted to hold them on the thin strip of land along the bank there. For hours, it was a close-run thing. We managed to kill hundreds of Janissaries, at least, and they were precious men the Sultan could ill afford to lose.

Vlad was everywhere, shouting encouragement as he rode from position to position. "We are holding them!" He rode close to the enemy and, taking a crossbow, shot at them before riding back to his cheering men. "Throw them back!"

While we focused on our side of the river, we did not pay attention to what was occurring across the water. The Sultan was there, and William and his Red Janissaries too, but we could not get to them and so we ignored them for now. But they had ordered up every one of their great cannons and positioned them in an arc. When the order was given, all one hundred and twenty cannon fired at once.

Our war wagons were hit, smashing them and sending shards of oak and limbs of hand-gunners spinning across our positions.

Wallachian cavalry were blasted apart.

The shock of it alone almost broke our poor army. Even I had never heard a cacophony like it. A hundred and twenty massive cannons firing at once seemed enough to shatter the very world, splitting first the air and then the ground beneath our feet. It did not shatter the Wallachians but we knew we could not stand against such a bombardment and so Vlad ordered a retreat.

Without those Turkish cannon on the far shore, I do not doubt we could have sent the massive army back over the river by the end of the day.

As it was, we were defeated. And the Sultan's army was in Wallachia.

∞

"There he is," Rob whispered. "Do you see him?"

"Yes, yes," Serban said at my side. "He is there. No, there, my lord."

Peering through the trees from a high ridge, I saw the banner and the man riding at the centre of the party. "By God, he looks just like him."

"Rather more handsome than Vlad," Eva said, squinting beside me.

"You cannot possibly tell at this distance," I said, glancing at her.

"Certainly I can," Eva replied. "He is a most striking young prince."

Vlad Dracula's younger brother, Radu, had joined the Sultan's army. Indeed, it was common knowledge that the Sultan intended to place Radu on the throne as Voivode of Wallachia once Vlad had been defeated. What is more, he had four thousand of his own horsemen with him. Radu was completely and totally under the spell of Mehmed and William.

"Do you reckon he's an immortal?" Walt whispered.

"Why don't you go ask him?" Rob said.

"What did Vlad say about it?" Eva asked. "Was his handsome brother turned?"

"Quiet, all of you. He is here, that is all that matters. With him here, it is worth the risk."

The Turks had moved slowly north from the river. We knew they were coming for Târgovişte. They were so focused on destroying Vlad's capital that they ignored the fortress at Bucharest and the fortified monastery of Snagov. Mehmed did not want to waste time and men on taking places that ultimately mattered little in his conquest. If Vlad could be removed and Radu put in his place, all the smaller places should either give up or could be conquered without consequence.

We knew we had little hope of winning a set-piece battle on the open field.

Instead, we started a type of war that I had fought before, in France and other places. Along the line of advance and for miles around, all grain stores were burned, as were the crops in the field. Every source of water was poisoned, and the livestock and peasantry were driven into the north where they would be safe.

As the Turks advanced up the valleys and through the dense forests, we harried them everywhere they went. Every scouting party, every group sent out for forage, we pounced on them and killed them.

Our purpose was to kill as many as possible, of course, but even more it was to break their spirit. To make it so that every man was afraid in his heart to face us.

We also damned small rivers and diverted their waters to create swathes of waterlogged marshland to slow down the progress of the army, especially of their supply wagons and most of all the dreaded but enormously heavy cannons.

Our peasants may not have been professional soldiers but they excelled at digging the earth. And so we had them dig man traps everywhere. Steep, deep pits with wickedly spiked stakes at the bottom which the peasants delighted in smearing with bog water and human and animal shit. These traps were covered with thin sticks and leaves to disguise them.

It was a scorching summer. By denying the Turks access to water, they suffered deeply from thirst and heat exhaustion as they advanced. The sheer size of their army worked against them and they spent thousands of men relaying water for miles and even then it was never enough. Without enough fresh water to drink, they certainly did not have enough to wash with, and they grew filthy and, rather quickly, disease spread. The camp sickness began killing almost as many as we did.

So their days were spent in misery as they crept forward in agonising thirst, afraid of each step and fearful of leaving the core of their army lest they be murdered most horribly.

And we made sure they suffered every night.

When they came to a stop for their nightly camp, they were exhausted and thirsty and short of food and then they had to dig their trenches and throw up their earthworks around their tents. And we made certain that they had to do it, for any man not within the safety of those defences we took and murdered and left for their comrades to find in the morning, often headless or skinless or somehow mutilated.

My *sluji* could see in the dark better than any mortal and they delighted in creeping up on sentries and drinking their blood while their screams echoed through the hills and forests. When the Turks took up their march again, they would pass scores of their friends, skinned, or headless, and impaled upon tall stakes. At first, the Turkish soldiers, outraged, immediately cut down every man we left for them but we knew we were breaking their spirit when they began leaving them until the slaves at the rear were ordered to do it. Thousands of men saw what conquering Wallachia would cost them.

The Turks we captured had begun referring to Vlad Dracula as *Kaziglu Bey*, which meant the Lord Impaler. It was a name we embraced. The Lord Impaler is coming to drive a stake through every man in your army, we would say to captured men, and then we would send them back to their men with the message on their lips but with their hands cut off or their eyes put out.

And yet we could not stop their advance. They were too many. Slow and shaken as they were, their sheer numbers combined with the relentlessness of the will driving them, they were inexorable.

"We must break their spirit," Vlad had urged us, on many occasions. "They must be made to see that even if they achieve victory it will be at the cost of their entire army. We are not their only enemies. The tribesmen in the east threaten them, and they have no friends among the Arabs. The Mamluks of Egypt would gladly see the Turks destroyed. We must break their spirit and they will retreat."

The bravest of his friends on occasion risked asking for reassurance. "What makes you so certain, my lord?"

"I know these men. I know Mehmed. I know Zaganos Pasha. They are men who carefully calculate the cost of their actions."

It was true, of William at least, I could attest to that. He was a man well versed in cutting his losses in order to save his skin.

But it was not working. Not entirely. Not enough.

The Turks pushed us back into the mountains not far from Târgovişte. If they turned from us to besiege the city then we could fall upon their rear and work away at them. But with their cannons and their sheer numbers they could break into Târgovişte and take it before our methods of warfare could drive them off.

More desperate measures would be required.

Peering down on Radu from that high ridge, I knew it was time.

"Are you certain we can do it?" Rob asked, scratching at his stump.

"Too risky," Serban muttered. "To risk all when we need not do it, it is too much."

"Târgovişte will fall if we do not," Stephen said.

"So what?" Serban said. "It is a city."

"A city full of people," Rob said. "Families."

"It is the heart of the kingdom," Stephen said. "When it falls, the kingdom falls. Where will we stop William then?"

Serban shrugged. "We would live. You would live, my lords. To survive is all."

"Enough talk," I said. "Now that Radu is here, that makes every leader together in one place. It is worth the risk."

"I doubt that Prince Vlad will see it that way," Stephen replied.

"Then I must convince him. Come, we must retreat before we are seen."

We crept backwards through the trees until we were behind the ridge and we rode north for the heart of the camp. Our army was spread over three valleys and each had at least one pass leading north into Transylvania. If the Turks attacked any or even all of the valleys we could retreat all the way out of Wallachia if we needed to. However, we also had prepared defensive positions all the way up those valleys so we could mount an effective fighting retreat with every step. If the Turks did attack us they would pay dearly for it.

Few of us believed Mehmed would be so foolish. All he had to do now was hold Vlad's army at bay, take Târgoviște and install Radu as the new *voivode*. Gradually, loyal *boyars* could be found to support him publicly and they would then be granted the lands held by the *boyars* in Vlad's army. The Turks would garrison every town so strongly that we could not take them and then we would be starved of supplies until our army withered into nothing.

"We should attack," I said to Vlad, pushing into the cool shade of his tent.

Vlad was sipping on a cup of blood while his armourer measured and fitted a new or repaired gauntlet on his other hand. I could smell the blood, though it was mixed with wine, and I am certain the armourer would have smelled it, also. There were rumours of Dracula's regular blood drinking circulating amongst the army and the populous but it disturbed me to see him doing so openly.

"Attack? They still outnumber us three to one," Vlad replied, waving his cup in the Turk's direction. "Each one of his soldiers is more capable than most of mine. We could not kill enough to win. Instead, we must drag them further into the hills."

"We do not need to kill many men to win. Only three."

Vlad grunted. He looked tired. "You mean Mehmed and William and..."

"And Radu. Your brother is here. I have seen him this morning, with the four thousand horsemen Mehmed has gifted him."

Vlad ground his teeth. "I thought they would keep him safe in the lowlands. If he is here then we need not kill all three. Killing Radu alone would put an end to Mehmed's great plans for Wallachia."

"It would not. Mehmed would find any one of a hundred other puppets to place on the throne. He could pluck one of the Danesti at will and they would gladly accept. If Radu alone is killed, it does not save Wallachia."

Vlad fixed his dark eyes on mine. "You would say anything if it meant getting what you wanted. And all you want is to kill William. You do not even care about killing Mehmed."

I kept my voice level. "That is not true. I have fought him and his father before him, fought the Turks, fought for Christendom as a crusader, for almost twenty years."

"You have. But only because William was by their side. If William dies, you will leave here and abandon us to our fate." He glared at me. I could see white all the way around his irises.

I shrugged, as if it was a matter of small importance. "If William dies then I have other business to attend to. Once that is completed, I would fight the Turks once more."

"I do not believe you. You are just like all the other Catholics. Only interested in each other. You will only care when the Turks are at the gates of Rome. Even then, no doubt, you would prefer to fight each other than to do your duty to God."

He glared at me and my anger flared up in response to his words. I had done more than any man and to be questioned and doubted by one so young was deeply offensive. I could have happily struck him a blow.

But I forced my blood to cool.

"Perhaps you are right," I said, surprising myself almost as much as him. "But the fact remains that you are about to lose your kingdom, Vlad. Nothing can stop Mehmed from taking Târgovişte."

He sneered, curling his lip. "If they reach the gates of my city, I will make sure what they find will shatter their hearts in their chests."

"You will. But supposing they can bring forward their cannons and knock down the walls. Will that not give them cheer enough to carry them through?"

He waved away his armourer who retreated as quickly as he could. "You would have me gamble the existence of my people on a single throw of the dice."

"If you do not throw the dice then your kingdom is lost. Your people will be slaves forever."

Vlad walked to the open front of his tent and looked out at his army. "It might cost half of them their lives."

"It might."

"Even if I kill Mehmed then William will see another Sultan put into his place. Another puppet. And William will come again."

"That is why we must kill William above all."

"Above Radu? Above Mehmed?"

"Do you doubt that he is the most dangerous of them all? With William dead, with his Blood Janissaries wiped out, then our enemies are only mortal."

"Very well, then." Vlad turned to me. "How could it be done?"

13

Night Attack at Târgovişte 1462

WE TORTURED TURKISH SOLDIERS AND OFFICERS that we had taken in previous raids and questioned them about the precise location and disposition of the enemy soldiers within their camps. We had so many that it took some time but we combined the reports until we had a consistent picture of where Mehmed's tents were, and those of Zaganos Pasha and also Radu Dracula.

For all their heart and for all the deaths and mayhem that they had caused, we knew that the peasant infantry would not be capable of attacking in the manner we needed. Their officers were for the most part excellent but the peasants did not have the discipline needed. Not only that, they did not have the armour and weaponry required.

Instead, we took every single remaining mounted soldier we could gather together. They had to be mounted. We needed to penetrate deep within the camp at multiple points, kill our targets and retreat before the remaining soldiers surrounded us and killed us.

For a time, it seemed we would have only seven thousand men. Even after all their losses, to us and to plague and thirst, the enemy still had seventy or eighty thousand soldiers in the field. Some of the captured officers swore that they had received reinforcements bringing their numbers back to a hundred thousand but I was careful to silence those men and discount their testimony.

"What's the difference?" Walt asked, shrugging, as I cut a Turk's throat for claiming such a figure. "Seventy thousand is already impossible. Might as well be seventy millions."

"Quiet, Walter, or your throat will be the next one cut."

"When a man threatens violence it means he has lost the argument."

"Shut up, Walt."

At the last moment, our numbers were boosted to almost ten thousand cavalry when two more great companies returned from their ranging. They were tired and their horses would be in a bad way but they would be coming with us that very night. We needed every man we could get.

Such an assault could only have a chance of success if it was carried out in the dark of the night. By day, we would be seen and the enemy would be prepared. By night, we had a chance. Slim, yes, but a chance.

Our attack took place on the night of 17th June 1462.

"This could be it," I said to my companions as darkness descended. The air was still warm from the day and the pines released their sickly-sweet smell into the sky. "This could be the night that we kill William and fulfil our mission. Or... this could be the end of our Order. Let us not pretend that this is anything other than a huge risk. We are outnumbered and we are riding deep into the heart of the enemy. While I pray for victory, I also fear that not all of us will escape with our lives. But we have toiled here for years for the chance to get this close to William. He is as well defended as any man on earth and so surprise is our only chance for ending him."

"We understand, sir," Walt said. "Death or glory, ain't it. Same as usual."

"Well, let us pray for glory and for victory," I said. "You know what to do. Keep a tight rein on your companies and keep in sight or sound of the next captain, if not me. Any questions?"

They went to speak to their detachments and to take a last draught of blood before the fighting.

"Serban," I called. "Where are you, you little bastard?"

"Here, sir," he replied, hurrying over.

"Listen, Serban. We are going into hell. Even the *strigoi* will struggle to make it out alive. I want you to wait here."

He frowned, wrinkles creasing like canyons. "I have not slowed you down yet. Not once, my lord. And I never will."

"That is true enough," I admitted. "Still, I want you to stay at the camp until we come back."

He bowed. "I will prepare the servants for your return. And if you die in the battle, I must say it has been an honour to serve you."

"I could still make you a *strigoi* before I go? There should be time enough."

"Very kind, my lord, but I would rather stay as I am."

"Fine, well, you get going now. It is soon to get dangerous around here."

Our army would attack in two flanks. My *sluji* would accompany Vlad in the main attack while a boyar named Lord Gale was tasked with assaulting the Turks from the opposite direction. Our horses and their riders swirled in the darkness, a great mass of flesh and steel moving out of the trees, our lance points raised to the stars. I had seen countless battles and ridden in more raids than I could remember and yet my heart hammered in my chest as we swept down from the hills. William was out there in the dark. So close, I could almost smell him over the reek of the sap.

Ahead of my men, each forward detachment took a handful of Turkish officers with them to allow us to get close to their outer sentries before killing them. The prisoners were then killed, despite our promises to free them for cooperating.

"Close now," I muttered. "Be ready to charge."

Word spread through our lines.

Be ready.

Once we reached the trench lines around the camp, our foremost men roared and their trumpeters sounded.

Our cavalry charged in. Cries went up into the night sky and the hooves pounded on the hard, dry earth. We streamed into the camp, rushing by the outermost Turks and leaving them for the men who would follow us.

Some men bore flaming torches which they whirled and tossed out into tents and stores. Other shot their crossbows in volleys to create confusion and terror before dropping them and charging in with sword and spear in hand.

We charged in with the *sluji* keeping tight in formation, their lances lowered only when we needed to force our way through, deeper into the camp. I was determined to keep our immortals out of the fighting for as long as possible so that they could focus on the Blood Janissaries, when we found them, but of course there were so many enemies in the way that we had to join in with cutting our way through.

The Turks were in a blind panic. Somehow, they had not expected we would attack in force. At least, they were certainly not prepared for it. The only men who were armed initially were those sentries we had quickly dispatched and overcome and the men further within all seemed to be sleeping in their tents or even out in the open air. Most men rushed from us in full retreat rather than standing to fight and those who did were in various states of undress, let alone in armour. Our blades cut them to ribbons and the air filled with the smell of hot blood and the screaming of the terrified Turks.

It seemed to be going even better than I had hoped but I knew the sands of time were swiftly running out. In the distance, a gun fired and then another. It would not be long before they organised themselves. We had to find William before then or it would be too late.

Smashing our way through a line of Turks, we came across a vast and colourful tent surrounded by properly equipped guards.

"Mehmed's tent!" Rob cried nearby. "Or William's?"

"To me!" I cried. "*Sluji*, to me!"

A handful of them rallied to me and without waiting for more to come I ordered a charge and raced toward the tents myself. Our numbers and strength overwhelmed the guards. I had a sinking feeling that it could not be William's tent. He would surely be surrounded by his blood-red slave soldiers. The tent was hacked into and my men pulled down the ropes and poles holding it erect and they rushed inside even as it collapsed. A dozen *sluji* came out dragging a pair of finely attired Turks.

"Who are you?" I asked them in Turkish, dismounting and coming at them on foot. On their knees with my men holding them fast, they cringed away from me. "Who are you?" I asked, slapping their turbans from their heads. "Who are you?"

"We are wazirs. I am the Wazir of—"

I slapped his face. "Where is Zaganos Pasha?"

"In... in his tents."

"Where are his tents? Point them out. Where, man?"

Their shaking fingers both pointed the same way, deeper into the camp. I sawed through both of their throats and threw them down.

"Find the other captains," I commanded Rob. "I want all the companies with me now."

There was hardly room in the avenues between the tents for so many men to ride abreast but to my right and left my men tore

428

into anything that stood in their way. We killed more men as we advanced, setting fires as we went. The flames lit up the night and also filled it with billowing black smoke. Sparks flowed up like a demonic rainstorm. In the distance, a mass of gunpowder exploded in an almighty blast that I felt through the very earth. We killed men and we killed horses and we killed camels.

The Turks came at us in confused charges, mounted or on foot, but these we beat back, though each time we lost a man or two. Some of the *sluji* were killed outright and others must have become separated in the confusion. Our numbers dwindled and always there were more Turks beyond the ones we cut down. Gradually, they became more organised and we came up against masses of heavily armoured men and their cavalry began cycling charges that slowed us down. At my flanks, my men were being killed and I could do nothing to protect them.

"Too slow!" Walt cried, riding toward me with his axe raised and dripping blood. "Too slow, Richard! We're getting stuck!"

"On!" I roared. "Kill them! Kill the Sultan! Kill the Pasha!"

We killed them and their screams filled the night.

"Great God Almighty," Rob cried, pointing ahead before pulling his visor closed. "Here they come."

Out of the swirling smoke and darkness, lit by the flames of the burning camp, the Blood Janissaries advanced with their hand-gunners at the forefront. Some knelt and others leaned into their weapons, bracing them against their chests or couching them under their arms.

"Beware gunners in front!" I shouted to my men but before the words were out of my mouth their weapons fired and my men and their horses were lashed by a hundred deadly shots. My men fell in their dozens, their lances thrown down as they fell. Some that were hit were wounded rather than dead but even those would bleed to death and expire without blood to heal them. And we lost many horses. Some horses could survive multiple wounds and continue to function but still they were mortal, and they collapsed under the onslaught.

The next two rows of Janissaries advanced beyond their front lines and they brought up their guns and lifted their sticks with the smouldering tapers to the firing holes.

"What do we do?" one of my men was shouting. "What do we do?"

Hesitation and uncertainty are the worst possible things at such times and so I made a snap decision. It was my default decision with regards to problems and which has caused me more trouble in my life than just about anything else.

"Charge!" I shouted. "Come on, charge them now!"

Perhaps I should have waited. Two hundred years later I might have ordered my men to dismount and to lie flat while the enemy fired but I did not yet have extensive experience with firearms. I imagined that if they saw three hundred charging cavalry they would be panicked enough to miss their shots or even to break altogether, seeing that they were without polearms in the front lines.

But they were far too disciplined for that. And all I succeeded in doing was ordering a partial charge from men who were not prepared that brought them closer to the guns that were shooting them.

Dozens of us were hit again.

As was I.

The flashes of the fire and the crashing of the weapons filled my eyes and ears. An impact hit me in the chest with such force it was like being kicked by a destrier. I found myself tumbling along with my horse who collapsed under me having himself been shot in the head and chest.

I smacked into the ground, the sound of my armour crunching filled my ears, and rolled until I was lying on my back, struggling for breath. Above, all I saw was darkness and the sparks from a hundred huge fires spraying up into it like the souls departing the dying.

Hooves drummed on the ground and men shouted and I rolled to my feet. My sword still in my hand, I looked about to get my bearings. It was hard to breathe and I instinctively touched my chest only to feel the metal of my breastplate. Whatever the damage was, it would have to wait. Bellowing horsemen rode past me at a gallop and crashed into the Blood Janissaries with an almighty crash of bodies and steel.

I hurried forward on foot to join them, feeling a mass of wounds all over me. I needed a horse but I could not see one spare and so I ran on toward the *sluji*. Our charge had ground to a halt by the density of the Janissary formation. We were better armoured and on sturdy horses but the hand-gunners were dead or had retreated and now they fought back with their long polearms. We could not break through.

Through the press of men, at their rear, I caught a glimpse of a large man on a large horse, directing his men.

It was William.

I looked around for my captains or any senior man and took a deep breath to shout for my companions to push on and kill my brother.

But the breath I took caught halfway through and instead of a shout I coughed out a mouthful of blood. I felt my breastplate again and found two holes had been shot through it, both in the upper chest near to my heart. A chill went through me. Would it be fatal? Would I be strong enough to escape from the enemy camp?

Pushing those unworthy thoughts aside, I looked for assistance.

Where are my bastard bodyguards? I snarled to myself before I remembered. *I made them charge to their deaths.*

A riderless horse nearby struggled to free itself from the press of men and I reached it just as another one of my *sluji* did.

"My lord!" he said. "Are you wounded? Where are your men?"

I tried to answer him and instead, blood welled from my mouth.

"Christ save us," he said and he helped me to mount and offered up his lance which I took with some difficulty. It hurt just to hold it but I had to try something, anything, to reach William. He was so close.

Walt's angry shouting reached me. "There you are, you daft bastard!"

He rode to my side along with Rob, both covered in blood and on exhausted or wounded horses. I pointed my lance, the point shaking with the exertion of doing so, at William where he sat behind his Janissaries. Both of my men shouted their understanding and their approval and they called in the others around us.

I waved a hand at Walt who hesitated just for a moment, no doubt concerned about my condition, before he ordered the charge. It was so clear to me in that moment. We would push through ten lines of immortal Janissaries and strike down my brother.

He saw me, I am certain. Through the darkness and the boiling smoke and the flickering radiance of the burning camp all around, he saw me.

I will kill you, I thought as I looked at him. I will kill you.

It was a mad risk but still I might have ended it right there. All those later centuries of death and horror inflicted by William could have been avoided. I myself might have been killed but at least William would have fallen also.

Instead, a thousand Janissaries dressed in white advanced out of the shadows on our flank.

"Watch out!" my men cried. "Look to the flank!"

They were in a wide formation, their white robes and long hats seeming to glow orange in the firelight. Already, they were prepared to fire. There was no time to react, no time to move.

The Janissaries took aim and fired.

We were cut down. The *sluji* were blasted, raked, from one side and all our men there were riddled. Their armour providing no protection and only their immortality preserving the lives of some. Had I been on that flank rather than the centre, already wounded as I was, I would certainly have been killed. As it was, only the presence of Walt and Rob beside me served to shield me from the attack. Even so, my horse was killed and Rob and Walt were shot. As we climbed, dazed and in pain, to our feet, we found the Blood Janissaries advancing in front and their mortal compatriots rushing on the flank.

Unable to speak, I signalled as best as I could that we should retreat. I need not have tried. Not a man among the *sluji* was fool enough to think we could stand against such an onslaught.

There was no way forward, only back.

We fell into a desperate retreat, fighting any who came too close and fleeing as fast as our legs would carry us.

A group of our brave *sluji* rode up, threw themselves off their horses and helped me and Walt and Rob into their saddles while they stood and covered our retreat. Those Wallachian soldiers saved our lives that night at the cost of their own. I do not remember their names.

We soon rode amongst thousands of mortal Wallachian horsemen who had also turned to flee. Our raid was finished and I could not speak to ask what had happened. All I could do was try to stay conscious as I coughed up masses of blood and spat it off into the darkness. We fell back and enemy cavalry pursued us into the hills even after sunrise.

All I wanted to ask was whether Dracula had killed Mehmed. And whether Dracula himself was still alive. But all that came from my throat was more blood.

It was hours before we were clear of the enemy and by then the day had turned hot. My blood caked inside my ruined armour and I was stiff as a board, sweat and blood mixed and ran into my eyes. All I could think was that I had failed. William was still alive.

We returned on exhausted horses with thousands of tired and wounded men to the camps we had prepared.

Eva stood waiting, her face twisted in aguish as she ran to my horse. Stephen was everywhere shouting commands to the servants. My men had to help me dismount and I could not speak a single word of command though they knew what I needed. They took me to my tents where some of my servants removed my armour and others bled themselves into cups that I might drink. This I did, greedily, and at once began to feel as if I might just avoid death, though I could still barely take a breath. After undoing the straps and removing my plate, they cut the blood-soaked clothes from my body and washed my skin.

I had been shot three times in the chest. One of the balls had passed right through me and I had a corresponding wound in my back that they claimed was big enough to fit a fist inside, with shattered bones poking out. The other two shots had entered my rib cage but had not come out.

One shoulder had been torn up by another ball and I had a long gash on my thigh that could have been caused by anything but I assumed was the result of being shot also, as my armour had been penetrated but remained in place.

"You did not find William," Eva said. "I can tell it from your face."

I gestured for more blood and guzzled down as much as they could give me. The pain was excruciating and I faded between wakefulness and unconsciousness as they tended to me. I felt an intense itching in my chest and looked down to see first one and then another piece of flattened lead, shining with blood, emerge from the wounds in my body and drop onto my lap and from there to the ground. A servant picked them up and stared, mouth open, at them.

"Blood," I said. "More blood."

A short time later I was cleaned and dressed and had a belly full of servant's blood and fresh wine. Still bruised and exhausted, I knew I would live.

"What happened?" Eva asked, stroking my hair.

"We came close," I muttered. "Not close enough."

"You lived. You can try again."

"What happened with the rest of the attack?" I asked.

"You will have to ask someone who was there. I know we lost many men. Perhaps too many lost to win the war. You shall have to speak to Dracula."

"He lives?"

"Ask Walt."

I got up to do just that but Eva placed a hand on my chest, looking me in the eye and then all over. She slipped her arms around me and held me tight for a moment before letting me go.

Walt was already up and walking around the camp, taking stock, checking on his company. My surviving men were being treated and were drinking every drop of blood and wine that they could get. They watched me with the grim faces of defeated men.

"Walt," I said. "Where is Rob?"

"In there," he said, nodding at a tent. "Shot to bits. He'll live, probably."

"Is this all there is?"

436

Walt sighed, placing his hands on his hips and looking around. "Ain't finished counting but looks like we have a hundred and thirty men here. Worst of all is that Jan died, poor sod. Garcia lives. And Claudin is still with us, sadly. But most of the rest of the Company of Saint George didn't make it back. Reckon a few more will come in today. But not many."

"A hundred and thirty? Out of four hundred and eighteen?" I felt sick to my stomach. "We lost two hundred and ninety immortals? And we did not kill William."

Walt shrugged. "Near enough wiped out his red bastards, though."

"We did?"

"Did you not see? Easily half of them, probably more. If it hadn't been for those mortal Janissaries coming up then." He shook his head. "We nearly had the bastard, didn't we. Still, come out about even, I would say. Our lads are a wee bit disheartened, though. Reckon some of them are realising that being immortal doesn't mean you ain't ever going to die. Don't worry, I'll have a word. Me and Rob will sort them out."

"What of Mehmed? What of Dracula?"

Walt looked up the hill toward the rest of the camp. "Dracula lives. I reckon Mehmed does, too, or else them lads wouldn't be looking so heartsick."

"I am sorry, Walt."

He nodded, looking the men over. "I been thinking, Richard. I been thinking that it might be we should get ourselves some of those hand-guns after all. Pretty useful, it turns out."

I ordered my servants to fill Rob with blood and to take care of him as if it were me and I moved to speak to my men. There was hardly a man who was not wounded in some way. And all of them had seen their friends die or had been forced to leave them behind in the enemy camp as they died. I said whatever I could and perhaps my words helped to lift their spirits a fraction, even though they no doubt felt angry at me for having led them to such a crushing defeat. The Company of Saint George was almost entirely wiped out and the *sluji*, after so much promise, had been reduced by seven tenths.

Making my way slowly up the hill to Dracula's tent, I felt every one of my three hundred years.

"I did not kill him," Dracula said when I was admitted into the inner part of his large tent. He, too, had been wounded and was drinking wine mixed with fresh blood. "I did not kill him."

"You were shot?" I asked.

Dracula sneered. "It is nothing. My men were killed. My *friends*. And Mehmed lives."

"As does William."

Dracula nodded. "And Radu. That bastard Gale did not break through on the other side of the camp. We were two thousand men fewer than we should have been and it is Gale's fault. I shall have him impaled the moment he shows his face."

"You will do as you must. But perhaps he has his reasons."

"Gale is no friend to you. Why do you defend him?"

I shrugged. "If he is at fault through incompetence or cowardice, then I would gladly see him punished. But it was a difficult task. Impossible, or near enough. Even so, we came close to victory."

Dracula turned his face up, squeezing his eyes closed. "I *saw* Mehmed. My men wounded him before the Janissaries attacked. We were a hair's breadth from killing him."

"He was wounded?" I said. "How badly?"

"Not badly enough. What of William?"

"We killed at least half of the Blood Janissaries. But I lost almost three hundred of the *sluji*. Perhaps more will yet return but it was a bloody exchange. I suppose our immortal armies came out with somewhat even losses."

Dracula scoffed. "You failed. And Gale failed." He stared at me, as if daring me to speak. The words hung in the air between us before Vlad sighed and spoke them aloud. "And I failed. I most of all."

"How many men did we lose?"

"Perhaps as many as five thousand, including men surrounded and taken prisoner as we retreated. We are in no better a position than we were. In fact, we have only lost by this raid."

"How many of the enemy did we kill?"

"I do not know. A great many. Twenty thousand? Thirty? Not enough. Not nearly enough. There will be no way to stop them from reaching Târgoviște. All we can do now is prepare the way for them."

The Turks advanced on Târgoviște. Vlad Dracula had spent his years as *voivode* building the defences of the city, at great expense and using vast numbers of slaves to carry out the hardest of the labour. And so the walls and the gates and gatehouses had been strengthened mightily in preparation for the assault that he knew would come.

Their advance cavalry came first toward the city while we stayed back in the hills to watch. We could not stop them by force of arms, we knew that, it was just a question of whether the force of Dracula's spirit would be enough.

For the final two miles along the road to Târgoviște, Vlad Dracula had impaled twenty thousand Turks.

There were dozens of rotting, impaled Turkish for every single pace the advancing army had to take and the closer they got to the centre the more there were. It was a crescent of impaled soldiers, growing to be half a mile wide at the centre, so that they walked through a forest of their dead comrades.

Highest of them all were still the rotten corpses of the treacherous Hamza Pasha and his Greek Thomas Catavolinos.

The advancing Turkish cavalry, thousands of them, faltered during their passage through the twenty-thousand impaled men and their hearts and stomachs were not strong enough to get them to the gates of the city.

They turned tail and fled back to the rest of the army.

South of the forest of the dead, they made their camp for the final time.

And in the morning, they retreated south.

What force of arms could not achieve was done through breaking the will of the enemy. On the Danube, the Turkish fleet ferried their broken army back across to Bulgaria. Their rearguard spread out to protect the army while it did so and this we attacked and defeated near Buzău.

While we won that final small victory, the main army burned

Brila and departed Wallachia, heading back to Edirne.

However, not all the army fled so far.

A detachment was left close to the border. This force of exiled Wallachian *boyars* and Turkish cavalry was commanded by Radu Dracula.

And he at once began agitating to take Vlad's throne.

14

The Throne

1467

"MY KINGDOM IS BROKEN," Vlad said. "And I am the one who has broken it."

The great hall in Târgoviște was empty but for the two of us and Vlad's guards and servants. Dracula drank off his goblet of wine and commanded that it be refilled. He gulped down half of that and leaned back in his throne.

"It was the Turks that broke it. You defended your people."

"I did. And at what cost? My people struggled and won and they are exhausted. So many crops and stores were burnt. Countless wells poisoned and all the while we fought the land has been untilled. There will be famine. Half of my best soldiers are dead or will fight no more. The bravest and strongest of the peasants who fought for me have been killed. Everywhere I go in my lands there are sons without fathers and wives without husbands. And worst of all, I have no allies."

"Your cousin Stephen of Moldavia will—"

Vlad chopped a hand down. "Stephen will do what is best for Moldavia. As he should. It is right and proper that he should. The Turks will turn on him soon enough."

"Perhaps if we go to Mattias Corvinus and—"

"Ha!" Vlad smiled but his eyes were filled with bitterness. "He considers me an enemy and always will. As do the Saxons. And half of the ancient families in my kingdom."

"They had to be driven out and frightened into submission. You could not have done otherwise."

"I was foolish to think I could unmake the ancient feuds of those lords. It would have only worked if I could have killed every one of them and their entire families. And that would be killing Wallachia herself. My methods enabled me to take and hold my crown. But now my people are shattered and my enemies gather."

"You shall weather the storm. You will endure."

"Yes. But why?"

"To defend your people."

He looked at me with something in his eyes. "You are not a subtle man, Richard. That is where you differ from your brother. You have cunning on the battlefield and in any feat of arms. But in politics, you have no subtlety at all."

"Of this, I am aware."

"And I am no different from you. I have never sought compromise or conciliation. It is not in my nature, as it is not in

444

yours. My brother, however, is a peacemaker. Radu is a diplomat at heart and always sought to ease tensions and calm conflict throughout our youth, whether in childish games or in training or when William and I fell to arguing."

"You argued with William often?"

Vlad sighed, looking up at the dark beams of the vaulted ceiling. "As a son might argue with his father, perhaps. A father and son of differing temperaments. And Radu would stand between us and profess his love for us both and beg that we calm ourselves."

"Radu said he loved William? Is that true? Was this before William... violated him?"

Drinking down his wine, he called for more. "No. I think William loved Radu almost as much as Radu adored William. I speak as if it were all in the past for of course it is so for me but I do not doubt that their love endures even now. Radu begged William to give him the Gift of his blood but William said always that Radu was too young and he had to wait until he had grown into his prime years. And even then, William was reluctant to grant my brother what he wanted."

"Why would he not do so? He uses his blood to bind followers to him. It is what he attempted to do with you."

"Indeed and my own immortality was a source of great despair for Radu. He could not understand why William would give me the Gift, when William and I disliked each other so strongly, and at the same time deny it to Radu. But it was because of his love for him that William did withhold it, of that I am certain. He did not want my brother to become like one of us. Drinkers of blood, tied to the consumption of it, and denied the hope of a natural life. He tried to explain it to Radu but my brother heard only rejection. You are so pure, so beautiful. It would be an act of desecration to destroy you. Words such as that. But Radu wished only to be with William forever and William eventually promised that he would give him the Gift, in time. If he did not change his mind."

"You said they had love for each other. But from the way you speak, it sounds almost as though they were tender with each other. I can scarcely believe it."

Vlad took a sip and stared down into his drink. "They were, at times, I am sure. Radu is the fairest man in the world and his nature was always sweet and gentle but he is not a weakling. He has a sharp enough mind. I think William set out to make him his by seducing him body and soul but somehow William in turn became bewitched by Radu. They were at times like lovers, yes, but also like brothers, or a father and a son, or friends of the deepest kind, in the Greek tradition. Like Achilles and Patroclus or Alexander and Hephaestion."

"And you did not try to save Radu from this wicked, perverse relationship?"

His head snapped up and he glared at me. I held his gaze and then he slumped, shrugging. "At first, I did try, but Radu would never speak of ending it. And soon my contempt for him overcame my pity. I resolved to abandon him to the fate he had chosen for himself in his weakness. As I say, I have never been a subtle man. Now I am older, I see that I should have tried harder. He is my brother and the bonds of family should be stronger than anything else. I should have sought compromise so that he was not entirely lost to me. But I did not and now I find that he is working hard to replace me in my own kingdom. And so now what should I do, Richard? Harden my heart once more and fight him to the death, throwing my surviving Wallachians against him and his Wallachians until only one of us is left alive?"

"Yes."

Dracula scoffed, shaking his head.

"What else can you do, Vlad? If you give yourself up, he will have no choice but to have you killed."

He pursed his lips. "I could flee. Take myself into exile."

"You are the Voivode of Wallachia."

It was as though he could not hear me. "I thought I could change the pattern. That I would be the prince for years, for decades, bringing stability and peace and safety to my people. Instead, I find I am just one more name in the litany of Wallachian princes. If I had been a shrewd prince, as Radu will be, then I might have turned the *boyars*, made them my allies, instead of enemies." He threw back his head and downed the contents of his goblet before waving his servant over for more. "But a man cannot change his nature."

I could scarcely believe what I was hearing. For years, I had thrown my lot in with this man and had helped him to defend his kingdom against the mightiest army on earth and just when we had won, he was throwing it all away.

"All you did here was for your people."

He nodded slowly. "That is true. I swore I would do whatever was needed to save them. I would take any action required, no matter if it was a great sin or if it caused me personal danger or even humiliation. And so I find that I must follow this oath again by giving myself up in the interests of my people. By staying, even if I win the battle for the throne, it will be they that will suffer most."

"But what about William? He must be killed."

He pointed a finger at me. "That is your sacred quest, not mine."

"But Radu will be a puppet of Mehmed and William. Our enemies are still the same. And you are simply walking away? Giving up everything we have fought for?"

He smiled. "I will not be dead, Richard. Merely biding my time for more favourable circumstances."

"Such as what?"

He opened his arms, as if gesturing at his hall, at Târgovişte, at his kingdom beyond. "The *boyars* will grow tired of Radu, in time. His heart is too soft to rule. There will be rumours of his blood drinking and he will make many errors by trusting this boyar or that one. And in time, my people will want change. They always do. And I will be ready. My lands will have healed by then and the people will have grown fat once more."

I could not think of anything that would change his mind. "But it will be as though Wallachia has fallen to the enemy. Radu will have Turks at his court. And he will do what William commands him to do."

"And if William is foolish enough to come to Târgovişte, we shall come back and kill him, you and I."

I scoffed. "You expect me to come with you? Into exile?"

He could not meet my eye. "If I asked it, would do you do so?"

"I cannot simply wait in the distance for years for things to change. I must stop my brother." I took a deep breath. "And to do that, I need the *sluji*. William still has his immortals and so I need mine. I must stop him, Vlad."

Dracula shrugged, as if it was no matter. "You must. And you should take the *sluji*. They are yours. Loyal to you. It is your blood in their veins, not mine."

"I will take them, then," I said. "But take them where?"

"You may go where you wish," he said, sipping from his goblet. "I would have you go to my cousin Stephen and aid him. The hammer blow will almost certainly fall upon Moldavia next."

"And where will you go?"

Vlad looked up again, leaning his head on the back of his throne. "I think I shall lose myself in Transylvania. Perhaps there will be some friends who will give me sanctuary. I will have to disguise myself in some way, perhaps as a merchant. Can you imagine such a thing? It might even be amusing."

"Radu will pursue you."

"He is not the soldier that I am."

"I will go with you. I will bring the *sluji* out of Wallachia along with you and we will fight off any attempt to take you. When you are safe and if Stephen will give us sanctuary, I will take the *sluji* to Moldavia and continue the fight."

Dracula leaned forward and held out a hand to me, which I grasped. "You have been a good friend to me, Richard. That is just what we shall do. We must make our preparations in secret and then move without delay. All those men loyal to me who will face retribution if they stay must be urged to join us or to make their own preparations. I will leave you to speak to the *sluji*."

When I returned to my quarters and summoned my companions, they were distraught to say the least. I had to have the same arguments I had just gone through with Dracula, and with myself, all over again.

"Are we going to, you know," Walt said, dragging a thumb across his neck. "After all, if he's not helping us no more then he's just one of William's immortals. And we all know what we swore to do with respect to William's immortals."

"I hate to say it but Walt is correct," Stephen said. "We did our best as far as this land is concerned but it could not be saved. It is time to take our losses and put an end to it."

"No," I said. "There is still more that he could do for us."

"I understand that you do not want to harm him," Eva said. "Because you like him."

"He is a good man."

Stephen scoffed. "How can you say those words without them sticking in your throat? He is a monster. Surely, you can see that, Richard? Or perhaps you cannot."

"Because I am a monster myself, Stephen, is that your meaning? Do not beat about the bush, if so. You may quake in your boots at the monstrous things he has done but they were enough to break the spirit of the Turks, were they not?"

"Our night attack on their camp broke their will. Wounded their Sultan."

"What is that you say, Stephen? *Our* night attack? That is very interesting as I do not recall seeing you there."

"You ordered me to stay away!"

"Because of your utter incompetence as a soldier, yes, which you display here again. It was a remarkable feat, beating that army with a band of peasants. Have you ever heard the like of it done before? Where has it been done? Is there word of it in your books of history? Tell me."

He stood before me, almost shaking, but he kept his voice level. "It was done by the *sluji* and by your skill as a captain in leading them, not our dear prince or his useless *boyars*. This is not a proper kingdom, Richard. It is a loose collection of mountain clans who can never be ruled. We should never have spent so much time and effort here. Now we must leave and nothing has been accomplished at all. Everything is precisely as we left it only tens of thousands now lie dead and this country is ravaged."

Eva spoke quickly so that I would not argue against Stephen's words. "What is done is done," she said. "It is in the past. We have fought William and his pet Sultan to a standstill where if not for our presence he would have conquered. We all agree that is true." She looked at Stephen and he avoided her gaze but nodded his assent. "And we also agree that Vlad broke the will of our enemy but he also broke the strength of his people. More than that, from what Richard tells us, it seems Vlad has broken his will also. This is a land, a people, and a prince who are shattered. All we must decide is what to do now. What now brings us closer to William's death?"

"Whatever we do next, we cannot do it from here," I said. "Vlad Dracula is fleeing his kingdom. We shall go with him. And then I shall decide where we go next. But know this. Our quest remains the same as it ever was. We will find a way to kill William."

Rob cleared his throat and spoke quietly from the corner. "We might never come back to this place. To this kingdom. Ever. It might be destroyed, overrun. It might become a new part of Rumelia."

We all stared at him.

"Yes, Rob," I said, knowing he would not speak unless he had something important to say. "That is so."

"Well, we never did go to that monastery, did we. Remember, that old dear up near Poenari with the story about her immortal husband. We always said we would go there when we had a spare few days. But we were so busy with the *sluji* and everything that we just put it off. Because it seemed there was always time in the future to do so."

I nodded. "But if we do not go now, we may never go at all."

"Leave it," Walt said. "Who cares about that batty old bird and her nonsense? We ain't riding down south with Radu and his cavalry charging about the lowlands."

"She said they knew about immortals at Snagov. If that is true, it is not an opportunity we should pass up."

"That may be," Stephen said, "but we do not have time to ride there before our prince and the rest of the men flee the city. We must not be left behind in the country. What if our route of escape is cut off? What then?"

"We can be there and back in three days. There is time enough."

Walt raised his hand. "Does any of us reckon there is anything to find? All we've heard is stories from old Serban and a mad old peasant woman. If once there was immortals in this country, they are probably gone. If they weren't, we'd have run into them by now, wouldn't we? And, I might add, if there are any sneaking around, so what? Why do we even care about them?"

"They would come from the children of Priskos," Eva said. "They might know something useful."

"That is true," Stephen said.

"Wasting our time," Walt sighed.

"It is three days, Walter," I said. "We will be back here in no time and thence to exile."

"Just us?" Eva asked. "The Order."

I nodded. "Just us, and Serban, if you can find him."

$$\infty$$

The monastery at Snagov was on a small island in the middle of a long, narrow lake and we crossed to it by an ancient boat moored on the shore for just that purpose. The people in the village said it was used to ferry supplies to the monks, who they spoke of in hushed tones.

Other than the stone buildings of the rather small monastery, the island was green with fruit trees and the kitchen gardens where monks or lay servants hoed the earth. It was actually quite lovely and I felt peaceful just looking at it and decided that no matter what the monks had to say on the matter, I was glad that I had come.

Vlad had not really understood my desire to visit, when I had gone to him before we left Târgoviște.

"If you are abandoning me, Richard, at least have the courage to say so."

I frowned. "You think that I would skulk away like a coward? Is that truly what you think?"

He sighed. "No. But why ask them about immortals? They have never mentioned anything to me about it and I have been there many times."

"You have?"

He puffed out his chest. "I gifted them a new bell tower, a chapel, and a new roof. I even offered to build them a bridge to the mainland. They declined."

"Very generous of you, I am sure. I heard a rumour that they have some knowledge of immortals. All I will do is ask them to share it and return here."

"Why would they have such knowledge?"

I shrugged. "Perhaps an old text in their possession?"

Vlad snapped his fingers. "That will be it. They have a magnificent library there. The monk in charge of it, decrepit old fellow, blind as a mole but sharp up here. Very well, then, I shall see you when you return. If they give you any trouble, remind them of the bags of florins their prince bestowed upon their house."

"I will do so," I had replied.

There was a monk in his black cassock waiting for us on the island landing as we moored the boat. He was a young man but he had a rather magnificent beard.

"You are welcome, my lord," he said, smiling but hesitant.

"No doubt you are wondering why I have come," I replied. "I have questions regarding certain legends and I am told that you men here know the answers."

He frowned and opened his mouth to answer, then closed it again. The monk looked over his shoulder at the monastery buildings and then past me out over the lake, still frowning. "Perhaps you should speak to the *hegumen*, my lord," he said, finally. *Hegumen* was their word for the abbot.

"Perhaps I should," I said, smiling. "Well, lead the way, brother."

As we set off toward the buildings, Stephen hurried up behind me and whispered in my ear. "Actually, the common form of address for a monk here is father, not brother."

I turned around to tell him to shut up and saw Serban was on the dockside still. "Serban, what are you doing? Come on, I need you."

He slumped sullenly up the bank. "Someone should guard the boat, sir."

"Guard it against these dangerous monks, Serban?" I asked. "Come on." Still, he hesitated so I grasped him by the shoulder and shoved him into motion in front of me.

The handsome buildings were of a pale golden sandstone and the trees, and fruit bushes were neatly pruned and the pathways smartly swept. Evening sunlight glowed from the walls of the new bell tower. Before we entered the monastery, three monks emerged from a dark archway and came to meet us. The foremost of them was a man of middle age, his beard tinged with white.

"Ah, here is the abbot now," the monk from the dock said.

"Welcome, my lord," the abbot said, as we drew to a stop in the long shadows. "I am Abbot Ioánnis."

"I am Richard Ashbury, a soldier in service of Prince Vlad."

"Ah," he said, his eyes widening. "I have heard so much about you."

"You have?"

"You have come far and arrived late. It is almost vespers and I am sure you and your men will require refreshments. Do you intend to stay for the night?"

"If you would allow it, father, and if you have space. The villagers will put us up if not."

"We have a rather fine new hospital building with space enough for all of you with some to spare. It was enlarged due to the beneficence of our generous prince. Come, I shall escort you there myself."

He led us around the perimeter to the hospital which had beds and even a dining table where guests could take meals separate from the monks' refectory.

"Abbot Ioánnis," I said as my men spread out in the dormitory. "May I state my business here?"

"If you wish to do so," he said.

"It is somewhat of a strange question to ask but I have been looking for certain stories." I trailed off.

"Stories?" he prompted, a smile on his face.

"Stories of a rather strange nature. You see, I am looking for tales of men who drink blood."

His smiled faltered and his eyes darted around. "Oh? What could you want with stories like that, my lord?"

I sighed, sensing that I had perhaps wasted my time on the ramblings of a mad old woman after all. "I was told that you collected such tales here. It may be nonsense and if so, I apologise. Have you ever heard of the word *strigoi*?"

He peered at me, his mouth slightly open. "Well—" he began before breaking off, staring behind me. "Is that you, Serban?"

All of us stopped what we were doing and turned around to see Serban slouching in the doorway, his head down.

"Serban?" I said. "Come here."

He came forward, almost dragging his feet with every step.

"It is you, is it not?" Abbot Ioánnis said. "Praise Christ, you have returned. Gracious, it must be, what, thirty years?"

"Returned?" I said. "What is the meaning of this?"

Serban bobbed his head. "Father Ioánnis. Long time. You are abbot now, I see. That is well."

"Oh," the abbot said, chuckling, as if that was unimportant. "So, it is you who has brought my lord Richard Ashbury to our house. How wonderful."

"No, no," Serban said. "It was not me. I did not bring him."

"Ah," the abbot said, his face falling.

"Serban, you serve me and I command you to tell me it all, now."

He shrugged. "Not much to tell. I was here. Then I wasn't."

The abbot scoffed. "Oh, Serban, you feel guilty, I am certain. Please, do not. My lord Richard, allow me to speak of it. There is really not much to tell. One day, a soldier arrived on our shore, terribly wounded. He managed to tell us that he was looking for a place to die. Well, we are not unskilled in the arts of healing and in time, the soldier was made whole again. He stayed after and we spoke of God and His son Jesus Christ. You see, the soldier's body had been healed but his soul was yet wounded from the battles and horrors he had seen. For a time, the soldier embraced life here. He became a novice, wore the cassock and carried his prayer rope and recited in prayer with us. He confessed his sins and, my lord, there were a great many sins to confess, as is the way with soldiers, and I had high hopes that we would welcome him as a full brother." Abbot Ioánnis smiled. "But one morning as we rose for orthros, we found that the soldier was gone. And we never saw him again. Until this joyous moment."

I stared at Serban, who was looking at his shoes. "You sneaky little sod!"

The abbot chuckled. "Many novitiates end their time at a monastery in such a fashion."

"I know that," I said. "But why did you not tell me this at any point, Serban? Is your shame really so great that you could not speak of it?"

He looked up at me. "I knew that you had to come here. I did not know how to speak of it properly. In the right way. But Ioánnis has done it well."

I shook my head. "If only your battlefield bravery was matched by your moral courage, Serban."

"Please, my lord," the abbot said, "do not be overly firm with Serban. I can understand his hesitancy. But he need not fear us. We mean him well, always. Now, you are looking for stories of *strigoi?* Then you must speak to Theodore. Your men should remain here and I will escort you to the library."

Vlad had not been lying about the library at Snagov. The walls were lined with shelves packed with scrolls and there were more codices than I had ever seen in one place. Some of the books were richly ornamented and some even encased in gold and jewels. One wall was lined with windows that opened on to a view of the long lake beyond and there were two monks bent over copying manuscripts. In the corner, sitting by an open window with his face half turned to the view, sat an ancient monk with an enormous white beard.

Abbot Ioánnis dismissed the two scribes and called out to the elderly fellow. "Father Theodore. I have brought with me one of Prince Vlad's soldiers named Richard Ashbury, the Englishman. He comes wishing to ask you if you have any stories of the *strigoi* that you may relay to him. Why he wishes to know this, I cannot say, because he has not told me and I have not asked him. Would it be well for him to speak with you about this?"

Theodore turned from the window and stared, glassy eyed, in my direction. The man was quite blind.

He dragged himself to his feet and I was surprised to find he was rather tall and, though his back was bent and his frame was frail, it was clear that his shoulders and chest had once been broad. Theodore surprised me then by offering his hand by way of greeting and when I took it I found his hand was even larger than mine and his grip was like iron.

"Richard Ashbury," he said, his voice thick with a strange accent. "I am Theodore. Welcome."

Beside me, the abbot spoke up. "Father Theodore, you will never believe who Richard has brought with him. It is none other than our old—"

"Leave us, Ioánnis," Theodore said, turning his cloudy eyes on the abbot, who immediately left without another word. "Come and sit by my window, Richard."

He strode back to his seat and eased himself down into his chair with a sigh, indicating that I take the chair opposite it, also by the window. The evening breeze ruffled the edges of the ancient monk's snow-white beard.

"Thank you for meeting with me, father," I began but he just spoke over me.

"What can you see, Richard?"

"Out of the window? Well, I see a small courtyard outside, well paved, with a low wall surrounding it. Beyond that is the graveyard, going down to the water's edge. A few trees there, looks like alder and a magnificent dark green pine, the top of which is lit by the sun. The trees are not enough to obscure the view of the long lake beyond, however. The water is clear and flat and hardly rippled by the wind. I see the sun setting off over the right bank where there is woodland and fields. I see sheep on the far bank and three shepherds, all boys, throwing stones into the water. Smoke from the village drifts across and catches some of the sunlight high above. It is peaceful. No danger. Everything is as it should be."

He smiled as I spoke and when I finished, he sighed. "Yes, that is what I see, also. You have good eyes, brother. A soldier's eyes. I would wager you watch always for danger on distant horizons, am I correct? Of course I am. And that is why you wish to know of *strigoi*, is that it? You fear these creatures?"

"Fear them? No. I would like to find them. If they cause others harm, I would kill them."

He seemed amused. "You would kill them, would you? You know that they have strength beyond that of mortal men, do you? So how would you do that?"

"I find cutting their heads off usually works."

Theodore scowled. "You have killed *strigoi*? Where? When?"

"I do not know if they were *strigoi*. What I do know is that I found them everywhere from England to Palestine."

The ancient monk's voice rose, incredulous. "And you *killed* them?"

"Most of them. So far."

He held himself still. "Well, Richard, if you are an expert killer of *strigoi* all over the earth, why would you seek stories from a simple old monk?"

Sighing, I sat back and looked at the lake. "All the ones I killed so far were created by one man. But I have heard there are more in these parts who, I assume, were not created by him. I would like to speak to those men and if you have word of them in your manuscripts then that might help me to do that."

Theodore eased himself back further into his chair. "You call them men. And yet you also say that you kill them. Is that not murder?"

"They are men, certainly. The ones I killed have all been murderers, also. Murderers who toiled at sedition and treachery and attempted to gain control of kingdoms so that they might rule as immortals for a thousand years. These I killed. If that is murder, then so be it. But you called them creatures. Perhaps we speak of different things."

Theodore sighed. "They have many names. All people have their own words for what these men are. The Wallachians call them *strigoi*. The Croats call them *mora* and the Czechs name them *pijavica*. In my homeland, they were called *vrykolakas*. And so on. But they all describe people who are turned from human into one who must drink blood to live. And they come only at night because the sunlight hurts their flesh and their eyes. Sometimes they are terrifying monsters, other times they are tragically cursed people. But they most certainly all describe the same thing."

"You seem to be an expert," I said. "I had assumed you would need to refer to some ancient codex. How is it that you know so much about them?"

He smiled. "I know so much about a great many things. All my life, I loved learning. Even when I was a soldier."

I had to suppress a laugh. "You were a soldier?"

Theodore frowned. "I was a fine soldier. I will wager I killed more men than you ever have, Richard the Englishman." He sighed. "But I was even better at fighting for lost souls. Alas, my time is almost up. I spent so many years in scriptoria and libraries like this one that I have wasted away into this frail creature before you. Yes, my time is almost up. If you learn nothing else from me, learn this. Never become a scholar."

I smiled. "Hardly much danger of that. But tell me, what do you know of the *strigoi* of Wallachia? How many are there here now, today? How might I track them and find them?"

"You do not fear them?"

"If anything, they should fear me."

"Because you wish to kill them all."

"No, not at all. If they live peacefully, I would have no quarrel with them. I merely wish to know how they came to be."

"What do you mean, son?"

"All *strigoi* were made into what they were by another. Do you know about this?"

Theodore sighed. "The *strigoi* drink the blood of the *vampir*."

"The what?"

"The *vampir* is the immortal lord who creates the *strigoi*."

"He is one man? Where is he?"

"No, no. He is not one man. There have been more than one *vampir*. No one knows where they come from but only they can make a man into a *strigoi*."

"Well then, yes, that is precisely who I seek. How can I find them?"

He hesitated for so long, staring out at the dusk, that I thought his attention had wandered. "I doubt even the *strigoi* out there know where the *vampir* are."

"You know something," I said, leaning forward. "There is something you are not telling me. Do you know where I can find one of these *strigoi*?"

Theodore turned his blind eyes to me and smiled. "It has been a joy to speak with you, Richard. Please do return another day."

"Thank you for seeing me," I said, annoyed that he was hiding the full truth. "I will come again if I can but it may not be for a long time."

"If God wills it, I will still be alive. And if not, I wish you peace."

"I am a soldier," I said, standing. "Peace is the last thing I want."

When I returned to the hospital, my men were eating. I sat at the table and gulped down two cups of wine.

"How did it go?" Eva asked.

"I am a *vampir*," I said.

"You did what?" Walt called out.

"The monk in the library knows all there is to know about nothing useful at all. I am sorry, my friends, this was a waste of time. In the morning, we will ride for Târgovişte and then into exile."

∞

It was not long before Radu III Dracula was recognised as Voivode of Wallachia by most of the *boyars*. He was cunning in a way that Vlad never was. Word was spread by his agents in advance of his arrival that under the rule of Radu III, Wallachia would remain completely free of occupation Turkish soldiers. What was more was his promise that the *devshirme* would never be paid. There would be no Blood Tax under Radu's rule, no sons of Wallachia would be taken by the Janissaries.

William's devious hand was behind it, there could be no

doubt. Only a friend of the Turks could get such concessions from them in order to secure his throne but the peasantry of any nation are a simple sort and they did not question the whys of this boon. All they heard was the promise of freedom from occupation and the freedom to raise their sons in peace.

And what man or woman in all the world would fight against that?

The only other option for the country was to retain their hero Vlad Dracula who many still loved but who could promise nothing more than a reign of relentless repeated invasions and further destruction of the land.

Before we had even fled far we heard that the people were calling their new leader Radu the Handsome. We did not get close enough to see his beauty but we were not far off. He and his soldiers pursued us right through the mountains and it was a close-run thing. First we raced up the valley of the River Arges and sought shelter in Vlad's castle at Arges. Radu's men were so close behind that we barely made it before they were encamped below the castle. By the end of that day they were bringing up small cannon with which to blast through the walls.

But Vlad was never a man to get himself into a situation he could not get out from and there was another exit from his castle that took us across the slopes to the north, with our horses and all.

We headed of all places to Brasov who Vlad—and I—had once terrorised. But after the peace had been secured with them it was neutral ground, of sorts and there we awaited the arrival of the King of Hungary Mattias Corvinus.

Vlad and he met in the town hall at Brasov and came to an agreement.

Radu had already sent word that he would favour and even extend the all-important commercial agreements of the Saxon colony towns and so they were inclined to back him over their old enemy Vlad. And Mattias Corvinus, cautious to a fault, was not one to pick an unnecessary fight. In fact, the king had signed a truce with Mehmed and had officially ended the crusade against the Turks. It was in his interest to do so in order that he could further concentrate his efforts on Frederick III the Holy Roman Emperor who still had eyes on Corvinus' crown.

Vlad agreed to give himself over to Mattias Corvinus as a prisoner.

It seemed like madness for him to do so but it was likely the safest course of action that he could take. Hiding out in one of his small Transylvanian castles would mean being besieged and taken by an enemy, eventually. And there were already plenty of Saxon enemies in addition to the Wallachian ones.

In spite of everything, it was to be a rather pleasant imprisonment for Vlad. He resided in the king's summer palace at Visegard overlooking the Danube and the Hungarians treated him well. He was valuable as a rival claimant to the Wallachian crown and that alone would serve to keep Radu the Handsome in check. The implicit and ever-present threat was that the Hungarians could remove Radu if he proved too troublesome and they had a ready alternative always at hand.

What is more, Vlad III Dracula was a name that stirred fear in the hearts of all Turks. He was Kaziglu Bey, the Lord Impaler, and Mattias Corvinus made sure that Dracula was at his side whenever he undertook diplomatic business with the emissaries of the Turks. I am certain that there was not a one of them who did not look upon the Lord Impaler without feeling a terrible itch beneath his turban.

Dracula was also offered a place in the Hungarian royal family on condition that he embraced Roman Catholicism in place of his Orthodox faith. They gave him an important position in the Hungarian Army where he served as a respected and feared senior captain.

As far as captivity goes, it was as comfortable and honourable as it was possible to get.

The Turks continued their work of encircling Hungarian territory, however, and as much as Radu the Handsome called himself a vassal of Hungary, I knew the truth. He was allowed to reign only by the grace of William de Ferrers, Zaganos Pasha.

Of all the kingdoms that might seek to resist him, the small and isolated kingdom of Moldavia, between Wallachia and the Black Sea, was perhaps the least likely to be successful.

But it was all we had.

1 5

Moldavia

1 4 6 7 — 1 4 7 3

"MY COUSIN WRITES THAT YOU ARE HIS FINEST soldier," Stephen of Moldavia said as I stood before his throne in the great hall of his palace in the city of Suceava. "Do you agree with that statement?"

"I am not a prideful man, my lord," I replied. "But it is the truth."

King Stephen looked rather a lot like Vlad Dracula, with his long nose and wide moustache but he did not have Vlad's piercing gaze and bulging eyes. Still, it was immediately clear that his men both loved and respected their king and I was sure to show proper deference.

"You are a mercenary," the king said. "And your men, the *sluji*, have fought the Turks and beaten them. And so I will have you, gladly. But I will not have you running around my kingdom causing trouble, do you hear me? I can use you but I do not need you. I can expel you at any moment and you must understand this?"

I bowed. "As you say, my lord. All my men want is the chance to kill Turks."

"All you want is to avoid the retribution of my cousin Radu the Usurper, you mean? Well, whatever you mean, you will have your chance. And perhaps you will have the chance to do both, for what is Radu if he is not the slave of the Sultan and Zaganos Pasha?"

"Indeed, my lord."

King Stephen smiled down at me. "I know all about Zaganos Pasha. My cousin and I spent years together before he claimed his kingdom and he helped me to claim mine and many a night we sat drinking wine and speaking about the evils of Zaganos Pasha." He lowered his voice. "Or should I call him William?"

"Call him what you will, my lord, all I ask is that, in your service, my men and I be used to counter the Janissaries of the pasha. It is why the *sluji* were created."

The king nodded. "You were right to come to me, Richard. Only Moldavia stands against the enemy. Albania, Bosnia, Montenegro, and Serbia have fallen. Wallachia is Turkish in all but name. And both the Turks and the Wallachians are massing on my borders."

"The Wallachians too, my lord?"

"Will it prove to be a problem for your men if they help me to defeat Radu, should he invade my lands? Your men are all

Wallachians, are they not?"

"Most of them, my lord. But they are loyal to me, now. And anyway, Wallachia is not one people but many. There are more clans than I can name and they harbour hatred for each other and they seem to enjoy fighting each other whenever there is no enemy without. You can trust my men."

"That is good. But it may be your men will not have to fight Wallachians at all, as the Turks have sent Radu thousands of soldiers for his army."

I could scarcely believe he would be so open about it, after all his promises. "Radu has claimed to his people that he is holding the Turks at bay through clever diplomacy. But if this is true then his people will know him for a puppet after all."

"He believes himself strong," King Stephen said, a smile on his face. "He thinks he will conquer Moldavia and be only strengthened." He laughed and turned to his lords in the hall. "What do you think, my friends? Shall we sit back and allow Wallachia to conquer Moldavia?"

Their roar of defiance shook the very stones of the walls.

The king smiled. "I shall not wait for Radu to launch his invasion of my kingdom. I will not have war on my land, on my people, when I might wage it on my enemy's soil and spill the blood of his people instead of mine."

I was surprised. "My lord, you mean to invade Wallachia?"

"His Turks are still arriving. Would you prefer to wait for him to gain his full strength? But I thought you were a great strategist, Richard the Englishman?" His men laughed.

"I would never claim that, my lord. But Radu will flee to the mountains and avoid battle."

The king threw up his hands. "Wonderful! Then we shall raid his kingdom and rob it blind. In the end, his own men will overthrow him."

I had fought to protect Wallachia for years and now I would be fighting to destroy that very land, those very same people. The thought twisted my stomach but it was not so unusual a turn of events for a mercenary. At least there could be some good to come of it.

"If Radu is removed," I said, "you will be able to reinstate Vlad Dracula."

King Stephen frowned. "Why would I want to do that?"

I hesitated, surprised. "He is your cousin, my lord. He is your friend."

The king pointed at me. "Your friend, you mean. With Radu gone and my armies in his lands, yes, I could perhaps restore dear Vlad. But is that best for Moldavia? Is that best for me?"

"Is it not?"

The king stroked the end of his moustache. "He can be depended on to fight the Turk, that is certain. And yet we cannot always have war, eventually we must have some form of peace with the Turk. And the Turk hates Vlad Dracula."

"They fear him."

"Yes and they will come again sooner and with greater strength if Vlad is on the throne."

I sensed that this was not the first time King Stephen had considered these points. "You have another lord in mind for the throne? Perhaps yourself?"

His men bristled and cursed my impudence but Stephen waved them down. "I would not step into that snake pit. There is another I would make Voivode of Wallachia. A man I have here at court."

I remembered that there was an exile in the city. "You have one of the Danesti clan."

"Yes. Basarab Laiot will be what Wallachia needs in order to pull together the warring factions within the kingdom."

"Can he be trusted?"

King Stephen scoffed. "He can be trusted to act in his own interest. As can all men. Do you not agree?"

"All men, indeed. To one extent or another."

"And so, knowing what I will do, who I must wage war on, and who I must put on what was my cousin's throne, can I trust you to join us? And to follow my orders?"

What else could I do? I had to work to bring about another battle against the Turks for the chance to kill William."

I bowed. "War is my business, my lord.

King Stephen dismissed me and I was escorted back to my companions in our quarters in the palace. The city of Suceava was in the north of Moldavia, just on the eastern side of the mountains that separated the country from Transylvania. Even though Suceava was on the edge of Europe, with nothing to the east but the Tartars and the Golden Horde, it was finely built, with buildings almost as magnificent as those of Buda, though on a far smaller scale. I had expected Moldavia to be halfway to barbarous but it was no more so than Wallachia, at least in the large towns. The country, too, was fertile and crossed by countless rivers that drained from the north down into the Black Sea. The small country's southern border was the Danube and where it met the Black Sea it was wide and the area around it was marshy indeed. It was no wonder the enemy intended to invade from Wallachia.

My men were enjoying the delights of a Moldavian tavern when I found them, sinking tankards of beer and gnawing on chunks of bread.

"I like it here," Rob said as I sat down. "Serban likes it too much."

The old soldier had his head on the table, snoring audibly even over the din of the ale room.

"What happened?" Stephen asked, pushing me a plate of half-eaten boiled pork in jelly. "Did he accept us?"

I related everything that the king had said in between mouthfuls of pork and beer.

"Basarab Laiot instead of Dracula?" Walt said when I was finished. "He will be worse than useless. Have you met him?"

"Have you?"

"I drank with him a few days ago. We played dice. I was not impressed by his wits nor his character."

"Why?" I asked. "How did you come to play dice with a pretender to the Wallachian throne?"

Walt grinned. "An attempt to woo me, wasn't it."

We stared at each other. "Woo you?"

Walt was enjoying himself. "Promised me great wealth. Swore he would grant me an estate near Buzau. Said I would be a great captain in his armies. All he wanted was for me to tell him what the secret was. What the power of the blood magic was that gave you your strength and the strength of the *sluji*."

Stephen gasped. "He wanted it for himself."

Eva leaned over and punched Walt on his shoulder. "You did not think to mention this, you witless oaf?"

Walt rubbed his shoulder, still grinning. "Hardly seemed worth it. Wasn't going to accept, was I?"

"Our agents brought word of him years ago," Eva said as Stephen nodded. "We dismissed him as neither a possible asset nor a risk. He is a nobody."

"Basarab is a duplicitous boyar who attempts to be cunning but is not competent at it," Stephen said. "And this is who we would be fighting for?"

"No. We would be fighting to kill Radu and so remove one of William's immortals."

"Assuming Radu is an immortal," Eva said. "We have no proof."

I scoffed. "Come on, he must be by now. William would never have given him this much authority were he not bound to him by the Gift."

"Very likely," Eva allowed.

"And even if he is not then we should destroy him anyway, for Radu is an important ally in William's plan of conquest."

Rob snorted a laugh. "More than an ally. More of a sweetheart, no?"

Walt grinned. "We're going to break his heart."

I fished a piece of gristle from the back of my teeth. "William feels nothing for any of his spawn, no matter what the fools believe."

"That is a point to consider," Stephen said, sitting up straighter. "Whether William feels any true closeness to Radu, will he not come to fight for him if his rule is at risk?"

"Zaganos Pasha is in the East with Mehmed," Eva said. "Waging war against the tribes threatening to overwhelm the Turks there. He will not come here until his business in the east is concluded. You see, William understands the value of patience. His plans for conquering this entire land are almost complete. All he needs is Moldavia and he will have subjugated the lands from the Black Sea to the Adriatic. He will not be rushing back here in a panic, even if we threaten his beloved."

I gestured with my tankard as I spoke. "If he does not return, we shall kill Radu with all the more ease. And if William does return to save his spawn, we shall kill him also. It seems to me that it is in our interest to join this war against Wallachia and to win it."

"What about our lads?" Rob said. "The *sluji* are Wallachian. They will not want to fight their former lord's brother and they especially will not wish to do it for the Danesti clan to benefit."

Rob's concerns worried me because if he felt them they were likely worth considering.

"The *sluji* have sworn oaths of obedience," I said. "They will obey or they will suffer the consequences."

"You might first attempt to explain to them that they will be fighting the Turks, as they have sworn to do, when they are fighting Radu."

"If you insist, Rob," I said. "Now, enough of this disgusting beer. Have them bring me wine."

∞

Stephen sent requests for aid to Mattias Corvinus, who was instead concerned with central Europe. Likewise, Moldavia's traditional overlords the Poles also declined to be drawn into the fight. Their concern was for the east and the north of Europe, not the Balkans to their south. They did not believe that the Turks could threaten them.

My men joined with companies of Moldavian cavalry and we raided the lowlands with hardly any opposition. Radu was careful to stay in his castles in the high places of Wallachia and no matter how many villages we burned and no matter how many crops we destroyed, Radu would not be drawn from his places of safety.

He sent companies of Turks against us, some of them Anatolian but mostly Rumelians from Bulgaria. When they were too many, we ran. When we had the advantage, we attacked them with everything we had and we destroyed them. And even then, Radu would not come to face us.

Eva and Stephen used their agents to spread word of Radu's treacheries and to seek *boyars* who would come over to Moldavia's side and many of the Danesti clan replied that they would be willing to turn on their prince, for the right incentives.

Still, Radu the Handsome stayed in the mountains.

Along with Moldavian captains that I rode with, I eventually persuaded King Stephen that only an all-out invasion would be enough to force Radu to lead his armies in person. In autumn 1473 we brought Radu to battle near Bucharest at a field near the River Vodnu. It was a rather sad and brief affair, with little glory to be had for anyone.

For all his charisma and personal command, Radu was not a bold general by nature. Far from it. But the presence of so many Turkish soldiers had emboldened him and we baited him into an attack in which we enveloped and crushed his army.

As his army crumbled, Radu abandoned his men and fled his camp. He fled in so much haste in fact that he abandoned his treasury and all of his wardrobe. The man had more clothes than a king of France. He left his battle standards and his new wife. He had lost all legitimacy in the eyes of his people and soon they would be willing to declare Basarab as the new Voivode of Wallachia.

But I would find out all of that later. First, I had to catch him and kill him. A company of Rumelian *sipahis* fled with Radu and I led the *sluji* after them. It seemed that they were making for the fortress of Giurgiu which Radu loyalists yet held and so we had to stop them before he reached it. No doubt King Stephen could besiege it and no doubt Basarb could command them to surrender but by then Radu would have been long gone across the Danube. And I wanted him.

"The woodland!" I said to my captains. "If we can reach the woodland before them, we shall have him."

I made half of my men dismount and told them to meet me at Giurgiu. We took their horses as remounts, stripped off as much armour and equipment as we dared and then set off across country. We stopped only in the darkest of night and I had them up again well before dawn, trusting their immortal eyesight to keep us on track. We cut across the marshland and finally reached the wood, exhausted and tired but ready.

We were hardly in position when Radu and his *sipahis* came cantering from the north toward the fortress. Radu, still the proud peacock that he was, rode at the head of them in shining armour and a great headdress upon his helm, with a glittering golden band around it studded with rubies.

"Do you reckon that's him?" Walt muttered before we sprung our ambush.

My *sluji* swarmed on the *sipahis* from both sides, pulling them from their horses and drinking their blood while they screamed.

I made straight for Radu and caught him in indecision. He began riding back to save his men before seeing the speed and strength of the *sluji* and he wheeled his horse about to make for the fortress. Instead, my lance point caught him in the flank and threw him from the saddle. He landed on his helm, his neck bending under him. I jumped down and was on him, pulling his helm from his head.

He looked so much like Vlad that for a moment I thought it was him but then I saw how the man's features were far more refined. His jaw was squarer and his brow higher and his nose less of a spear point. He roared at me and drew his sword half out of his scabbard before I wrestled it from him and threw it aside.

Still, he got to his knees and pulled a long dagger from his belt. I grappled with him as he rushed me and I knew at once that he was an immortal. Radu was strong and a well-trained fighter. He tried to trip me and twisted to get inside my guard. But I butted his face with my helm, crushing his nose and he released his grip. Tripping him, I forced him down and slipped his own knife under his throat.

Blood streamed down his face.

"Not so handsome now, are you, boy?" I said. "I am going to send William your head."

I was about to slit his throat when Eva stayed my hand.

"Richard!" She held my arm. "Let us not be so hasty."

"He is an immortal, Eva. He must die."

"And so he will," she said, trying to get me to look at her. "But why not speak to him first? He may know William's plans."

Radu's eyes glanced back and forth between us. "I will tell you nothing!" he said, in French.

"Quiet!" I said and cracked his broken nose with the butt of my dagger, causing him to flinch and wail, though I held him fast. "The world knows William's plans. Conquer Christendom."

"He may have some secret. Something. We should question him."

"Perhaps. But the Moldavians will not wish him taken prisoner. The Wallachians opposed to him would see him dead also, lest his continued existence give heart to his faction and to the Turks and so prolong the war. And what is my status that would allow me to take a royal prisoner? I cannot take him and expect to keep him unchallenged. He must die."

Eva looked around at the *sluji*, who were feasting on the *sipahis* or rummaging through their equipment. "What if we take him in secret? Tell the world he is dead and only we shall know he lives."

I hesitated, looking down at Radu. "They will expect to see his body. Let us provide one. We could use one of his men, although I doubt any of those filthy Bulgars could pass for Radu the Handsome."

Eva nodded to herself as she thought it through. "We must mutilate the corpse's face. We shall dress him in Radu's shining armour and fine underclothes and carry away the real one."

"But carry him to where? Where can I keep him for questioning that he will not be seen?"

Stephen stepped forward. "Richard? We are not so far from the monastery at Lake Snagov."

"Yes?"

"Perhaps that abbot would hide him there."

"Why would he do that?"

"All the money that Dracula showered on that place must count for something. The abbot loved Dracula, you could tell by the way he spoke about him. He's loyal to Vlad Dracula and I bet he would hold Radu as his prisoner without giving him up. The monks are, of course, utterly loyal to the abbot and none would speak of it."

Eva looked down her nose at him. "Radu is an immortal."

I sighed. "Oh yes."

"What's the problem?" Rob asked. "Ah, he needs blood. Well, you said the old boy in the library knew all about us. About *strigoi*."

I shook my head. "I imagine if we tell the monks we brought a cursed blood drinker into his house, he would throw us into

Lake Snagov. He would have to bleed his brothers to keep Radu alive."

Eva sighed. "I suppose it is worth the attempt."

Rob nodded down at Radu. "Exactly. And if it all goes pear shaped, we'll just kill the bastard."

I ordered Radu's clothing swapped with a soldier of similar height and frame and stood admiring the finery he was now dressed in, Walt smashed his face in with his mace. As the false Radu's body was delivered by my men to Stephen, I took the real Radu north to Lake Snagov.

∞

The abbot came down to the dockside and watched us row across the lake to his island. Behind him came first half a dozen and then a score of black robed monks, spread out across the bank.

"Richard Ashbury," he said, his face grim. "It has been some time since we saw you last. Do you mean us harm?"

"Harm?" I asked, confused, and then looked at my men as the abbot would. We were all, to one extent or another, wearing armour. Our men waiting with the horses behind us at the village were likewise arrayed for war. "My apologies for coming to you in this manner. Of course I mean you no harm, father. Why would we?"

He looked us over again, still not trusting my word.

"We come straight from the battlefield," I explained. "Hence our appearance."

"There has been a battle?"

"Not much of one. We have defeated Radu Dracula and have taken him prisoner."

"I see. I am sure that his brother is pleased. But what does this have to do with us?"

I hesitated for a moment and then gestured for the prisoner to be brought forward. Walt and Rob picked him up from the bottom of the boat and carried him up to me. Dressed in a commoner's undershirt and hose, he was bound with rope around the wrists and had a leather bag over his head. I nodded and Walt pulled the bag off to reveal Radu Dracula's face, swollen and covered with dried blood from his broken nose.

"Abbot Ioánnis, I am pleased to introduce Radu Dracula."

The abbot recoiled and the monks behind cursed and muttered until the abbot silenced them with a glare.

"Why bring him here?"

"The new Voivode of Wallachia will be a man named Basarab. He is a Danesti and he will have Radu killed. Basarab was placed on the throne by King Stephen of Moldavia, who will also have Radu killed. We preferred that he live. And so we left a defaced body in Radu's armour on the battlefield and brought him here in the hopes that you would keep him safe."

The abbot stared at me. "Why in the name of God would we do that? We survive here in peace precisely because we stay out of the dynastic wars of the Wallachians. If we are discovered harbouring a former prince, we shall not survive here much longer."

"No one will know. It is a secret known only to my men and yours."

The abbot was amused. "Secrets always come out, Richard."

A disturbance behind him made us turn and I saw the old librarian, Theodore, coming down to the dockside with a hand outstretched on the shoulder of a young monk walking before him. He walked with the aid of a long stick, his unseeing eyes staring into nothingness.

"Did I hear Richard Ashbury?" the old man said, his voice raspy from his aged throat but still deep from his barrel chest.

"You did, Father Theodore," I called. "How delighted I am to see that you are still alive."

The abbot bristled but Theodore chuckled as he came to a stop beside him and his guide sidled away. "And did I hear you say you have Radu Dracula as your prisoner, here?"

"You have good ears, father," I said. "He is here beside me. Angry beyond words."

"Free me," Radu said, his voice thick from his wounded face. "Free me, brothers, and it will rain gold on your house, I swear by—"

I punched him in the stomach, knocking the words from his mouth. Walt and Rob held him aloft, else he would have collapsed.

"He can offer you nothing because he has nothing to offer. He has lost his kingdom. But I would very much like to speak with him and I hoped you could find space in your house and in your hearts for a poor wounded soldier."

The abbot scowled. "It would not be an act of charity to put my brothers here in mortal danger."

I sensed it was not going well so I decided on a final throw of the dice. "Would it change your mind overly much if I told you that Radu here was a *strigoi*?"

The abbot and all the monks stirred and looked to each other, disturbed indeed.

"Even if that is true," the abbot said, his voice almost a growl. "Why should that concern us?"

Theodore placed a massive hand on the abbot's shoulder. "We would be glad to welcome Prince Radu into our house. I think we have a spare cell, do we not, Ioánnis?"

The abbot dismissed his brothers and led us through the monastery down into a corridor with a row of four cells, one of which he led us into. There was a bed, a low table with a lamp on it, and a high, narrow window at the top of the far wall. I pushed Radu into it, forcing him down to his knees, and was followed in by the abbot and Theodore. My men and a handful of monks crowded outside.

"Periods of solitary contemplation are required for all of us," the abbot said. "Especially for novices. You will be comfortable here, Radu."

"There is something I must make clear," I said. "Being that Radu is a *strigoi*, he will require regular cups of human blood for consumption."

Radu snarled at me from his knees. "Your men are all *strigoi* also, Englishman. And you are worse. You are the father to them all! But you will be defeated. My master will come for you, traitor, he will come and he will–"

I kicked him in the guts and he fell forward and curled into a ball.

"We will have no violence here," the abbot said and moved to help Radu onto the bed.

Theodore had a smile on his face.

Neither of them asked me about Radu's accusations nor questioned the need for him to drink blood.

"I must return to my men. King Stephen will be looking for me. Before I go, I must question my prisoner."

"If he is in my care," the abbot said, "he is not your prisoner but my ward. And I refuse to allow you to harm this man, whatever he may or may not be."

"I must question him," I said, staring at the abbot. "And I will question him."

"You will leave, sir," he replied.

Theodore cleared his throat. "I must say that I am most curious to hear what the *strigoi* has to say. You can question our new brother here but only if I am present to hear what is said."

I shrugged. "Fine with me, father. I will try to avoid spilling too much of his blood."

The ancient monk smiled. "That will not bother me."

Abbot Ioánnis straightened up. "Yes, do what you will and then go. But I will have no part in it."

"Do not mind him," Theodore said. "He is young and is burdened by responsibility for the safety of his brothers."

"He is a good man," I said.

"Indeed he is. I wonder, Richard, are you?"

"I try to be. Although, I cannot deny that I have also done

much evil."

"Haven't we all," Theodore said as he closed the door and latched it. He stood before it like a sentinel. "You may begin."

I nodded and turned to Radu who was now sitting on the bed, his bound hands before him. "Hold out your hands," I commanded him and proceeded to saw through and unpick his bindings until his hands were free.

"William always said you were foolhardy. And I see it is true," Radu said, rubbing his wrists. "For I am now free to kill you."

I smiled. "You are free to try."

"Perhaps I will bash the old man's head in before you can stop me. Do you think the monks would let me stay after that?"

I looked at Theodore. "I expect that old man knows a trick or two. Besides, you are not a killer, Radu."

He scoffed, outraged. "I have killed a hundred men."

"Perhaps you have but the fact remains, you are not a killer. I know a vicious, murdering bastard when I see one and you are not it. Your brother, now. Vlad Dracula is a killer through and through, down to his marrow. He can kill women and children without flinching. Even I could never compare with such a monster."

"Even you," he said, sneering. "Even you, with your three centuries and thousands of deaths at your hands? I doubt there is any who can compare to your evil."

I shrugged. "Perhaps there is only one who has surpassed me. Your master."

Radu spat on the floor at me feet. "Your brother."

"Where is he?" I asked. "Why did he not come to help you

keep your throne?"

Radu said nothing but looked up at the narrow window high on the wall.

"I shall tell you," I continued. "William is in the east with his brother in arms, Sultan Mehmed. His truest friend in all the world. I hear that they lie together like man and wife. Tenderly, so it is said, and with great passion."

"They hate each other!" Radu snapped. "They are at war with each other. It is not love. It was never love."

I shrugged. "Not what my agents tell me."

"Your agents are wrong. William holds Mehmed in contempt and Mehmed has grown tired of William."

"But William has won him all Thrace up to Hungary, or near enough."

Radu scoffed. "Mehmed is sick of Europe. His armies are ground into dust here."

I smiled. "Because of me. I am the one who has ground his armies into dust. I smashed his armies at Varna, at Kosovo. I killed thousands even at Constantinople. I defeated him at Belgrade, smashing his army into nothing. I killed fifty thousand of his soldiers when he invaded Wallachia. All because of me. And now he despairs." I laughed.

"William could have defeated you a dozen times!" Radu said. "But Mehmed would never let him lead. He was ever jealous and held William back. But no longer." Radu smiled. "Soon, you will feel his wrath unleashed."

"Mehmed will unleash William?" I said. "How?"

Radu shrugged and looked away, a smug smile on his bloody

488

lips.

"Listen, Radu," I said, crouching down across the room from him so that I was level with him. "Look at me, Radu." He turned his eyes to mine, smirking. "You mean to say that Mehmed is going to give William an army of his own? But I thought they now mistrusted one another, so why would he give William an army? You are lying."

Radu shook his head. "It is a chance to prove himself. To finish the conquest once and for all."

"And if he should fail, what then?"

He laughed. "He will not fail."

"Where will he lead it?" I watched Radu closely. "To Moldavia?"

Radu's mouth twitched. "He knows where you have been hiding. You and your pathetic little immortal company. He knows and he is coming for you and for Moldavia. You will not stop him. If you had any sense, you would run. But William knows you too well. He knows that you will stand and fight and that will be your downfall."

"Yes, William is the one who runs. I have defeated him before and each time he has fled like the coward he is."

"He could have killed you," he said. "A dozen times, William could have killed you but he did not because you are his brother and he loves you and he wants you to live."

I smiled, genuinely amused. "He has lied to you about that just as he has lied about everything else. He lies. It is what he does. He lies to all the poor fools who he subjugates and forces to do his bidding."

"Not me," Radu said. "He will come for me. He will find me and he will come for me here and he will kill all these monks and then he will kill you."

I glanced at Theodore who stared into nothingness.

"He will never know you are here. No one does. William will hear that you died in a grubby little ambush in the woods and he will believe it because he will know that you make for a pitiful soldier. And he will not mourn you. He will not give you a moment's thought."

His face was twisted in anguish. "Kill me, then! Why keep me?"

"I am sorry, Radu. You may prove useful one day. And I think that your brother would rather you live."

Radu sneered. "That bastard will have me killed the moment you tell him where I am. He cares nothing for me, nothing at all."

"You would be surprised. He feels guilty for abandoning you when you went over to William. Perhaps he would like to make amends."

"Nonsense," Radu said but quietly.

"I may be gone for a good while," I said, standing and looking down at him. "I suggest you make the most of your time in solitary contemplation."

His head snapped up. "I will kill you one day, Richard Ashbury."

"I told you, Radu. You are not a killer."

He sat slumped on the bed and I called my men in. We trussed him up again, this time tying him to the bed post by a length of rope. He gave us no resistance and did not look up when I said farewell.

Outside, Theodore turned to me with a smile on his face. "A most illuminating conversation."

"I must hurry to King Stephen and from there prepare Moldavia for an invasion." I pointed at Radu's cell door. "He will require a cup of blood every two or three days to stop him falling into illness and madness."

"I think we can manage that."

I peered at him. "You do not appear surprised or disturbed by any of this. You or the abbot. Are you not afraid of him? I said he was not a killer but I fear he may harm you, all of you, in an attempt to flee this place."

"We may be monks but we all answered this calling from a question we heard out there in the world. I am not the only former soldier amongst us and between you and me, Richard, we have a couple of ruffians here who would make even this William knock his knees in terror."

I smiled. "I doubt that. Remember, he has the strength of ten men."

Theodore leaned in. "But we, Richard, we have the power of God."

16

The Battle of Vaslui

1475

THE SULTAN HAD LONG BEEN ON CAMPAIGN in the east and north of Anatolia against the forces of the powerful warlord Uzan Hasan. By all accounts the eastern nomadic horsemen were numerous and ferocious but they were not enough to overcome the discipline and sheer firepower of Mehmed's army.

There was now nothing to stop the Turks in the east and they ranged around the Black Sea to threaten the flanks of the lands of the Golden Horde and the Genoese outposts around the coast.

But the core of Mehmed's forces came back to Europe and William began his move to crush Moldavia. The Sultan even ended his siege against the Albanian city of Shkoder in the north in order to free up more soldiers for William's great horde. Those soldiers were not in a fit state, so our agents said, and we knew that it would take at least a month to march them to Moldavia. But Mehmed expected his soldiers to do extraordinary things and they usually managed what he demanded.

"I did not wish to tell you until I was certain," Eva said. "But now one of Stephen's men, that Genoese merchant with the nose, has confirmed it."

"Confirmed what?" I asked them.

We had a very large, very old house in the Moldavian city of Suceava that served as our residence and headquarters for the *sluji*. Our hall was almost large enough for every soldier to squeeze inside for meetings and ceremonies but that morning it echoed to the voices of the Order of the White Dagger only.

"Confirmed that the Turkish army assembled at Sofia and now marching here is being led by Zaganos Pasha."

I nodded. "So Radu was not wrong. William commands the army personally? And where is Sultan Mehmed?"

Stephen shrugged. "Possibly Constantinople. Possibly Edirne. But not at the head of this army, certainly. And it means that William walks into our arms once more. If he joins his men in battle, which he no doubt will, he is in danger. This benefits us."

"It means more than that," Eva said. "This perhaps confirms Radu's claims that William and Mehmed are indeed now in conflict about the direction of the empire. If Mehmed has given William one final chance to complete the conquest and if we defeat it, then William may have to find a new master."

Walt grunted. "Or kill his current one and take over."

"The Turks would not follow him," Stephen said. "They hate

him enough as an advisor. If he attempted to rule directly, the empire would collapse."

Walt opened his arms. "Even better."

"Let us not get ahead of ourselves," I said. "We have to defeat this army first. Do we know how big it is?"

Stephen glanced at Eva. "The precise number is not yet known," he said, "as more are coming in to support the campaign but from the amount of grain they have requested, it cannot be less than a hundred thousand fighting men."

"Likely more," Eva said. "A hundred and twenty thousand, probably."

I whistled. "He has winkled out the biggest army the Turks have ever fielded, has he not? What soldiers does he have?"

Stephen unrolled a long piece of parchment and peered at it. "By meticulously calculating the cartloads of straw my Bulgarian merchant has been commanded to transport through Rumelia, it is like that—"

Eva spoke over him. "Thirty thousand *sipahis* for the core cavalry. But also Bulgarian, Serbian, and Tatar cavalry in support."

"Infantry?" I asked. "The Janissaries are the Sultan's personal troops so presumably we do not have to contend with them."

Eva and Stephen shook their heads in unison. "Janissaries for the core," Stephen said. "Thousands but we do not know how many. They are supported by an enormous number of *azabs*."

"Guns?"

"Many in number," Eva said. "Every size of field gun that can be transported has been assembled. More than Moldavia has in the entire kingdom, certainly."

"This is a conquering army," I said. "With William in command, it is one to be feared. How long before they reach our southern border?"

"They have dragged in thousands of Bulgarian peasants who are at work clearing forests and shovelling snow. They are building bridges across the marshlands in the south."

"Bridges across the marshes? Remember when they attacked Wallachia, their cannons were bogged down and they could not move. So, William has learned his lesson. They will move swiftly, for all the great number of the host. Do we really believe he will attack in winter and not spring?"

"He's coming now," Stephen said. "Perhaps he means to catch us unprepared. Perhaps crossing the marshes is easier when they are frozen. Perhaps the Sultan has given William a deadline that he must meet. But they are coming now. No chance he maintains a force that size for months of winter while they sit and do nothing."

"We will have to share all of this with King Stephen," I told them. "He will not like it."

They looked at each other, throwing meaningful looks. I knew they were each urging the other to speak.

"For the love of God," I snapped. "Spit it out."

"King Stephen will like this even less," Eva said. "It seems also that Basarab III Laiot has welcomed a large detachment of Turks across the Danube and has himself committed seventeen thousand Wallachian soldiers to the army."

I laughed and covered my eyes. "So, Basarab is another traitor to his people and to Christendom. I will never understand Wallachia. What is wrong with those people? Why do they continue to do this?"

"At least he has shown his true intentions," Stephen said, shrugging. "He is an enemy of all those who oppose the Turks and so in time he can be removed."

Walt scoffed. "Easier said than done. We just have to defeat this great army first. How many does old King Stephen have, anyway?"

I sighed. "He had word this morning from Hungary that the Pope's call to crusade has been answered by Corvinus who sends a paltry two thousand men from Hungary."

Walt shrugged. "Better than a kick in the bollocks. Is that it?"

"Poland has likewise sent two thousand. King Stephen has recruited five thousand mercenaries, though many of them look to me like nothing more than desperate fortune hunters and outlaws."

"Takes one to know one," Rob quipped, to much amusement about the room.

I ignored him and continued. "The Moldavians can field fifteen thousand of their own soldiers and Stephen's heavy cavalry can beat anything the Turks might field. There are just not enough of them. And the peasant recruitment of all able men aged fourteen years or older has resulted in thirty thousand sullen and incompetent sons of Moldavia assembling."

"Vlad defeated the Turks with less."

"King Stephen has heart and he is a bright fellow but let us not be fooled into thinking he is the equal of Vlad Dracula on the battlefield."

"Well," Walt said. "We'll just have to see, won't we."

"Are the *sluji* prepared?" I asked them. "In that case, we must assemble them. The weather grows ever colder and William will not hesitate to strike hard and soon."

∞

The battle would be fought near Vaslui, deep inside Moldavia. But first, we had to draw the Turks to it.

We were by now experts at this type of warfare. When William's great army of Turks crossed into Moldavia, they found nought but burning fields and poisoned wells. Every resident had been removed north and there was not even a single animal larger than a cat in the entire country. Those people who could not fight were sent into the mountains in the northwest where it was hoped that they would be safe.

Every step that William's army took, we made them pay for by endless sudden raids. Every point that we held in force, they gathered a detachment with which to attack and when they did we fought briefly for a time before retreating. Every company that did so retreated toward Vaslui over prepared ground, stopping only to delay the massive army pursuing them. We used the *sluji* in some light skirmishing that helped to prepare them and also supplied us with enemy blood to drink. But I wanted them fresh and ready for the main battle to come.

The town of Vaslui had been well fortified by King Stephen. In addition, he had ensured that of all the lands for miles around across the march of the enemy, the fields and villages around Vaslui alone would remain whole. Livestock remained on the outskirts and stocks of grain filled storehouses, like a trail of breadcrumbs.

It was all a trap and the Turks, starving and cold and desperate, surged toward the city in their thousands, drawn by the promise of grain, meat, and fodder. Whether William knew it was a trap or not, he must have known he needed to capture the supplies we were sitting atop in order to complete his conquest and so save his plans for total domination.

What was more, our army blocked the route to Suceava, the capital, which William no doubt expected to use to quarter his army over the bitter winter.

They had to cross the River Barlad to reach Vaslui and our constant harassment of the massive army had served to funnel them into a narrow crossing over the river. The High Bridge was the only way across into the valley beyond and the fact that we had allowed it to stand was certainly a giveaway of our nefarious intentions. No doubt, William and the other commanders expected that whatever we planned by way of mischief could be overcome by their numbers and their hundreds of artillery pieces.

In comparison, we had twenty-one cannons.

The Turks needed to strengthen the bridge before they risked bringing their massive army and heavy pieces across it. And while they did that, our army waited anxiously unseen over the hills beyond. It was cold and damp and deeply unpleasant weather to be waiting around in but we could do nothing else until William took the bite and crossed into our trap.

"He will not take the bait," I said for the hundredth time.

"Stop saying that," Rob muttered, shivering.

"He ain't got no choice but to take it," Walt replied.

We peered at the vast army on the other side of the river from our vantage point on a ridge, hidden by the trunks of an unruly stand of scruffy pines. On our side of the river was a boggy valley almost entirely empty of soldiers. Across from us, though, William's army filled the plain as far as the eye could see. Low cloud and drizzling rain hid the full extent of the forces but even so it was enough to make my heart race.

"By God there's a lot of the bastards," Rob muttered, echoing my thoughts. "Have you ever seen so many men in one place in your life? Got to be a hundred and fifty thousand, all told. More than Stephen reckoned with his bloody idiot calculations."

"If only we could knock down the bridge while all their biggest cannons were on it," Walt said.

"Or when the Blood Janissaries cross," Rob said.

I snorted. "And William, also, but no doubt they would survive the fall and the dunking and come up merely smelling sweeter than when they went in. Come on, their woodworkers are almost done with the bridge and they will be across today or tomorrow. We must prepare for battle."

"Thank the Lord," Walt said. "It's bloody freezing."

We had discussed the battlefield for weeks and months. It was one the Moldavians had used in years past to defeat the Poles and it was as good a place for the purpose as I have ever seen in my life. The valley was surrounded on three sides by steep, densely wooded hills and the ground throughout the valley floor was soft and in many places marshy indeed. Horsemen would find their pace slowed to a difficult walk and even infantry would have difficulty fighting or even coming to order. I had walked it myself, lifting my knees high to make headway and found myself quickly exhausted. Yes, it was a fine trap but even so the odds were severely against us.

We waited overnight in our camps for them to come on but as the night ended and sunrise approached we were greeted by a thick blanket of freezing fog.

It was hard to see from one tent to the next, let alone across the battlefield.

"We must continue as if they will," King Stephen said as we stood sipping warm wine in his tent and stamping our feet. Outside, the Moldavian and allied forces prepared themselves and within the king's tent their lords and masters were subdued and apprehensive. "You will at all times listen for the trumpets and send riders with messengers. We must stay in contact. You each must send a rider to me at intervals to tell me where you are and what is happening. Do you all understand? You must select sensible men and give them good horses. Each must know where my position is before the day begins."

It was good advice and I was impressed by his command of the situation and of his commanders.

"Are the cannons in place?" the king asked.

"They are, Your Grace," said the Hungarian artillery commander. "Every one of them aimed at the bridge. We will knock a few of their heads off as they come over, will we not, my lords?"

They muttered their assent and some smiled. Still, they were subdued. No man feels victory is near when they are so outnumbered. I resisted attempting to give them good cheer. They did not like me and it was not my place.

"Cuza, you will keep the cavalry back here until it is needed," the king said. "We will send all the mercenaries out, infantry and cavalry, to screen the cannon. Send the mercenary captains in and we shall explain it to them."

Everything was in place and yet so was the fog. The reports coming back all morning confirmed that the Turks were probably waiting for the air to clear, afraid to march into what they could not see.

King Stephen called me to him. "If Zaganos Pasha is truly your brother, perhaps you know a way to encourage him to cross the bridge today."

I sighed. "He knows we are waiting in the hills to descend on him and yet he means to cross anyway, convinced that his strength will overcome ours. But he would be mad to march into it while he cannot see us coming. It costs him nothing to wait for the fog to clear. Once he can see, it might give him confidence to march across but he is by nature a cautious soul and he would rather delay than risk disaster."

The king scowled and sipped his steaming cup of wine. "I know all that. I asked you if there was a way to encourage him across today."

"Have you tried praying for the fog to lift, my lord?"

His men bristled but the king ignored my tone. "I have," he said. "And my priests are praying for that very thing as we speak. Very well, that will be all."

I did not obey him as I was beginning to warm to the idea of tricking William further. "If we could make him believe we have left the field, he might advance." One of the king's men scoffed openly but he ignored them, staring at me as if urging me to continue. I did so, thinking out loud. "How could we make him believe that? Why would we ever abandon such a perfect spot? Any army placing itself down there will be enormously disadvantaged. After all, that is why you did not—" I broke off.

The king stared, waiting. "Yes?"

"If we brought our army down into the valley, he would attack."

The king's men groaned and told me to get out.

"Of course he would attack," King Stephen said. "We would be suffering that very disadvantage which you have mentioned."

"But we have the fog," I said, still thinking as it came to me. "And the Turks could not see us assembling even if we did so." I clicked my fingers and grinned. "Your Grace, can you please summon all of your musicians. And all of those of the peasantry with loud voices for singing. And serjeants and captains who might be spared."

King Stephen peered at me. "I do not know how it is done in England but in Moldavia it is our tradition to hold the festival celebrating victory after the battle has been won and not before."

I could not help but laugh, briefly. "Please, my lord. Other than praying for the fog to lift, this may cause the Turks to act."

Taking the mounted *sluji* with me, simply as I did not wish to be separated from my men, I marched the hastily assembled drummers and trumpeters down into the boggy valley and advanced toward the bridge. There were hundreds of us and more came running after us down from the wooded hills.

"Spread out and play," I shouted at them. "Play for all your worth. Make enough noise to startle God in Heaven!"

I had the peasants sing together whatever working songs they knew and to raise their voices louder and louder. Other men amongst us were various captains and serjeants with mighty battlefield voices who I commanded to roar out imaginary orders to their imaginary companies.

In very little time, we had made a sustained and mighty cacophony that echoed through the valley and across the river.

"God help us but that's a nasty noise," Walt cried, his hands over his ears.

"Tell them to sing louder," I shouted to my Moldavian detachments. "Command the trumpeters to sound an advance and the signal to form a line. Send the serjeants forward to sing their orders. Hurry!"

Whether it was truly my scheme that motivated them, I cannot say, but all of a sudden from out of the fog came our riders who shouted that the Turks were now crossing the bridge.

Rob burst out laughing. "You mad bastard, Richard. You mad old bastard, you've only gone and done it."

"Back!" I shouted to the drummers and trumpeters and peasants, sending my men along our makeshift line to repeat the orders and get them out of the way. "Get back, now! Flee for the hills. Back to your companies!"

I grabbed a handful of messengers. "Ride to the cannon masters and tell them the enemy crosses. They must fire now, do you understand? Go!"

By the time we had pulled back, the twenty-one Moldavian cannons opened up from the flank, firing through the fog at the bridge itself and the bank on our side where the enemy would enter the valley and assemble. Our forward positions of archers marched into range and began to shoot, raining down volleys into the massed ranks of Turks who crossed and sought to assemble on our side. It was difficult to get a sense of what was happening down there but I was certain the enemy would be falling in their hundreds under such a barrage.

"I bet you he'll pull back from this," Walt said to Rob, shaking his head. "How much money have you got on you?"

But a handful of cannons and archers could not slow thousands of soldiers for long and so they advanced slowly, company by company, from the bridge and into our valley. Into our trap. Whether we would be enough to stop them, I still had no idea.

Through the swirling fog, I caught glimpses of the *azabs* advancing. The king brought up our hand-gunners and these men fired their guns from the front and from the flanks at the advancing companies, their filthy, stinking weapons massed together and scything down the *azabs* that marched like lambs to the slaughter into them.

Wherever the *azabs* managed to close with our infantry, our men turned and fled, retreating as far as necessary before turning to shoot or to hold position once more. It appeared through gaps in the fog that the *azab* infantry were running hither and thither like a leaderless mob and everywhere they went, they were killed by crossbows or by guns.

Behind them though came hundreds of *akinji* light cavalry. They too attempted to break through the infantry and cannon arrayed before them but again they found themselves surrounded on three sides and were no doubt confused about where our fire was coming from.

Our cannons kept firing at the bridge itself, blasting away continuously so that any who crossed were in danger of being blown to pieces before reaching the field beyond. Even when they crossed the bridge they would find more cannonballs crashing amongst them if they tarried there in order to assemble their companies.

"Fog's lifting," Walt said, his mouth full of slices of dried sausage.

"Reckon it's the cannons and guns blowing it away?" Rob asked.

"Do not be absurd," I said but perhaps he was right for in the coming centuries I would see that very thing happen for certain. Whether it was the gunpowder or the wind, the fog was rapidly thinning.

Perhaps it was this which gave William the confidence to send his Janissaries and sipahi cavalry across. They were superbly equipped veterans, professional horse soldiers who had fought everywhere in the empire and had won countless victories for their sultans. And William had thirty thousand of them.

They thundered across the reinforced bridge in a seemingly endless mass, their mail and lamellar armour a dull grey and their lances held high above them.

"Time to get to work," I said to my men and we called for our helms.

A great cry went up everywhere at once and my own men beside me cried out.

"By Jesus the Christ and all His saints!" Walt shouted. "Would you look at that!"

Through the swirling banks of fog, the High Bridge was collapsing before our eyes. It was jammed with *sipahis*, packed flank to flank and nose to tail along its entire length. Whether it was the weight of horses alone or if a few lucky cannonballs had helped, the bridge supports snapped and came apart and the entire bridge tilted and slipped, spilling men and horses from the side as it went before the entire thing collapsed and sent them crashing into the river below.

Every man around me crossed himself and sent his thanks to God, for half the enemy army was yet on the far bank and they now had no easy way to cross. William was there and would be unable to send orders to his soldiers on the other side.

But even though it was not the whole army, we were still outnumbered by those who had crossed already. The *sipahis* on our side rapidly organised themselves in, I must admit, a rather impressive fashion. A testament to the professionalism of the officers and obedience of the men. It was impressive and worrying in equal measure. The mass of surviving *azabs* were arranged into some semblance of order and they advanced on our flanks, pushing away the hand-gunners and archers by their sheer numbers and their mad bravery. This allowed the *sipahis* to advance out into the valley toward our mercenary infantry and cavalry. Behind them the Janissaries formed up and followed, ready to exploit any opening the horsemen created.

I ordered the *sluji* to fall back and we kept our distance, watching as the *azabs* finally engaged our infantry. It was hard fought but the Turks were driven back once more, suffering incredible casualties. *Azab* bodies littered the field already.

"What are we doing?" Rob asked, prompting me for orders.

"Keep the men back," I said. "Keep our distance. This is not yet our fight."

William was on the far bank with his immortals and I now doubted we would get the chance to kill him that day. Still, the enemy threatened to overwhelm the Moldavians and so we might well have to fight a retreat all the way back to Suceava, which might present more opportunities to come at him, so I thought I should keep the *sluji* fresh and unharmed. On the other hand, if we won the battle, we might destroy William's partnership with the Sultan. All I could do for the moment was hold my men ready at the flank.

Though the ground was soft, the *sipahis* advanced quicker than our infantry in the centre could retreat and so our mercenaries were ordered to hold their ground and fight off the cavalry. The *sipahis* began to charge and retreat in companies and larger formations. Cannons blasted continuously, sending their projectiles flying overhead and the hand-gunners fired at the enemy in front of them.

Behind the *sipahis*, the Janissaries began to manoeuvre out to both flanks. It appeared as if they meant to encircle our infantry while the *sipahis* kept them engaged. Our infantry were already being pushed back by the Turks and even if they were not surrounded by the Janissaries, their line might well have been broken and the order of the battle would disintegrate and in that chaos the numbers of the Turks, especially of mounted men, would mean the end for us.

It was the high moment in the battle, where most soldiers of both sides were engaged and only the reinforcements would decide the outcome. In the wooded hills all around us, King Stephen and his heavy cavalry waited for the moment when their charges would turn the tide in our favour.

But the enemy had tens of thousands of men close at hand, just across the river. If they could somehow be brought across before the day's end, while the king's cavalry was engaged, then everything might change.

"Rob?" I called. "Take ten men and ride around back to the river. See if you can see what William is doing. Do not engage anyone, even if it means returning without reaching the river."

He called out the men he wanted and they thundered off toward terrible danger. I wondered if I would see him again.

"He will cut his losses," Stephen said, riding forward to give me his opinion. "He will retreat. It is his nature."

"He needs a victory," Eva said in response, "or all his work with the Turks will have been for nothing."

"What is a century to William?" Stephen countered. "Even if Mehmed orders him from—"

"Enough," I snapped. "We shall see."

Trumpets sounded from the trees, echoing through the hills. From the fog-filled woodland ringing the valley, the sounds of horses and men built until I could make out the colours and banners emerging from the shadows between the pines. King Stephen's Moldavians in the centre, with the detachments of Hungarians and Poles on the flanks. As they advanced, I saw masses of the peasant army marching behind with their spears and flails and mattocks in hand.

Walt called to me. "Rob's returned, Richard."

A company of *sipahis* chased him but they broke off when they saw how many we were and retreated, allowing Rob and all ten of his men to approach.

"Turks trying to ford the river," Rob said, breathing heavily from his gallop. His horse shook beneath him, its chest heaving, and Rob patted and rubbed its neck with his stump. "Thousands of them trying to use pieces of broken bridge and other timber and rocks and anything to make a dam or a ford at least."

"Will they succeed?"

"Men being swept away. Water must be colder than ice. But there's thousands of them. They'll do it eventually."

"Damn him!" I growled. "He will win the battle."

"Should we stop them?" Eva said. "Take the *sluji* and stop them coming across?"

"They have cannons and guns. And he will send his Blood Janissaries to sweep us away while he remains unassailable on the far bank. No, we shall assist in the destruction of this army as swiftly as possible. Ready the men. We will assault the enemy after the nobles and the *boyars* complete their charge."

"Who do you fancy?" Walt asked. "Get us some sipahi officers, you reckon? Lots of nice stuff on them, jewels and gold and the like. Nice for a drink, and all."

I considered charging the *sluji* at the enemy cavalry but discounted it. "We will flank these Janissaries and wipe out as many as we can. They are the Turk's best soldiers. The more we kill, the better it is for Christendom. And tell the men to steal their hand-guns, the ammunition and the gunpowder. If we survive this day, we should arm ourselves properly."

The Turks had advanced so far into the valley that a good number of the Hungarian and Polish cavalry and Moldavian peasant forces emerged fully behind the main body of their army. There was no escape for them.

I brought the *slujis* close and arrayed them in two lines while the Polish horsemen rode by us, two thousand of them in whites and blues and reds, with pennants fluttering above them. The wealthiest lords were clad in shining plate and even the lowest of the riders were superbly armoured, as were their horses.

Like storm waves crashing against a promontory, the heavy cavalry crashed into the Janissaries, the *azabs* and the *sipahis* in the centre. The enemy were overwhelmed and crushed by the weight of the charge. Our men-at-arms were fewer in number than the enemy but were still unstoppable.

Their great charge flattened hundreds of Janissaries, many fell dead from lance strikes or were bowled down and crushed by the horses themselves. Those that avoided the first charge were met by a second line which brought down even more. The Poles slowed and turned about or moved through the Janissaries, thrusting with their lances or using their swords or axes or maces. Others formed up beyond them and prepared to charge the thousands upon thousands of *sipahis* in the centre.

My *slujis'* war cry had often been the name of Vlad Dracula or that of their country. But considering there were Wallachians fighting in William's army, we needed something else that would proclaim which side we fought for. There was one that all men knew, that was even older than I was.

"Christus!" I shouted, lifting my lance high over my head. "Deus vult!"

My men took up the cry behind me and we advanced on the Janissaries. I knew I would not need to tell my men to end the fight by taking a number of our enemies prisoner so that we might later drink their blood. We had fought together for years and they knew their business.

Despite being mortals, exhausted by their slog through the sodden ground and the shock of the heavy cavalry, the Janissaries put up a strong and sustained resistance. They were strong and well-trained individuals and even broken by our attacks they formed groups and fought back to back. None wished to surrender. For the thousandth time I cursed the Turks from ripping these fine men from their Christian families as boys and turning them into Mohammedan slaves, their minds broken and infested by the infidel religion. But my anger at the Turk and the sympathy for the boys that were and the men they might have been did not stay my hand when it came to cutting them down.

In time, all the living Turks in the valley broke and tried to flee. All were chased down and killed or captured.

And despite his attempted crossing of the gorge and freezing river, William did what he always did.

He took the remnants of his army, and he fled.

They all rushed south, back toward Bulgaria where they would be safe. All but Basarab and his Wallachian horsemen who abandoned William and rode west for Wallachia.

With William on the run, we knew we had a chance to catch him and kill him but he had a half a day head start and he somehow managed to keep his army in good order throughout the retreat. Though they were no doubt distraught by the loss of so many of their comrades, and the fact that they rushed through a winter landscape devoid of food or water, they maintained their cohesion. We attacked the rear guard repeatedly and each time we killed hundreds of them but our horses were no less exhausted than theirs were. The Poles and Moldavian light cavalry that rode with us were excellent soldiers but they were exhausted also by the battle they had fought. It was bitterly cold.

Four long days and nights, we whittled away their rear guard. We lost hundreds of men through enemy hand-gunners and ambushes and through accidents and exhaustion. We could not have pushed our people or our horses any harder. And still the Turks, and William, got away.

When the reports came in to King Stephen of the enemy losses, he had them checked again by his own priests and monks. And yet it was true. Our small army had killed forty-five thousand Turks in the valley and during the retreat. We had killed four pashas in the valley and a hundred enemy battle standards were taken.

In addition to the dead, we took thousands of prisoners of both low and high rank. The lords, King Stephen kept, while the commoners he had impaled.

It seemed he had learned a thing or two about frightening Turks from his cousin.

Unlike Vlad, though, he soon after ordered them cut down and burned rather than leave them rotting.

By any measure, it was a great victory, and King Stephen could do as he pleased without hearing a word of criticism from anyone. Indeed, the Pope proclaimed him an *Athletae Christi*, just as old Janos Hunyadi had been years before.

In Hungary, Mattias Corvinus did everything in his power to claim the victory as his own. In truth, not only had he not been there but he had sent the barest minimum of his men to fight the battle and yet he wrote a series of letters to the Pope, to the Holy Roman Emperor, and to all manner of other kings and princes of Europe telling them that he, Mattias Corvinus, had defeated a large Turkish army with his own forces. It was truly an incredible bit of dishonesty and whatever lingering flicker of respect I had for the man was gone the moment I found out.

King Stephen on the other hand not only refused to celebrate his victory but instead he fasted for forty days in order to show his devotion to God.

"It is to God that this victory should be attributed," he said when I saw him a week after it was fought. "It was God that brought down the High Bridge."

"It was your well-placed cannons that brought it down," I

replied, frowning. "And Zaganos Pasha sending too many *sipahis* over it at once in his eagerness to crush us."

The king would not hear it. "God smote the bridge with his own hand."

"Perhaps he did but it was the drummers and trumpeters that brought the enemy across."

King Stephen smiled. He looked tired. "Yes, and I am certain that you would like to claim this victory as your own, Richard. But who placed that thought in your mind?"

"I did."

His smile dropped. "God put it there, Richard, so that Moldavia would be saved."

"Well then, My Lord King, I shall praise God for his deviousness and his martial cunning."

Stephen frowned. "For his wisdom, yes. Now, you asked to see me and I believe I know what you wish to discuss." He leaned back in his chair. "Wallachia."

"Basarab turned traitor. He must be removed."

The king sighed. "And your friend must be returned to the throne, is that it?"

"My friend and your cousin, yes, My Lord King."

He leaned forward. "What will Zaganos Pasha do now?"

"Our agents suggested that this was the last chance he had to conquer Christendom. Now he has failed, Sultan Mehmed will take his armies east and south."

King Stephen closed his eyes. "Then we shall have peace. Praise God."

"If those things come to pass, perhaps. But if the Sultan takes his army a thousand miles away and leaves only garrisons, would this not be the best time to launch a reconquest?"

The king interlocked his fingers and peered at me. "We would struggle to fight off another invasion at this point. Launching one of our own is out of the question. Do you comprehend the size of Bulgaria? What would you have me do, besiege and conquer Sofia?"

"To begin with, yes. But not alone. With an ally on the Wallachian throne and support from Hungary and the Poles, it would be possible to—"

"No," he said. "It would not. We have been ravaged by these wars. We need time to heal. Years, you understand, not months. By the time we are recovered, Sultan Mehmed may have defeated his enemies and then returned to assault us once more."

"Precisely why we must attack now."

King Stephen smiled and then laughed but it was with a certain affection. "I have long admired your military vigour, sir, and your relentless enthusiasm for war and conquest. But you have never understood us and our kingdoms here. We have been beset by the Tatars of the Golden Horde to our north for generations. The Turks have been at our gates in the south for almost as long. This is our life. Our burden. God is good to us. He has given Moldavia the wealth of the plains and the safety of the mountains. He has given us wheat and sheep and timber. He made our men courageous and our women strong. Moldavia will endure these barbarians from this day until the end of days and we shall prevail."

"I pray that you will."

"You want Vlad Dracula on the throne of Wallachia and I would not object. But he is bound to Corvinus, now. It is not my words of support you require but the assent of the King of Hungary."

"Perhaps you might consider sending—"

"Yes, yes," King Stephen said, waving his hand. "I shall have letters written."

"There is of course the small matter of Basarab occupying the—"

"If I can spare the men when the time comes, I shall spare them. You have my word. Is that all or would you like to cut my purse while you are here?"

I bowed deeply. "Your wisdom and generosity is matched only by your prowess commanding armies, My Lord King. I will take the *sluji* west and do what I can to restore Vlad to his throne."

The king nodded as if he did not much care either way. "And what will you do with regards to your brother? Our dear defeated Zaganos Pasha?"

"I pray only that he flees far from here along with the Turks."

King Stephen pursed his lips, nodding slowly and regarding me closely for a few moments. He then abruptly dismissed me without any courteous words and I was escorted from the hall with Walt at my heels.

"Not true, is it?" Walt asked me, following me out. "We're not praying William has fled with Mehmed?"

"Of course not, you bloody fool."

"What will we do then?" Walt asked, lowering his voice. "How are we going to kill William now?"

"I have a notion," I said. "But we will need to see Dracula return in order to achieve it."

17

Dracula Returns

1476

AFTER THE SNOW THAWED, I took my men into Transylvania to meet Dracula, where he had been residing. When we arrived, however, Dracula was not there. Instead, he had travelled to Bosnia with Mattias Corvinus and an army of five thousand soldiers.

We set off immediately for Bosnia but arrived too late.

The Hungarian forces had captured the city of Sabac and Corvinus declared his campaign a success and left Dracula in command with the task of taking the city of Srebrenica from the Turks. The area around the city was teeming with silver mines so it was no wonder Corvinus wanted it.

Any doubts that Dracula had lost his edge during his long relegation from the front lines was dispelled when we heard what had happened next.

He disguised his soldiers as Turks and sent them into Srebrenica during the monthly market day. Those men quickly captured the gates and then Dracula himself came charging in at the head of thousands of soldiers. While the gates were held open, Dracula and his Hungarians rode inside and caused chaos until the Turkish garrison surrendered the city.

Dracula had every Turk impaled. The city was burned to the ground and everything of value taken.

It was a brutal sacking that deprived the Turks of a key regional source of income and extended the strategic reach of the Kingdom of Hungary. What was more, it declared to the world that Vlad III Dracula was back.

When we returned with him to Transylvania, we set about building an army to retake Wallachia. With support from Hungary and Moldavia, plus soldiers from Serbia and loyal Wallachians, Dracula assembled a force of twenty-five thousand men.

King Stephen, good as his word, brought his army of fifteen thousand into Wallachia from the east while we swept in from the west in order to crush Basarab between us. In addition to his native forces, Basarb had eighteen thousand Turks.

Our armies met near a small town named Rucr in the Prahova Valley. Half of the battle was fought in a woodland and there it ended amongst the trees. It was hard fought and bloody but the *sluji* helped to win it, as they had done so many times before. This time, fifty of them were armed with hand-guns which added a considerable tactical advantage.

Each army lost close to ten thousand men. Basarab fled south and ultimately escaped to the Turks but his rule was over after that battle.

It was devastating for Vlad to witness so many of his people dying. In the aftermath, I found him sitting on a fallen tree, watching the wounded and the dead being carried away by their friends. He was alone but for his bodyguard standing at a respectful distance.

I sat next to him in silence for a while before he spoke.

"Wallachians slaughtering each other." Vlad shook his head. "Those men there should have been brothers and yet they died with each other's blades buried in their guts. I have come back to take my throne but, Richard, I wonder. I do wonder. The longer I go on, the more I think this war is nought but madness."

"They are fighting for survival," I said.

His gauntleted hands made two fists before him. "Why will they not unite against the most dangerous foe? Why can they not see it?"

I grunted. "I have been asking these same questions for thirty years."

He turned to look at me then. "Is that how long you have been in Wallachia?"

"In Hungary, Transylvania, Moldavia, Serbia, Albania, Bulgaria, Constantinople, and yes, most of all, in Wallachia. All of these kingdoms I have found peopled with strong, proud men and beautiful, terrifying women." When I said this, Vlad smiled. I continued. "On the one hand, these lands are wild and virginal and on the other it is as though the feuds within and between the peoples are as old as time. I know these lands, have fought in them, have fought for them, for longer than some men live. And I will always be a thorough outsider. I must admit that I do not understand your people and I never will. My own people, the English people, I know them in my heart. Although it is three hundred years or more since I was born and raised there, the people are the same as they ever were and I understand their concerns and their interests. I can predict, without conscious thought, how my people will respond to any given difficulty or boon. Whether commoner or lord, I know their sense of humour for it is also my own. They frustrate me and even enrage me at times with their manner but it is in the same way that a family feels about itself. For they are my family. Each time I return, the faces are new but the people are the same and I know that I am precisely where I am supposed to be. Your people are, I am sure, just as fine as mine. But I will never know them nor will I understand them."

Dracula ponderously raised a steel-clad finger to point at me. "You, sir, miss your homeland."

"I do. I think perhaps I am heartsick for it."

"And even though I am home, and victorious, and newly made Prince of Wallachia, I too am heartsick for my homeland. For a people who can live in peace. For a time, I thought I could give them peace and good fortune. But now I know I cannot. I shall never be able to do so."

"You may have peace if you crush your enemies."

Vlad shook his head. "I did that, many years ago. I killed two hundred lords and their families. It did not bring peace. I see now that I never could. How long will I go on, bringing nothing but war to my people?"

"Your people will have war whether you lead them or not."

"Yes, yes, that is true. But when my presence as their prince is the cause for war, how can I say I love my people? It is nought but pride, is it not?"

"What else can you do?"

"That is what I have been asking myself for years, Richard. What lies in my immortal future? To seek to be prince for a hundred years? How would I accomplish it? By killing hundreds and thousands of my own people? I have been thinking of William. And of you. How you keep to the shadows and let other men, mortal men, take the glory and the fame that should be yours. The Pope names this king or that lord as *Athletae Christi* when it is you who are the true champion of Christ. And yet you are humble enough to let it pass."

"I do not know that any man has ever named me humble."

"And yet you are. If I could but control my pride then why could I not do the same? Watch over my people from afar, protecting them, keeping them from harm where I can. Learning true patience and humility while I do so. Is that not a good life to lead?"

I looked at him, the mixture of hope and despair in his eyes, and wondered if I would have to kill him myself one day soon. He was spawned by William and so I was sworn to end his days. I still needed him in order to battle William but after victory was achieved, I would like as not have to cleanse the earth of him and his ilk. But was I bound to that fate? It was an oath I had sworn but what was to stop me from ignoring it in this case?

"It may be a good life, Vlad. But you will only get to live it if William is first killed."

Vlad nodded. "You think he would come for me?"

"I do not know what he will do now. What do you think?"

"Me? You are his brother."

"And you were his friend. His protege. You spent more time with him than I ever have."

Vlad raised his thick eyebrows. "Is that so? Well, for a long time after I abandoned him, I expected that William would come for me. Or that he would send his men to kill me. But he did not. I do not know why. Perhaps he feared me."

"Perhaps."

Vlad peered sidelong at me. "You do not think so."

"If he wanted to kill you, nothing would stop him trying. He may wish you dead but he would weigh the possible dangers of making it so and if it did not benefit him in some way, he would not take action. William has never let pride stand in the way of his continued long life. And I am sure that you are not as important to him as you might imagine. I have met many that he turned. He promised them the world and they loved him and were convinced he would return, even after a hundred years or more."

"And these people you killed."

"Yes. Like you, he swore that they would be the ones to help him bring about his new kingdom. He swore to so many that they would be the one sitting at his right hand to rule over millions of worshipful subjects for a thousand years. Some of the women he seems to have promised undying love for and they remained convinced they would be the immortal queen to his king."

Vlad nodded. "He knew enough to never promise such a thing to me. His honeyed words spoke only of power. The power to rule over my people and keep them safe. He knew me, I suppose, even before I did." He looked up at the sky. "Radu, on the other hand, wanted William's companionship. Craved it. And William was quite convincing in his own professing of friendship. I certainly believed their admiration and respect was mutual, though of course they were far from equals."

"Radu is also convinced of the sincerity of William's friendship."

Vlad turned slowly and scowled. "When did you speak to Radu? Before you executed him?"

"I have deceived you for a long time, Vlad."

He got to his feet and looked down at me. "In what way have you deceived me?"

"I did not kill Radu."

"Where," Vlad said through gritted teeth, "is he?"

I glanced around at Vlad's bodyguards. "He is somewhere safe."

Vlad breathed hard as he stared at me. "Why?"

I tried to make light of it. "I believed he might prove useful. But I am glad to tell you now that he is alive."

"You feed him blood?" Vlad hissed. "Whose blood?"

"His gaolers keep him well."

"Take me to him. Now." He clenched his fists as he spoke but I did not move or respond. "I command it."

I looked at him, careful to keep my expression neutral. "You are the Prince of Wallachia. But I do not answer to you. Despite appearances, I never did."

Vlad curled his lip. "So. Not so different from your brother after all."

"I will take you to Radu. I am sure he will be glad to see you."

Vlad nodded slowly, his lips curling with rage. "And then I will impale him myself. I wonder how long it will take an immortal to die upon the stake. Well, we shall see."

I stood, moving slowly lest I anger him further. "You must do as you see fit, of course. But, you see, my friend, I had hoped that we might use him first."

"Use him?" He scowled. "Use him for what?"

"To kill William."

1 8

A m b u s h

1 4 7 6

TOGETHER, WE JOURNEYED TO THE MONASTERY at Snagov. Our men waited in the small village and Vlad and I crossed with just a couple of men apiece, who rowed us smartly across the lake. The abbot and his monks had seen our huge party galloping up and they stood ready to greet us as we moored up.

"My Lord Prince," the abbot said, bowing to Dracula. "It is a great honour to see you again. We have all prayed for your return to your rightful place upon the throne."

Vlad nodded. "How fares my brother?"

The abbot glanced at me but his smile never wavered. "He does remarkably well, my lord. We pray together often."

"He *prays* with you?"

"Oh, yes, indeed. We converse every day and I or one of my

brothers prays with Radu. If only we could allow him from his confinement, I believe he would enjoy our communal services."

Vlad scowled, horrified. "You have made him into a monk? He is a prince of Wallachia, not some black-clothed kneeler."

"Is that what he is, my lord? You are certain? Radu the Handsome, Voivode of Wallachia is dead. Slain by some brute of a Catholic mercenary years ago." The abbot smiled at me as he spoke. "We have here a man seeking to find peace and forgiveness."

"Have you considered that he is deceiving you with his good behaviour," I said, "and intends only to get you to drop your guard so that he might make his escape?"

The abbot smiled. "But of course I consider it daily. And that is why he always remains chained inside his cell."

"Chained?" I said, surprised but pleased. "That is well."

"Not much of a life," Vlad muttered.

"On the contrary," the abbot replied. "It forces a man to look inward. He must commune with his soul. And as I say, he is confined but not isolated. What is more, he has devoured every text in our library and is keen for more."

Vlad raised a finger and jabbed it in the abbot's face. "You have made my brother, a knight and a prince, into a scholarly monk. It is shameful."

To his credit, Abbot Ioánnis did not so much as flinch. "Do you believe, My Lord Prince, that taking holy orders is shameful?"

"For one who was a prince, yes indeed."

The abbot lifted his chin and stared back at Vlad. "The prince is dead. Only the man remains. The man and his soul. I can think of no greater pursuit than to attempt the mastery of the self. Especially for one who may find himself walking the earth, ageless and powerful, for all of time. Men such as yourself, my lord."

Dracula scowled at me.

I held my hands up. "I never said a word about you, Vlad."

The abbot stroked his thick beard. "Your brother speaks of you often. Almost as much as he speaks of your brother, Richard."

I sighed. "My brother wraps himself around these poor people's hearts so that they can never untangle their soul from him."

Abbot Ioánnis nodded. "He does have an unusual power, that is true. But we pray for the disentanglement. You will find Radu much changed, Richard, from when you saw him last. As will you, my prince."

"Take us to him," Vlad said. "Now."

We followed him to the monastery and down into the corridor with its row of cells. When the abbot opened the door, we found Radu in black monks' robes on his knees, facing away from us.

"Radu," the abbot prompted. "You have guests."

It was only when Radu climbed to his feet that I heard his chain dragging across the stone floor. He turned as Vlad stepped forward and they faced each other.

Radu had become thin, his handsome face now gaunt and his cheeks were deep hollows beneath sharp bones. Yet, for all that, he looked well. He had a composure and stillness to him that he had entirely lacked before.

"Look what has become of you," Vlad said, his voice breaking.

"If our father could see you."

Radu's eyes flicked to me. "Your companion murdered our father. Otherwise, perhaps our father could see me."

Vlad half turned. "I thought he had killed you, also. I am glad that he did not."

"You are glad that I am kept chained like a dog? Whether you are here to kill me or to free me, please be about it. I have waited long enough."

I heard the abbot laugh lightly at my shoulder.

"We will do neither," I said. "We will use Radu in order to bring William to us."

"What do you mean?" Abbot Ioánnis said.

"My comrades have let it be known that Radu is alive and that he is held here."

"You have done what?" the abbot said, turning on me, furious. "You will bring an army down upon us, you great fool."

Radu likewise growled at me. "What is the meaning of this, Richard? You saved me and kept me here and now you wish me dead at William's hand?"

I waited until they had stopped. "You are nothing but bait, Radu. And William and his men will not reach Snagov because we will ambush him before he ever reaches this place."

Radu was incredulous. "And what if William evades your ambush and does find me here? He will slaughter these good monks to reach me, of that I am certain. But what then? I am no longer his man. I no longer share his vision. He will slay me also."

"Truly?" Vlad asked his brother. "You mean you will follow me?"

"No. I follow God, and myself. Under the guidance of the Abbot Ioánnis here and also Father Theodore who has wisdom greater even than William's, and that which he has is far more Godly and true. William will come for me, if he knows I am alive, but my love for him is at an end. Truly."

"Listen again," I said. "If William does reach Snagov, then you are in no danger. For you shall not be here. Not you, Radu, and not you, Abbot, nor any of your monks."

The abbot raised a single bushy eyebrow. "And where, pray tell, shall we be?"

"At the fortress of Bucharest. It is not twenty miles from here. We will leave at sunrise."

The abbot was calm but firm. "My brothers will not leave this place. It is their home. We have the laity to consider also."

"All will come. If necessary, they will be trussed up and carried off in sacks but they will come. I shall not have your deaths on my conscience should William avoid our ambush and fall upon this place."

An aged voice in the doorway made us all turn.

"How can you be certain William will come?" Theodore stood there, his hand on a young monk's arm.

"Theodore," I said. "You look just as well as ever."

He ignored my greeting. "How do you know, Richard?"

"My companions Eva and Stephen have sent messages alluding to Radu's presence here. Messages intended to be intercepted and they were. What is more, Vlad's coming here will also have been noted by Turkish spies. There is no doubt that they are everywhere in this country."

"That seems to me to be a lot of hope and no surety, my son," Theodore said.

"Well, there is also the fact that William has abandoned the Sultan with all of the Blood Janissaries. Our agents confirmed it. Whether he has left Edirne without orders or is acting still for Mehmed, we do not know. But there is a force of Turks newly stationed on the southern bank of the Danube. It is likely William will take command of them and rush here, to Snagov, to rescue Radu and kill you, Vlad, at the same time."

"So," Vlad said. "You have used me as bait. You have deceived me. Manipulated me. And now you expect me to *allow* it? You are so much more like William than I imagined."

"Perhaps I am. But just as you have acted immorally to achieve a greater moral good in the protection of your people, so I have betrayed your trust in order to put an end to his existence. It is not right but I will pray for God's forgiveness."

"It is not God's forgiveness you need but mine. In order for your ambush to be successful, you require my men and they are of Wallachia."

"I do, yes. But if you do not help me then I will use the remaining *sluji* alone. They will follow me and together we will overcome the Blood Janissaries and kill William. But I very much doubt he will come into Wallachia without those mortal forces in support. And so I would really rather also have the support of your small force out there. Together we will spring the trap. And together we will kill William, who is my enemy, and yours, Vlad, and yours, Radu, whether you accept it or not."

Vlad strode away from me and his brother, crossing the small cell in just a few strides. He went to the high, small window and looked up through it.

He grunted. "You cannot see anything from this useless window, Radu."

Radu smiled. "I can see the sky above my homeland. I see clouds and birds and the sun. I see rain and snow falling. A taste of God's creation is enough to remind me of it all. And that slice of blue sky, no larger than my outstretched hand, is all the kingdom I have needed since I have been here. Never in all my life have I felt contented before being brought here. I may have this chain upon my body but my soul is free."

I glanced at the abbot and Theodore who stood smiling proudly at their ward.

Vlad said nothing for a while before turning to Radu. "Brother, if your words are sincere then it brings me great joy to hear that. Perhaps, if you prove that you are loyal then when the time is right your existence can be declared to our people and you may be welcomed at my court. Or, if you prefer, I will found a monastery and you can be abbot there and live in peace."

Radu bowed his head. "Nothing would give me greater joy."

"Richard." Vlad turned his terrible gaze on me. "We will kill William together. But your manipulation of me I shall never forgive."

"I understand. Now, let us prepare to leave this place. Tomorrow, we ride to Bucharest."

The monks were incredibly efficient and had their valuables and victual packed and ready well before dawn. Being monks they were used to rising for midnight and matins services but still they worked through the darkness as if they were half-bat and half-soldier.

Still, with so many men, monks, soldiers, and servants, it was a somewhat chaotic departure from the side of the lake that morning.

"Where is the ancient one named Theodore?" I shouted at my men, not seeing the blind monk in the crowd.

Stephen called out from over the sea of heads. "The abbot said the old man is too frail and blind to travel."

"Too stubborn, more like. Well, may God damn him, then," I muttered. I knew if William managed to get by us and reach the monastery, then he would not take pity on the blind man's frailties. But we would intercept William before he reached Snagov and anyway I had too much on my mind to think of one surly old monk a moment longer. "We must hurry," I cried out, repeatedly. "If it is not essential, leave it behind."

Rob nodded at a group of servants carrying squawking baskets. "Would you say chickens are essential, Richard?"

"In the name of Christ, sort the daft bastards out, will you?"

Waving his stump at them and babbling in his appalling Wallachian, Rob scared them into dropping their baskets.

"Where the bloody hell is Serban?" I asked Walt as I pulled myself into his saddle.

He shrugged. "If you haven't noticed, the old bastard's always off somewhere when there's hard work to be done."

"Will you take some men and take position at the rear of the column, Walt? If there are any stragglers, whip them along. If they won't keep up then you have to truss them up and bring them forward."

Walt rubbed sleep from his eyes. "Can't we just leave them to it? They'll come up eventually."

"Absolutely not. Not a single one can be left behind. What if one of William's men scoops him up and questions him about Snagov? Better to kill them than let one risk the entire plan. Our only hope is through springing an ambush and trapping him. Do you understand?"

"None will fall behind. You can trust me."

I did trust him. Him and Rob, as well as Eva and Stephen. They had been with me for so long because they were trustworthy, reliable and competent. My captains in the *sluji* and all the surviving men had given every indication of similar reliability but I still could not trust them as I could one of my own countrymen.

We rode out in a long column, with the vanguard far ahead out of sight consisting of Vlad's cavalry and behind them a core of lightly armoured veteran infantry, mostly survivors of Vlad's peasant armies and led by his peasant officers. Then Vlad and his bodyguard rode at the head of the rear guard which was formed mostly of his bodyguard and fine troops they were.

I rode behind with the *sluji* and at the rear traipsed the monks and the lay brothers and other servants, some pushing hand carts and others leading ponies.

Radu I kept hooded and chained at the rear of my company, guarded by two trustworthy *sluji* under orders to keep him safe but above all to stop him riding off. Despite his seeming sincerity and newfound piety, I could never trust a man who had been for so long under William's thrall.

If all went well then we would sleep within the safety of Bucharest that night and in the morning could send out scouting parties to watch for the approach of William's Turks and begin planning our ambushes.

By the middle of the morning, Vlad rode back along the column and fell in beside me. We rode along a track with trees close by each side, the shadows beneath cold and still.

"I understand why you did as you have done," he said without preamble. "Until this morning I had not understood just how well you played your part."

"My part?"

"Your performance as a mortal man. As a crusader and a mercenary captain. Even though I knew what you were, how long you had lived and what you had done, I still believed in your subservience." He smiled, his moustache lifting, and a brief laugh escaped from beneath. "And yet it was all pretence. You see yourself as a man above kings. You obey what orders you wish and ignore the ones that do not meet your aims. And you manipulate your superiors into doing what you wish. Even the lords and princes that do not really care for you, still they see you as a straight speaking and morally upright man. But all the while you hold our hierarchy in contempt while you stand above it."

I rode in silence for a while to collect my thoughts while Vlad rode smiling beside me. We left the close confines of the wood and came out onto a long section of road where the woodland had been cleared. On both sides were wide and long meadows but they were covered in nothing but clumps of low weeds. The rear guard ahead of us filed through the woods where they closed tight by the road again beyond the meadow.

"I will not disagree with all you say," I said, finally. "There is truth to much of it. But I do not see myself as above a king. It is impossible for me and my close companions to fit within a mortal nation. We have many times attempted to do so but as you say it is more a dramatic performance than it is truth. We live in a city or pose as a lord but we have no father and mother that we can admit to and so we seem to come from nowhere. We have no brothers and cousins with which to make a family. And we can make no children of our own to raise and any that we might adopt will age while we will not. Not in a natural sense. When we fight as mortal soldiers, we must hide our need for blood from our comrades and so we can never be at peace amongst them. As for kings and princes, I have known so many, both good and bad, that the inherent power of their authority has somewhat lost its ability to cower me. We are not above anyone, as such, but we are outside of them. We are the eternal mercenary, doomed to wander and to never fit within a nation, even our own."

"What of my future as a prince?" Vlad asked. "If we as immortals are doomed to live outside of our nation, do you believe it impossible for an immortal to sit on a throne?"

"Impossible?" I sighed, thinking of Priskos and his claims that Alexander the Great was his grandchild, just as I was. Alexander and Caesar and other kings. All met their brutal ends. "How many kings have—"

I was cut off by the mighty blasts of coordinated firearms on both sides of our column. Hundreds of hand-gunners discharged their weapons and the men and horses around me, in front and behind were hit. Steel pinged and men cried out in pain and panic.

Horses fell and men fell with them. Ahead, I watched the cavalry of the rear guard riding one way and another in panic.

"We must charge the enemy!" Vlad shouted, drawing his sword and pointing across the meadow to the edge of the trees where clouds of smoke drifted from the shadows.

It would ordinarily be good advice but I knew it had to be William commanding this force. My mind rushed with realisations. William had somehow discovered my own plans and ambushed me instead from a prepared position. There could be stake pits, trenches or other defences that would cut charging Wallachian cavalry down before it reached the Janissaries beyond.

"Ride back for the *sluji*!" I shouted at Vlad and took my own advice, wheeling my horse and urging him back towards my immortal company.

Another blast ripped through the air and then another., far mightier than hand-guns.

They were cannons, firing from the head of the column behind me. Whether it truly was William or Basarab or Turks, they had planned their ambush well.

"Where is Radu?" I shouted at Eva.

"Who cares?" Stephen cried out. "We must flee!"

"William will be after him, you fool. Perhaps coming for him in person. Where is Radu now?"

"Rear," Eva said, pointing. "Put your amour on, first, Richard, please."

"There is no time," I replied.

"A helm at least," Eva said, fighting to control her horse.

"I will go get Radu," Rob said. "Bring him here."

"Very well. While you are there, tell the damned monks to flee into the woods if they have not already."

He nodded and wheeled his horse around. I called to my captains.

"Put on what armour you can, quickly. We must act decisively but not foolishly. And listen, we must use the *sluji* to kill William. Zaganos Pasha is here and here is where he will die. Your enemies the Blood Janissaries have come to kill Prince Vlad Dracula but we will kill them. Arm yourselves, now. We will ride around this flank. Bring up the hand-gunners, we will advance behind them."

Two of the *sluji* came galloping up from the rear. "My lord," one cried. "Master Robert sends word. Please forgive us, my lord, we did not know."

"Know what?" I shouted. "What is the message?"

"He said you had sent him for the chained monk and we released him to him. But then Rob came and asked for the same thing. He has chased after him and the monk. Heading due east, into the woods."

"Can you understand what these fools are saying?" I asked Eva. "Who did you release the chained monk to? Who is Rob chasing?"

"It was Serban, my lord. Please, forgive me."

My mind raced. Serban had freed Radu and led him away? What it meant, I did not know, other than one thing.

"We are betrayed," I said to Eva. "Serban has betrayed us."

"Let him go," Eva said. "Rob will catch him."

"One handed? No, I will go and I will bring Radu back here."

"He is not important!" Eva cried.

"He is our bait," I snapped. "William will take him and run. I will not lose him again."

"Let someone else do it."

I ignored her. "Vlad!" I rode quickly to where he was shouting a stream of orders. "Radu has been taken from the rear. Taken to William. I will bring him back."

"Why?" he said.

"William wants him. He is my bait. You command the *sluji* and attack one flank of the enemy, there. Break through the men there and join the rest of your army. If we are separated, I will see you at Bucharest."

I turned and rode toward the rear, past my immortal soldiers. It seemed wrong to abandon them but I knew Vlad would lead them well enough and I would return to them soon. Worse would be abandoning Rob and losing my one chance at snaring my brother.

Walt, Eva and Stephen fell in behind me and a handful of squires came with us. The group of monks were standing together at the rear with the lay brothers in the centre, the abbot at the forefront. He waved his hand to beckon me to him.

"You should flee, you fools," I shouted, "you will be killed."

"We shall stay," the abbot said, firmly. "None shall kill us."

"The bloody Turks will," I cried. "Where is Radu?"

"Gone. There." He pointed through the woods. "You should flee also, Richard. Do not pursue him. Let Serban go, he is nothing but trouble."

I left them to their impending deaths and rode in the direction he had indicated. We had not gone far into the cold dark of the woodland before I found three bodies upon the ground.

Throwing myself from the saddle I found Rob on his back with a sword thrust up through his neck and out of the top of his skull. His eyes were open and unseeing and he lay soaked in blood.

"God, no," I cried. "Rob!"

A few steps away, Radu lay on his back in his monk's robe, alive for the moment but clutching at his throat where it had been cut. Blood gushed through his fingers, soaking his robe, and when his eyes met mine they were wild. He knew he was about to die.

Serban crawled away on his belly through the pine needles, though he glanced over his shoulder and sighed, rolling onto his back. I strode over to him and saw his loins were drenched with blood. His guts were spilling from the wound and he stank of his innards. He should not have been alive but he was and I knew then that he was an immortal.

"He should not have tried to stop me," Serban said, snarling. "I warned him but he would not—"

I reached down and wrapped two hands around his throat and pulled him up, lifting him off his feet and throttled him. His eyes bulged.

After a moment, I threw him against a tree trunk and released my grip enough for him to breathe.

"Why?" I growled through clenched teeth. "Why betray me? Why kill Rob?"

He coughed. "Never betrayed you. Was never yours."

A chill seized my heart. "You are William's?"

He smiled. "Not his either. Our people have been here since before the Christ was born."

"Your people? What people? Immortals?"

"Tried to make you see. Understand. But you want only to kill us all."

I leaned down. "Did you tell William we were coming? Where to ambush us?" I saw in his eyes that it was true. "You must have, you have been gone since we reached the monastery."

He coughed blood and clutched at his slippery guts. "I wish it did not have to be so."

"Why take Radu? Why kill Rob?"

"You have lost. William will control Wallachia. Radu was... a gift."

I grabbed his hair and pulled his head back. "Where are the other immortals? Who are the other *vampirs* in Wallachia?"

He smiled again and winced. In the distance, the guns fired and men shouted. Hooves drummed on the earth. Steel rang out on steel. I had already tarried too long.

I drew my dagger and sawed through Serban's neck until his head was cut from it. I threw it down, disgusted with him and with myself.

Walt cradled Rob in his lap after having drawn the sword from his skull. Eva knelt beside him and had one arm around Walt's shoulder and her other stroked Rob's blood-soaked hair. Walt wept freely but I was numb. From beside Radu, Stephen shook his head. Radu Dracula was dead also.

"We will return for Rob's body," I said to Walt. "And bury him properly. But now we still have work to do."

Walt cuffed his cheeks and when he looked at me I saw white rage and black despair.

We rode back through the wood directly toward the sounds of battle to find hundreds of bodies lying in the meadow. The *sluji* had dismounted and were fighting in a ragged line against the Blood Janissaries. So many had fallen on both sides and more were being killed every moment. With horror I realised that the Janissaries had the upper hand. There were more of them alive and the *sluji* were dying quicker.

I looked for Vlad as I advanced and saw him hammering his sword against the breastplate of a fallen figure in elaborate Turkish armour.

William.

My brother fought against Vlad, one against the other. Dracula in his magnificent plate and William on his back, his face twisted in hatred as Vlad whipped his sword down on him. William held his blade up to defend himself, holding it with two hands, one on the blade itself.

The men around them fought their own desperate battles to the death, bodyguards fighting bodyguards, and immortals against immortals. My *sluji* were almost wiped out. My captains had all fallen.

And yet Vlad had almost achieved victory. He had William down, almost at his mercy.

I aimed my horse for their fight, drew my sword, and charged at them.

Vlad's sword blade broke and he fell upon William with a dagger in hand and they grappled. Vlad worked his arm down and his blade under William's helm, cutting and stabbing into him.

By God, I thought with a thrill as I came closer. *He has done it.*

Just then, four Janissaries rushed forward, raised their hand-guns and fired them as one into Vlad from a yard away.

The shots ripped through Vlad's armour and through his flesh, deep into his body. He jerked and fell back from William and the Janissaries pulled their fallen master away.

"No!" I roared, almost upon them.

Vlad lay as if he was dead and I was running out of time before William's men got him away from me. My horse was nervous of the noise and the stink of smoke and the mass of men I was forcing him towards but I had to force my way through the line to reach William. Vlad had wounded William severely and there would never be a better chance to finish him once and for all.

My horse fell under me, shot by a dozen Janissaries behind the line. The beast went down hard, as if his legs had been cut off, throwing me and I fell on my neck. It hurt like the devil and I was dazed but I rolled to my feet to find a company of Janissaries rushing me with their swords and axes.

I killed one as I fell back and then Eva and Stephen arrived on horseback, flattening some and driving the rest back. We rushed into them together and killed them.

But the rest were fleeing. Some mounted, others on foot.

"I need a horse!" I shouted and a squire rode over, leaping off and offering me his hands to boost me into the saddle. Once seated, I looked for the fleeing enemy. They were retreating through the woods, with companies of Janissaries covering the escape.

"*Sluji*! Form on me!"

We had been all but obliterated. Many of my men lay wounded and were calling for blood but there were dead squires all over the field and my immortals were bleeding to death in their dozens. Others were dead and limbs and heads littered the field.

Vlad Dracula lay on the field with two of his men at his side. His helm had been removed and his eyes stared up at the sky, blood soaking his hair.

"Is he dead?" Walt shouted. "Is he dead?"

His men seemed stunned. I could not spare time to deal with Dracula or his men.

"*Sluji*!" I cried to any that yet lived. "Our enemies flee. There. We stop for nothing. Every one of them will fall."

Despite all they had been through, they found their horses and formed up on me. We were so few and they were exhausted and wounded but still they formed up and we chased the enemy into the woods.

The Turks had engaged the Wallachian army further along the track and the fighting there continued. Whatever the outcome, it did not matter to me. All that mattered was catching William. I prayed that he was already dead, killed by Dracula's blade and his men carried nothing but William's corpse back toward the Danube, but I doubted God would grant me such luck.

A half dozen immortal Janissaries rushed suddenly from hiding behind a stand of trees with their lances up and we had to pull up and cut them down before continuing. Two of my men were killed in the exchange. But then we were on again.

Every half a mile or so we crashed into another ambush in the woodland. Each time we killed them but I lost men in turn and so our numbers dwindled and our progress slowed.

"His men spend their lives to grant him a few yards more," Walt shouted, wiping his blade off on a Janissary's red robes.

"And mine spend theirs to gain it back," I said, looking at the few men I had left. Our horses were hanging their heads and if they survived the day, not one of them would be fit for anything other than food for the hounds by the morrow.

"Be full dark soon," Walt said, looking up. "How will we find him then?"

"When we reach the Danube, we will follow the bank in both directions. You will take half the men one way and I the other. If you find him, send a man back to me and I will do the same."

Walt puffed his cheeks and shook his head but we rode on for the river and came out of the trees with the moon already up. It was cold and my men shook and there was not one of us who was not disheartened.

"By God," Eva said, riding up to my side with her hand outstretched. "Is that them?"

"It is. A score of the bastards."

"They see us," Eva said.

I squinted, trying and failing to see what their eyes could. "Is he with them?"

"Can't tell," Walt said, drawing his sword and sighing. "Is that a boat drifting across the river?"

A dark shape moved slowly out there, not far from the bank.

"William may be within?" Stephen suggested.

"Another boat is drawn up on the bank," Eva cried. "I see it in the grass."

"And twenty Janissaries guarding it," Walt growled. "Letting their master get away."

"Dismount," I ordered. "Form a line!"

We pushed our useless horses away and formed up with the Danube shining in the moonlight nearby. From the long grasses by the river, the remnants of the Blood Janissaries advanced. They outnumbered us two to one but I would not let them stop me. William was so close, I could almost taste him.

I led the charge, pulling ahead of my tired men.

The Janissaries were superb and fought with ferocity and skill. My men fell, fighting with every last breath.

I cut them down and killed the last of them, running my sword through his face.

All that remained of the *sluji*, who were once five hundred, were three badly wounded men who sat on ground soaked with the blood of their brothers and their enemies.

William's dark boat was crossing the river, a single rower within, moving slowly.

Wading through the grass and into the freezing mud, I

reached the boat which was pulled half up onto the muddy bank. It was big enough for thirty men, with four oars aside. Clutching my sword I pulled myself up and over the side, splashing into deep water within.

They had hacked holes through the bottom of it, rendering it unusable.

"William!" I shouted across the river, standing in the ruined boat. "You coward!"

Out in the gloom, he stopped rowing and stood. No more than a shadow upon shadows. "Damn you to hell, Richard!" His voice was loud, travelling across the water and the still night air.

"Find a hand-gun," I muttered to my men. "Crossbow, anything." They splashed away toward the corpses on the bank and I raised my voice again. "I will find you, William. No matter where you run, I will find you."

"Ha!" he shouted. I saw him raise his hands to his mouth as he did so. "You leave me be, brother!"

"I defeated you, William," I shouted. "Again and again, I defeated you. And now you flee. All your men, dead! Your Sultan despises you. You are finished!"

"I have barely begun!" he cried out.

Walt splashed over to me, hissed, and held out a hand-gun. "The only one still dry. Loaded. You aim, I will fire it." He had the end of a burning match cupped in his hand.

I took it and squeezed the wooden end under my arm and looked down the iron barrel. It was practically full night and William was drifting further on the current with every moment. The river and the boat and the man had blended into one shadow.

"Radu is dead!" I called.

He said nothing in return. I scanned left and right while Walt blew on the match, ready.

"Did you hear me? I killed your only friend in all the world, William. He died in agony!"

Silence, and then. "And my men killed Vlad!" he shouted. "And he was your—"

"Now!" I hissed at Walt.

He touched the match on the firing pan and the gun banged in my hand. Across the river, William cried out and I was sure I heard him fall into the water.

We stood and listened. There was nothing but the wind in the trees behind me and the gentle sound of the great river in front.

1 9

The Vampir

1 4 7 6

IT WAS MORNING WHEN WE cautiously returned to the battlefield. Exhausted beyond measure, our horses dragging their feet with each step.

We were dejected and heartbroken.

I was not certain whether William had in fact been killed but I strongly doubted it. At least I had given him a parting gift. Whether Dracula was dead, I was not certain either but it seemed likely, considering the lifeless state I had last seen him in. Either way, I had to return to the field. Above all, Rob had to be buried. I would not leave him to be tossed into a mass grave or allow his body to be scavenged and lay unburied.

We crept through the dark trees to the edge of the meadow and found the usual sight after a battle. Figures crouched over the dead and dying, collecting bodies and weapons and armour. Hand carts trundling along, horses standing here and there. Locals mixed with soldiers and servants. Crows hopped and squawked and were chased away, only to land on some other poor body.

"Where is the prince?" I asked a Wallachian captain who stood at the edge by his horse.

"My lord?"

"Where is Vlad Dracula?"

The captain was somewhat out of his wits and he stared for a moment, despair in his eyes. "We fell back. The Turks came up here to this field. We gathered the men and pushed the Turks off. They fled south, back to the river."

"Where is he?"

The Wallachian frowned, looking at me. "They took his head."

"The Turks took Dracula's head?" I asked. "You are certain?"

He shook as he recalled it. "They had it raised on a spear. They celebrated as they fled."

"You recognised him?"

"It was his helm, yes. The only one like it."

I sighed, rubbing my eyes. "What about the rest of him?"

"My lord?"

"Where is your prince's body, sir?"

"The monks took it."

"What monks? They took it where?"

He stared. "Monks."

I sighed. "Where are your friends, Captain? Where are your

servants?"

"Dead." He looked around. "Or fled. Or..."

Walt approached and patted him on the shoulder. "Come on, son. Let's find your mates, shall we." He led the man away across the meadow and passed him off to a group of soldiers.

We retraced our steps back along the track to find the place where Rob fell. He was right where we had left him. However, the others were not.

"Where is Radu's body?" Eva said.

"Serban's is gone also," Stephen said. "Head and body both. Could Radu have been alive after all?"

"Not a chance," I said. "His people must have taken him."

"And Serban also?" Stephen asked. "Why would they do that?"

"Where shall we take dear Rob?" Eva asked, kneeling by him.

"What about the monastery at Snagov?" Stephen said. "He appeared to like it there."

We all instinctively turned to Walt who nodded his assent. "The monks will bury him proper."

The sun rose as high as it would on that winter day by the time we reached the monastery at Snagov. We rowed across the lake and moored up, leaving Rob's body on the shore while we approached the buildings, calling out for any of the monks or servants who had stayed or, we hoped, had returned from the battlefield with the bodies of Vlad, Radu, and Serban.

It was deserted.

Walking through the empty buildings, I called for anyone. I called for Theodore, who had stayed, and headed for the library.

"They were not at the battlefield," Stephen said beside me, his dagger in his fist. "And they are not here. So, where have they gone?"

"They must have come here," Eva said. "Where else could they go?"

"There is nowhere else," Walt said, his face a mask of anguish.

We stopped as one at a noise up ahead. The screeching of iron hinges and the shuffling of feet.

"You have returned, my dear brothers," a raspy voice called out up ahead. It was Theodore. The ancient, blind monk stood filling the doorway to the library, like a bag of bones beneath his robes.

Walt scoffed behind me. "Silly old sod."

I raised my voice as I continued toward him. "It is not your brothers who have returned, Father Theodore. We also are looking for them. It is I, Richard Ashbury, who fought with—"

"I know who it is returning," Theodore said, his voice seeming suddenly stronger. "Come and speak with me a while, Richard Ashbury, the *vampir*."

I followed him into the library in time to see him ease himself into his chair by the window, the place I had first seen him. It was open and the cold afternoon air smelled of pine and woodsmoke.

"You call me a *vampir*?" I asked him, crossing the library to stand over him. "Why do you say that?"

"Have a seat, brother," he said, indicating the seat opposite.

I ignored him. "You called me a *vampir*. And you are right. But how did you know it?"

Theodore smiled. "I know it, Richard, because I am a *vampir*, also."

A chill spread up my spine. I was shocked and at the same time, it seemed as if I already knew. With a sigh, I sat across from Theodore while he smiled through me. Cold air poured in through the window but the old man did not seem to feel it.

"You call yourself a *vampir*, Theodore?" I looked at his lined face and the broad yet bony shoulders under his robes. I wondered how he could be an immortal and also aged and infirm. "What did you do to the other monks? Did they return here after the battle?"

"They came with men to bury," Theodore said, pointing toward the graveyard outside his window. "And then my brothers had to leave. You see, they were afraid of you and your brother and what you might do."

"Afraid of me? But it is William who means to conquer your people."

Theodore smiled. "And you, Richard, are the one who is hunting *strigoi*. You are both young and dangerous. Both of you are quite mad."

"I am not young," I said. "But I am dangerous. And yet William is the mad one."

He raised a large, bony finger. "Both of you are tearing through the world like mad bulls, not knowing our ways. It is not your fault. But you are a danger to us and my brothers had to go into the wild once more."

"The wild?"

Sighing, he turned his unseeing gaze to the world. "We were here for a good while. We dwelled here in peace, our lives safe from notice, from interference. They will go on, at least for a time, but I am tired of this life. It is time for mine to end."

I shook my head, more confused than ever. "You call yourself *vampir*. How can that be so when you are so..?" I gestured at him, searching for the right word.

"Aged?" he said, smiling. "Decrepit? Frail?"

"How old are you?"

"I do not remember. Is it eight centuries? Or nine, now?" He shrugged. "Enough. Yes, enough, now."

"Do you drink blood? You feed on your monks?"

"You misunderstand. Our lay brothers, the servants, provide our blood. When it is required, some few of those are chosen to join us and so we go on."

I laughed at my own idiocy. "So you were all immortals? All the monks? The entire time I was searching for *strigoi* but I already found them all?"

"All of my brothers are *strigoi* but not all the *strigoi* were here. They are everywhere in these lands. The places they now call Albania, Serbia, Hungary. In all these places they have their own names for us. The Hungarians call us izcacus, the blood drinkers, and believe we are demons. Others that we are risen from the dead."

"How did you come to be made?"

He opened his arms, presenting himself. "I am like you. We are born *vampir*, from our *vampir* fathers, though we must die in our lives to become all that we might be. We have greater power and the ability to make *strigoi* with our own blood. But we, you and I, are lesser than our fathers. We cannot mate with woman.

As you will know."

I rubbed my face and sat back. I did not know where to begin. "Who is your father?"

"A son of a creature that we call the Ancient One. The First *Vampir*. He has many names. My father was born of him and later my father made me. My father taught me many things. But he is long dead."

"So we are... cousins, you and I. We share a grandfather. The Ancient One." I hesitated. "Did you meet him, Theodore?"

"Alas, no. He has not been heard of in a thousand years. Lost and likely dead, though some say he will one day return and rule over all *vampir*, *strigoi*, and human alike. If he does, I shall not be here to see it."

I almost told him that Priskos yet lived but I held my tongue. It seemed to be an even greater secret than I had imagined.

"So you made your brothers? The monks? I thought the abbot led them?"

"Ioánnis is young. Not yet four hundred years. He has heart enough to go on. I have remained to guide my brothers, my sons, for many years beyond my desire to do so. But they have to go into the wilderness once more and to wander until they find a new home. I am old and broken and do not wish to travel. Only to die."

"I do not understand. How it that you are an immortal and yet you have aged?"

He sighed. "Aged, yes. But slowly. Some *vampir* live for a thousand years and seem to hardly age a decade, as did my father. But for centuries now I have drunk only the blood of lowly servants, many of them old men. In my youth, I was a warrior and I drank the blood of the warriors that I defeated. If I had continued to drink the blood of the strong, I would have my sight and a straight back and the strength of my legs. Alas, I chose the path of peace."

"You ceased to be a soldier in order to become a monk? Why? To hide from those who would harm you?"

"If I had continued to live as a warrior, I would have died many centuries ago. Even a warrior as strong as we cannot cheat fate forever. All those I made died. I came to a monastery in Constantinople and discovered the rules of Saint Basil. I was entranced. For a time, I was consumed by it. I raised my head and argued with matters of Church and the empire. I argued with emperors and wrote and wrote and wished to reform this rule or that. So many words. You will find my writings here and elsewhere." He smiled, his wrinkled face creasing deeply as he turned his blind eyes to the scrolls lining the walls. "It seems so foolish now. Self-indulgent and naïve. And I angered one emperor too many and then I had to leave Constantinople and I took some of my brothers with me. We have lived in many monasteries in the centuries since. And we were here so briefly but this was a good place. A good place for our troubled souls to search for peace. And it is a good place to die."

"You are the one who created all the *strigoi* in these lands? And they were all were monks?"

"No, they do not all come from me. Once, I had brothers. My father had brothers and so we had cousins. We *vampir* of Rome made many *strigoi* and with them we fought to keep the barbarians from Rome's door. My father and his brothers were soldiers and strategoi for many emperors but we could do only so much as the empire slowly declined. It took us centuries to realise that it is not military power but moral supremacy that keeps a people strong. We did not do enough to stem the moral decline of our people and when we realised, it was too late. My father, his brothers, my brothers and cousins, they all died fighting the enemies of Rome. I believed the *vampir* were all dead, other than me, for it seemed I found only *strigoi* in my travels. Some I gave sanctuary. Others, wild and mad, had to be killed. But then you came to me and I knew."

"You knew what I was? How?"

"Even without my sight, I could see it in you. In your bearing, in your manner, I could feel your age. You reminded me of my brothers. Even so, I was not certain but young Serban confirmed he had seen your power. You were young and yet somehow you were *vampir*. I must ask, who is your father, Richard? Can it be that one of my father's brothers survived after all and you are his son?"

"No, I have a different lineage. My father did not know what he was and he died in ignorance. And so I did not know either. Neither did my brother William. We had to be killed before we discovered the truth about our nature."

Theodore smiled. "The truth? To be raised in ignorance must have been terrible. And even now, you have discovered so little, I pity you. And you have sworn to kill your brother, and his *strigoi*? That is not our way."

"It is my way. Besides, you said not moments ago that you

killed your own."

He made a growling sound as he cleared his throat. "Only when the rogue *strigoi*'s actions threatened to bring down us all."

I leaned toward him. "And William's actions threaten to bring down Christendom. Even if they did not, he has committed murders that must be revenged."

Theodore's thin lips drew even thinner. "Revenge, is it? Ah, I see."

"It is justice."

"Because he broke the laws of man?"

"Because he sinned. He killed innocent women and children. Many times."

"Ah, children." Theodore tilted his head back and breathed deeply. "It has been so very long since I drank a child. I remember the sweet taste upon my lips. Such power in a child's blood."

I swallowed my revulsion. "So I have heard. But why is it so?"

"God is mysterious. But the child is like a sprouting seed, is it not? Within the acorn is the strength of the oak."

"Whatever the benefit, it is wrong, surely you see that? You profess to be a man of God, do you not believe the murder of children to be a sin?"

"It is a sin, for men. But are we men, you and I?"

"I do not know. Once, I knew I was a man but as the centuries have gone by, I have begun to wonder. Am I to understand that you do not believe the laws of man, the morality of God, applies to us? To *vampir*? You are convinced, then, that we are not men?"

"For centuries, I have asked this question."

I waited for him to continue but he did not. "And you have

an answer?"

"I have many answers. But which is the truth? I do not know. Perhaps I was incapable or perhaps I needed more time. But my time is up, and so I must die without knowing. I am ready to die and you will kill me."

"You want me to kill you?" I said. "Why?"

"I cannot kill myself. That is certainly a sin, for men and for *vampir*. And yet I cannot go on in this broken body. Can you do this thing?"

"Killing men, or immortals, has never troubled me. And yet I have so many more questions before you die."

"I am so tired, Richard. After my eyes failed, I wished to die and yet my brothers begged for me to stay with them. I have given them decades against my will. If you wish for another hour of my life then when our time has run through you must give me what I want in turn."

"And what is that?" I asked, though I could guess.

"I will answer your questions and then you will end my life swiftly, striking my head from my body and burying my remains in the manner I wish. Do you agree to grant me this mercy in exchange?"

"Certainly."

"Then go on with your questions, Richard."

"How many of us are there in the world?"

"*Vampir*? Only me, you, and your brother. There were many but they all died. Their offspring are yet walking the earth."

I knew of at least two sons of the Ancient One still serving Priskos but I said nothing about that. "And their offspring? The *strigoi* that they made? How many of them are there?"

"I know of a mere few wild ones still out there but they have learned to be wary of me and my brothers. They cannot be very many."

"What about Serban? Did you place him in my service? I was deceived by him and because of my foolishness, he murdered my friend."

"Serban came here, dying and Ioánnis asked me to save him. I believed he would stay and become one of us but he fled and stayed away, fearing I would have him killed for his betrayal. When you brought him here, he told us what you were, hoping to find favour with us. He wished to know whether he should side with you or with your brother in this war that you are waging. I told Serban to embrace peace, to join his brothers in contemplation of God, and to devote his life to prayer. He cursed me for a fool and said that he would have power and wealth instead."

"You could have warned me," I said. "Because you did not, my friend is dead."

"It is no fault of mine. I can tell you are naïve and trusting and entirely without cunning. In truth, I am surprised you have survived this long. I doubt you will live much longer. Why not come to an understanding with your brother? Make peace and live."

"As you have chosen peace, Theodore? It is peace that has withered your body. Peace has withered your mind and your soul. Man was not meant to live in peace. Only through struggle and conflict and war can we find our fulfilment and live as we are meant to."

Theodore smiled as I spoke. "My father and my brothers spoke as you do. They all died."

"I see now it is your fear of death that has made you this way. Death is not failure. To give up is failure. All of you here, this brotherhood, it is failure. It is contemptible. While you sit here in contemplation, Constantinople fell to the barbarians. If you had fought, if your monks were soldiers, perhaps it would yet stand. You are nothing but a coward."

"The difference between you and I is that I once thought as you do." Theodore sneered. "My time is almost up, oh great soldier. Ask your questions."

I sighed and looked out of the window, thinking on what might help me to know. "I have met immortals in my life, *strigoi*, who themselves turned mortals by their blood. These men so turned became like savages, filled always with a madness for blood. Their skin would blister and burn in the sun. We named them revenants, for they resembled creatures from stories told in England that went by such a name. Do you know about these creatures?"

Theodore scowled. "These are *moroi*. They are abominations. They bring nothing but destruction and chaos and so we do not allow such creatures to live."

"Oh? When have you seen them made?"

"Ah, many *strigoi* grow lonely in their isolation. They make a companion out of lust or love. Sometimes the *moroi* turns on their creator and kills them. A *moroi* is always mad. My brothers and my *strigoi* have always done their duty and killed all *moroi* that are made. We hear of their madness and murders and track down and kill the abomination. This you must do always."

"So just as I kill *strigoi*, you kill *moroi* but you believe only I am at fault."

Theodore's brow knitted over his sightless eyes. "Your ignorance is vile, cousin. A *strigoi* keeps his soul. He may lose it through his actions, just as any man, but a *moroi* is nothing but a man made into a beast. A beast in the likeness of a man. Like a wild beast, it acts without thought. And like a wild beast, it must be slain to protect the people. It is our duty, *vampir* and *strigoi* alike, to do so. My brothers have cleansed them from the world for centuries and they will continue to do so after I am gone, until they themselves dwindle into nothing."

"There was an old woman up near Poenari who told me her village was almost destroyed by two *strigoi*. She sent me to Snagov. She said her husband went away for a long time and returned to her as a *strigoi*, for a while. Do you know about this?"

Theodore frowned. "Petru, yes. It was not long ago. Forty years, perhaps. Two of my brothers fled and it took Ioánnis and the others days to find them. Weeks, perhaps, weeks of murder and violence against the peasants. When they found them, they were bleeding Petru. Once, in his youth, Ioánnis was a desperately violent man and he unleashed that violence on our rogue brothers. Petru was almost dead when they brought him to me. He took his oaths. But he did not stay more than a few years."

"You let him go? Why?"

"He was quiet. He lived with his wife, for a time, supping on her blood. Then he went away and found some way to feed without causing trouble. Or he was killed, or he murdered himself. I should never have made him, and I should never have made Serban. Saving a man's life is not reason enough to make him *strigoi*. But my sentimentality and my weakness in the face of my brothers' compassion is the least of my sins. They take pity on others far more than I ever could but I find myself indulging their compassion, as a father indulges a son who brings home a wounded animal."

I nodded at the graveyard outside. "Your monks took Serban, Radu and Vlad from the battlefield and buried them here?"

"They buried Serban here, yes."

I was confused. "Where did the abbot take Dracula's body?"

Thedore smirked. "His body?"

I sighed. "The Turks took Dracula's head but the monks were seen removing his body from the battlefield. So where is his grave? His tomb?"

"Ah," Theodore smiled. "Our poor former ward Radu was killed in your little skirmish, yes. His body was swiftly exchanged for Vlad Dracula and the men guarding their fallen lord were killed."

I could barely believe it. "By the monks?"

"They sought to rescue one of their own. They left the body of Radu in Vlad Dracula's armour so that the people would believe their prince was dead. My brothers returned here with him and he was submerged in the font."

"The font?"

"The blood font. It required a number of sacrifices to fill it but then Lord Dracula was close to death. He rose stronger than ever and left with my brothers."

He rose.

"Vlad is alive? Where did they go?"

Theodore smiled. "You will not find them."

"They can have no more than half a day on me. I will track them."

I stood and he thrust his hand out to grasp my wrist. His grip was iron. "Why do you wish to slay your family?"

"I wish only to slay my brother and the evil that he spawns with his blood."

"Vlad Dracula is *strigoi*. Made by your brother. You will kill him?"

"He has been my ally. My friend, even. I wish for him to help me in slaying William but if he will not then perhaps he must die also."

"But why?"

"He has done evil. Great evil."

Theodore tilted his head. "What evil has he done?"

"Killed innocent women and children."

"Those of his enemies. It is the work of kings. A kingdom cannot be maintained without sacrifice. Indeed, my young cousin, nothing of value can be maintained without it."

"You speak of peace and yet you have no sympathy for the innocent. Are you a man of God or not?"

"What is a kingdom, Richard? What is a nation? A people?" He paused, expecting an answer.

"It is... a family."

Theodore made an approving growl in his throat. "Yes, good.

And what is a family?"

I sighed. "I do not know."

"A man, a woman, their sons and daughters, this family is a stone. One stone amongst others just like it forming the foundation of a clan, a tribe, a people, a nation. The family and the nation both are the foundation of order. Outside it is chaos and destruction that will shatter any family or nation that is not united, and which does not protect itself against the chaos. It must be strong and maintain itself at all costs. At all costs. Maintenance of family and nation takes sacrifice. It costs blood. But it must be done or all comes crumbling to dust and ash."

"Dracula sacrificed a little too much, do you not think? Spent so much blood and yet his people are not safe now, no safer than they were. What did he achieve with his bloodletting?"

"It is not something one ever achieves. It is something one does. It never ends. Blood sacrifice every day until the end of days. How old are you to not know this? Did you never have a family of your own, Richard?"

"You want me to let Dracula live because he did his best?"

"You must let them all live because they are your family. They are your people."

"The English are my people."

"The English would kill you if they knew what you were."

"Perhaps. But they are my family all the same and I will maintain them through my sacrifice. The *strigoi* who do not protect Christendom are my enemies."

"You would kill my sons, though they do that very thing for their own people? They serve the Vlach, the Serbs, Albanians,

Bulgars. We bring them wisdom and guidance."

I could barely believe how wrong he was. "Your people are being overwhelmed by the Turks as we speak. They will be no more if Dracula and your sons do not *fight*. Perhaps I will not kill them but they must be brought into the fight so that the Turks can be defeated and your people can have peace."

"This is the crux of it, Richard," Theodore said. "The fight will *never* be won. I pray it will never be lost also but it will never end. In my youth, fighting for the Emperor, I thought as you do. But I learned there is no end to these things."

"You were a Greek. You fought for Rome and lived in Constantinople but because you stopped fighting your great city has fallen to the Turks. So your homeland is conquered by an enemy who wants nothing but the eradication of you and your people and everything you ever achieved and you decide only that it is time now for you to die? You may have once been a warrior but you hid yourself away for so long that you have grown weak not only in body but in your soul. And now you abandon your monks to their fate. You even admit that without you to make more of them as they die off over time, they will dwindle into nothing. You are nothing but a broken old man who has given up."

"My body is dying. I did not understand until it was too late that I needed to drink the blood of warriors or infants to maintain my strength. Whether I wish to abandon them or not, that is what has happened. They will endure for centuries yet, I hope. And perhaps you might one day help them. If they need more *strigoi*, you might grant them your blood."

"No."

Theodore smiled, sadly. "We shall see. If not you, perhaps your brother would grant his."

"He has no interest in maintaining this world, Theodore. William is the chaos swirling outside."

"Perhaps. What will be, will be. It is in God's hands. But my time is long past. Now, I have answered your questions at length and it is time that you do as you agreed."

I was sick of him and his weakness. But still, he was family, of sorts. "You are certain you wish to die?"

"It pleases me that you do not wish to kill me, cousin. I pray that you one day feel the same way about all of your family. Now, help me to stand."

"Would you not rather kneel?" I asked.

"Help me to the lectern." I held his bony elbow and supported him as he shuffled across the room. Once beside the lectern he felt for the book that lay upon it. A liturgical gospel book, closed, with a cover of wood and leather inlaid with rubies and shining with gold leaf. Theodore sighed as his fingers brushed the cover. "Make the blow clean, brother. Take my body and bury it well with my head between my feet and with a rod of iron driven through my heart so that I will not rise before God raises me by His hand." He closed his eyes. "I am ready."

I felt as though I should say something, offer him something in his last moments. But he wanted only one thing from me and I could see no good reason to deny him it.

His fingers brushed the cover of the book and he smiled, with a prayer on his lips, as my sword cut through his neck. Theodore's blood sprayed across the gold cover and his body fell while his head rolled and came to a stop by his chair. The smile still on his lips.

∞

As the sun went down on a cold, clear day, we buried him as he wished in the graveyard, overlooking the lake.

There, also, we buried poor Rob. As good a friend and as good a man as any who ever lived. My heart ached to know he was dead and to have died in such ignominy instead of in glory. But then he had lived a long life filled with glory on the battlefield and nothing, not even an inglorious death, could take that away from him. Sir Robert Hawthorn had saved my life more times than I could count and he had given his hand when he killed the lunatic immortal Joan of Arc, saving an innocent young woman and captive children by his actions. Off the battlefield, he had been my constant friend and I could barely believe he would be at my side no longer. In his mortal life, he had fathered and raised children and been a faithful husband to his wife, leaving them prosperous, secure, and respected, which is the most honourable duty a man can fulfil. The world was a worse place now that he was dead but he left it a better one because he had lived.

"It is a good place," I said over his grave.

"He should be buried in English soil," Walt said. "Ain't right that he is here. Ain't right that he died here, amongst these people. They are mad. They are hopeless. He should have been fighting for England."

"You are right, Walt," I said. "You are right."

"Still some food in the kitchens," Eva said. "Sleep here and go after William at first light?"

I nodded, looking at the wooden crosses we had pushed into the earth.

"Why not go after Dracula first?" Stephen suggested.

"We will not find him," Eva said. "This is his land."

"I am inclined to leave him and the monks alone," I said. "For now, at least. Not only are they a distraction from William, they are doing no harm and may be doing good."

"William, then," Stephen said. "Who has either returned to Sultan Mehmed or fled elsewhere."

"Probably burrowed into the mud," Walt said, "like the worm he is. Don't really expect to find him, do we?"

None of us answered for a time. We watched the sun sink beyond the hills and almost at once the air grew colder.

"Wherever he has gone, we will pursue him."

Walt was right, of course. William slithered away and abandoned all he had worked for.

Sultan Mehmed had grown tired of Zaganos Pasha and instead turned his attention elsewhere. In the years that followed, he conquered the Mamluks of Egypt and the Turks, known as the Ottoman Empire, dominated the entire region for another four hundred years until its eventual collapse.

Mehmed's sons and grandsons would conquer in all directions. They pushed Christendom back all the way to the gates of Vienna, first in 1529 and then for the last time in 1683, which was the point that the tide finally began to turn.

Every Christian kingdom in the Balkans fell to them, from Serbia to Albania and even much of Hungary, these places were subject to direct Ottoman rule. It was only Wallachia, Transylvania, and Moldavia that remained as vassal states with their own rulers.

I am certain that Vlad Dracula and his *strigoi* monks were to thank for that, and they continued to watch over their people for generations. It would be centuries before I saw Dracula again.

William fled to Greece and from there to Italy. We followed his trail for a long time but we could never corner him and after many years had to admit defeat. Having lost William's trail, I returned to England once more. So much had changed in our absence and yet it was a delight to return home, to be surrounded everywhere by my own people.

In my long absence, the Plantagenets had been overthrown and England had a new king, a miserable sod named Henry VII. Stephen and Eva wormed themselves into the machinations of the new lords during the reign of his son, Henry VIII while I fought in a handful of minor wars. We recruited men, I made some into immortals and built the Order of the White Dagger for the day when William emerged once more.

That day would come during the reign of Queen Elizabeth. Unbeknownst to us, William ingratiated himself at the courts of Spain and worked to create an army of immortals large enough and powerful enough to conquer England for ever.

It would be my greatest challenge yet.

A vampire armada.

AUTHOR'S NOTE

Richard's story continues in *Vampire Armada the Immortal Knight Chronicles Book 7*

If you enjoyed *Vampire Impaler* please leave a review online! Even a couple of lines saying what you liked about the story would be an enormous help and would make the series more visible to new readers.

You can find out more and get in touch with me at dandavisauthor.com

BOOKS BY DAN DAVIS

The GALACTIC ARENA Series
Science fiction

Inhuman Contact
Onca's Duty
Orb Station Zero
Earth Colony Sentinel

The IMMORTAL KNIGHT Chronicles
Historical Fiction - with Vampires

Vampire Crusader
Vampire Outlaw
Vampire Khan
Vampire Knight
Vampire Heretic
Vampire Impaler

For a complete and up-to-date list of Dan's available books,
visit: **http://dandavisauthor.com/books/**

Printed in Great Britain
by Amazon

45090041R00350